I0582647

Needing you Always

LIZZIE MORTON

Boxes are for packaging, not people.
The best person you can be, is yourself.
Don't let anyone tell you otherwise.
Dance to whatever song you want.
When you can, laugh till it hurts.
On the days where smiling feels impossible …
remember the days that you did.
Seize every moment.
Forget the words of those who don't matter.
Don't fly, soar.

Prologue

When the words 'urgent action' glared at me from my laptop, I hesitated before opening the email.

Ange—my superior—has never dropped me from a project.

Yet here I am two weeks later. Crammed in the back of a cab, crawling through the clogged streets of Nuremberg.

My colleague, Abby—who's also my roommate and best friend—huffs as I divert my gaze away from the diary sitting open in my lap. The scribbles covering what should have been our schedule for Johannesburg's first major fashion week make my eye twitch. The carefully crafted client list has been swapped for a summer centered around unprotected sex, drugs, sweaty dreadlocks, and tattoos.

When the cab slows to a stop in the staff parking area of our first festival, I smooth the line between my brows and lift the corners of my mouth into a tight smile. Nuremberg might challenge the Bermuda Triangle seeing as it's eating all the scheduled flights. The rest of our PR team might still be on the other side of the Atlantic, and the group of rockheads we've been forced to work with might be nowhere to be found—but I refuse to allow these things to be more than a hiccup.

At least we have Abby's childhood friends—Sophie and Zoe—on hand to help unload the gear from the trunk. The fact I'm thankful for these small mercies, when the two of them together regularly out-drink a football team, adds to the absurdity of the situation we're in.

"You need to go to the front-stage area and get set up," I tell Abby when we're almost backstage.

Her feet remain glued to the trampled grass. She's short-circuiting. I would be too, if I were her. About to face an ex. The ex. The one that got away and the sole reason we're in this mess to begin with.

I'd also be more accommodating if we weren't working on borrowed minutes.

We should already be ready for a musical performance, but the likelihood of there being actual music is slim to none, because we still don't have a band.

"Now!"

Abby springs to life and hurries away.

The second she disappears, I'm tempted to call her back. After casting a quick glance around to check no one is watching, I dab at my sweaty top lip with my finger and wipe my palms against my white linen pants.

You've got this.

Feeling more Zen, I make my way to the VIP tent where the band is due to arrive.

My positive mood evaporates when all I find is a group of B-list celebs dressed in a mixture of boho and nineties aesthetic clothing—festival chic at its finest. The people who aren't lounging in multicolored egg chairs with cocktails are drinking beer beside a pop-up bar, which is being manned by a bartender living his main character moment.

"Come on," I mutter. "Where are you?"

I'm mentally planning my speech to Ange to explain how we've messed up before the tour's started, when the fake pretentious laughter surrounding me drops a decibel.

My heart stutters when four guys enter the tent.

S.C.A.R.A.B.—Warped Record's rock babies.

"Hey!" I call out when the band begins walking in the wrong direction. I wave, hurrying toward them. "Sooz, PR." I smile and hold my hand out to the guy I know to be Jake—the lead guitarist.

It's the weak, lack luster handshake I receive in return that has me deciding against the same intro with the rest of the group. The guy on Jake's left, with less-tangled-on-the-top dark hair—Zach—looks like he's going to be sick. Things improve when I get to the lead singer—Sam. He swipes some dirty blond locks out of his face and gives me the kind of smile that makes his eyes crinkle.

Then I concentrate on the guy in the background. Ryan Alvarez: the drummer.

Tattoos aren't my jam, yet I find myself transfixed by the flames curling up the side of his neck, wrapping around the symbol of death, front and center. Blinking, I drag my attention away. Clearly, no one ever explained to him the idea

9

behind less is more. Everything about him is loud. Ink-covered skin. Blond highlights in otherwise dark hair. Styling products in said hair. The spikes he's sporting could take someone's eye out and gale force winds couldn't move those babies.

His abundance of everything physically is counter-balanced by his lack of anything emotionally.

He's cool. Calm. Maybe not collected. But chilled.

The one who looks …

Rest of the band forgotten, I stalk in his direction. "Do you mind giving us a minute?" I ask the cowboy he's started talking to through gritted teeth. I'm gifted a hat tilt before he leaves us. "Are you stoned?"

Ryan watches me. His eyes are lazy, and his gaze lingers on my hair. I'm tempted to raise my hand and check some hasn't fallen from its bun. The rest of the band walking over stops me. They seem totally unphased that their band mate might as well be floating in the clouds.

"You know about this?" I direct at no one in particular, receiving a round of shrugs in return. "Unbelievable."

"It's not an issue," says Jake, as if being stoned before performing in front of thousands of people is normal.

I purse my lips, deciding with the little time we have, there's no point turning it into one.

"Fine. Wardrobe." None of the guys move. "Now!" I power behind them as they follow one of the stage crew members. Even Mr. Super-Chilled manages to move like someone's lit a fire under his gluteal region.

"The basics," I say to the team of make-up artists, and they get to work straight away.

There's only time for a quick powder job—pointless, as it's going to melt off within a couple of songs—but it's part of the process, and I don't want to step on anyone's toes. When the make-up team has done their part, wardrobe jump straight in.

We're finally catching up, and my stress levels have dropped when the loose cannon fires.

"I'm not wearing that."

I agree to one of the stylist's suggestions for a black shirt with a skull in the center for Zach. Then, after a steady inhale followed by a slow exhale, I turn and walk to Ryan. The stylist beside him gives me a sour look as I approach. His stage outfit is still clutched in her hands.

"What do you mean, you're not wearing it?" I ask. Stay cool, Sooz. Be cool. I smile and keep my voice even. "It's the wardrobe we have planned for you."

Ryan looks past me, bored, like he couldn't care less what we have planned. "I like what I'm wearing."

I take in his shirt. It's no good.

"It's creased. And you have a ..." I lean in closer, inspecting the white material right in the center of his chest. "A stain ..." He looks down his nose to where I'm leering. "Right here." The temptation to prod him is strong. I keep my arms locked at my sides.

He shrugs. "I got hungry."

"You need to change," I reply, drawing back.

"I don't need to do anything." Huh. For someone who appears super chilled, he's oddly defiant. "I like my shirt."

A stage crew member in the background signals that we have three minutes.

I try to meet Ryan halfway. "Why?"

11

"Why what?"

"Why do you like the shirt so much?"

The lazy smile he's wearing lifts to a grin. His eyes twinkle and I have a feeling I'm going to hate his answer. "Because the ladies love a good gun show."

I chew on the inside of my cheek.

"Two minutes!" calls the same stage crew member.

I glower at Ryan. "Fine. The shirt stays."

It's the comment he makes next which solidifies that he's what I despise in a man. "I knew you'd come around, baby." He places a kiss on each bicep. "No one can resist them." I turn and walk away. "I'm Ryan, by the way."

'I don't care' is what I wish I could say.

"Great," I call back, leaving him behind.

A deafening roar fills the air as S.C.A.R.A.B. finishes their set.

I have an eclectic taste in most things: music, books, TV, movies. The only limitation I've ever had has been with rock music. Now I know it's because I've not heard the right type. The type I'd like. And I don't like what I've heard, I love it.

There's no denying the band is good, ridiculously so. Like there's no denying that my foot tapped to the beat throughout the entire set. While high, Ryan managed to perform at a standard most musicians struggle to achieve. The whole band did. Hopefully setting us up for what will be a successful summer.

Unfortunately, in the hour of knowing them, I've quickly learned that when it comes to this group of guys, the term polar opposites applies.

After a stellar performance and coming out on top, we're now plummeting following a disastrous reunion between the lead guitarist and my colleague. It's the kind of reunion that has my positive hopes for the coming months slipping through my fingers. The marijuana-loving drummer is the least of my worries, because at least he's amenable to the outside world.

Following a verbal truth dump with Abby's ex, one that results in him skulking away, I spin around ready to check on the rest of the band. The air is knocked out of me when I collide with a wall of muscle, and I fall back. Eyes snapping shut, I brace myself for pain. One second passes, and then another. The impact never comes. When I prize my eyes open, I find a pair of hands locked around my upper arms, holding me in place.

"Darn it," I murmur, staring at a familiar stain in line with my forehead.

A throat clears and I lift my chin, finding myself lost in pools of dazzling green. Ryan's eyes narrow. His lighthearted, high-as-a-kite self is nowhere to be found. His fingers moving a fraction, serves as a reminder of how we're standing. I move my attention away from his face, dropping my gaze to where our skin is touching. The tips of his fingers dig into my muscles, the pressure making the surrounding flesh white. It should hurt, but I don't feel anything, too busy trying to figure out whether Ryan's holding me up or holding on to me.

A clatter in the background has his touch being snapped away while I remain stock still.

"You need to get changed." Ryan doesn't argue when I continue, "No gun shows for the press. I have a shirt waiting."

Stage crew race around, preparing for the next band to go on stage. Out of the corner of my eye, I see Ryan's drum kit rolling by. He raises his right arm, wiping away the sheen covering his brow with the back of his hand. It's impossible not to watch the way his bicep shortens and bulges.

"No riveting comments on our set?" Ryan asks, dropping his arm back to his side.

The small, unprofessional part of me is disappointed the show is over. It enjoyed watching the damp material of his shirt catching on the deep rivets making up his torso.

I plaster on an unaffected smile. "Singing, exceptional. Guitar and bass, very good. Drums ..." Ryan stands a little taller. Puffs out his chest. "Average."

"Average?" he splutters.

When I move my left leg out to the side, ready to move around him, he mirrors my movement.

"Yes," I confirm, frustration edging its way into my voice. "Average."

Ryan's eyes become slits. "Do you even like rock music?"

I try to move away, but find myself blocked again.

"Some."

"What does some mean?"

"The good stuff."

"And S.C.A.R.A.B.?"

Laughter floats in from the VIP tent to my right.

"There's potential."

The first guitar chords from the next band's opening song rip through the atmosphere.

"For?"

"Success. If the drummer spent less time getting high and focused on what he was supposed to be doing."

"Right." Ryan scowls. "Thanks for the wonderful insight."

"My pleasure." I smile before serving him with his final reminder. "You need to get to wardrobe."

The floor of the tent rustles when I start to walk away, but my steps slow when a final question reaches my ears.

"Any tips for handling the interviews?"

"They'll go better if you're not stoned."

I don't turn to check if he's heard me. His huff is answer enough.

Chapter One
4 Years Later

Eyes set on my lap, I shift uncomfortably in the backseat of the town car.

My blonde hair is in a tight knot and the material of my skirt suit is wrapped around my body like a vise. I went for the finest bouclé weave I could find. If it weren't for the color, Mother would be in her element.

A pair of blue eyes sparkle at me through the rearview mirror.

"You look beautiful, as always," says Andre, the Van Rensburg family driver.

"You're paid to say that."

"I'm paid to *drive* you. No charge for the extra compliments."

The light banter loosens some of the tightness in my chest. "What a gentleman."

As we continue to move further away from Cape Town, flying along the R310 toward Stellenbosch in silence, I jab my finger against the window switch. The tinted glass starts to roll down. Warm air billows in and the last remnant of direct sunlight warms my skin. When the window's a third of the way down, I realize I'm going to ruin my hair. I close my eyes, press the switch harder and let it roll to the bottom.

It's when the car slows and Andre turns left that I open my eyes again. My nails bite the soft leather of the seat as we move along the sprawling drive. Dust clouding around us forces me to roll the window back up. We stop beside a set of red, stone steps leading up to an old Dutch architecture building. The whitewash exterior stone glows against the fading blue sky, framed by the mountains in the background. My childhood home.

The car's been still for over a minute, and I still make no attempt to move.

I could tell Andre to take me away. After twenty years of the same dynamic, I know he would.

Mother will murder you if you don't turn up.

I also promised myself that this time, I'd leave the country with the two of us being on good terms. Well, as much as the two of us can be.

The choice of disappearing is taken out of my hands when the front door opens and my brother steps out. Willem waves. It's a small one—to minimize the risk of crumpling the suit he's wearing. I mimic his movement, also hating creases.

"I'm proud of you," says Andre, breaking through my bottomless thoughts. "And everything you've achieved …"

"Thanks."

Before I have the chance to think of a better reply, he's out of the car and opening my door.

God, I hate this place. The thought has me frozen on the spot. *One night, and you're free.*

Taking a single, deep breath, my grip on the leather loosens. I don't bother checking for the damage that's been inflicted. After another breath, my lungs fill with enough oxygen that I no longer feel like I'm going to pass out.

Andre's, "Have a wonderful night, Ms. Van Rensburg," follows me when I've climbed out of the car and I'm walking toward the house.

"Wow," says Will when I'm closer. "You look amazing."

"It's the bouclé."

"No." He chuckles. "It's the person wearing it. Come on, *sis.* You're late."

With a last, wistful glance toward Andre, I follow Will's lead and we step inside. My heels click against the marble floor and echo off the high ceilings. There's nothing soft to absorb the noise. The blinds are venetian and upholsteries minimal. No surface has been left untouched by Mother's designer.

Only when we're at the back of the house are we greeted with noise. The clinking of glass and light chatter. Will's steps slow as we approach the dining room and he gives me a small, side-on smile.

A horn may as well have blared, announcing our arrival when we pass through the door. What little noise there is disappears as I become a spectacle at my own party. Heart beating a little faster, I cast a quick glance around, confirming what I already anticipated. No one is here for me.

It's not like you expected anything else, I remind myself, as my eyes move over the board members and managing partners from South Africa's fastest expanding law firm.

They settle on the person standing in the center, in the predictable outfit, hair matching my own, wearing a look of disdain. Cape Unity's pillar of strength. Leader. Chairwoman. Annika Van Rensburg. My mother.

"Suzanne," she says, with a well-practiced smile. The *finally* that follows is so only I can hear.

"Mother."

I hold my breath and wait for something. Anything. An ounce of affection. Unfortunately, her motherly warmth wasn't discarded temporarily for the boardroom. It was discarded altogether.

Two half-filled Champagne flutes are in her hands when she covers the room. Transparent beige liquid sits in each. There's *just* the right amount of everything. Sheen to the glass. Liquid filling said glass. Bubbles soaring to the surface. Even the quantity of hors d'oeuvres doing the rounds have been carefully calculated.

"Thank you," I reply politely when she passes my drink.

Our eyes lock, and an eerie silence settles around us. The state of our relationship—or lack thereof—isn't an unknown, especially within her firm. When my eyes start to burn, I give in, blink, then divert my attention back to the room. I don't need to watch the corner of her mouth twitch like I know it will. Her warm smiles and reassurances were swapped for smirks a long time ago.

Will—the true professional he is—raises his flute in the air. It's a white flag, signaling that the first of the night's battles is over. When he lowers it and takes a drink, a non-audible sigh passes over us. Conversation sparks back to life.

Mother drags her attention away from her favorite offspring and puts on the performance of a lifetime, softening her eyes and leaning in toward me. She stops at the last second, leaving only millimeters between us. "Why are you wearing yellow? You're a part of the Van Rensburgs, not the solar system."

For my brother's sake, and the fact the room is filled with his guests, not only hers, I make my eye roll an internal one.

Will clears his throat. "Mother."

She pulls back, lips pursed. "I have guests to see to. If you'll excuse me."

The faint sound of a sniff follows her as she walks away. My shoulders slump and I take a sip of my drink. Any relief provided by her absence is temporary and my anxiety levels start to rise again when my eyes lock on a man in his early fifties. Our uncle spreads his arms wider than his midriff as he walks over.

I'm cursing our family genetics and the fact I bear some resemblance to him, when he says, overly loud and too enthusiastically, "My favorite partner." An unnatural number of teeth are flashed in my brother's direction. "Happy birthday, Willem."

I start to count in my head. I'm at five when I accept that I'm going to have to add on the second part myself. "And Sooz." I raise my glass, instigating my own toast. "Happy birthday, *Sooz*."

Will coughs, then, with a smile that doesn't reach his eyes, says, "Si. How are you doing?"

Our uncle lets out an out-of-place chortle, and I'm hit in the face with the overwhelming stench of rum. I wrinkle my nose while Will's smile remains set in place. Not one facial muscle moves. There's a reason he's secured his position as partner in Cape Unity, and it has nothing to do with my helping him over the past few months.

"Good," Simon replies.

"And we'd be even better if we didn't have to deal with you," I say under my breath.

The loud 'what?' from Simon makes it clear I wasn't speaking low enough.

His eyes widen a fraction when he turns his head in my direction.

Yes, Uncle Si. There's a third person supposed to be taking part in this conversation.

"We're so happy to see you!" I beam.

Will's guard slips and his brows drop to a shallow frown.

"And I, you," Simon replies. I blink. "You're returning to the UK, yes?"

"The *U-S*." I keep smiling while imagining introducing him to my middle finger. "New York. Day after tomorrow. Unfortunately, I couldn't catch a flight sooner." Will's elbow finds its way into my side, and I bury my wince in my Champagne. After drinking more than an acceptable amount in one, I raise my practically dry glass in the air. "Oh. Would you look at that? I'm out of the old champers. If you'll excuse me, I have to go …" Simon gives me an encouraging nod, while Will shakes his head. "And drown myself in it," I finish, out of earshot.

Catching sight of my empty glass, one of the waiting staff zeroes in. The suit the poor guy's wearing is as pretentious as his position. Getting closer, he raises the bottle he's carrying. He confirms his intentions to fill my glass with a solid, "Miss."

I shake my head. "No need. I'll take it with me and save you a job."

His mouth drops open when I whip the bottle out of his hands. The words 'join me' burn my lips. A rebellious streak that only appears when I'm here.

I ignore it and instead, when I'm happy no one is looking, slip out of one of the doors that leads to the large terrace. Garden seats and a long table are strategically placed to make the most of the vineyards.

I fill my glass to the top, then lean back and close my eyes, pretending I'm anywhere I want to be.

Anywhere but here.

Chapter Two

I'm not sure how long I spend outside. It doesn't feel like long until I hear a pair of footsteps tap along the terrace, stirring me from a faint, Champagne-induced slumber. The steady increase in volume makes the owner's target clear.

"Still torturing your poor uncle, I see." The voice is warm and familiar, belonging to one of the only people I care for here.

My eyes remain closed. "He deserves it for being …"

"A prick?" Henrik finishes for me, knowing I won't say it out loud.

"Yeah." I giggle.

Opening my eyes, I turn and take in my oldest friend—like, three decades old. He fills the expensive suit he's wearing perfectly, and his mousy brown locks are swept to the side. It looks effortless. I know otherwise; he parts with a fair chunk of money each year for styling products. There's a price to be paid for looking natural.

"You're glowing," he smiles, and his eyes drop to my outfit. "Literally."

"It was all the shop had in stock."

Henrik's face scrunches up as he tries to hold in his laughter. "Bullshit."

"Mother will kill you if she hears you cussing like that." He slides into one of the chairs next to mine, grabs the bottle of Champagne off the table, then gives the glass in my hand a skeptical look. "How refined of you." I snicker when he raises the bottle to his lips. He lets out an overdrawn sigh after drinking, then lowers the bottle and wipes his mouth with the back of his hand. "So, really, are you finally branching out from the monochrome vibe she's tried to instill? Or is it something else? Why the yellow?"

I smile into my glass. "A couple of weeks back, she caught me wearing a yellow dress and said it made me look like the sun."

"She isn't wrong." Henrik chuckles. "I wondered why the room got brighter. I turned, and there you were."

I roll my eyes and drain my drink.

"You'll be drunk if you carry on."

Henrik and I both still as Will walks around the table, stops in front of us, and shoves his hands in the pockets of his suit pants.

"I don't think I could ever be drunk enough to deal with this," I reply.

"Dramatic much?" There's a challenge in Will's gaze that would have most backing down. Unfortunately for my brother, the fact we shared a womb for nine months has me not caring who he is or what he does.

"I'm allowed to be dramatic. Tonight is supposed to be *our* birthday party, but Mother seems to have forgotten there are two people in the definition of twins. *Again.*"

Will lets out a long, suffering exhale. "Sooz. Stop."

"Willem." I glare. "You stop. For once." The disappointed look he throws back has me struggling to hold in a sigh as I turn to Henrik. "Could you give us a minute?"

Henrik's gaze flickers between the two of us. I shouldn't enjoy the poorly hidden daggers he gives my brother, but I do. Henrik gives my shoulder a squeeze when he stands. Then, knowing how to diffuse the situation perfectly, stops at Will's side and rests his left hand, palm flat, against his abdomen. The silver band on his ring finger glints in the light, and my brother relaxes. Henrik leans in to whisper something in his ear, and Will sags into his husband's touch. Warmth fills my chest, watching them together. They deserve this. The hidden moments—and all the rest—after the struggle it's taken to have their relationship accepted in Cape Unity.

A breeze picks up as Henrik leaves, rustling a couple of the oaks in the distance. Distracting myself, I tilt my head back, absorbing the feel of the warm air coating my skin as Will takes Henrik's place. Once settled in the rattan chair, he goes to take the bottle I'd forgotten was in my hands. I grip it like a vice.

Our eyes lock. His narrow. "I'd like a drink." My brow twitches. Waiting. "Please."

"Fine." I hand him the bottle and wave my glass in the air for him to take. "Got to keep up appearances, *bro.*" We both know Mother would have kittens if she or, God forbid, anyone else from the firm, witnessed him drinking from the bottle.

After grabbing the glass, Will fills it carefully, then hands the bottle back. "Why are you being like this?"

"Do you really need to ask?"

"People aren't mind readers, *sis*. If you're upset about something, then you're going to have to tell me."

"What?" My eyes widen. "You mean twintuition isn't a thing?"

Will scowls before unleashing a hard truth. "You're being a bitch."

My spine straightens and my lips pinch together as I wait for him to take it back or state he was joking. Neither happen. "I've yet to hear the words '*Happy Birthday*' be sent my way. It's a *joint* birthday party. I think my prickliness is justified."

Will groans, then goes to drag his hand through his hair, a color match to my own—vivid blonde. He stops right before the tips of his fingers touch the strands. "I'm sorry."

"It's fine."

The reason why I'm here, giving up time working on my own career so he could secure the position he deserved, has me slumping back into my chair. Will deserves this party tonight, and in a perfect world, I wouldn't have been needed the past few months. But the world isn't perfect, and neither are we. Neither am I. Far from it. Which is why, despite knowing all these things, the sting created from knowing how the night is going to continue to unfold doesn't get any less.

"It's not fine." Will shakes his head. "Not really. But I couldn't have done any of this without you. Are we good?"

"Always." And we are, even when my own successes are overshadowed by his, like our moment is overshadowed by the smell of searing meat wafting toward us from the house.

Springbok. Will groans as I wrinkle my nose. Joint party my behind. "We should go back in. People will be wondering where the guests of honor are."

Will goes ahead.

I spend a few more minutes outside, knowing ninety percent of the party couldn't care less where I am if he's in there with them.

Around dessert, the proverbial dump hits the fan.

The ninth eye clash with the woman sat opposite is when I'm tempted to slide the candelabra closest to me across the table. But, because I really do want to leave on as close to good terms as I'm able to with my mother, I don't.

Besides the candelabras, there's festive detailing on the high-end disposable napkins. When everyone is consuming their springbok, I conclude the gold foil has a carat count. A carat count that will quickly find its way into the trash, because Mother will have any sign of Christmas—only a couple of weeks away—disposed of the second her guests are gone.

"You two look so alike ..." the woman opposite me says, drawing my attention back to her. The Pinotage I'm midway through swallowing gets caught in my windpipe. "It's uncanny."

"We're twins," I deadpan when I've stopped coughing.

I wince into my glass when there's a sharp stab in my ankle.

"Fraternal," says Will as I set my glass down. "Easy mistake."

A parfait appears in front of me, and I clap my hands.

"Are your tastes similar in other things?" asks the woman, ruining my special moment with the first course I've been able to consume.

My spoon hovers in midair and Henrik scoffs around his own dessert.

"Excuse me?" I croak, lowering my spoon.

Mortification takes over as her words sink in. She's referring to Henrik. The point completing the triangle. Our childhood trio that has become more of a duo for obvious, marital reasons.

"Like hobbies and interests." She smiles sweetly, a poor attempt to cover up her insinuation.

I school my expression and raise my spoon back to my mouth, moaning when the creamy dessert coats my tastebuds. I really do love Parfait.

"No," I reply when my mouth is empty. "We're two completely different people. With different … *interests.*"

The tip of her spoon moves through the raspberry reduction decorated artfully on her plate. "And you work in law, too?"

"No." I hold her gaze. "Like I said. We're different."

"So then, you work in …?"

"PR." Because the two letters together don't appear to spark any kind of recognition, I expand. "Public Relations."

The next smile she gives me is bordering on sympathetic. "That's … nice …"

The temptation to throw my spoon across the table is strong. My target would be the raspberry sauce, so it splatters all over her white blouse.

"Sooz is the best in the business," says Henrik.

"Time to retire to the drawing room!" says Mother, jumping to her feet at the head of the table. Her chair falls back from the force, sounding out like a snare drum when it hits the ground.

I turn and give Henrik a look. We don't have a drawing room.

Will pushes his chair back carefully and stands. The rest of the room follows suit. Even the woman opposite me.

"Stay out of trouble," says Henrik under his breath before departing.

When everyone has left to celebrate Will's birthday, I pick up my spoon and tuck into my parfait, celebrating mine alone.

Two hours later, the guests leave. Their laughter is obnoxiously loud, disturbing the peace of the night.

I'm packing a few extra things I didn't take with me when I left South Africa three years ago, when there's a knock at my bedroom door. My skin prickles, the tell-tale sign of hives brought on by one person. I ignore it, praying Mother assumes I've left already and disappears to bed.

"Suzanne." *Bummer.* "I know you're in there."

The Van Rensburgs are known for three things: drive, persistence, and stubbornness.

Mother is as Van Rensburg as it gets. Her blood runs pure. Her drive is unquestionable with what she's achieved over the years with the firm. Her stubbornness is a given, being that she refused to take on our father's name. Her persistence is what has me scrambling to my feet from where I've been packing. She won't be going anywhere until I talk to her. The sooner we get this over with, the sooner I can leave.

When I reach the door, I hold my breath with my hand resting on the handle.

Two minutes. That's all it is. You've got this.

There's an overpowering smell of roses when I open the door. I wrinkle my nose as she drifts by.

"Mother," I say, my voice clipped.

As she moves around the room, I watch her, questioning if we're truly related. She stares at a couple of discarded pieces of clothing strewn across my bedroom floor like a hurricane has devastated the place.

"You're really leaving." There's an extra bite to her tone and I can't figure out why. She hasn't exactly been at the top of my call list, trying to overcome our communication difficulties in the past decade.

"Yes." I walk past her and grab a rogue camisole, then place it in the case Andre brought up for me at some point during the evening.

She does her usual pursing of the lips and—after giving my room another disdainful look—focuses her attention on me. "Stay."

I open and close my mouth. After swallowing harshly, I manage to say, "What?"

If Mother picks up on how she's rendered me virtually speechless, she doesn't show it.

"Christmas is soon." She sniffs, and I gawp. "What?"

"We haven't celebrated Christmas since Dad left."

"And?" No part of her face moves. Her recent Botox treatment is partially responsible.

"Well …" I pause. "I thought it was a given that we wouldn't be celebrating this year either."

"We could. You're back home." I feel a flutter of hope. "There's a function at the firm on Christmas Eve. Some of the board members are impressed with how well you handled Will's situation."

"Sorry. You know my flight's booked." I shrug her off and focus on my case, trying to ignore the burning sensation behind my eyes that's getting stronger with each second that passes.

Mother clasps her hands together. If only her intentions were as angelic as the look she's trying to portray. "This could be the chance you need to make something of yourself."

I suck in a breath. She might as well have slapped me.

"My flight can't be changed," I lie.

Her hands run over the double-breasted blazer she's wearing, part of a matching set. The pencil skirt fits her like a glove, skimming over hours of hard work in the gym and a limited calorie intake. "You could come home. Permanently."

"Brooklyn *is* my home."

"The firm would like to offer you a position."

My nostrils flare as I struggle to keep a grip on my emotions.

Van Rensburg's don't show weakness.

Mother watches me unphased.

"So …" I swallow, needing to calm my voice. "Let me get this straight. I give up what I want to do with my life, to help you?"

"Suzanne. The firm has employee benefits, they're reput—"

"No." I hold up my hand. It trembles ever so slightly in the air. "Don't *Suzanne* me. Don't treat me like a child."

"You could do great work with us."

"I'm already doing great work." I hate the words that work their way out of my mouth next. They make me sound spoiled, ungrateful. But there's so many years of resentment fueling their departure, that once I start to say them, I can't stop. I'm done trying when it comes to the two of us. I've nothing left to give. "The firm will have to find someone else. It's a no." I shut my case and zip it up, letting out a hiss of air when I catch my skin.

"Why are you behaving like this?" Mother snaps, as I set my case on the ground, ready to leave.

Because I'm a grown woman with the ability to make my own choices. Choices that, so far, have proven to serve me well in life ...

I stop after I've passed through the door and turn my head, angling it so she can hear what I say next without me having to face her. "There were two birthdays being celebrated tonight."

"It was a joint party, Suzanne." Her voice raises. "I threw it for you and your brother! What more do you want from me?"

The urge to walk away without another word is strong, but the urge to give her a verbal slap back is stronger. I turn so I'm facing her.

"I want you to respect that the choices I make are mine."

The tip of my nose tingles. *A few more minutes, then you can cry.*

"Suz—"

"When you call, if you ever decide to, I want you to call because you're interested in what I've been doing. I don't want you to call because you want something from me, or for me to do something for Will." My gaze catches on the way her neck muscles tense. It interrupts my flow. "But most of all …" I pause before delivering my final blow. "I want you, for once, to remember that I'm a fucking vegetarian."

As I walk along the hall, away from my room, her voice hits a pitch I've never heard, when she calls after me, "Where are you going?"

"Back to Brooklyn," I call back. "On the next flight I can catch."

"Wait! Suza—"

"Goodbye, Mother."

Andre doesn't say a word during the car ride to the airport and I don't bother asking where my other cases appeared from.

I also don't ask how he knew I'd need them.

Chapter Three

My flight from Cape Town to New York takes an eternity longer than usual.

I feel like an empty shell until we're halfway over the Atlantic, according to the in-flight map. The latter part of the journey picks up thanks to the three bottles of flight-sized spirits. Thank you, international flights, for the free drinks.

A wobbly step out of JFK and a yellow cab later, the tightness that's been sitting in my chest since I left Brooklyn months ago starts to ease with each mile I get closer to home. The one that feels like one. Even the battle with my bags up the many stairs can't ruin the moment I enter the three-bed apartment I share with Abby.

Especially not when a blur of brown and multicolor barrels toward me, jumps, and almost takes me down.

"'Tee Soo!" screeches the small person that's safely in my arms thanks to a good set of reflexes.

Laughter floats into the living room from our small kitchenette. "I think she's happy to have you back."

Where most would go the more civilized route with a hot beverage in greeting so early in the day, when my roommate Abby steps into the room, she already has the caps popped off two bottles of beer. The stained, oversized nightshirt and black leggings with a hole at the knee suggest my homecoming is barely the excuse she needs. The toys covering all surfaces and the small puddle of milk sitting on the coffee table turn the suggestion into more of a solid, confirming that Hurricane Clara has been on top form while I've been gone.

"What gave it away?" I reply, setting Clara down while trying to ignore the mess.

Eager brown eyes lined with the thickest, darkest lashes I've ever seen, stare up at me. I start to count in my head. I'm at three when she looks ready to burst. "Presents?"

"Clara …" Abby warns with a tight smile.

I puff my cheeks out, trying not to laugh.

"Pwease," Clara adds, missing the point entirely.

Her hopeful expression and uncanny timing, mixed with some serious sleep deprivation, are too much. My shoulders tremble and the air I've been holding in flies out of my nose.

Abby shakes her head while crossing the room toward us. I take the beer she's holding out for me and she ruffles Clara's hair when her hand is free. "This is Jake's fault for bringing something back each time he goes away."

"It's cute," I reply.

It's not a lie, or even a stretch of the truth. Clara is cute. Exceptionally so. I have a feeling it's intentional, so she can get away with whatever she wants. She's a force to be reckoned with. Not that a single person in our group would have it any other way.

Our bottles come together with a clink. "It's ridiculous is what it is," says Abby. "He's getting worse. Now he does it if he goes away for a day."

I laugh right before I go to take a drink, cursing inwardly when I almost chip my tooth against the glass. "Rockstar boyfriend being super cute with his daughter after it's taken the two of you over a decade to find a happy ending ... I'm not sure what the issue is?"

Abby's eyes lower to Clara, who is still staring up at me, waiting. I don't think I've seen her blink once. "He's spoiling her."

The corners of my lips twitch and I struggle to keep them in a line when I crouch so I'm at Clara's height. I set my bottle down on the coffee table and reach back to grab the bag I used as hand luggage. I drag it toward me. Then, so slowly that Clara starts to vibrate with excitement, pull out a stuffed rhino I bought from the tacky gift shop at Cape International. It rounds her Big Five collection up to three. There's a lion and elephant sitting on her bed.

My thoughts drift and I find myself questioning if I'll ever get to complete the set. The pity party is in full swing when I remember the promise that I made to Clara before I left for South Africa. I told her that one day she could come home with me, with Abby, and that we would go see the animals on a safari in real life. None of these things seem like a possibility now, after how I left things with my mother.

Clara's eyes widen when she sees the overpriced ball of gray fluff and she screeches, breaking me from my thoughts when she snatches it from my hands before racing to her room.

36

Carefully stepping over the stacking bricks scattered across the floor, I head to the couch, rubbing at my ear. "I think she burst my eardrum."

"You've only yourself to blame." Abby chuckles, and we both drop to the couch at the same time.

We land on the couch cushions with such force we almost bounce back up again. Thankfully, no beer is lost in the process.

"Beer before eight," I say, taking in the state of the room. "What's the special occasion?"

"My sanity hopefully being restored," Abby replies. If her voice didn't already give away her exhaustion, the dark panda circles beneath her eyes would do the job.

"It's good to know I'm missed somewhere." I laugh, then grimace when I take a drink of the liquid that's warmer than the temperature of the room. "Sorry. I can't do it." I set the bottle back down and twist my body so I can face Abby. "Want me to watch Clara while you get ready?"

Her shoulders droop. "Does getting ready include a nap?"

"Depends what time she has to be at daycare."

Abby taps her phone screen and then a "crapper" fills the room. "We're late." She clambers off the couch. "Are you coming into the office or sleeping?"

"Office," I reply without a second's pause.

"Of course." She hides her amusement as she walks in the direction of her room. "Do me a favor?"

"Yeah?" I call after her.

"Get rid of the beers in case Jake comes by."

"What?" I mock horror. "He's not a fan of early morning beer? But he's a rockstar …"

Abby turns back, laughing when she catches my expression. "He's been reading the parent bible again. If it's not in the book, we don't do it."

"Sounds delightful."

"Yeah, it's not." She disappears into her room.

Doing as asked, I make quick work of getting rid of the beers in the kitchen.

My body hums with excitement when I grab what I need for the day and leave the apartment, making my way to the one thing that's been reliable and consistent in my life. Work.

It's funny that when you're away from a place you miss, time seems to slow. Minutes feel like days. Days like years. But the moment you're back, it's like no time has passed at all.

That's how it feels as I walk into Next Level's offices. Like I'm being reunited with an old friend. Maybe without the old, as the offices are relatively new thanks to rapid business growth and necessary property expansion.

It was a risk, moving here and giving up my position at the old firm I worked at in Cape Town, where I first met Abby. There's something to be said for gut instinct, because we've been named New York's PR company to watch two years in a row. I feel a strong sense of pride as I bypass our glowing blue company sign that hangs in the lobby, framed by two potted palms.

The niggling desire to have my mother here to see all that I've accomplished keeps reappearing like a weed. Thinking it is a waste of energy. She's indicated her disapproval of my expat life all along, but when she offered me the position in the firm, her feelings became crystal clear.

I push through the glass doors and let out a sigh of relief when I see everything is how I left it. The intern's desks are still central in the main room. The life size #bekind framed canvas is still sitting on the large, exposed brick wall, after I spent two hours agonizing over its position. Admittedly, the spider plants in front of the windows could do with some TLC, but overall, I'm impressed. Zoe—our beauty guru and one of Abby's childhood friends—hasn't burned the place down leaving her hair styling appliances unattended, and the new interns who've been recruited in my absence all look happy.

But rather than feeling euphoric like I thought I would, I feel flat.

Brushing off the negative emotions that seem to have followed me from South Africa, I move through the lofty space, waving at the new interns as I go. They wave back, suggests they know who I am. That, or they're really good at pretending. I'm too jet lagged to figure out which, so I continue toward the back room. The designated office for Abby, Zoe, Amanda, and myself.

When I step inside, I blink as my eyes adjust to the rainbow in front of me, otherwise known as our office decor. The desks are as bright as I remember them. Then I take in the empty white one that used to belong to another of my closest friends—Sophie.

Get it together, I tell myself, trying to ignore the sinking feeling. She's chasing her dreams in the same way I moved here to chase mine.

The room is also empty, but a time check reveals I'm twenty minutes early. I make quick work of taking out what I need from my bag and setting it down on my desk—the yellow one. After, I head to the small kitchen area and make the strongest coffee I can stomach.

I re-enter the office with two minutes to spare, so I sit and fire up my laptop, then tap my fingers against my desk, waiting. Thirty-seven seconds before the hour, I hear Zoe before I see her. Amanda's laughter follows. There're slapping noises that sound suspiciously like high fives— likely with the interns—then the click of heels against the distressed wooden floors, which gets progressively louder.

"She's back!" squeals Zoe when she fills the doorway.

The surge of joy I feel seeing her for the first time is short-lived. She starts jogging on the spot—impressive given the heel size she's sporting—then crouches and shows some spirit finger action.

She looks like she's going to …

Oh God, I hope she isn't …

She does exactly what I don't want her to, sprinting across the room and diving into my arms. I let out a "oomph" when she collides with me, sending my desk chair into a literal spin.

"We've missed you!" My response is non-audible, because she's squeezing my face into her chest. "What did you say? I couldn't hear you."

"I said," I reply, pushing her away. "That we spoke every day."

"It's not the same." She pouts, walking over to her orange desk. "Go on. Admit you missed us, too."

"Of course, I did."

She drops into her chair and spins back round to face me, wiggling her brows. "How much?"

Amanda is busy starting up her laptop and pulling what she needs out of her beige Chloé shoulder bag. It's like

40

watching an Elle Woods-Mary Poppins crossover. She takes a moment to look up from what she's doing, and some of her platinum hair falls forward, covering her face. "Ignore her. She's been needy since Sophie left."

Zoe huffs. "I am not being needy."

"Yes ..." Amanda sets her bag into her bottom drawer, because Chloé never goes on the floor. "You are. I have to remind you daily she still wants to talk to you, even though she's not here."

"Fine. I miss her," Zoe admits. Sophie leaving has been a sore spot for her after they'd only just managed to repair years of damaged friendship.

"And that's fine," Amanda responds. "But you're now defusing your neediness onto Sooz." Zoe scowls. "Take all that energy and plow it into something useful, like the New Year's Ball checklist I emailed over last week that you still haven't read."

"You can't know I haven't read it," Zoe says.

"I put an open alert on it," Amanda fires back. "Yes, I can." She starts typing in her password.

I seize the opportunity to interrupt. "I missed you, too," I say, knowing it's what Zoe needs to hear. "Even after the daily calls." Her expression lifts. "I also like the violet." I gesture at her hair. "Definitely winter vibes."

Zoe frowns. "Winter vibes? I'm transitioning into Hit-Girl." My silence gives away that I don't have a clue what she's referring to. "Mindy McCready ..." I give her a blank look. "For the Ball ... It's who I'm going as. She's from *Kickass*, and it's our first major event, so I wanted to get into the spirit and be a kickass character."

A dull headache builds behind my eyes.

41

"I told her she could have saved her hair health and bought a wig," Amanda says over her shoulder, opening her calendar on her screen.

"I'm getting into character," Zoe explains. "Like method acting." I pinch my brow, trying to relieve some of the tension. I'd forgotten what the office chaos felt like. "What's wrong?"

"Headache," I reply. "Can we discuss costumes another time? We have bigger things to worry about, like organizing the event."

The event being the New Year's Ball, which Next Level decided to organize at the start of the year. At the time, it seemed a great idea—a way of leveling up, showing the industry what we're really made of. Getting the cream of the celebrity world under one roof and promoting the hell out of ourselves. Then life started to get in the way. Now we're permanently a team member down, it's safe to say my daily heartburn episodes aren't unwarranted.

"Fine," Zoe replies. I ignore the huff she lets out after.

"Great." I stop with the pinching and give her a genuine smile. "Onto the agenda. Catch me up."

Zoe and Amanda share a look, remaining silent.

"What?" The fact Zoe talks at all times, even in her sleep, is a clear indicator there's something wrong. "Why are you both looking at each other like that?"

"So, agenda!" Amanda says, pitch high, brows higher.

"Why do I get the feeling I'm not going to like what's on the agenda?" I stare between the two of them.

Amanda is better at masking her emotions than Zoe, so when she shows no sign of cracking, I face the alternative. As predicted, Zoe looks like she's going to break out in a sweat beneath all her foundation and contouring. I think I've got her when Abby bustles in, looking more put-together than back at the apartment. She's wearing her standard skinny jean, vest and shacket combo. No holes or stains to be found. The bun sitting on top of her head is strategically messy, compared to the struggling-with-life kind.

"Sorry. Clara refused to go into daycare." She drops into her chair with force and hits the power button on her laptop. "Again." When she receives no response, she spins her chair, glances around, then smiles in my direction. "Has Zoe told you about the office decoration bonanza she has planned?"

"No." I shake my head. Zoe still looks like she's going to pass out from guilt-ridden stress. Whatever part of the agenda she was going to reveal, it had nothing to do with Christmas decorations.

"We wanted you to get settled first," says Zoe, holding a defensive finger in the air.

"Yeah. Right." I narrow my eyes and look around them all. "What's going on?"

Gesturing in the direction of her screen, Amanda starts to explain. "All our diaries are jam-packed, as you can see."

"Okay …" Her screen is a rainbow of color, more vivid than our desks. The only space that is white is the column where my name reads at the top.

Abby goes all in, straight to the point. "A new job has come in."

"What is it?" I ask. The girls look between each other again. "What aren't you telling me?"

"There have been a few issues while you've been gone." Amanda waves her hand in the air, as if she's swatting said issues away.

"What kind of issues?"

43

Zoe coughs, then opens her mouth. Whatever she was going to say gets lost in the ringing of my phone.

I give them all a hacky look before grabbing it off my desk, frowning when I see the name 'John West' flashing on the screen.

"Hello?" I answer, hesitantly.

"Sooz! Hi!" says Abby's father—one of the big dogs at Warped Record Label—cheerily. My shoulders drop ever so slightly with relief. Whatever he's calling for can't be that bad, because he sounds his usual self. "Good trip?"

"Great," I lie. "What can I do for you?"

"Do you think you could come by the label within the hour? I need to talk to you."

"Um …" My bottom lip finds its way between my teeth. So much for this not being a big deal. "I could. But we have a lot on here. If there's any chance, could we do it over the phone?"

"Sorry," John replies. "I need you to come here."

Warped Records are our biggest client. There's no way I can say no. "Okay. No problem. I'll try to get to you as soon as I can."

"Thanks, Sooz. It's appreciated. I'll see you soon."

We say a quick goodbye and then both hang up. The girls each look guilty as charged. They confirm as much when not one of them says a word.

"This better not become a thing," I say to the little traitors as I slide my laptop and chargers back in my bag. Still, no one says a word. They simply drop their heads, pretending to be absorbed with their laptops. Zoe has yet to turn hers on.

Accepting I'm going to get nothing from them, I leave, preparing myself to jump straight into the deep end. I just hope that whatever John needs me for isn't going to make me sink.

Chapter Four

Trudging through Times Square, I feel dead on my feet. I pull my coat tight around me as rain bounces off the sidewalk, splashing against my boots. The only negative of my abrupt South African departure: I didn't get to enjoy a final day of summer before returning to *this*.

Sure, New York has its moments of beauty outside of my favorite warm season. Like Central Park in the fall, when the leaves on the trees resemble licks of fire hanging in the sky. Or the multicolored lights around the giant tree at the Rockefeller Center, brightening the darkest of days. I could come up with a long list.

But the euphoric feelings that come with experiencing the magic New York has to offer are, more often than not, dulled by the dank weather and bitter wind chills. When you're caught in the full throes of a winter here, it feels never ending.

With a shiver working its way through my body, I still can't hide the smile tugging at my lips. The thing about the Big Apple is, it's a fighter. It doesn't care what anyone thinks, finding a way to turn a negative into a positive. Like now. The crowded sidewalks are providing some reprieve from the wind whipping through the streets. Tight bodies press in around me, helping to hold in what little heat there is.

When I'm at the right place, I crane my head back. Clouds obscure the view of the top of the building. Nerves kick in with the anticipation of what I'm going in to. This place houses TV networks, film production companies, animation studies, the odd talent agency. But, most importantly, it's the home to Warped Records.

Pushing my nerves down, I make my way inside. My boots click against the gleaming marble floors, the sound making my stomach clench while the contents of it swirl more than the white and black pattern beneath my feet. It gets worse when I step inside the elevator and watch the number on the small screen increase the higher up I travel. The stop the elevator comes to is so seamless I don't realize it's happened until the doors sweep open, revealing the coolest set of offices I've ever had the privilege of setting foot in. Sorry, Vogue. Warped Records are the trend leaders here. Psychedelic carpets. White surfaces. Floor-to-ceiling windows. They all complement the cream of the music business, floating around like they're taking part in a trip to the grocery store.

Gracie Ray smiles when our paths cross and I do an internal squeal. I'm a total fan girl. Not that I'd ever let it show. I keep my composure. I'm the epitome of cool. But damn, Gracie Ray smiled at me! I'm still swooning when I approach the front desk.

After checking in, the receptionist leads me through the offices. They cover so much floor space it feels impossible we're still in the city. But those are the expectations of younger me, the one who would devour books based in New York, drinking in all the little details, including the emphasis on the lack of space. Younger me didn't realize this only really applied to the literal living situation, and my first trip here cleared up any misconceptions. Nothing about the city is small.

When we come to a stop outside a glass door, the receptionist taps her knuckles against it. John West looks up. He might not be *my* father, but I pick up the small details making his expression grim.

The contents of my stomach set into motion once more, when my eyes laser in on one of the two chairs facing John's. The one on the left already filled by a figure.

A figure with a broad back, wearing a worn leather jacket.

A figure with messy hair. Hair I hate. Hair that's been causing me issues since the day I moved here, because of the owner's refusal to do anything with it apart from what he wants, even for a front-page cover for the biggest magazine in the country.

A figure that, when the glass door opens and the barrier is removed, will make my nose wrinkle from the earthy, woody scent of marijuana he carries with him wherever he goes.

Ryan-feckin-Alvarez.

Because we've avoided each other wherever possible, it's instinctive to turn and walk away. John West nodding captures my attention, though. And no matter how much I want to, no matter how much my gut tries to tell me this is going to be the start of something I want no part of ... I

47

don't leave. My feet remain rooted to the spot. When the receptionist opens the door and moves to the side to let me pass, I still don't move. I remain where I am, stuck in limbo with my jaw clenched, trying to decide what to do.

"Sooz. Hi." A muscle in John's jaw twitches, like he's torn between saying an overly earnest please or holding himself back from dropping to his knees and begging me not to leave. "Come in."

He slides his chair back and stands, reducing the odds of me darting. Even his movements seem wary. There's a slowness to the way he brushes a hand over his already straight navy tie. Reluctantly, I approach the right-hand chair, hating that it's where I'll be sitting. Left is where it's at. It's the seat I have the most success with, because the majority of clients I deal with are right-handed. Because of this, their gaze naturally falls ever so slightly to the same place. Right. My left.

It's not a legitimate thing, but I've put a lot of my success down to this small detail.

John's eyes dull as he gestures for me to take the dreaded right seat.

I do. Hesitantly.

"Thank you for coming by on such short notice."

Clasping my hands in my lap, I try to ignore the way my palms slip against each other as much as I try to ignore the person at my side. The one who might as well not be here, because for the first time since I've known him, he's saving us from hearing the many delights that often find their way out of his mouth.

"No problem," I reply.

A small clock sitting on John's desk ticks, filling the silence.

"We have a potential issue. Well ... *issues*."

A sideways glance at S.C.A.R.A.B.'s drummer has my gut stirring again. His hair's unrulier than usual. Not the fake I-don't-care-what-the-world-thinks-of-me unruly, the I-haven't-bathed-in-a-week unruly. What's covering his jaw doesn't look far off catching up in length. I sniff, assessing with my senses the severity of what we're dealing with. One of the muscles in Ryan's jaw flickers at the sound.

His eyes remain focused on the window, a dancing cannabis leaf fills the digital billboard directly opposite. Suddenly, it bursts into flames, revealing a tortured cartoon figure. Cue the dancing bottle of CBD and the cartoon figure miraculously becomes a happy, relaxed version of itself.

An irony-fueled snort slipping out is what gets Ryan's attention. He turns to face me. I match his movement and our gaze's lock. His vivid green eyes narrow. If he's trying to intimidate me to keep my opinions to myself, he'll have to try harder.

"Are they marijuana-related issues?"

Ryan remains silent. John West looks like he wants to be anywhere but in the same room with the two of us.

"Somewhat," John replies.

I hold back an eye roll. "Figures." I ignore Ryan's huff. "What are we dealing with?"

The clock continues ticking. With each second that passes, it begins to sound more like a bomb. I brace myself, ready for it to detonate.

I hear Ryan draw in a breath when John West opens a drawer to his left and pulls out a brown manilla envelope. He slides it across his desk. An invitation to take part in whatever disaster is going to unfold. I give it a long, hard stare.

Do I want to see what's inside?

Do I want a part in this?

Next Level already have enough to deal with, and we're about to find ourselves amidst the full throes of the festive season. The fact Ryan is still at my side, remaining unnaturally silent, is a warning. I go to shake my head, apologize to them both and leave, when I catch Ryan's hand gripping the arm of the chair so hard his knuckles are white.

Mentally blocking John out, I shift in my seat. "Am I going to hate what I find inside?"

Ryan faces me again. "Yes."

"Why am I here?"

A shadow crosses his face, turning the green of his irises from a shade somewhere between grass and mint to a dark green mulch. "Because I need you." A boulder lodges in my throat. "Will you help?"

I frown at his abruptness. "You're asking me to help when I have no idea what I'm going to be dealing with."

"No," Ryan says. "I'm asking you to decide whether you care enough to help, regardless of what's inside."

"We hate each other." The words come out more of a whisper and I curse at the slight falter in my voice.

"You fuck me off at times …" He trails off, and I wait for more words to follow. I'll be waiting a lifetime, because instead of continuing, he stands.

I shoot John West a confused look when he doesn't stop him from walking toward the door, then crane my neck so I can ask, "Where are you going?"

"I can't be here when you make your choice," Ryan replies.

"Why?"

"Whatever you decide needs to be because you want to help me. Not because I'm here, making you feel like you have to."

Forget the verbal slaps Mother delivered forty-eight hours ago. These are worse.

The Ryan Alvarez I know is a waster. Unpredictable. Painful.

He isn't reasonable.

"And what happens if I decide not to help?"

Ryan shrugs. "Nothing. Things stay the same."

A simple nod is all I'm capable of giving him before he slips silently out of John West's office. I twist my neck so I'm back facing forward. John West's eyes drop to the envelope waiting on the desk for me. When I pick it up, there's a slight tremble to my hand. It turns to a full-blown shake when I lift the lip and drag out a thick wad of images.

The bomb detonates.

"Oh …" I say, taking in the first distorted image. Even with the fuzziness, there's no denying it's Ryan standing tall, powerful, overbearing, with his anatomy in the mouth of a woman who looks old enough to be his mother. "My …" comes out when I thumb through a few more. I stop at a crisp image of him unconscious on the floor of what is undeniably a brothel. "God …"

"It's not ideal," grimaces John.

He pushes back his desk chair and walks over to the wet bar stationed in the corner of his office. He grabs two crystal glasses then looks over his shoulder. "What would you like?"

"Vodka, please," I answer.

He fills the glass with three thick fingers worth of liquid, so clear it could be mistaken for water. I'm ready to guzzle it down like it is. Four fingers of Scotch fill his own glass.

"This will destroy the band's reputation," I say, stating the obvious when he hands over my drink.

The pad of my thumb skims over the exquisite diamond cut in the crystal, the pattern identical to the glasses my father used to have me hand him. I block out the harsh reminder, raising the glass to my lips and letting the ice-cold liquid pass them. The burn the vodka creates is like the previous owner of the seat at my side. Polar. Subtle, yet harsh.

"The label's too if we don't handle this right," John says, breaking me from my thoughts.

"Where are they from?"

John takes a long drink of his Scotch, leaving less than two fingers' worth behind. "They appeared in the label's mailbox a few days ago."

"Do they want money?"

He shakes his head uncertainly. "We're unsure. That, or ..."

"Or?"

"We think they've been sent by a competitor." John drains the final fingers of amber liquid from his glass.

A competitor would know what they're doing. Have the means to do whatever they want, and stop at nothing until they reach their end goal. Legal fees and whatever else will come from the fallout of these images making their way into the world will be pocket change to a competitor.

What isn't pocket change ... the dreams of the four guys who have done nothing but bleed themselves dry to get to where they are.

"Another label?" I croak. "Why?"

"There were whispers a month ago that with S.C.A.R.A.B.'s success following the performance at Orensanz, and the forecasted pre-tour sales for next year,

Warped Record's profits would start to take over the majority share of the market."

"Things change all the time. Players get knocked off the top spot in any industry."

John leans back in his chair, clasping his hands in front of him and interlacing his fingers. "What do you know about Warped Records?"

"That in the past decade they've moved from ranking at the lower end of the top one hundred record labels in the world to the top ten," I reply instantly. One of the main parts of my job for Next Level—locking in new clients—means knowing everything about them. "That Wayne Rogers started it ..." John nods. "Why do I feel like this is more important than how much of the market Warped Records is dominating?"

"Not more important." John smiles. "Neither acts as a singular in this."

Hello cryptic. I don't say that out loud. I go for, "Sorry, what?"

"It's what the two together mean." He glances at my glass. "Another?"

My eyes widen when I find it as empty as his. When did that happen? Because the past few days have been downright terrible, I say yes. Spirits aren't my go-to, especially not during stressful times, but I've been tipped into a place I'm unfamiliar with and it feels like the only way to cope.

When John is back in his seat with both of our glasses replenished—with significantly less liquid—he exhales before delving back into his confusing explanation. "Wayne Rogers, Warped Record's founder, is also one of the main reasons we're working alongside Sophie, funding Singing to

Heal. He had a vision. He wanted to create a label where image meant nothing, and talent meant everything."

"Why?"

"For a while, he worked for one of the big dogs."

"I didn't know that," I admit.

"Only those closest to him do. Part of him getting out of his employment contract was that if he wanted to work in the industry, it would be with a name no one knew."

"But everyone knows his name ..."

"His new one."

I frown. "He *literally* changed his name?"

John takes a sip of his drink. "Legally. Yes. He wanted to change the music industry with Warped Records, and he was willing to do whatever it would take. His vision is coming to life now more than ever thanks to S.C.A.R.A.B."

"Figures?" I squeak, needing to know exactly what I'm dealing with.

"Pre-tour sale predictions have beaten a certain blonde you passed in reception."

My eyes practically pop out. "S.C.A.R.A.B. are beating Ray Ray?" John gives me an amused look. "She's my favorite ..." I explain. "Which is why I find it hard to believe what you're telling me. Those kinds of pre-sales don't happen in alternative music. *Especially* not rock alternative." The corners of John's mouth lift. "And I'm judging."

"The reason why this is happening is because the band is focusing on the music *they* want to create. Want to know what takes a talent to the *next level?*" I smile at his play on words. "Passion. But you already know that with what you've achieved with my daughter."

"I'm assuming we're not allowed to say her name, so all I'm going to do is state the obvious. She's not with Warped."

Of course, I'm referring to my fan girl moment and the reason why it threw me.

"She wants to be," explains John. "She wants a label that support her values and goals. Who she is over the image she's presenting. And that's what this all comes down to. But the rest of the industry doesn't like it. For too long, artists who started with a dream have been forced into whatever box was trending, into becoming something they didn't want to be. Whoever their label made them."

"Which leads us to this …"

"A battle between image and talent …" John says grimly. "Because if the most successful artists figure out the biggest label in the world is letting their artists focus on talent …"

"Then they will jump ship."

My airwaves feel like they're starting to close up. "You think they're going to threaten to leak the images unless you drop the band. And if you don't, they're going to use cancel culture to prove image does matter and destroy the label." John drains his glass a second time. "S.C.A.R.A.B. will be collateral … People will hate Ryan …"

"Unless we fight back …" All the dots start to connect and a bitter taste that has nothing to do with the vodka I've downed fills my mouth. John leans forward, resting his elbows against the rich wood of his desk. "So, what do you say?"

I stare out at the colorful display of Times Square. My bones ache with tiredness, but it doesn't stop me remembering why I'm here. Because I, like the band, refuse to be put in a box.

When I make my decision, my eyes find John's.

"Tell me what you need me to do …"

Chapter Five

My time traveling from Manhattan, back to Brooklyn, is spent on my phone—when the Subway signal allows—trying to figure out where Ryan left to.

I'm in Riff's—Sam's older brother Shaun's bar—no closer to finding him, when my chest expands with hope at the sight of Jake through the top glass panels of the door. He walks in, and at first, I don't think he sees me. I use the moment to remain where I'm standing at the bar and take him in. Where the eyes are often the windows to someone's soul, Abby once told me Jake's window is his clothing.

My gaze lands on black jeans first—his usual pair, but clean and pressed relatively well. I then move to his white t-shirt—it's a positive that it hasn't been replaced by a black one. If it were red, any attempts at a conversation would be a no go. His dark hair is its usual level of messy. My overall assessment: he looks too clean and put together for the band to have been on a blowout. Yet. It's only been an hour, if that. There's still time.

Unfortunately, Abby's claim might not quite be hitting the mark in these circumstances, because the deep-set lines framing his eyes and covering his brow give away his anxiety that matches my own. He scours the small groups that have congregated, despite it only being afternoon. After a second, his eyes stop moving, landing on their target, and it registers who he's looking for. Me.

He makes short work of moving through the bar and stops in front of me abruptly, rubbing the back of his neck, like his second home is the last place he wants to be.

"You've spoken to John?"

I give him a tense nod and shift the straps of my bag further up my shoulder. "I left the label an hour ago. Ryan left before that. I stopped by your place but there was no one there, hence why I'm here." Jake looks troubled. "Where is he?"

His attention moves behind me and he signals to one of the bartenders for a beer.

I exhale through my nose and count to ten. Somewhere between four and five, I lose my patience. "We're on a short timeline."

Jake's attention snaps away from the bartender and back to me. "Do you think I don't know that?"

I narrow my eyes. "How much do you know?"

He lets out a huffy laugh, doing an excellent impression of the guitarist I first met before he got his act together and grew up. If only his drummer had followed his example, then maybe we all wouldn't be stuck in this mess, drowning in his mistakes.

"He mentioned a picture."

"Ten," I clarify.

Jake pales as the bartender appears with his beer. He grabs it from the bar and downs half the contents in one giant gulp. "Fuck."

Folding my arms over my chest, I soften my approach. "Worse than you thought?"

He grimaces and takes another drink. "Yeah."

I wait until he's set his beer down before broaching my next line of questioning. "Did you know?" I search his face. "About this habit …"

The muscle in his jaw ticks. It's tiny. But it's there. "Everyone has a past, and some of us aren't lucky enough to put it behind us."

Pushing this isn't worth the effort. Any information he gives me will take time to get. Time which we don't have on our side. I decide to go for a different angle.

"I can't help if I don't know where he is …" I hold my breath, praying Jake will pick up on my hint.

A wary look is what I get in return. Then, silence. I'm ready for giving up when Jake says, "Where do you think he is …"

"I don't know. Which is why I'm here, and he isn't," I quip.

Jake chuckles. It's not a humorous chuckle, but it's light. He seems less standoffish than before. "He's not home." His fingers graze his stubbled chin. "And he's not here." He's mocking me, but I guess it's better than him hating on me. "Where else could he be? Where do S.C.A.R.A.B. spend most of their time …"

"The Wreck."

"Ding, ding, ding." He pushes the boat out, mimicking a lightbulb moment.

The word starting with A and ending with hole is on the tip of my tongue. Mother's expectations have embedded themselves in deep over the years, though, so I keep the insult to myself. Spinning on my heel, I hurry in the direction of the exit before Ryan can change his location.

"A 'thank you' wouldn't go amiss," Jake calls after me.

His laughter follows me into the streets of Williamsburg when I use my middle finger in place of my mouth.

For a long time, I've questioned why S.C.A.R.A.B. practice at The Wreck.

It's a rehearsal room in Brooklyn—if you can even call it that—that's two floors up with non-existent security. That's after a trip along a beaten-down alley through too many smells. Weirdly, it's the hammering of drums, usually used to amp up an audience, that calm me.

Now I know Ryan is here, I kind of want to put off the inevitable. In the time I've spent frantically searching for him, I've not really thought about what would happen once I found him. I'm halfway up the second flight of stairs when I pull out my phone.

Any hope of a quick check is gone when I see how many notifications I have. Ignoring the never-ending stream of emails coming in, I open the messenger app. There're a few notifications in the Next Level group chat.

Deciding I'll speak with the girls later, I open the message from Henrik.

Are you alive?

I smile at the GIF he's sent of a panda searching with a pair of binoculars.

Just, I reply.

Knowing, because of the time difference, I won't get a response straight away, I slide my phone back into my bag, then cast a glance up the remaining stairs. My pulse thrums beneath my skin, as fast as the beat Ryan is smashing out on his drum kit. I don't get nervous. So why now?

Because it's personal.

We might not always like each other. We might not always see eye to eye, but ultimately, I do have his best interests at heart.

After telling myself I've got this, I make my way up to the rehearsal room. I wrinkle my nose at the overwhelming smell of weed that gets stronger the closer I get. It's going to take at least two washes to remove it from my clothing.

When I'm hovering at the doorway, Ryan continues playing, none the wiser to my presence. I watch while the rings, pops and thumps vibrate through the air. His inked arms glisten with exertion in the light, as he remains lost in the beats he's creating.

Never one for extended personal moments, I cough. My timing is off, because he rolls into a somehow louder section of whatever it is he's playing, drowning out my efforts. I don't attempt to catch his attention again. I opt for walking deeper into the rehearsal room, remaining a safe distance back when I stop.

His arms stop moving when he looks up. I wave halfheartedly.

"We need to talk." I might as well be talking to myself. Ryan just sits. Watching. When he doesn't even blink, I start to wonder how high he is. "Did you hear me?"

He moves, setting his drumsticks down on one of the drums. They make an echoing clatter. I go to ask what he's doing, when he raises his hands up, toward his ears, then pulls out a pair of yellow ear plugs.

"You could have taken them out to start with," I say, face blank.

Ryan sets the plugs down next to the drumsticks. "If I'd known these are all it would take to block you out, I would have used them sooner."

"You're hilarious," I deadpan.

He smirks. "Most people seem to think so."

"Is that how you have so many women falling at your feet? With all your humor?"

"Wow." He blinks. "You can't find it in you to be nice to me even for a few minutes after you've found out my life is going to be ruined?" His words come out as lazy as his movements when he stands up from the small stool where he's been sitting.

"You're assuming I decided to help you."

"Why else would you be here?"

"Unfortunately, I don't have a few minutes to play nice, thanks to *someone's* poor choices." I cast a glance to the side, finding more of his poor choices sitting on display on a small table—for anyone to see. There are two joints already finished. I bet if I were to touch them both, one might still feel warm based on the ripeness of the fruity scent filling the room.

"Whatever." Ryan moves around the drums and walks toward me.

"That's it." I smile, overly sweet. "You *whatever* this situation and continue getting stoned."

I catch his fist clench at his side out of the corner of my eye. "You don't know what you're talking about."

"There's an old saying." I move closer to him, so close the smell of weed clinging to his clothing makes my eyes start to water. "A picture speaks a thousand words. Lucky me. I got to look at all ten of them. You messed up. Admit it. Own it. Move on from it."

Ryan scowls down at me. "Is that the genius plan? I thought you were paid for things like this?"

"And I thought you were supposed to be a world class musician. Act like one." I pause. "Or don't. Maybe that's what the issue is here? You've let fame get to your head? Think you're above behaving like a rational human?"

Ryan dips his chin. Too far. So far, our noses almost touch. I can feel his warm breath on my lips when he says, "Leave it, Sooz."

I give him my most passive aggressive smile, playing a game of Russian Roulette, when I lift my own chin, virtually eliminating the last of the space between us.

"Unfortunately, I can't. You ensured that the second you let multiple women suck you off and were stupid enough to get caught." My chest rises and falls. Ryan's jaw ticks. While I have the upper hand, I roll my shoulders and take a step back, getting ready to put the first part of the plan I came up with on the way here into place. "John hired me for a reason. I suggest you follow the advice of the one person I know you respect. Now, if you'll excuse me, I need to go, because *some* of us are trying to save your career, while it appears *you* have no problem continuing to destroy it."

With the cold hard evidence of his harem of women and addiction sitting in the small brown envelope in my bag, I leave him behind.

Chapter Six

"The board wants to handle things in house," says John West a couple of minutes into our conversation.

"But you don't," I finish.

I called him the second I received his assistant's voicemail, explaining that he needed me to contact him regarding an update on Ryan's situation. The update, I now know, is that Warped Record's board members don't trust Next Level to handle the situation.

It's not necessarily a shock, considering most of them are old enough to be *John West's* father. Old and stuck in their ways.

But what is a shock is what John hits me with next.

"You're the only person Ryan trusts."

My "Excuse me?" mingles with a snort.

"Yes?"

"You said Ryan trusts me …"

"I did," John replies, unfazed. "Unfortunately, we can't ignore what the board wants, given the circumstances. It will make an already fragile situation worse. We need to play this out carefully."

"Ryan doesn't trust me," I say, needing John to understand the situation. Surprised that he doesn't already.

"By the time the PR department prioritizes this," John continues, "it will already be too late. Plus, the odds of Ryan doing anything they ask are minimal."

"Because the odds of him listening to me are so much higher." I laugh.

"Sooz," John says. His voice comes out slow and weary. "The fact Ryan allowed you to witness a situation where he's at his most vulnerable speaks volumes."

It's my turn to pause. "Most vulnerable? Those images are the result of his poor choices."

"Nothing about what you've seen is his choice. You should know better than anyone that an image is a snippet of a bigger picture. Often without context."

"Then tell me what it is I'm really dealing with here," I say quietly.

"I can't," he answers. "It's not my story to tell."

My alarm sounds out two minutes after I've closed my eyes. At least, it feels that way, thanks to my phone conversation with John West at the end of yesterday.

Blinking into the darkness, the minimal light spilling in behind my blinds confirms it's too early. But time is of the essence. After allowing myself some more time buried in my sheets, I ignore my body's protests and force myself up.

"Morning," says Abby, looking a stark contrast to what I witnessed during our reunion yesterday.

She's the epitome of shabby cool in an oversized shirt and lounge pants. Her hair's a tumble of soft, dark waves around her shoulders. I look like a gremlin.

"Thanks." I smile when she slides my yellow 'Sooz' cup, filled with coffee, across the kitchen counter. Once I've dumped a ton of sugar in it, I wait for it to cool, tapping my fingers against the worktop impatiently.

Abby waits until I've drunk a third of my caffeine, necessary for functioning, before asking, "How did yesterday go with my dad?" I attempt to hide behind my cup, but my expression gives it all away. Abby's mouth twists. "That bad?"

I set my cup down and decide vague is the answer. "It could've gone better." I know she knows. I just don't know the extent of what she knows. I have a sneaky suspicion the implications of all this have been toned down by John a significant amount. The last thing he will want is her worrying about what this all means for Jake. "I assume Jake's mentioned the pictures …"

"Yeah."

"I can't believe he was stupid enough to get caught." I'm unable to keep the bitterness from my voice.

Abby's brows knit together. "He made a mistake, Sooz."

"He made a lot more than one," I mutter, staring into my cup. When I lift my head, I squirm under the disapproval she's sending my way. "Why are you looking at me like that?"

"He's not a bad guy …"

She has a point. A valid one. But I'm overtired, grumpy, and more anxious than I've been in a long time about a work-related issue. Needless to say, the combination isn't bringing out my best side. Snappy, irrational Sooz is working to the max. "Message understood." I salute, and Abby's frown turns to a smile. "I swear to be the queen of professionalism."

"There's only one problem," Abby says, as I walk out of the kitchen.

"Which is?" I call back over my shoulder.

"You don't swear." Her laughter filters through my bedroom door when I've closed it.

While getting ready to take on the day, I pray Ryan decides to be on his best behavior. Otherwise, it will be impossible for me to be on mine.

Knowing Zoe is the one in Next Level with the most flexible workload, I fire off a string of messages to her with my plans, detailing exactly where I need assistance. She shoots back an 'Okay', and, just like that, I have a partner in crime.

My relief lasts all but a few minutes, ending abruptly when I step out of mine and Abby's apartment block into the cold, dragging the bag representing what is going to happen next down the front steps. My new job role is the last thing I want to be doing, but I have no choice. We can't control the situation if Ryan goes off the rails like he's been known to. So here I am, ready to become his live-in babysitter.

When I get to S.C.A.R.A.B.'s place, the first round of knocking does nothing. Neither does the second.

On the third round, I go for more of a hammer approach. It seems to do the trick, because shortly after, a weary-looking Sam—S.C.A.R.A.B.'s lead singer—answers, wearing a pair of basketball shorts and an old band shirt.

"Sooz?" He rubs away the sleep clogging the corners of his eyes and stares at me blearily.

Folding my arms across my chest, I give him a look of mock concern. "Sophie's kicked you out already?"

"The troops rallied together." He groans the second he realizes he's let slip what he shouldn't have. Rubbing his hand back and forth through his sandy blond hair makes it stick up in all directions.

"You mean you got wasted," I reply with a glare.

"There were some beers."

"*Some*." Throwing in air quotes, I attempt to keep my voice light.

Sam shrugs. "We're pro's ..."

"That's what I'm worried about." With his frame filling the doorway, I glance over his shoulder, signaling that I want to enter. He doesn't budge. "Are you going to let me in?"

Sam narrows his eyes. "Are you going to be kind?"

"When am I ever not?"

"Always." He grins and goes to turn away, mumbling under his breath, "That's what I'm worried about."

"Fine." Before he disappears I hold my right arm out between us and wiggle my little finger. "I pinky promise." He eyes my smallest digit like it's a lethal weapon. "Come on, Sam. I won't bite."

"*Fine*," he says, wrapping his much larger pinky around mine quickly before stepping to the side so I can enter the house. His eyes catch on the huge travel bag I hoped he wouldn't notice, but is an impossibility not to, as it's the same size as my lower torso. "Do I want to know?"

"No. So, don't ask."

I hear him mutter under his breath something that sounds like 'I shouldn't have let her in' before he shuts the door after me and turns. "Ry's still in bed. Top floor." He tilts his head toward the stairs, adding on, "Attic room."

"He's been relegated as far away as possible?"

"Something like that." Before I can come up with any smarter comments, he shuffles toward the kitchen, calling back, "You know, if we were with any other PR company, they'd be nicer."

"Ah yes …" I start walking up the stairs and peer at him through the white spindles. "But then, you wouldn't have the best team behind you, helping in impossible situations like this."

I don't include the part where Ryan said he needed me. It feels unnecessary. Plus, the fewer reminders I have mean I can block the comment out.

"Confident much?" Sam laughs.

"Very much." I grin as I continue trekking up.

Out of all our clients, Ryan aside, S.C.A.R.A.B. are my favorite to work with. The banter they bring makes the long days with impossible clients feel less impossible. Not that I would ever tell them that.

Four floors up, my lungs and quads protest. It takes me a minute to get myself together before knocking on Ryan's bedroom door. Like down at the front one, there's no answer. I give it a minute; in case he's taking his time to get out of bed, then, before knocking again, I press my ear against the door, listening out for any kind of movement. There isn't even a shuffle.

Instead of knocking again, I wiggle the handle to see if it's unlocked. The door opens and the overwhelming smell of weed hits me as I stare at the dark hole that is Ryan's room.

"Hey, Ryan?" I call up the final flight of stairs leading to the attic. Nothing. "It's Sooz, you there?"

When there's still no reply, I make my way up, squeezing my eyes together in a bid to avoid seeing anything I really don't want to. At the top, it's so dark, there's little risk of being scarred for life, so I prize my eyes open again. What would be worse than seeing something I don't want to? Feeling something I don't want to. I'd never live it down.

"Ryan?" I repeat when the ends of my boots hit what I think is a bed.

I squint, trying to make out what I'm doing, but it's no good. I can't see a thing, and if I keep going like I'm doing, I'll still be here this afternoon. Fumbling in the dark, I move my hand around in my bag until I find my phone. After pulling it out, I drag my thumb down the screen and turn the torch on, praying Ryan isn't naked. The room's illuminated enough I can confirm I am, in fact, standing by Ryan's bed.

My eyes settle on a sock-covered foot, then move up to the hem of the leg on a pair of denim pants. Everything after that is covered by sheets. I shuffle alongside the bed, stopping when I get closer to where Ryan's head is peaking out, twisted slightly to the side. Looking so peaceful and still, I could forgive him for the mess he's caused. He doesn't look capable of any of it.

I'm tempted to leave him alone and come back in a couple of hours when my brain returns to the whole *still* thing. I freeze, watching him intently. Nothing moves, not even the sheets covering his chest for the rise and fall of a breath.

Oh my God. I think he might be …

My chest tightens, and I try to figure out what to do. He doesn't look corpse-like pale, but the light isn't the best, so I can't be sure. Resting one knee on the part of the bed that's free, I carefully lower myself over him. When he still doesn't move, not even a millimeter, I hover my cheek right by his face. The warmth I want to feel blowing out through his nostrils isn't there.

"Boo!"

I shriek and fall forward, face first into Ryan's chest. Pain shoots through my nose, straight into my head. My face rubs against warm skin and I'm tickled by coarse hair when Ryan shakes with laughter so hard he's wheezing.

Of course, Sam races up to find out the cause of all the noise as Ryan continues howling. Consumed by pain and partly by humiliation, I refuse to move. I don't know which is worse. My face smothered against Ryan's chest or being *found* with my face smothered against Ryan's chest.

"Am I missing something?" I can hear the suspicion in Sam's voice, which makes my cheeks burn hotter.

"Just Sooz doing whatever she can to get a piece of me," Ryan replies. "You should have seen yo—" He doesn't finish whatever he was going to say, because he starts laughing again.

I'm too mortified to move.

"Right. Well. Yeah." If I could see Sam, he'd be scratching his head, trying to figure out what's going on. "I guess I'll leave you both to it."

His feet hammer their way back downstairs and I try to work up the courage to lift my head.

Ryan goes still. "He's gone. You're good."

There's a soft kind of seriousness to his voice that I'm not used to. It has me moving away warily. As I do, the peachy skin I expect to find where my face was stuck isn't there. There's a swirling mix of blacks and grays. I'm hit with the urge to trail my fingers over them. I blink the thought away when I look up and find Ryan watching me.

"You need to get up."

He groans and pulls the sheets over his head, covering both his face and the awkwardness of whatever that weird moment was between us. While he's busy burying himself, I glance around the room again. From what I can tell, it looks like it smells; like he doesn't care. Clothes cover the floor. There's so many, I find myself wondering how I managed to make it over here in one piece. When my eyes settle on the roof window, I come up with a plan.

Ryan must feel me move from the bed, because he asks, "What are you doing?" at the same time I pull up his shade and let in the blinding daylight. With my path clearer and less dangerous, I walk back over to his bed, bunch his sheets in my hands, and rip them away.

"Rise and shine!"

The groan Ryan let out earlier is nothing compared to the one he lets out now. He rolls onto his side so his back's facing me, and balls himself into the fetal position. "It's too early."

"It's nine."

"Like I said, too early."

I go in for the jugular. "For wasters, yes."

The muscles in his back tense at my choice of words. "I'm not a waster."

"There's that much second-hand weed floating around in here I think I'm high." It's the only explanation for why I want to giggle at the sight of him still curled up in a small ball.

He must realize I'm not going anywhere, because he rolls over onto his back—with his eyes still closed. Somehow, he manages to unfurl himself gracefully. With his limbs stretched out, he's so long the tips of his toes reach past the end of the bed. The tips of his fingers look like they could reach the ceiling.

When he opens his eyes lazily and catches me watching, I snap my gaze away, not missing, at the last second, the smirk that curls the corners of his mouth up. "Could we have found the secret to your happiness?"

I don't need to react, because Ryan laughs at his own joke. He's always been the only person in the room to appreciate his comedy genius.

"You need to get ready."

"Why?" he asks, suddenly more alert.

Plastering on the biggest smile I can manage, I reply, "Because today we transform you into someone the press will love."

Before they have a reason to hate you, neither of us acknowledge out loud.

Chapter Seven

Over an hour after I entered Ryan's room, we're making our way through the Baltic streets of Brooklyn to our first destination.

"Where are we going?" Ryan asks, hurrying beside me.

"You'll see," I reply, turning left off the block, toward the subway.

It's when we're walking through Manhattan, in the direction of one of my go-to boutiques for clients, that Ryan figures it out. The neon pink sign glaring straight ahead of us is a dead giveaway.

"Clothes shopping? I thought the whole point of you working with me was that we were going against *image* ..."

"Yes. But there's only so far that will stretch. Being caught with your sausage in a woman twice your age's mouth, unfortunately, but not unexpectedly, is a red card—even to the most forgiving audiences." I exhale away some of the tension from my body. "We need to make you look …" I drag my eyes over what he's wearing, my gaze zeroing in on the greasy, too-long locks falling over his forehead. "… put together."

"You missed a word out."

I give him an amused look. "Which was?"

"More." He scowls. "More put together."

Stepping in toward him, I reach up and brush the hair back from his face. Ryan's eyes turn to slits, right before I say softly, "Nothing about you looks put together right now. 'More' doesn't come into the equation."

I step back with a smile and continue walking, expecting Ryan to kick up a fuss or start to protest. He does neither, following me silently into the store.

"Hey!" calls Zoe, her purple hair causing a major color clash with the store's interior. Focusing on the uncomfortable-looking drummer at my side, she beams. Ryan gives her a small wave. He looks around like this is the last place in the world he wants to be. With his attention elsewhere, Zoe turns her attention to me. "You're late."

I refrain from commenting that the statement is ironic coming from her.

"He wouldn't get up," I reply.

"*He* also didn't know we were coming *here*," Ryan chips in. The glare that finds me serves less as an explanation of our tardiness, doing more to reinforce exactly why I didn't tell him. Had I, there'd be a strong chance he wouldn't be standing here with us.

Zoe grins, her eyes flickering between us. "Not gonna lie, I was worried about this plan. But I think it's going to be fun."

Ryan huffs and opens his mouth. Before he can utter a word, one of the store assistants walks over. I'm grateful for her help, because Ryan seems more amenable and accepting of her wardrobe suggestions than he does mine. Five minutes later, she leaves the three of us alone. The list of potential hits on clothing includes shirts with sleeves that are an adequate length, and jeans that are considerably less ripped.

Unfortunately, Ryan's optimism toward a new wardrobe ends abruptly when it comes to trying things on.

"I like my old shirts," he mutters, stepping out from the changing room wearing a black Henley covered in semi-transparent writing.

"It's understated," I say, taking in the way it complements the new, clean black denim covering his legs.

Zoe nods in agreement. "It looks really cool." She walks over to him and raises her hands to adjust the shirt where it's hanging out of place. Ryan pulls back and Zoe huffs. "Chill FlinchyMcGee, I'm trying to sort the collar. You've managed to get it twisted."

"I can do it myself." Zoe's brow arches and he grunts out a "Fine," allowing her to work her magic.

"You look sexy," she says when she's finished. At my snort, she spins around, giving me the hackiest of looks. "Tell him he looks sexy, Sooz."

Questioning why I requested her help, I find myself saying, "You look sexy."

It's not a lie. The fit is exquisite, wrapping around and pulling tight in all the right places. Muscles carved to perfection are now on display, and there's no denying the effect they have on the women in the room, including myself.

If a panty assessment were carried out, the results would come under the same damp theme.

Never have I been more aware of Ryan's rock and roll status than I am now. Feeling rattled and infuriated by my body's reaction to him. I'm ready to leave the store. More so when I find myself the recipient of Ryan's signature smirk before he disappears back into the changing rooms.

A-hole.

The next hour goes pretty much the same. There's lots of huffing from Ryan, lots of excited nodding from Zoe, and me … I'm contemplating purchasing a new pair of underwear and doing a quick change. It's only the thought of being caught by Ryan, and how it would inflate his ego, making it impossible to get him back out of the boutique, that stops me.

When I've forced him to hand over his credit card and the store assistant has arranged to have all the items Zoe and I decided on delivered to S.C.A.R.A.B.'s place, we step out into the warmer, early-afternoon air.

With him clutching the bag holding his old clothing like it's a lifeline, I smile as we make our way to our next destination.

Ryan grumps his way through Soho, then kicks up a stink in the hair salon when I inform him that he's having the '*highs*' of his lights lifted, and the ends to his length chopped. Predictably, he's silent when it comes to the facial.

"Remind me why we're doing this again?" he moan-groans when the beauty therapist begins massaging his temples—an extra I'm sure she's thrown in for free.

Glancing over my checklist, happy we've achieved what we need to, I say under my breath, "We're getting rid of all the damage your weed habit has caused." My comment isn't quiet enough, because the therapist's hands stop mid circle.

Ryan opens one eye, arching his brow as if to say 'seriously'.

Zoe shakes at my side.

"What's after this?" Ryan asks, when the therapist goes back to working her magic on his lingering hangover.

"We go home." I purse my lips, waiting for him to take the bait. He's too lost in a world of bliss. Zoe shakes her head at my side, waiting for me to strike the match. "Together."

Ryan's eyes snap open, and he stares at the brunette hovering over him. "Can we pause?"

"Sure." She smiles and grabs a fluffy towel, wiping the remaining oil from her hands. "Let me know when you're ready to start again. We can work on other areas."

Her eyes drop to his crotch, but her insinuation's wasted. Ryan's too busy trying to murder me with his eyes.

When the three of us are left alone, Ryan scowls. "What do you mean, *together*?"

"I'm your new roomie," I chime, sliding the list I've been working on into my bag in preparation to leave.

He stands, catching the towel that had been covering his front as it falls. He drops it on the treatment chair. "Nope."

"What's wrong, *Ry*? Scared all the forced proximity might get too much?" I flutter my lashes while Zoe's head snaps back and forth between us.

"Not happening." He shrugs on his new gray hooded jacket and walks away. After catching the therapist's attention—much to her disappointment—he pays for his treatment and leaves without another word to me or Zoe.

"He's going to lock you out. You know that, right?" says Zoe.

I dangle my spare set of keys in the air. The ones Sam gave me when I went over my plan while Ryan was getting ready. "There's no bolt on the back door."

En route to the exit, I grab Ryan's bag of old clothing while Zoe laughs at my side. "Please take a photo of his face when he finds you sitting in the kitchen."

"This is serious, Zo."

Outside, I hail a cab. One pulls up straight away.

Game on, drummer boy.

"Go easy on him, yeah?" Zoe says, adding herself to the ever-increasing tally of people advising me to take the less aggressive route.

"Of course," I lie, because there's a long list of things I'd rather be doing with my time, like helping the girls organize the New Year's Ball.

Instead, I'm left babysitting someone who has no intention of helping themselves.

I hit the jackpot with S.C.A.R.A.B.'s home, because there aren't many in Brooklyn with a back entrance.

I'm sitting in darkness at the central island in the kitchen when I hear a key slide into the front door and unlock it. My pulse starts to race.

The shuffling of feet toward the kitchen has the few butterflies awakened turning into a swarm. My heart all but stops when they pause outside the door. Because we're deep in the house, Ryan's outline is faint as the daylight outside disappears at a rapid rate.

With a huge grin sitting on my face, the lights turn on.

"Fuck!"

Ryan drops his keys, and they hit the ground with a clatter. He collapses with his back against the door frame, then bends over. His forearms rest against the tops of his thighs as he tries to regain control of his breathing. I laugh. So hard my ab muscles spasm. What follows is a serious round of cramp as I struggle to catch my own breath.

Luckily, I'm in the company of the person I care least about seeing me this way. Being around Ryan—weirdly—is easier than being around most other people. Maybe it's because I don't have to put on a show or false pretense of having everything together. Whatever I do have in order is a million miles away from where he's at.

"You're not staying here," he says when he's able to do so.

I tap my fingers against the kitchen worktop, making sure my nails catch and make an innocent clicking sound that, in the right situation—like this one—is irritating. "It's already done."

"It's my house."

"John West's request trumps everything."

"I'm pretty sure he didn't ask you to live with me."

"I quote … 'Do whatever it takes.' If we thought we could trust you not to screw up further, then it wouldn't come to this. We're stuck together. Sorry, *Ry*," I finish with a smile.

If looks could kill, I'd be on the floor, ready to be carted to the mortuary thanks to the one I get in return.

"If you're not going, then I am."

I tilt my head to the side and tap my nails again. "You're being dramatic."

"Says the person moving into *my* house so she can babysit me."

"You made your bed, now you have to sleep in it. If you didn't want things to be this way, then maybe you should have kept that …" I gesture at his lower body, specifically at the hip region where his zipper is covering what I'm referring to, "tucked away. Or at least been more discreet."

"I didn't know the photos were being taken."

"But they were," I say, minus the nail tapping to hammer home my point. "Now, we have no choice but to deal with it."

"I think we can do that without you living here."

"I repeat … John West's request. I didn't exactly have a say in the matter either." The last part comes out more of a mutter.

"You're making me feel like I'm unhinged."

My left brow pops with a silent 'aren't you?'. Ryan scowls, and I sigh, accepting now isn't the time for our usual back and forth. If I want him on my side on this, I need to be gentler in my approach.

"Look, people make mistakes. And everyone has different ways of dealing with things. But yours, for whatever reason you're doing all this, aren't working. And not only that, but the choices you're making also have the potential to harm others." Ryan's scowl deepens. "You know what I mean. You're in a band, Ryan. You're 'a team', like I've heard you tell Sam more than once. Right now, you're not acting like a team player. You're forgetting that your actions reflect on your friends. And the label. And Next Level."

My words must hit a nerve because his shoulders droop. He looks as tired as I feel when he walks across the kitchen and sits on the stool two over from mine. "You think it's going to be that bad?"

"Do you want the truth or a fluffed-up version?"

"I want you to answer as my PR manager, not as my friend."

"The press loves a scandal. If these images get out … this is their favorite kind."

Ryan stares at his lap. "Will people believe what they see?"

His weird phrasing makes me pause. Why wouldn't they? What's happening in them is there, clear for the eye to see. Then, I remember what John said about photos in the media often being a snippet of the bigger picture.

"Some will," I answer, opting to keep him on my side with careful wording. "Because people can be vultures. But there will be others who don't, if you prove from here on out that they have no reason to." The urge to reach over and give his hand a squeeze hits me out of nowhere, and I don't know what to do with it. Sitting on my hands would be weird, so I go back to tapping my nails against the counter. "I wouldn't be here if I didn't think I could help."

He lifts his head and turns to face me. "Do you *want* to be here, though?"

I purse my lips, taking in the hard set of his brows and the way the muscles in his jaw clench tight.

"You left me so I could make an unbiased choice, and I did," I reply. "I might not want to be here, but given the circumstances, I still am."

Without another word, Ryan slides off his stool and leaves. When he's gone, I try not to acknowledge the disappointment I saw in his final glance my way.

It's only later when I'm lying awake that I realize what's been bugging me all night.

We're the definition of polar opposites.

The two least compatible beings that could ever be thrown together.

But, despite our muddy, less-than-amenable history, he referred to us as friends.

It's already two AM. I should be tired. Exhausted. I've been running on fumes since leaving South Africa. Yet here I am, horizontal on the couch, working on my laptop, with sleep a long and distant (but much needed) memory.

"Working?" says a familiar voice, one I can't decide is welcome or not.

Regardless, I have no choice but to engage with him, because of the not-so-minor detail that this isn't my home.

"Yep," seems an adequate response in that it's an answer. It's also kind of dismissive, suggesting conversation isn't something I want to engage in.

"What on?" Given that I'm working on my laptop, without the main lights on, I can't read Ryan's expression. But his voice sounds light, playful.

I decide to go with it, and reply, "A scandal …"

He leans against one side of the doorjamb. "Bad?"

"The worst."

"You should tell them to go to hell." He folds his arms over his chest and crosses one ankle over the top of the other. Somehow, he manages to make not wearing socks look cool.

"That's what I keep telling myself. Yet here I am …"

"Dedicated to the cause?"

I tilt my head to the side. "I guess."

Ryan pushes away from the frame and enters the room. "Are you really working?"

"Yes," I admit, no humor whatsoever in my voice, signaling that our ceasefire has come to an end.

"It's ridiculous o'clock in the morning. You're making me feel bad."

"Save the pity party, Ryan." I sound cold and abrupt, but I'm here to do a job. Encouraging him won't help either of us. His shoulders slumping only fuels my frustration. "You were pictured with multiple women and that's not the worst of it. You messed up."

"Is that what you think?"

"That you could have fucked your career? Yeah."

At first, Ryan doesn't look at me. When he does, I wish he hadn't, because I find myself ignoring the logical, work-driven part of my brain, and want to take everything I've said back.

"The worst part of what you've just said is the cussing."

"It felt necessary." I feel like I'm glowing as I reflect the blue light from my screen. "We could change people's perception of the situation ..."

Ryan's eyes close. "If—"

"If you trust me," I say, testing out the theory following my call with John.

"I barely know you."

Huh. Torn, I navigate my way back to the professional route. Personal has no place in this conversation. It has no place with us. "The fact I'm here, when most people would already have walked away, should give you enough reason to."

"I don't trust anyone."

"You trusted hookers."

Ryan goes to leave. Before he disappears, he rests a hand on the frame. The muscles in his arm tense. "You have no idea what it is you're really looking at."

I shift up the couch and raise my voice. "Then trust me. Tell me what it really is that I'm seeing."

"No."

"Ryan …"

He's a foot out of the room, but I'm able to hear what he says next. "If I could trust you, you wouldn't have come up with your own conclusion."

"And what exactly was I supposed to do?" I call out.

"You were supposed to ask me first."

Chapter Eight

After a restless night over-analyzing everything, I come to the conclusion that, if Ryan and I are going to get through this ordeal without murdering each other, then I need to change my tact. Less cold and professional, more … friendly? Thinking the word makes me nervous.

With my glutes planted in the same place they were when Ryan left last night, I smile as he enters the kitchen.

"You look perky for this time in the morning." I chime. Ryan ignores me as he walks in the direction of the freshly brewed pot of coffee, wearing a pair of black jog pants and a black muscle vest. "Maybe the party-less lifestyle will work for you after all."

My phone rings out as Ryan pulls a bottle of almond milk from the fridge. It then goes on to chime another three times in quick succession.

Ryan turns and stares at it as it flashes with one notification after another next to my bowl of cereal. "That's kind of annoying. Can you turn it off?"

"Forget perky. Hello grumpy." The flash of my pearly whites does nothing to lighten his expression. "It's called work. And all of those notifications are related to *you*."

He continues to glare at it when it chimes again. "Fine."

"You know, you're more jovial when everyone else is around."

Ryan ignores my comment, and Zach picks the perfect moment to enter the room. I half expect Jake to appear, but quickly figure out that with me gone, Abby will be taking full advantage of having an empty—barre the toddler—apartment.

"What can I say," Ryan mutters under his breath, "you bring out the best in me."

"I've been told that before." I grin.

Ryan blinks. "And you believed them?"

Chuckling to himself, Zach grabs a bowl from the cupboard, then the cereal and almond milk from Ryan.

"FYI," I say to them both, "I'm all for the dairy-free vibes, but you're out of milk. I thought you'd want to know."

"This is a dairy free house," says Zach, pouring his cereal.

I look between them. "Why?"

My phone chimes again. I divert my attention to it at the same time Zach says, "Because R—"

When I find the notification is a message from Will, I set my spoon down and check what he wants.

How's things?

Wow. His twin communication has reached stellar levels since I left.

Fine, I type back quickly to appease him, then lock my screen.

I look back at Zach. "Sorry, you were saying?"

"Cholesterol. It's better for it," Zach answers. I give him a blank stare.

"Seriously?" They both nod, and I laugh. "I don't mean to be judgy, but …" My eyes flicker between them, finding nothing but seriousness in their expressions. "Ryan owns enough weed to run a marijuana farm. Forgive me for assuming that health *things,* like diet, might not be a top priority for you guys."

"You know what they say …" says Ryan, "it's all about balance. Overindulge in one thing, then something has to give."

I open my mouth, and before I can stop myself, the words are tumbling out. "The same could be said ab—"

"Don't." Ryan holds his hand in the air, giant palm facing me, all flat and authoritative. It's then that something distracts him. He leans to the side, glancing around me. "What's that?"

"What?" I turn and find nothing.

"That thing on the floor."

"That," I say when I realize what he's looking at, "is a mat."

He rolls his eyes. "I gathered that much. What are you wearing?"

I look down at my matching peachy-pink yoga set. "Fitness gear? Is there something wrong?"

"You look like a walking Lululemon ad." He picks up his bowl.

"I like to do yoga in the morning," I start to explain. "Then meditate." I slide off the stool and walk over to roll the mat up, feeling two pairs of eyes watching as I go. They're still watching when I have it placed safely under my arm. "It helps manage my stress levels."

Ryan blinks. "Then why are you still stressy?"

Zach chokes on a mouthful of cereal.

Because of his passive aggressive quip, I take great pleasure in delivering my next bit of news. "Anyhoo …" Both guys watch me with intrigue, Zach with watery eyes. "John West called an hour ago. A headlining band pulled out of a gig at the last minute, something to do with food poisoning. You'll be filling their spot."

"Says who?" Ryan asks, looking less than happy with the news.

"Warped Record's board members. They think it will be an excellent opportunity to give people a refresher of your talents before the feces hits the fan."

"Where? When?" asks Zach, while Ryan remains stewing in his foul mood.

"New Orleans. Tomorrow." My voice comes out light and overly cheery. It's impossible to hide my excitement over the fact I'll be wandering around NOLA in a little over twenty-four hours. Both guys groan, and I roll my eyes. "Please. Anyone would think, the way you're going on, that traveling and seeing the world is a hardship."

"It is when you have a million presents still to buy," huffs Zach.

"I think a million is being a bit dramatic," I reply. "Take those lemons and turn them into lemonade. We can go shopping along Canal Street." I clap my hands. Nothing can dampen my mood. Not even the surly drummer standing across the central island from me. Walking on air, I head to the kitchen door. "Chop, chop, boys. Time is of the essence!"

Making my way along the hall, I'm too happy to be offended when I hear Zach say, "Did you lace her fruit loops?"

My euphoria carries me upstairs to the bathroom to take a shower, and somewhere between shampooing and conditioning my hair, I forget how bizarre it is that Ryan knows what Lululemon is.

When John West said we'd be in New Orleans two days *max,* as if there was the possibility it might have been less, what he meant was that we *would* be in New Orleans for two days.

Forty-eight hours.

Two thousand, eight hundred and eighty minutes.

One hundred and seventy-two thousand, and eight hundred seconds.

No ifs, buts, or maybes about it.

Which means I have two intense days with my least favorite person.

The one who has the ability to grate on me more than the blistering midday heat.

Vying for top spot as my biggest challenge yet …

The person who, impressively, is managing to taint what should be a magical trip to the one place I've always wanted to visit, and he isn't even here yet.

The source of my irritation: the article he's managed to make the front page of every gossip magazine overnight with. The one with the crystal-clear, full spread image of him with a stunning Victoria's Secret model—giant assets, legs like ladders and hair thicker than a horse's mane, the works—while a joint rests behind his ear, and one hangs between his lips. They really set off the rugged look he's working with the crinkled gun show shirt and paint splattered denim pants that look more ripped than put together.

I read the headline for a fourth time: *How the Z-generation does the farmer's market.*

Of course, the Z-Gen reference isn't related to Ryan. It's the model who—depending on who is reading the article—could be classed as way too young to be hooking up with him. It's a simple case of morals and values, and I'm all for being open-minded when it comes to love and relationships. I have my brother and Henrik to thank for years of lessons as to why the path of love isn't always linear or predictable, and can't always be packaged with a bow on top.

However—with a capital H—there are certain expectations that come with being in the public eye. Something Ryan seems to keep forgetting, being that he's parading his drug habit around like it's the same as carrying a bottle of H_2O. Even for him, it's out of character. I want to grab him the second I see him, shake him hard, and ask what he's playing at.

S.C.A.R.A.B. has come so far, and after Sam's blip in the summer, they're back on track. They have an eight-month world tour scheduled to start at the end of January to promote their new album. It's less than eight weeks away.

There's no doubt in my mind that this has been leaked as a warning. This image, combined with the wad safely tucked away with my things back in Brooklyn, will cause carnage. It's a warmup. Pre-game. Whatever you want to call it.

And the goal: to cause a wobble with the band's fans, so when the main images leak, it will destroy their confidence and make them question their loyalty.

People don't want perfect. But they also don't want unhinged, which is exactly what all these images, as a collective, are portraying Ryan as.

A bead of sweat trickles down my back because, apparently, New Orleans didn't get the message it's December. The only sign Christmas is on the horizon are the fairy lights wrapped around the palm trees lining each side of the wide road, and the faint sound of festive music spilling out from the many restaurants and stores.

Hot and frustrated, I go to shove the magazine back on the stand where it caught my attention. A hand swoops in, stopping me. I look up to find an old guy in his seventies, wearing an *I-don't-think-so* expression. He pulls his hand from the stand and turns it over, then waits. I huff and hand over the right money for the magazine, grumbling to myself as I walk away, that now, not only will I have Ryan by my side, but I'll have to carry him around with me too.

After shoving the magazine in my bag, I pull out my phone and double-check the text Jake sent with where to meet. With the flights being so last minute, sadly, I was unable to travel with the band. I fully reveled in being gifted a few extra hours of solitude regardless of the soul-destroying wake-up call at three AM.

Unfortunately, my reprieve has come to an end. As has my short but sweet amble along Canal Street. After casting a wistful glance at the tease of the Old French Quarter, I move toward the central business district. Google Maps predicts a lengthy-ish walk, so I opt for keeping my phone out, with the hope of catching up with a couple of messages en route.

It seems like an easy task in my head, but trying to navigate the crowds of tourists is virtually impossible. I give it up as a bad job when I almost take part in a major selfie collision outside The Ritz. I stop beneath a tall palm in the shade so I can catch a quick break and read my screen properly. A red and yellow tram rolls past, and I curse that the place Jake picked for us to meet isn't on the hop-on, hop-off route.

The first couple of messages are ones I've been cc'd in by one or two interns. I mark them as read and move on.

Abby: *Is Ryan still alive?*
Me: *Only because I haven't seen him yet ;)*
Abby: *Oooo a winky face. Maybe the odds are in his favor?*
Me: *As long as he behaves.*
Abby: *Get cracking that whip baby!*
Me: *Don't call me baby.*

I close our message thread and skim through my one with Zoe. She's sent a string of messages regarding mixology for the New Year's Ball, as well as three purple hair shading image updates. I send back a simple 'X' to let her know I've read them, then reply 'yes' to all of Amanda's additional guest list suggestions. Going through my inbox is taking more time than predicted, and I'm considering dealing with the rest of the messages if I have some free time later, when my eyes catch on a name I can't ignore.

Will: *Why didn't you say goodbye before you left for Brooklyn?*

I chew on my bottom lip, considering my answer. I wind up going for the easiest out, because the last thing we need is to get into a Mother-related argument via SMS. They're hard enough to navigate in person.

Me: *Something came up with work. Sorry X*

I click out of my inbox, reopen the map, then psych myself up to keep moving through the heat with the promise of a cool beverage when I reach my destination. Preferably of the alcohol variety.

A sticky ten-minute walk later, I'm majorly regretting my packing choices. The trickle of sweat on my back that appeared at the magazine stand has been joined by a flood. I dread to think what the back of my blouse looks like. White silk and heat aren't a good combo. At least the restaurant has air con, and as I step through the doors and temperature wall, cool air coats my skin. I let out a sigh of relief.

"Sooz! Over here!"

The temptation to turn and walk straight back out of the restaurant is strong. The many eyes now facing in my direction stop me. I plaster on a smile and glide toward the band. Never have a group of guys looked so out of place. Their black shirts and inked skin stand out against the white pressed linen and gleaming silverware covering the table.

Where most customers have glasses of crisp white wine sitting on their tables, S.C.A.R.A.B.'s is filled with bottles of beer. Judging by the quantity of empties, this isn't their first round.

"Hey, Sam," I say when I reach where they're sitting. He pulls me into his side for one of those brief greeting hugs people do when they're familiar, but not overly familiar. It's awkward. When he pulls away and scratches the back of his neck, I clear my throat. "So glad to be here!" Three faces beam back at me. Their smiles are bright. Too bright. I move from Jake, to Sam, to Zach and frown. "Erm … where's Ryan?"

"He went to get food," replies Sam.

Jake shakes his head and Zach looks like he wants to face plant the table.

"We're in a restaurant." I hold Sam's gaze, trying to figure out what's going on and why he looks like he wants to disappear.

"He doesn't eat the food here," Sam continues.

"You've been here before?" I frown to myself, because Abby's not mentioned the band performing in New Orleans.

"What Sam's trying to say," interrupts Jake, throwing his band mate a 'shutthehellup' look. "Is that Ryan doesn't like this kind of food."

"Then why are we here?" I narrow my eyes.

"We thought you'd like it here?" Sam squeaks.

I give the room another once over, trying to figure out what it is that made them think that. When I don't have an answer, I voice my question out loud. "Why?"

"It has chandeliers." Jake kicks Sam under the table and he winces.

I go to ask why they think I like chandeliers, when a waiter walks over, and I have no choice but to sit. Sam looks surprised when I order a beer.

"Is Ryan getting stoned?" I ask Sam, because he's the one most likely to sing. All puns intended.

"Yes." The table shifts and one of the bottles wobbles dangerously. His pitch raises a level. "No?" I arch a brow. "Maybe." His brow is rapidly developing a sheen. "Stop staring at me like that. You're making me nervous."

"People only get nervous when there's something to be nervous about," I reply. Sam's saved when the waiter returns with my drink. I momentarily forget what we're discussing, because the lure of the cool amber liquid is much more appealing after the walk. "Where is he?"

Sam stares at his place setting, Zach makes a show of playing with the label on his bottle. Meanwhile, Jake keeps glancing around the room. Each time his gaze finds its way back to me, it's assessing.

"He's meeting us at the rehearsal," Jake says, finally.

"Okay," I reply. A brief look over the menu has me wrinkling my nose. "So, the beer's great, but I'm not really feeling the food options." Three pairs of surprised eyes stare at me. "I could nail some fast food."

Jake laughs and raises his hand to the waiter, signaling for the check. "Looks like we have something in common after all. Let's stop somewhere on the way to rehearsals."

"One thing though ..." Jake looks at me expectantly. "Can we please get an Uber?"

With a belly full of fries, fish bites, and beers, my mood is the best it's been since I left South Africa as we make our way to S.C.A.R.A.B.'s rehearsal for their show tomorrow night.

John West managed to secure a small rehearsal room last minute. Normally, a sound check is all that's required a few hours before. But with the band's latest album so fresh, Jake informed me they wanted to get in as much practice as possible.

The hammering of drums, spilling out through the crack in the door as we approach the room has me frowning to myself. More so when I catch the looks thrown between Zach, Sam, and Jake. There's no structure to the rhythm. The only way to describe it is noise. Angry noise.

I startle when there's a loud clatter and a "Fuck".

"Here we go," says Jake as he approaches the door.

There's something in his tone, akin to reluctance, which has me feeling nervous for what we're going to find. With each step I take, images of Ryan flash behind my eyes, sporting a similar appearance to the one in the magazine. I'm pleasantly surprised when the door opens, and he looks the same as he did after his transformation. He's even wearing one of the outfits I picked out. He hasn't fallen apart in forty-eight hours. At least, not yet.

Visually, he seems fine. Too fine. Suspiciously fine.

There are no outward signs that suggest a reason why his band mates are eying him warily. He doesn't even look high. He looks as sober as I've ever seen him, which I find oddly alarming. If it were anyone else, it wouldn't mean a thing. But the guy I've gotten used to seeing over the past few years isn't who's sitting behind the drums right now.

I hold my breath, waiting for when he looks up and finds me standing with the rest of his bandmates.

It takes longer than I anticipate, and when he does say something, all I'm greeted with is a simple, "Hey."

The frown I'm wearing is at risk of becoming a permanent one. I've never wanted to hear the word 'baby' more than I do right now. I hate the word and the letters that spell it, but there's something about its absence I hate more.

"Where've you all been?" he asks, when Jake is getting set up on guitar, Zach on bass and Sam is adjusting the height of his mic.

I've settled on the small couch at the back of the room. The only piece of furniture besides an equally small coffee table. It's the definition of bare bones. Ryan looks over, and I shift, trying to get comfy. My fingers itch for something from him. The usual remark. Some kind of banter. A beat passes and his gaze drops away. He leaves me with nothing.

Two hours pass, and the practice runs smoothly, without a hitch. You could question why I'm here. But therein lies the problem.

There has always been something predictable about the unpredictable nature of S.C.A.R.A.B.'s drummer.

I can deal with high Ryan. I can deal with drunk Ryan. I can deal with doesn't-think-before-he-speaks Ryan.

He's an expected. A consistent inconsistent.

But right now, the guy sitting behind the drum kit might as well be an imposter I don't have a clue how to handle.

My gut stirs and the hairs on my arms raise as I watch him hammer the drums like he wants to destroy them.

And I can't help feeling like this is the calm before the storm.

Chapter Nine

After rehearsals, the band has one thing in mind: decompressing.

In bars.

With alcohol.

The stringent part of me wants to put my foot down; to tell them they can't, because they have a big show tomorrow. The part of me going into a tailspin because Ryan's been on his best behavior and hasn't made a single out-of-place comment has me agreeing that it's a good idea. I'm fully aware I'm potentially setting him, and myself, up to fail. But I need to see a glimpse of the Ryan I know. What I've seen so far suggests he's far from okay. Sure, the world might be about to see his assets, but he's not seemed as affected by it all as he is now, and I don't have a clue why.

As we slowly make our way to the French Quarter, and the late afternoon turns into a balmy evening, the mood is flat, the vibe as far from party ready as it can get. Jake and Zach talk in hushed voices a few steps ahead, while Sam keeps making random observations and pointing out things he thinks Russ—the child he's adopting with his girlfriend Sophie—would like as we walk. He gets particularly animated over a brass band dancing on a couple of benches, and joins the crowds, pulling out his phone to film them.

Meanwhile, I can't take my eyes off the colorful buildings. The disappearing sun reflecting off the yellows and terracottas draws attention to the beauty of the old architecture. The ferns hanging from the cast-iron balconies are impossibly large, the sweet potato vines draping down, impossibly long.

There's so much to take in that the guidebook I picked up when I arrived isn't needed. It's wasted effort carrying it around, so, while Sam is still filming, I stop walking and open my bag wide, shifting a few things around so I'm able to fit it in. I'm so busy rearranging, I don't notice Ryan standing close by. When I look up, my eyes widen in surprise, then fill with confusion at the way his brows are furrowed. Following his line of sight, my insides knot at his front-page debut peeping out.

I open my mouth to explain, or apologize, but I don't get a chance to do either, because Ryan walks off. As I watch him go, I can't figure out what's more unsettling; the fact he seems upset by the magazine, or the fact I'm upset that he's upset. A familiar tension headache starts to build. I rub at my temples, which throb to the beat of the music spilling out from the bars as I follow Jake and Zach. Conversation and laughter create an atmosphere that's palpable. I can taste the excitement, like I can taste the Shrimp Creole wafting out from one of the restaurants we pass by.

We're halfway along Bourbon Street when Jake points at a corner bar that's caught their attention.

The word Absinthe glares at me, and I hold in a groan. After what I've witnessed this afternoon, it's very much clear this is needed. I keep my mouth shut and follow the guys, saying a small prayer that John West doesn't find out about this, because right now, I will not be winning any sitter of the year awards.

Where the exterior is bright white, the inside is dark, and a mash of old and new. The ornate wooden bar is lined with stools equally old, judging by the holes and wear of the upholstery. Business cards cover the musty brick walls, and football helmets hang from the exposed cypress beams, complementing the game playing on a screen above the rows and rows of liquor bottles.

With my business vibe attire, I feel as out of place as the fiberoptic Christmas tree sitting on the bar top, with half its branches missing.

"Whatcha drinkin', Sooz?" calls Sam, sliding a drinks menu across the bar to me. The movement is smooth, seamless, until it gets stuck on a sticky patch. I climb onto an empty stool and peel the laminated plastic away from the bar.

Zach perches on a stool to my left. Jake and Sam remain standing next to him. The three of them give the bartender their drinks order and he gets to work while I scan over the list of cocktails. I still when Ryan takes the stool on my right. When I've decided what I want, I go to pass the menu to him.

I frown when he says, "I'm good, thanks."

"Do you not want to look? There are some great sounding cocktails." My voice comes out unnaturally high with the effort it takes to keep it light. No part of this interaction feels natural.

Ryan's muscles tense before he swallows. The ink patterns covering his skin tighten and stretch. "I'm good."

"Oooookay," I murmur. Right now, he could give Abby, Queen Cranky Pants, a run for her money.

When the bartender has finished with Jake, Zach and Sam's drinks, he turns his attention my way.

"You order first." I smile at Ryan, who gives me a sideways glance. "I think you need it more."

I wait for a quip back, but I get nothing. "Beer, please," he says to the bartender. "Bottle."

"We have some great ones on draft," replies the bartender.

The muscle in Ryan's jaw twitches. "I'm good with a bottle." His eyes flicker my way. "Make it two."

The bartender walks to the fridge to get Ryan's order and I give the menu a final glance. He returns a minute later with Ryan's beers, then looks at me, waiting for my order.

"An Absinthe Frappé, please." I grin, and the bartender gives me a smile back that suggests he's happier with my order than he is Ryan's.

"You know that's strong, right?" Ryan says, twisting on his stool to face me.

"Wow," I say.

"What?"

"You said more than two words to me." My mouth talks to Ryan, but my eyes watch the bartender intently as he fills the bottom of a goblet-style glass with green liquor.

If Ryan wants to reply, he doesn't get a chance, because the bartender spurs into a long speech, explaining the process of making my drink. I watch, fascinated, as iced water drips steadily from a French vintage fountain onto a sugar cube sitting on a slotted spoon, which is resting on the glass.

"It's called louching," says the bartender, sliding my glass across the bar when it's ready.

I pick up the glass, now filled with a cloudy white liquid, and smile. The glass hovers in front of my lips. "Sounds dirty."

"As dirty as you'll feel in a couple of hours if you drink too many of those," mutters Ryan at my side.

With an eye roll I don't care if he sees, I take a small, hesitant sip of my drink. The green fairy comes with many a debaucherous tale, and I expect to fall flat on my back. Or at least splutter from the burn of what I assume is on par to battery acid. I'm pleasantly surprised when only the faint taste of licorice coats my tongue.

"Wow." I give the bartender a thumbs up. He laughs and walks away to deal with another group of customers further along the bar. I turn to Ryan and offer over my glass. "You have to taste this."

"I'm good."

I scowl at his reply. "What's with all the short answers? Usually, I can't get you to shut up."

Ryan's face goes all dark and broody. "I've had a bad week."

"You and me both, *buddy*."

The slam of his empty bottle against the bar top has me jolting in my seat. Ryan grips it tight as Jake clears his throat from behind. My eyes move over to the other bottle, finding that one empty, too.

"Another beer, please," Ryan says to the bartender. So much for my assumption that he isn't in a partying mood. He's nailed two in ten minutes.

"What's going on with you?"

Ryan sighs and lets go of the empty bottle, which miraculously hasn't shattered. "Nothing." His eyes clash with mine and his gaze says otherwise. "Can we leave it and have a good night?"

"Are you going to be your usual annoying self and go back to irritating the life out of me?"

"Sure," he replies with a tight smile.

I ignore what I think is disappointment flickering across his face at my question when I look away.

"Perfect."

An hour in, my blood hums from the Absinthe I've nursed carefully.

My limbs feel lax, and unfortunately, my mouth is laxer.

"I vote we head back to the bus," says Jake. "We've got a long day tomorrow."

The flights might have been *virtually* impossible to get, but hotel rooms were *literally* impossible, meaning I have the delight of sharing a too-small tour bus that looks like something from the eighties.

"I'm done too," agrees Sam.

"Party poopers," I cough into my glass.

While we've been sitting in the bar, it's become alive. So many bodies are crowded in the small space, you can barely breathe without skimming against someone. After the past few months in South Africa with Mother being all work, no play, the last thing I want to do is call it a night. The Green Fairy is working her magic.

"Yeah, you're definitely done," chuckles Zach, sliding off his stool.

Sam says the drinks are on him and signals to the bartender that he wants to settle the tab we opened.

"I think I'll stay," I say, playing with one of the beer mats on the bar as I anticipate the guy's reaction.

"Why?" Zach asks.

"It's dark out," I reply.

Five beers in, Ryan's body language is less glacier, and he arches a brow. "Meeting with some of your fellow blood suckers in the shadows?"

"Yeah." I blame my fairy friend for when I brazenly trail my eyes down to his neck. My attention locks on the symbol of death, sitting front and center. I want to ask what it means, but instead I give him my best passive aggressive smile. "Better watch out. You're first on my list."

After his mood earlier, I expect that to be it, for him to shut my game down and demand we all go back to the bus together. He takes me by surprise when he says, "I'll cross over to the dark side with you."

"Great, well, make sure she gets back safe. Yeah?" Sam gives Ryan a look, a knowing one, with a warning thrown in.

I'm tempted to laugh at Sam's concern. Miraculously, even without my usual shield of composure, I manage to hold it in.

"Sure," Ryan replies.

The hairs on my arms raise slightly when Sam, Zach and Jake leave. It's just the two of us and a room full of strangers. We've barely spent any time alone. At least, not time alone that doesn't involve fighting over things he refuses to do, or things he has done that he shouldn't have. I'm questioning my decision to stay out with him, and do a quick mental calculation, trying to figure out if we could still catch the guys up if we hurry.

Unfortunately, as much as I wish I wasn't most of the time, I'm very much my mother's daughter.

The biggest character trait I inherited from her? Stubbornness.

Swallowing down a ball of nerves, I begin rummaging through my bag, being careful not to display the magazine again. I feel better when I have my trusty ally in my hands, because it gives me something to focus on that isn't him.

"Of course you have a guidebook," says Ryan, shaking his head. A hint of a smile pulls at his lips as I flip through it.

"What's wrong with a guidebook?" I ask, with a quick glance at him out of the corner of my eye.

Ryan shrugs. "It's fitting, that's all."

When I find the pages I'm searching for, the ones dedicated to Bourbon Street and the French Quarter, I skim over the text, which is admittedly a little fuzzy around the edges.

The absinthe is doing crazy things to my judgement, because rather than being sensible and suggesting we go back to the bus, I find myself saying, "Fancy being wild with me?"

A mischievous sparkle appears in Ryan's green eyes. Eyes that, beneath the light spilling down from the antique chandelier hanging overhead, appear greener than the cheaper absinthe in the bottles lining the back row of the bar. Momentarily disorientated by their beauty, I find myself wondering if his actions ever match his mouth and cause as much chaos.

On paper, and on a professional level, this might not be the best idea, but seeing a glimmer of his normal self, I realize tonight is what *he* needs. And that's all that matters.

The words that come out of his mouth next warm my insides. "Baby, I've been waiting years to hear you say that to me."

There's a reason the Big Easy's signature drink is called Hurricane. It triggers a storm with my insides. Nothing I'm feeling right now is easy, and mixing it with the Green Fairy was cocky.

"I'm done," I declare, halfway through what is most definitely my final drink of the night.

"Lightweight." Ryan coughs, a poor attempt to hide his comment. "You still have the complimentary shots."

We both look to my left. He's right. There they are, sitting on the bar, untouched. Perfectly clear liquid, sitting in glasses, acting innocent to all the indiscretions they're capable of causing. Sneaky little buggers.

"I don't do shots."

"Not even a taste?" His tongue darts out, skimming his bottom lip.

My eyes follow the movement, albeit lazily. I blink rapidly when it hits me what I'm doing.

He's gorgeous. A gun show performing Adonis. Thick, inky lashes line his eyes. Eyes that are the key to his soul. Where his expression is stoic, his words deadpan, his irises are a storm of green, tumultuous waters that have the ability to drown you if you dare to get lost in them.

I have a feeling it would be impossible to lose him, because wherever he walks, there's likely a trail of broken hearts following. The not-so-subtle slightly drunken moves he keeps making scream 'player'. Throw into the mix a bad weed habit, the promise of too much money and a lifetime of fame … he has the potential to be the worst kind.

And apparently, when I'm tiptoeing the line of being drunk, I've also become super deep. Spectacular.

I watch him, watching me. "Stop it."

"Stop what?" His eyes glitter mischievously. That, or he's drunk, because I already know when he's high they're more like a glazed donut, lacking the sugary glint.

"Looking at me like you are doing."

"Which is …"

He's flirting, and he needs to stop. Whatever outcome he's gunning for would heighten his rock and roll asshole status. Not necessarily a bad thing for him, but for me … it would ruin my reputation. I'm here to do a job, the aim being the opposite of what we're doing.

"I'm not having this conversation," I reply.

"Okay." He lets out a huff of air.

I narrow my eyes. "Why are you being huffy?" He raises his bottle and drains the remainder of the beer. His go-to response over the years. Consuming any kind of substance as an excuse to avoid real life. "Of course."

I have a feeling the white flag we raised temporarily for the night is going to be lowered.

"Are you finished trying to psychoanalyze me?" he asks, giving me a side-on glance, bottle hovering at his lips still.

"That depends …"

"On?"

"Are you finished acting like a spoiled B-list celebrity? The broody rock star image isn't on trend anymore."

He throws his head back and laughs. I decide to hell with being sensible, grabbing my Hurricane and guzzling some more. I instantly regret it. The neon signs are making me woozy.

I slide off my stool and, as I do, my foot tangles with Ryan's and I stumble.

"Careful!" Ryan catches me before I fall, taking me by surprise, because I would have fully expected him to enjoy watching me hit the deck over saving me.

"Thanks," I mumble, straightening as something akin to humiliation tries to take over my complexion.

"Hey." A sharp breath catches in my throat when Ryan's hand darts up and grasps my chin.

It's a moment. A second. But one that prevents any oxygen from entering my body.

I snap my chin away from his grip and grab my guidebook off the bar. Trying to keep my movements steady, I bend to grab my bag from the ground and, when I'm safely upright, I shrug it up my shoulder, gripping the strap for dear life.

"Thanks," I say, giving the bartender a small wave, blocking out all thoughts of the drum-playing brute at my side.

"Are you okay?" asks Ryan from close behind.

I push through the doors of the bar into the night, leaving behind only a, "Yeah."

Outside, the signs are brighter than in. There's a chance Bourbon Street could compete with the lights of New York, and as we walk, we're bathed in an orangey yellow glow.

"We should get back. It's late," I state, trying to come across as casual and sober as possible.

The hint of mischeviousness in Ryan's eyes reappears. "Feel free to go back. I'll take in the culture on my own." He starts to walk along the street. The throngs of people dancing around and taking selfies—most with reindeer antlers sticking out from their heads—engulf Ryan, and all I can see is his head, which bobs above the crowds. The highlights in his hair sparkle like a forbidden treasure.

I chew on the inside of my cheek. It takes a split second to go against my better judgement and follow him. "You wouldn't know culture if it bit you in the behind."

He stops abruptly, and I almost slam into his back. "Say it."

I step to the right so I'm at his side, rather than standing with my face practically plastered against the black material of his shirt. The smell of soap and musk tickles my nose and it's tempting me to inhale. "No."

He must read the indecision written all over my face, because the corners of his mouth twitch. "Just because you go to the beat of one drum, it doesn't mean you can't enjoy another."

A large group of drunken guys stumble by laughing. I'm collateral to their fun and find myself thrust into Ryan's side. For the second time tonight, he stops me from taking a tumble, wrapping an arm around my shoulders to keep me steady while shooting daggers at the culprit.

"Sorry dude!" The drunk guy sways, then there's the moment I've been waiting for since we arrived. A flicker of recognition.

With his arm still wrapped around my shoulders, Ryan pulls me away from the group before they can create a fuss that will be impossible to get away from. We stop under a sign that reads 'Babes' and he drops his arm.

"Fine," I say, drawing my eyes away from the silhouette of the naked woman above me.

Ryan grins and shoves his hands into the pocket of his pants. He looks casual. Cool, but still rugged, all boxed into one package. "So …"

"So?"

"There's this place that might be cool to visit. Full of Christmas lights. They call it 'The Miracle on Fulton Street'."

"I'm good." Ryan searches my face for an explanation. "I don't like Christmas," is all I give him with a shrug.

When we've been standing for an awkward amount of time, neither of us attempting to move, Ryan lets out a ragged exhale. "You're the tour guide," he says, gesturing at the street ahead. "Lead the way."

"Um …" I glance around. "One minute."

Sliding the straps of my bag down my shoulder so they rest in the crook of my arm, I reach inside to find my guidebook again so I can double check where we're going.

Ryan's hand snaps out. His grip on my arm is firm, stopping me. He wiggles his brows, a move which, for most men his age, would make them look like a pair of jiving caterpillars. On him it screams sex appeal. "What happened to being wild?"

"What exactly are you suggesting?" I hold his gaze, trying to ignore the fact he's still gripping my arm, and the way his touch is making the temperature of my skin rise.

"We wing it."

"Wing what?"

"Everything." Ryan grins. "We walk. Explore. Without knowing where we're going."

Ignoring the excitement building inside me, I focus on logistics. "How will we get back?"

For a second, I think I've got him when his expression turns thoughtful.

Maybe he will give this up as a bad idea. A large part of me wants him to, but there's a small part shouting louder, wanting to dive into the waves and see what unchartered waters I'll end up in if I go with the current.

"Have you got your phone?" he asks, holding out his hand.

I slide it out of the pocket of my white denim pants.

After unlocking it, I pass it over. My phone is then raised high above us both, the screen mirroring and capturing the bemused expression on my face as Ryan beams.

"What are you doing?" I call out, scurrying after him when he walks away with my phone still in his hand.

"Making breadcrumbs." Tapping the screen, he flips the camera's perspective and takes another picture. "After you, my lady."

He gestures ahead and I hurry off so he can't see the smile threatening to take over my face.

"I'm not your anything," I say, taking a sharp right, leading us away from the hustle and bustle.

As we carry on walking, Ryan continually ignores my protests, forcing me to stop for orange-hued, breadcrumb selfies. When the sun dropped, the temperature didn't. I'm sweating like a pig multiple pictures in.

"You're glowing," he says, referring to the most recent image he's captured.

I purse my lips. "I'm back to not liking you."

With a smirk he points up. "I was talking about the streetlights."

"Sure, you were." I give him a playful scowl. "Come on."

"Why do I feel like you know where you're going?" he calls after me.

"I memorized the map," I call back.

"Of course you did."

His laughter follows me in the direction of the Mississippi river, and I blame my inebriation for why I enjoy the sound so much.

Chapter Ten

My skin grows damp as we continue walking. I want to believe it's from the heat, and not because of Ryan's arm, brushing against mine.

"What's the real reason you wanted to stay out until dark? Or do you actually have a thing for creatures of the night?" he asks at my side.

"What do you think?"

Ryan stops and I think I hear him huff. "Are you going to keep answering my questions with questions?"

Glancing over my shoulder further ahead, I find him watching me, eyes narrowed. The streetlight he's standing beneath highlights his frustration.

"We're almost there."

Weirdly, I feel more unsure about having him with me than walking alone in a place I don't know. A small part of me prays he decides not to follow.

Prayers unanswered, I can still hear him somewhere behind, when I think we're close to where I've been searching for.

"This is it?" Ryan asks as my steps slow.

We both take in our surroundings, which admittedly feel shady, and not because it's dark.

"You know, you don't have to go to this extent …" he continues.

Ignoring him, I keep moving forward, albeit a little slower, past the final line of buildings.

"If you want to have your way wi—"

His feet stop moving next to me and, thankfully, so does his mouth.

"Wow."

With the Mississippi calling to me, I walk toward the riverbank and stop at the railings. Leaning against the cool metal, I wait for Ryan to join me, keeping my eyes focused on the dark water when I feel him at my side.

The view's got nothing on New York, but that's what makes it special. Here feels serene. Stark lights have been replaced by a soft glow from the bridge to our right. The calm water reflects the moon and there's the faint sound of music drifting through the air, from a jazz cruise, alight in the distance.

"If I'd known this is what it would have taken to get you to be quiet, I would have come earlier."

"How did you know this was here?" Ryan asks, ignoring my joke.

"Guidebook." I chance a sideways glance at the same time he does. Our eyes connect. "They're useful."

"I'll take your word for it."

We both look away and go quiet.

114

"Are you ready?" I ask, when I start to feel uncomfortable with the silence.

The surface of the river is like a millpond and there isn't even the sound of water sloshing against the wall to listen to.

Ryan turns and faces me. "For the gig?"

I nod. "And the world tour."

"What's there to be ready for?"

There's a glint in his eye, like he's challenging me to react to his arrogance. Managing to stop myself taking the bait, I gain a few extra seconds by rolling my lips before I respond.

"Some people might find the enormity of what's happening nerve wracking," I reply.

"Yeah, well. I'm not most people."

I watch him reach into his pocket and pull out a joint. He places it in his mouth then lights it. The tip burns orange when he sucks in, darkening when he drags it back away. I cough over the smoke.

After taking another drag, Ryan lowers the joint, then extends his arm, holding it out between us. I stare, unable to decide what to do. It's the thought of what Mother would say if she saw me, that makes up my mind.

Reaching over, I pluck it from between Ryan's fingers.

The joint's at my lips when uncertainty kicks in.

"You don't have to," he says, sensing my hesitation.

Instead of answering, I inhale. If he's surprised by my choice, his face doesn't show it. When I exhale, a small, pathetic bit of smoke swirls from my mouth. Amateur.

"This is new to me." I try to explain it away like it's nothing. "I've never smoked before."

A muscle in Ryan's jaw twitches but he doesn't make a comment.

The coughing that follows my second drag is evidence I've done it correctly.

"How is this enjoyable?" I splutter.

Waving a hand in front of my face, I try to clear the smoke obscuring my vision.

"Here." Ryan pulls another joint from his pocket and lights it. "Watch."

I do as he tells me, fascinated by how he makes the process look effortless when he inhales then blows out a thick cloud. It disappears and I lose myself in his eyes. They're more beautiful than any of the stars hanging above us in the clear night sky. The sound of Ryan's laughter wraps around me, creating a warm and cozy feeling. Everything feels fuzzy.

"That will be the weed talking," he says, then his hands are wrapped around my arms.

He maneuvers me so my back presses against the railing, lining the river. The contrast between the hot surrounding air, coating my skin, and the cool metal, penetrating my blouse to my back, has me yelping in surprise.

"What are you doing?"

Ryan's standing so close the front of his body presses into me.

The calm that's begun to take over my body waivers. It doesn't stand a chance against the riot of emotions that come with his legs pressing against the side of mine. Or with him lifting his hand to clasp a lock of hair that's fallen from my bun and tuck it behind my ear.

"Want to forget with me?" His voice comes out gravelly and low. The only way I can respond is by nodding. "Relax."

My body goes rigid.

I'm jostled by Ryan's laughter as he takes the still burning joint from my grip. I've no idea where the other one he pulled out has disappeared to. Time feels like it's sped up, and with my brain working at half capacity, I'm struggling to keep up with what's happening. Unfortunately, my marijuana-induced high doesn't stop me forgetting why we're here, and images of the women in the pictures invade my thoughts.

As if he knows what I'm thinking, Ryan's empty hand wraps around my left. His thumb begins drawing small circles against the back of it and my eyes flicker shut.

"That feels good," I murmur, his featherlight touch soothing my uncertainty.

Somewhere in my haze, I feel Ryan tense, before his breath tickles the skin close to my ear.

His next words come out a choked kind of rasp. "Open your eyes." I do what he says and tilt my head back. "Now your mouth." My lips part and he holds the end of the joint between them. "Relax." His thumb continues to draw circles and my muscles go slack. "Block everything out and breathe in."

Drawing in a long deep breath, I let the bitter, yet sweet smoke fill my mouth. The taste of berries mixed with chocolate and mint coats my tongue. This time my lungs fill with ease.

"Hold it." Ryan's eyes lower to where the joint is still resting. He pulls it away, then his mouth is mirroring mine, leaving barely a centimeter between our lips. "Breathe out."

He drinks in my exhale, keeping the moment our secret a few seconds longer, before blowing it back out into the universe.

"How do you feel?"

"Corrupted." I giggle at what was possibly one of the hottest moments of my life. "High," I then admit.

Another rumble of laughter fills Ryan's chest as I bury my face in it. We must be in a parallel universe, because rather than pushing me away, or asking if I've lost my mind, he rests his chin on top of my head. Neither of us move, until Ryan goes to stub out the remainder of the joint and pocket it. His shirt rubs against my cheek.

How can something so simple feel like sensory overload?

It's instinctive to hold back a shiver. To hide how the unexpectedness of us being together like this is making me feel. Unfortunately, what I'm able to hide from Ryan, I can't hide from myself. Like I can't hide from the disappointment I feel when he draws back. It's temporary though, because then he's grasping and lifting my chin. Staring at my lips as words spill out of his own that I never thought I'd hear.

"I really want to kiss you right now."

I want to ask why because I thought he despised the ground I walked on.

Instead, I sweep my tongue across my lips. Ryan tracks the movement and my body goes slack. My eyes flicker shut as I wait for him to seize a moment I've never imagined wanting, let alone needing. I want to know what his mouth feels like against mine. I need to taste him. Somehow, I know a kiss from him will be the kind you don't forget.

Sensing his lips hovering near, ready to close the final gap, I wait.

And wait.

Then wait some more.

When nothing happens, I open my eyes, finding the hunger that filled Ryan's, is gone.

"I-I can't."

His body slumps causing our foreheads to collide with a force that makes me wince.

"I'm sorry," he chokes out, stumbling back. "I can't."

Fear transforms his face into someone unrecognizable. My chest grows tight as I watch him gasp for air.

Get it together, Sooz. He needs you.

Stepping forward, I place a hand on his shoulder. He shudders and his next breath comes out ragged. I tell myself he's okay. But he's not. Not really. Nothing about this moment is, because I don't know what's happening and I don't know how to help.

"Ryan. Talk to me. Please."

Giving his shoulder a firm squeeze, I pray it helps him find his way out of whatever dark place he's gone to. It does nothing and neither do my words. He struggles to suck in another breath.

Doing the only thing I can think of, I reach up, grab both sides of his face and force him to look at me.

"Ry!"

Vacant eyes stare back.

"Ry!" I snap again.

He blinks and some of the tension in my chest eases.

With his attention on me, I lower my voice. "It's okay. It's fine. Everything's fine."

His eyes dart around.

"It's okay," I repeat. "It's okay. Breathe."

Listening, he draws in a long, slow breath, which he lets it out even slower.

My voice comes out wobbly when I ask, "You good?"

Appearing more present with each second that passes, Ryan nods before his gaze drops to the ground. Gut instinct tells me not to voice my next question. But if I stand any chance of helping him, of us moving on from this, I need to.

"Why can't you kiss me?"

Ryan sweeps his hands across his cheeks, but it's too late. I've already seen the tear tracks. Without answering, he pulls out another joint. An escape.

Leftover adrenaline fuels my reaction and I snatch it away.

"Give it back." The look he gives me is as dark as his voice.

"No." I shake my head. "Answer my question."

"I can't." He swallows and I catch sight of something on his neck, beneath the tattoo.

Raising onto my tiptoes, I reach up to touch the masked skin. Where my fingertips move over, is raised.

"What are your tattoos hiding?"

"My scars," he croaks, verging on a plead not to pry for more information.

Unsure what to make of his answer, I find myself distracted by the hand tapping his thigh in a rapid beat. Pretending I haven't noticed, I take a step back because he's closed off. I can feel it. There's no way he's going to give me any more answers. I don't know if he ever will.

"Maybe you need this after all," I say bitterly.

Giving him an out, I hold the joint between us. After he takes it, I turn and walk away.

The journey back to the tour bus feels long. I do what I can to ignore the smell of weed that follows me, refusing to acknowledge what it says about Ryan. That despite the fact, in all the time we've known each other, I've given him more than one reason to hate me, he still makes sure I get back safely.

Chapter Eleven

I t's late morning and I'm retracing my footsteps from last night before the preparations for the band's performance begin, needing air and space to collect my thoughts and recover from the dull ache of my hangover.

The second I see Ryan standing by the riverbank, I decide the universe is messing with me.

I don't get a chance to even contemplate walking away. The universe continues to intervene as I trip on nothing, yelping as I stumble, forgetting the need to remain inconspicuous.

Ryan turns, and I'm left with no choice but to face him.

"Hey," I say, as far from cool as I can get.

"Hi," he replies before turning back to face the stormy waters.

The calm of yesterday is a long, distant memory. My eyes drop to the joint in his hand, taking in the way he rolls it between his fingers. The heated breeze hits my skin and I shiver as I walk to his side.

"You good?" I ask, staring out at the Mississippi.

"I guess."

While he isn't looking my way, I give him a sideways glance.

Everyone knows 'I guess' means no. I want to assume his sour mood doesn't have anything to do with me being here. But in the broad light of day, I can't convince myself it's true. Not when his scowl is as thunderous as the heavy clouds above us, threatening rain, which, right now, I'd welcome with open arms. It would provide a break in the humidity and give me a reason to scurry away so I can pretend this encounter hasn't happened.

Ryan is making it perfectly clear he doesn't want to be around me.

"I'll go," I say, gesturing over my shoulder.

"Stay."

That's it. No explanation. No expression. He doesn't even bother looking at me.

"No." I shake my head, wishing there was more conviction behind my voice.

Ryan doesn't react, simply continues staring out at the water while I struggle to fight the magnetic pull between us that tempts me to stay by his side.

Nothing good can come from me staying. So, I don't.

Before I can second guess my decision, I leave him and whatever thoughts are plaguing him, behind.

With ten minutes until the scheduled pre-performance photoshoot is due to start, everything is in place. Everything is ready—apart from the drummer.

"Where's Ryan?" I ask Sam.

He shrugs. "Trying to find food, I think."

My mouth parts. "Food? When you have a photoshoot and then you're headlining a set? He's finding ... food."

Sam shrugs, not understanding my urgency. "He was hungry?"

"Gah!"

"Are you mad?"

"What do you think?" I all but hiss, letting my frustrations from last night get the better of me. "Why can't he behave like he's supposed to?"

I mutter the last part under my breath, but not quiet enough.

"Because I'm not a dog," replies a voice behind me.

"And that's my cue to leave," says Sam, disappearing before I can tell him to stay.

"Where have you been?" I snap when I spin around and find Ryan towering over me.

He's back to wearing one of his favorite shirts. The gun show ones.

"Trying to find food," he replies, confirming what Sam said.

"Could you not have done that earlier?"

He scowls. The intensity in his eyes could melt a solid chunk of metal. I scowl right back.

"I couldn't find anything I liked." He starts to walk past me.

I outstretch my arm, almost, but not quite, touching his middle with my hand, stopping him from going any further. Heat pours off him, warming my palm.

"I have a chocolate bar in my bag."

There's a flicker of something in his eyes. It disappears as quick as it appeared. "I don't need your help and I don't need a babysitter."

He sidesteps my hand and walks off in the direction of the photoshoot, leaving me questioning if what happened last night was a figment of my imagination.

After the photoshoot, there's some spare time before the show. The guys decide to go for a drink in the bar next to the venue.

"What do you want?" I ask, eying the drinks menu.

"You decide." Sam beams.

"Hmm."

A familiar rumble of laughter, smothering the noise in the bar, makes my skin bristle.

"Sooz?" says Sam, and I realize I've been staring at the menu too long for a simple choice.

When I look up, the bartender shifts his weight between his feet, waiting for my order.

"Um, sorry, I'll have …" There's more laughter; louder, closer. I turn my head. Just a little. But enough I'm able to find Ryan a few feet behind us in the small crowd that has congregated, thanks to my indecisiveness. Our eyes lock. Mine widen. His narrow. I blink and snap my head back round, focusing my attention on the menu still sitting in front of me on the bar. "A coke, please. And a beer."

Less than a minute later, our drinks appear.

"Is everything okay?" Sam asks quietly, grabbing his beer bottle.

"Yep!" My voice reaches a pitch that suggests otherwise as I pick up my coke. "Can we sit down?"

"Yeah, sure."

We both turn to move through the crowd. What follows next is a moment, a completely unavoidable one. One that throws me off kilter, regardless of the rapid mental preparations I do. The coke I'm holding sloshes over the rim of the glass when I bump into a wall of muscle. Ryan has a habit of being everywhere I don't want him to be.

"Woah, dude. Want to get any closer?" chuckles Sam, sidestepping around him.

"You're blocking the bar," Ryan replies, keeping his gaze focused on me.

I do my best to avoid looking up, but Sam's right, he's standing so close I'm left with no choice. When I meet Ryan's eyes, I struggle to breathe. The noise filling the room disappears.

"Sooz." Sam clears his throat. It's like a bullet being fired, echoing around us, ringing in my ears, and bringing me crashing back down to Earth. "You good?"

"Yeah!" I answer, shrilly.

Stepping my foot out to the side to move around Ryan, I'm stopped when a hand finds my waist and grips it firmly. *His.* Making it clear he has ideas that don't involve letting me walk away.

"I'm sorry for earlier," Ryan says, his voice low and serious.

He's infuriating. Irritating. But it's more irritating when he isn't either of those things and he gives me the look that he's throwing my way now. It's filled with remorse. His eyes tell a story his lips won't. Last night made that very clear. It makes me panic, and I spurt out a remark I instantly regret. But it's necessary. Vital to re-establish our usual 'Sooz and Ryan' dynamic.

"Sorry suggests I'd have to care about what you say to me."

A deep line appears in the middle of Ryan's brows, and he takes the bait. "I can't decide if you're really a bitch, or pretending to be one."

I give him the tightest smile I can muster and walk away without replying, before either of us can cause the kind of damage that will be impossible to reverse.

We need to get the show tonight over with and get back to the normality of New York.

Standing in the wings, I tap my foot as S.C.A.R.A.B. begin another song of their set. The crowd roars their approval and I take the moment to reflect on how far they've come since the first summer I met them.

They've proved they're far from being the underdogs. Having found their groove, they pour everything into their music, and then ten times more. They've clawed their way up the industry ladder with no sign of slowing. It's no wonder Warped's competitors are breaking out in a sweat. The truly inspiring part is that, even though each time they go out on stage they run the risk of losing everything if they make one misstep, especially with the industry leaders watching their every move, they don't fear it. They face the risk head on.

They're true professionals, setting standards other acts struggle to follow, walking an extraordinary path toward a level of success no one ever could have predicted in their early days. Being a part of it all, watching them chase their dreams in a way few have the courage to do, is magical. Because in a world where image has become worth more than talent, they've set their own beat.

Their riffs tear through expectations and their melodies act as a soothing balm to the most damaged souls. When it comes to this group of perfectly flawed individuals, I have a feeling we've barely scratched the surface, and when we get to the core of who they are and unlock their true potential, it will ricochet through the music world in a way that's beyond comprehension.

Standing, I drink it all in. The music. The atmosphere. The start of it all, of everything to come.

Feeling the euphoria of the crowd, I let it pass through my body. It's then that I get it. The why. Why people might want to do this. Perfect their craft. Do something different. Put the thing they believe in out into the world, when there's the potential to be judged. Because there will always be those who don't get it. But when you find those who do, see the awe on their faces, hear it in their voices when they truly connect with something you've put your heart and soul into, I imagine there's no better feeling.

The beat is what takes the song to the next level. It vibrates through the ground, pounding in rhythm with my heart. My lips twitch as I watch Ryan giving the performance his all.

My foot continues tap, tap, tapping away.

Until my tapping falls out of sync. I frown. Assess.

I continue watching Ryan, but now it's for entirely different reasons. I block everything out. The guitar and bass, ripping through the crowd's noise. Sam's voice lulling every set of ears into a false sense of security, making it appear like everything is right. Really everything is wrong. My foot taps against the ground still and I focus on Ryan's face. Sweat rolls down his temples, but he doesn't look hot or flustered. He looks pale. Too pale. His eyes are wider than they should be.

He misses another beat and all the pieces slot together. He's stoned again.

"Unbelievable," I mutter.

I'm too upset to keep watching. Annoyed for the rest of the group, and everyone supporting them, that he can't keep his act together for a few hours.

He's worse than a loose cannon.

He's a faulty one.

Ready to misfire at any second and devastate everything around him.

Backstage, I hold my breath as the set finishes, praying the crowd haven't noticed how many times Ryan's messed up.

Their roar of approval makes it clear they haven't.

The guys all walk off stage, and I give each of them a warm smile to try and counteract the coolness in their gazes. Until I get to Ryan. I go to launch into a long speech about responsibility when I take in his pallor. I can't decide what he looks more likely of doing. Puking or passing out.

Jake moves toward him. His jaw is clenched, but his face is concerned. "Are you okay?"

"I don't know," Ryan replies, shaking his head.

"Do we need to get you some help?"

Ryan grimaces. "Not here."

Jake glances at me over his shoulder. His face hardens when he realizes I'm standing watching their whole interaction. He turns back to Ryan. "We need to get you somewhere private."

Ryan goes to step forward, but stumbles and mutters out a "Fuck!"

I groan. If anyone catches wind of this and it gets back to the label, we're all screwed.

Ryan sags against the wall. "Sorry."

"Stop with the sorry shit," Jake says. My ears prick up at what I hear next. "Before we left, you said you had this under control. You don't do you?"

"No," Ryan replies. Guilt pours from him like the sweat making his skin glisten.

I walk away, because I don't have it in me to watch any more.

When the meet and greets are over, I corner Ryan away from the others, and launch my attack.

"What the hell was that?"

Ryan's hand trembles as he raises it and drags it through his hair. He sways a little on his feet, but nowhere near as bad as he was before.

I narrow my eyes, taking it all in.

The rest of the band appear and stop in their tracks. Jake squares his shoulders and steps forward. Of course, he'd protect his drummer, even when he's in the wrong. This is ridiculous. They're enabling his habit. They might think they're helping their friend, but all they're doing is making things worse.

Ryan gives the guys a resigned look, then says, "Can you give us a minute?" I receive a round of wary looks and not one of them moves an inch. "I'm fine. Swear."

They move away, throwing daggers over their shoulders at me as they go. The way they're acting, you'd think it was me who'd messed up their set.

"What's going on?" I snap, at the end of my tether.

"Nothing," Ryan replies. "I had a bad set."

My eyes feel like they're going to pop out of their sockets. "Bad set? Bad set!" My voice grows higher in pitch. "A bad set is for amateurs. You're going on a world tour! There's no room for bad sets."

Ryan scratches at the stubble lining his jaw then salutes me. "Got it. Won't happen again, Ma'am."

"Hilarious," I deadpan.

It's when he pulls a joint out of his pocket and sparks it up right in front of me that there's a serious risk I might lose it. My jaw drops and I stand, watching him make quick work of the first half.

"You're unbelievable, you know that, right?"

He doesn't respond. He doesn't need to. The evidence is there in the form of bloodshot eyes and extra-large pupils.

"You'd miss a lot less beats if you didn't do that."

He laughs and rolls back his shoulders as he takes another long drag.

"You're not going to answer?"

"I've got nothing to say."

"You messed up."

He holds my gaze. "Fear got in the way."

"Fear of what? You're … you. What exactly could you be afraid of?"

"You don't know anything about me."

A beat passes.

"You're the gun show guy. The big strong drummer."

This time, when he laughs, he throws his head back. It's overexaggerated. Bitter. Suddenly, he stops. "Even the strongest people have something that can bring them to their knees."

"Ryan …"

My chest rises and falls at a rapid rate. My heart pounds as I watch him, watching me. His eyes lower, dropping to the sandals wrapped around my feet. His nostrils flare and then he takes two large steps toward me.

"Yes?"

My breath comes out in short pants. He's standing so close they're coating his skin with damp warmth.

"Why do you smoke weed?"

His eyes become unreadable as he considers his answer. Then the clouds part and he's back to being his usual self. "It's medicinal."

"For what exactly?"

"Anxiety."

"You do know anxiety means you have to care about something."

He tenses. Leans in. "You should try it. You're so stressed, it stresses me out … *baby*."

I suck in a sharp breath, despising him for using the term of endearment that made last night that little bit more special, and tainting it. "Bite me."

"Gladly." He grins and his eyes do a lazy perusal of my body. He's a virtual stranger. "Tell me where."

"Actually," I reply, lining myself up, ready to wipe the smug smile from his face. "I prefer to be bitten by men who won't require me to have a tetanus shot after."

He shrugs. "Your loss."

The words "I hate you" come out in a snarl. I'm so angry I can barely breathe.

"Careful throwing all that hate around."

My feet remain glued to the spot. "Why?"

He fixes a smile in place, then drops his head. I feel his breath on the shell of my ear. "Because it's a thin line between love and hate."

He might as well have lowered a pin into the Sooz shaped balloon that is me, because all I hear is pop.

"Jake! Wait!" I call, hurrying to catch him up as the rest of the band disappear inside the tour bus to call it a night before our early flight in the morning. Jake stops, turns, and gives me a look that says the last thing he wants to do, is to talk to me. "Can I say something?"

After what happened back at the gig, I need to clear the air with at least one member of S.C.A.R.A.B. because the rest have made it perfectly clear they don't want anything to do with me.

"Sure," he replies, eyes narrowed, making it clear he doesn't want anything to do with me either.

"This is my job." My shoulders slump as exhaustion kicks in. "I'm trying to help." Jake's gaze softens and he rubs a hand across his jaw. "I'm not the enemy."

"Why do I feel like this conversation is tailored more toward another member of the band than it is me?"

"Because it feels like he's doing whatever he can to make my job harder …" I admit.

"I'll have a word." Jake glances along the dark street. "I should go."

"Okay."

Neither of us move until Jake stubs his toe against the ground. "Sooz, he's not a bad guy."

Before he disappears, I'm hit with a realization. Something I think I've known all along but haven't wanted to acknowledge because it complicates things.

"I know he isn't," I reply.

Jake disappears onto the bus in the same way I wish I could make the memories of this trip disappear.

In the early hours of the morning, my alarm sounds out.

Sleep barely found me, making getting up less of a chore. The same can't be said for the guys. Two of which continue snoring, even though I let my alarm ring on for longer than usual.

My stomach growls, reminding me of its lack of fuel after I crawled into bed post gig, avoiding all of the band members. There's no way I can make it to the airport without getting something, so I make a quick plan to use the small kitchen to make a sandwich.

The bus is dark and silent as I move through it. I exhale, relieved, when I get to the kitchen. If you can even call it that. I'm pulling out a knife from a drawer when I hear an out-of-place snore. Moving further down the bus, toward a flickering light, I find a small TV running late-night informercials. The source of the snoring is Ryan, flat on his back in the booth. He'll need to get up within the next hour, but the fact doesn't stop me grabbing a blanket and placing it over his legs carefully. He's out cold. Doesn't move an inch. Whatever program is playing in the background continues, and there's the sound of light laughter. The bus illuminates, highlighting his cheekbones. His dark lashes rest together, creating a half-moon shadow on his skin.

I cast a quick glance around, searching for the TV remote. When I come up with nothing, I look back at Ryan, and find it peeking out from beneath where his hand is resting on his chest. I've almost pulled it out successfully when he stirs. His fingers wrap around it, and he lifts his arm. His elbow bends and the back of his hand settles over his eyes.

He lets out a long breath, then goes still again. My eyes move over to the familiar bands on his wrists. The ones he always wears. As the bus illuminates again and my eyes focus, there's one band in particular that stands out.

The vivid red one that has my eyes burning when I read the word 'milk' in bold white text.

With the TV still on, I back away, trying to figure out in the four years of knowing Ryan, how I could have missed this.

Chapter Twelve

I give Zach twenty-four hours of being back in Brooklyn, waiting until the following morning when the sun is starting to rise, before I go in with my planned attack.

The floorboards creak as I make my way upstairs, but thankfully, the house remains silent. I wait an extra few seconds before I carry on moving in the direction of Zach's room. Luckily, his bedroom door swings open with considerably less noise, and after closing it behind me, I tiptoe over to his bed. The journey comes with less risk than the one carried out in Ryan's room last week, being that he's considerably tidier than his band mate. The soft blue glow coming from the digital clock on his nightstand helps too, and I'm able to make out my path.

Zach's mid-snore when I tap his shoulder. My first time is too gentle, and it does nothing. The second time, I tap him harder. He almost snaps my wrist when his hand clamps round it as his eyes fly open. He bolts upright.

"What the fuck?!"

I flinch at how loud his voice comes out, praying he hasn't woken Ryan up. We *need* to have this conversation.

When he relaxes, I narrow my eyes down at him. "Tell me what you know."

I can barely make out his expression, but from what I can tell, he's looking at me like I've lost my mind. It's confirmed that's exactly how he's looking at me when he reaches over to the lamp beside his bed and turns it on.

"You're giving me serial killer vibes right now …" He rubs at his eyes. "What time is it? Is it even morning?" I glance at his clock, and he turns, reads the digits and groans. "Seven AM? Seriously? What couldn't wait till nine?"

"This conversation." I narrow my eyes again. "Cholesterol my buttocks." I point a finger in his direction, tempted to jab him in the chest. "Don't pretend you don't know what I'm talking about." He pales. "Who else knows?" I didn't think it was possible, but he goes a little paler. "Everyone?" He shakes his head no. "The band?" He nods. "John West?" His right eye twitches.

In for the long haul, I lower myself and perch on the edge of his bed. "That first tour in Europe. The night before last." Another brain synapse fires to life. "Do the images have something to do with this?"

"This isn't my story to tell," Zach says.

"Then who is going to tell it? Because it's very clear, after all this time, Ryan isn't."

"How do you know?"

"Deflecting. Really? When your band mate is putting himself at risk?"

136

Zach's gaze hardens. "Please, just answer. How do you know?"

"Why is it so important?" His eyes drop to the sheets covering his lap and it hits me. "He doesn't want me to."

"You need to talk to Ryan." He looks torn. "I know you want answers, but you won't get them from me."

I raise my chin. "And what if he refuses to give me any?"

"Then you have to accept that, for whatever reason, he doesn't want to tell you."

After my very short and not-so-sweet conversation with Zach, I make my way back down to the living room.

Ten minutes are spent pacing back and forth before it hits me how exhausted I am. Passing out on the couch seems reasonable, so I sit, then lean back with my head propped on a cushion resting against the arm. With my hands clasped on top of my middle, I stare to my right out of the living room window, watching as the light changes and the snippet of sky I can see transitions through all the shades of blue, until it becomes bold and bright.

Eventually, exhaustion takes over and my eyes drift shut.

When I wake up, close to noon, the house is empty, but my inbox—one of the constants in my life—is full. The message that captures my attention, spurring me into action and jumping off the couch, is from Abby, declaring an emergency.

Not long after reading it, I barrel into our apartment, expecting to find the place burning down, or at least a body from the phrasing she used.

All I find is her. And caffeine. Clara is nowhere to be found.

It might not be quite the emergency she declared, but something feels different. I struggle to figure out what it is.

"You survived!" Abby chimes, settling down on the couch, placing the two steaming cups she's carrying on the coffee table.

"Just," I reply when I've closed the door behind me.

Abby's excited expression slips away. "That bad?"

Before answering, I disappear into the kitchen, only returning when I have a stack of the dirtiest snacks I can find bundled in my arms. "Worse." I sit beside her, about to tear into a pack of cookies when a four-letter word highlighted in the listed ingredients has me setting them back down. "It was weird."

My phone bleeps.

"Ignore it." I hesitate when my phone alerts me to another text. "They can wait." She leans over and takes a cookie from the pack. My mouth waters with jealousy. It's not enough to have me reaching over and taking one, though. "I've barely seen you since you've got back. I am officially your number one priority."

When I laugh, Abby does too, causing a few crumbs to fly out of her mouth. She scowls and picks them up from the floor, then places them beside her cup on the table. I glance around. Sniff. I narrow my eyes and sniff again.

My eyes widen. "Can I smell bleach?"

The domestic side of life isn't her strong point. Now, with Clara, the apartment, when I'm not around, is a disaster. In her defense, with the little person in her life, there's not much point. Clara Ross is destruction personified. And right now, judging by the reappearance of Abby's holey leggings, she's destroying her mother.

"I tried to get on top of things while she's in daycare," Abby admits. "I didn't want you coming back to a mess."

"I could have helped." I don't continue when Abby frowns, knowing the conversation will go down the usual path of her declaring Clara isn't my child to clean up after. Something has to give though, because Abby is trying to juggle everything, and it's clear by the low set of her shoulders and the dark circles beneath her eyes, everything is going to fall apart.

"I wanted to get our first real tree." Her voice comes out wistful, and I know there's a big but coming. "But Clara would destroy it."

"Trees are overrated," I reply, waving my hand in the air playfully, dismissing such a ludicrous idea.

Abby laughs. "Only you could make me feel better about not having anything ready for Christmas." She's not wrong there. After the deepest of cleans, the apartment is bare. There's no clutter in sight, and no baubles.

Everything is the way it should be. Well, everything apart from me.

"Tell me about being home now we have time," Abby says, as if sensing I need a subject change. I never thought I'd see the day where I'd be happy to talk about something associated with Mother.

"You mean South Africa," I correct her, as she passes over my coffee, which is now drinking temperature. "Thanks." I take a couple of sips before diving into my three-month summary, allowing the warm liquid to raise my internal temperatures.

"Okay, so your mother is still your mother," confirms Abby, standing up from the couch. She disappears into the kitchen for a few minutes and reappears with another two cups of more than needed caffeine. "Now, tell me about New Orleans."

Midway through taking the cup from her, my hand jolts. The liquid inside sloshes dangerously close to the rim. Sucking in a quick breath, I tell myself to get it together, then finish retrieving it safely, while trying to figure out how to explain something I'm not really sure of myself. "It was okay."

I might as well have fired off a round of bullets for how unsubtle I'm being. Abby sees through my attempts to school my expression. "Which means it wasn't."

Knowing I can't get anything past her, like she can't get anything past me, I take a deep breath. "I got drunk."

"Interesting." She smiles behind her cup, but her eyes give away exactly what she's thinking. "I'm excited to see where this goes." She'd pass out if she knew I got high. Choosing to keep that tidbit to myself, I give her a look to try to throw her off track, and she giggles. "Was there hot, steamy hate sex in an inappropriate place?"

"No." My face remains stoic. I will not let her see how frazzled New Orleans has left me. It would mean talking about the thing I've been refusing to think about all morning, because every time I do, I feel like I'm going to vomit. "I thought I'd leave that as your thing."

"Touché." She lowers her cup and switches on her serious. "Okay. Now, tell me what really happened? I know you don't think you're getting away without giving me the rest of the story."

Mother trucker. I knew coming here was a bad idea. Already cracking, it won't take much for me to crumble.

"Did you know Ryan has an allergy?"

So much for keeping it to myself. Face planting seems justified.

"Yes."

If the couch wasn't so deep it's impossible to get up from at times, I'd fall right off.

"Wait. You actually knew?" Abby nods slowly while I try to figure out why Zach said she didn't. It doesn't take a genius to figure out that Jake has told her. "And you didn't think to tell me?"

I'm met with another eye roll as she sets her cup down. The way she shifts her position on the couch so she's facing me full on suggests she's going all in. She means business. The authoritative finger raised in the air and the "Firstly," that comes out of her mouth next, seals it. I brace myself for the reprimand I know is coming my way.

"You've made it clear, constantly, for three—almost four—years, that you hate the ground he walks on." I purse my lips and accept her first point as correct. A second finger joins the first. "Secondly, I only just found out, like, days ago. You haven't been here, and it's hardly the type of thing you dump on someone over the phone." My lips flatten. Also correct. A third and final finger, judging by the way her posture slumps back, joins the other two. "Finally, it's not for me to go around telling."

"What do you mean?"

"I've known Ryan since high school. I'd like to go as far as saying that since Jake and I got over all our crap, we've

141

become friends. And even though most of my friends' actions at times are questionable …" She isn't wrong there. "I trust them. If Ryan hasn't told me himself, then there's a reason for it. I'm choosing to accept that he will when he's ready. And if he never is, that's fine too."

"How mature of you," I quip, still feeling a little on the back foot.

Abby reveals some of her frustration when she says, "Everyone has a story, Sooz. We both know that. But whether someone decides to tell theirs is their choice. We have to respect the reasons why they might not want to."

"Why do I have a feeling this has something to do with the football player on our screen?"

Abby looks sadly at the muted television across the room, running through the last NFL season's highlights. I watch Michael Becket—Abby's ex—score a touchdown. We rarely talk about him. Abby gets too upset, because his story would break the strongest person. Their relationship ended on bad terms, but she still follows his career, and he has a regular virtual spot in our living room. The reminder of everything he went through and how he came back from it all resonates with me on a much deeper level now, knowing what I do about Ryan. He's never fitted into one of our conversations more. He's a perfect example of a person who shows the world what they want to see, instead of who they really are.

"Ryan stayed out with me. In New Orleans," I say, starting to give Abby some of our story. I blink. When did we become an 'our'? A duo? I don't have chance to over-analyze my brain slip, because Abby's brows twitch, and I can tell it's taking everything in her not to shake me for more details. "We kind of got along."

"There was no arguing?" she says, using her words to smother a smile.

"I mean, there was some. But there were also spells where there wasn't."

"Interesting."

"Weird." I'm not sure why I choose to set my cup down over revealing the almost-kiss detail. Embarrassment? No. Protective of a moment that could barely be called one? Maybe. "What was also weird was that he's kind of good company."

"Told you." Abby grins and holds a finger in the air, signaling that the point, in our four-year debate, is hers.

My phone starts ringing before I have a chance to say anything else. Zach's name flashes on the screen, and Abby looks confused.

"I may have cornered him for more details," I explain. "He's now terrified I'm going to tell everyone what I know. He won't leave me alone." The call cuts off, there's a beat, and then his name fills the screen again. Knowing he will keep blocking the line if I don't talk to him, I grab my phone and tap the green button on the screen, setting the call on speakerphone.

"Sooz. Hi." Abby muffles her laughter into her hand. "Where you at?"

"I'm telling Ryan's story to the New York Times." Zach squeaks, and I huff. "You need to stop. I'm not going to tell anyone. I'm with Abby, who, FYI, also knows, and no, it wasn't me. Take it up with your guitarist."

I hang up, and Abby frowns. "I'm assuming all this emotional turmoil over the person you thought you hated has you not sleeping?"

"That obvious?" I reply, rubbing my eyes.

143

"Tired Sooz is cranky Sooz." I shoot her a 'takes-one-to-know-one' look, which she responds to with, "Don't be a bitch." After a minute, she says, "You should talk to him about it. Ryan, I mean, not Zach."

"Yeah," I muse. "Maybe."

Abby shrugs as she stands. "It will be the easiest and quickest way for the two of you to get back to normal." I don't miss her smile as she turns to walk to the kitchen. "If that's what you really want."

All the way back to S.C.A.R.A.B.'s place, my brain goes haywire. No matter which way I spin it, I can't figure out why the thought of Ryan and I not being a part of each other's lives, leaves my heart feeling heavy.

Chapter Thirteen

A text alert comes through on my way back to the band's place. I pull out my phone to check it's nothing urgent, chuckling to myself when Zach's name reads on the screen. He's relentless.

Zach: *Gone out. Back later.*

Hanging up on him clearly got my point across. I shove my phone away with a smile and there's a spring to my step for the latter part of my journey. Nothing can bring me down. Not the heavy clouds hovering above. Not the stench of garbage as I pass an overfilled trashcan. Not the rat that runs across my foot—thank you, New York. Even the dirty orange hue everything is basked in, promising a fall of snow, can't dampen my mood.

Not when I know I'm going to get the band's place to myself for an extended period. Compared to Abby and my place, it's a palace. I've found myself on more than one occasion questioning why she hasn't moved in with Clara. There's an abundance of everything she needs: space. I'm tempted to message her and ask, when I remember she's as stubborn and proud as I am. It's why we clicked the first time we met and it's also why I don't bother asking. She won't move in, because it's not *her* place.

Too excited for the same space, I struggle to get Sam's key into the lock. The lock where, when I do manage to force the key in, won't budge. Just my luck I'm going to get stuck out, the first time I want to be in.

Despite what I was telling myself, I can feel my good mood slipping away. With nothing else to do, I sit on the top step and look up at the clouds. They seem to be growing thicker the longer I stare. Three minutes in, and I remember the key I all but snapped in the lock is for the back entrance.

Good mood firmly back in place, I make my way round to the rear of the house. When I'm inside, with the back door locked, I set my bag down on the kitchen central island and sag against it. I love living here, in Brooklyn, but the one thing that irritates the life out of me is the weather.

When I left earlier, I'd layered up against sub-zero temperatures. Four layers worth. But I'm sweaty now, so I decide to shower.

I grab what I need from my travel case, which is still in the living area. The house is so quiet as I make my way upstairs with my wash bag in one hand and a fresh towel and clothing in the other, I find myself tiptoeing. I go as far as flinching when my right foot catches on a loose floorboard and a loud creak reverberates off the walls. Laughter follows when I remember I'm the only one home. I'm being ridiculous.

Inside the bathroom, I set my things down and pull out my shower gel, placing it carefully on the side of the tub, ready to be used. When I'm in the shower, I let the water cascade over me, washing away more than the sweat. It's only when my body's lathered and I sniff that it hits me I've picked up the wrong body wash.

Taking another deep inhale, I absorb the notes of ylang-ylang and black pepper. The dark, sensual scent feels more familiar than I would like it to be, even without the overlay of pot odor. I should let the water wash the suds down the drain. Instead, my hands move over my arms, up to my shoulders, then down to my pelvis and lower. I try not to think how wrong it is when my hand moves between my legs, leaving traces of Ryan Alvarez in places I'll never allow him to go.

My legs move closer together. The ache low in my core is disturbing, so I turn off the water abruptly and clamber out of the tub. I grab a towel and wrap it around me.

I'm leaving the bathroom when there's a loud bang from somewhere in the house. My foot slips against the tiles. A moment later, I hear another bang after I catch my balance. Stepping out into the hall, I hear more banging, followed by the crash of a cymbal. It takes a moment, but I put the pieces together and realize that I'm no longer alone in the house. I'm not sure I ever was.

It's the loud crash, decibels higher, that has me heading in the direction of Ryan's room. Almost at the door, I pause when everything goes silent. Turning to go back down and get dressed, I freeze when a loud 'fuck' comes from his room. Heart thudding, I stop with my hand on the doorhandle, contemplating whether I should go up. Greeted

147

with another F-bomb, I decide I can't leave him, and open the door.

A cloud of smoke greets me. Jesus. It looks like he's lit up a marijuana farm. Weed fumes swirl around me as I make my way up, bracing myself for what I'm going to find. My footsteps slow as I reach the top. I hear a grunt.

Maybe it's not that bad?

More wasted hope. It's worse than I thought, because Ryan is on his bed, naked apart from the thin material of his boxers.

As I struggle to adjust my eyes, I could be convinced he's asleep. The noise I heard moments ago tells me otherwise. I start to open my mouth, ready to announce my arrival, when I freeze. He moves, and I hear a groan. There's another groan as he moves again.

In the dim light, I just make out what he's doing.

Himself.

Oh-my-God-oh-my-God.

I go to bolt, but my foot catches on an empty glass bottle. It makes a loud clatter as it rocks unstably, spinning across the room. The groaning stops and is replaced by light pouring from Ryan's bedside lamp.

"Sooz, baby. Enjoying the show?"

His teeth flash in the light. Then his smile goes slack, and his eyes roll back. He's so gone, I take the opportunity to scan the room. Three joints crowd an ashtray on his desk and a half empty water bottle stands beside it, which, judging by the performance he's putting on, isn't filled with H_2O. I make out the three large letters on the label of the bottle I kicked. Rum.

I go to ask what he's playing at when he emits another moan. A guttural one so intense I feel it throughout my body.

This isn't what I signed up for.

I'm half tempted to call John West right now and tell him, because his drummer is a lost cause. But all positive intentions fly out the shade-covered window when Ryan groans again. Unfortunately, my brain and my body don't want to work in unison. The smarter of the two is repeating over and over for me to leave. The latter is having ideas I can't ever be held responsible for.

I chew my lip. Ryan's back to palming himself, his breathing quickening as his hand picks up its pace.

"What are you doing?" I ask, gripping my towel. A bead of water—ice cold—falls from my hair and rolls down my skin. My skin prickles, and I try not to shiver.

Ryan tightens his grip on himself. His knuckles are white as his hand moves up and down. "I think you know what I'm doing."

A wave of irritation starts to build inside me. I seize it, because it's the only normal thing going on here.

"Stop," I say with a level of authority I didn't know I could achieve. I try not to think about what it means that he does. No questions. No arguing. When he's covered and my heart has settled, I soften my voice. "What's wrong?"

He stares at the ceiling for a moment, then sits up.

"What isn't wrong?"

I inhale, struggling for composure as strong alcohol fumes fill my lungs. When I exhale, enough tension leaves me that I'm able to keep a calm edge to my words.

"Ryan, please. Talk to me."

I pull the towel around me distractedly. Ryan doesn't miss the movement.

"Is this to do with what happened when we were away?"

He ignores me, dropping his head into his hands, folding in on himself, away from the world.

"Tell me what happened in New Orleans."

I wait a beat. Then another. I'm about to ask another question, anything to bring him out of the dark hole he's falling into, when he heaves in a deep breath and raises his head. His eyes are dark, unrecognizable.

"I was fucking myself with my hand, Sooz. Don't turn this into something it isn't."

"And what's that?" I snap, my anger rising.

"You believing we could be anything more than what we are."

In the years I've known him, I thought I hated him.

Right now, what I'm feeling is something more—more intense, more everything.

I don't dislike him. I don't hate him. I resent him. I realize I resent everything about him, including the whiplash of contradicting emotions I get whenever the two of us are alone together. At least, I do, until all those feelings are swept away by an image of him lost in a panic attack on the bank of the Mississippi River.

What happened to make you so scared? I want to ask. His blank expression stops me. I'm not going to get answers today. Not when he's like this. It's all I can do to get him to talk to me without him losing focus and his eyes rolling.

"You need help, Ryan."

"What I need is for you to leave. Permanently."

I square my shoulders, refusing to let his words affect me, especially when I'm not sure he even knows what he's saying. His next comment proves my assumptions correct.

"Or maybe I need you to fuck me."

Frustration bubbles inside me when he starts fisting himself again over his boxers.

"All for you, baby."

His eyes roll, and it hits me that he's too drunk and stoned for anything. Too lost. Lost in whatever pain he's been hiding. Taking in a breath, I brace myself, ready to guide him back to where he needs to be.

No matter what it takes.

Even if it means selling my soul.

Doing something I never said I would.

Becoming the kind of person that I've never wanted to be.

"You look so big when you do that," I say, setting the train into motion. My grandmother would turn over in her grave.

Ryan's eyes widen, alert. *Bingo*.

With a confidence I didn't know I had in me, I let my grip on the towel slacken and it drops to the floor.

Ryan, the cocky-wasted-high-as-a-kite-bastard he is, smirks as I stand before him in the most vulnerable state possible. I smirk right back.

"You won't leave because you like me."

I'm not sure if he's referring to why I won't leave now—this second—or generally.

He gives me a familiar smile. The same one I was gifted the first time we met. The smile which set our enemy status into play. It's a reminder, that when he wants to be, when he doesn't give a damn—or maybe it's when he does—that he can be terrible. It's also a warning that I should prepare to hate him more, and ignore my body saying otherwise.

The flash of heat between my legs makes me take the safer option. "No. I won't leave, because this is my job."

"Careful, Sooz," he warns, "or I might start thinking you want to be one of the women in those pictures."

The insinuation dripping from his words has me choking on a gasp as I try to block out the vivid images that appear.

Dark eye circles. Smudged make-up. Filthy, barely there clothing.

This is what he wants, I tell myself. *He wants you to hate him because then you'll leave, and your unanswered questions will leave with you.*

"Admit it," he continues. "I can tell by the way you're staring at me." His hand continues to fist his erection. It looks bigger. Harder. "Do you want to be those women? Are you jealous because you like me?"

No. I'm looking at you differently because I feel sorry for you. I pity you and the person you're allowing your fears to turn you into. A person who, if New Orleans hadn't happened, if you hadn't shown me who you really are—who you can be, when you aren't blocking the world out— I wouldn't believe existed.

But empathy doesn't have a place here. Not when Ryan won't remember any of it. It's wasted energy to achieve an unreachable outcome, at least for now.

"I'm turned on by you. There's a difference." It's not exactly a lie. "It's something I have no control over. Especially when you're doing that." I gesture below his midline.

Ryan's hand stops moving, and he stands abruptly. "Fuck me. Now."

My confidence evaporates with a blink. "Excuse me?"

His muscles tense in a way that's different from when he's drumming, and my eyes lock on the ink covering the inside of his left arm. There's an eye nestled in the crease, fading into the lower part of a woman's face as she touches her lips.

Her other hand skims the top of an hourglass, the last grains remaining in the top. The details and design signal it's expensive and intentional. They have a meaning.

They're telling a story I'm not sure I want to hear but can't stop myself from trying to read.

Ryan provides a much-needed distraction when he inhales, causing the lightning tattoos wrapped around his ribs and covering some of his chest to stretch. I reach out. The touch is electric. It paralyzes me.

"What does it mean?" I stare hard at his chest, trying not to think how we wound up standing so close.

"It's about tempting fate." My fingertips remain glued to his skin. "They say lightning never strikes in the same place twice." He swallows and the overly smooth patch of skin on his throat shines against the lamplight. "I'm hoping it's true."

I drop my hand when he lets out an awkward laugh. I've never wanted to hear someone laugh more. I want him to do it again. Hope fills my chest that maybe this is a sign we're done with the irritating Ryan. He's tiresome. This Ryan, the emotionally tortured one, makes me feel like I'm drowning, even as I anticipate his next move or verbal lashing. I can see the promise of reaching the surface, breaking through to the real person and understanding what's really going on. What the pain reflected in his eyes means. But it doesn't matter how hard I swim, how much I struggle, I can't get there. I can't reach him.

"I need you to fuck me and get it out of your system. Forget New Orleans."

Apparently, the reprieve is already over.

"No."

"Why?" He narrows his eyes.

"I don't fuck."

"Ah."

The sound is soft, soothing. An apology in the form of understanding?

"Ah, what?" I ask, treading carefully.

"You're the making-love kind. I should have figured you'd be the type to take it seriously."

So much for understanding. My temper flares. "And how else am I supposed to take having someone's penis inside me?"

I realize my mistake when he gives me a grin—the-shit-eating-kind—and brace myself for the vulgarity I know is coming my way.

"From behind? On top?" He winks. "I bet you'd love to be in control of exactly where the head of my dick hits. In control of how long and hard I make you come."

"Ry, stop."

He groans. If it were possible to be devoured with a look, the only evidence of my presence left behind would be the towel at my feet.

"You have no idea how hard it makes me when you call me *Ry*."

His chest brushes against mine. His erection presses into my thigh, his legs on either side of me. How is he closer? This wasn't supposed to happen. We weren't supposed to end up here. Me naked. Him hard as a rock. Him groaning like he keeps doing, making me forget why nothing can happen between us. Why nothing ever should.

Needing to grasp some control of the situation, I gift him with an eye roll. Then, instead of giving into the ache building low in my core, I say, "Please, save the dirty talk for someone who wants it."

I jolt when Ryan's palm wraps around the small of my waist. His thumb skims over the mole to the right of my bellybutton. His attention drops to where my nipples, hard and dark, give away what my words won't.

"These say otherwise." He brushes his thumb across a nipple.

He's awful. What's more awful is the surge of heat that floods through me. Why am I getting turned on by this? I'm supposed to be helping him. Not wanting to hump him until I forget my own name.

"There's a reason your body is responding to me, baby."

"Enlighten me," I croak.

"You want this for what it is." His thumb keeps moving back and forth, and my body agrees. He leans in and goosebumps cover my skin as he speaks, his breath feathering my ear. "Let me show you how good it can be. Let me fuck you 'till you're raw. I promise that after, you'll be begging for me to do it again." A small moan slips out of my mouth. "You drive me fucking insane. Love has no place in all the things I've been wanting to do to you."

His final statement is the ice-cold bucket of water I need.

Blinking, I come crashing back into reality.

"I'll make you a deal." Amusement crosses Ryan's face as he waits. "You can fuck me if you kiss me."

His hands drop away from my body as he pulls back. Like I knew he would.

"Get your towel." Venom laces his words. "Leave."

It might be the reaction I was gunning for, but it doesn't stop the disappointment I feel.

The two of us together like this are as toxic it as it gets.

Worse. Because even though I should walk away, leave things how they've always been between the two of us, I can't.

"You hate me that much you won't kiss me?"

"I hate myself." He says it so quietly I wonder if I've heard him right. But then he continues, "I hate myself when I'm around you. I hate myself for wanting what I can't have."

I step forward to whisper my own truth.

"And what if I want you back?"

"You need to leave." Ryan grabs the towel and wraps it around me. "Please. I can't give you what you need. I want you to go, Sooz."

Because I have no understanding of what's transpired between us, I do.

Chapter Fourteen

F inally clothed, I pace the band's living area for half an hour.

The house remains silent, and I can't decide which is more unnerving. Hearing Ryan falling apart earlier or having no idea if he still is.

My phone ringing stops me wearing away the floorboards, and I grab it before it can ring off. I'd talk to my mother right now if it provided me a break from reliving what happened in Ryan's room on repeat. It doesn't stop my heart from picking up its pace, though, when I read the name John West.

"Sooz!"

"Hi!" I squeak.

"How are things going?"

You mean besides Ryan messing up a set and potentially about to die from alcohol poisoning or a weed overdose ...

"Fine! Perfect!"

If Henrik were here, he'd call me a lying little hussy.

"Great …" I can't decide if John sounds totally unconvinced, or like he's going to deliver bad news. "So, we have an issue."

Of course it's the latter, when I have a million other issues already stacked on my plate.

"Is it a 'the pictures are about to be leaked' kind of issue?"

Please don't let that be it. Ryan going off the rails couldn't come at a worse time.

"Yes." Bummer. "There's no clarification on who is responsible for them, but there's been contact with the label for money."

"How many days until they want it?"

"Seven at the most."

"Which we all know means less than four." Because time is of the essence and I no longer have a clue how to handle this situation, I find myself opening up to John as the person he really is to me—my best friends' father—rather than him being someone I'm working with. "Ryan's not in the best shape."

John's sigh floats down the line, doing little to improve my positivity. "I didn't think he would be."

"Does he already know?" I ask, some of the pieces slotting together, making the picture clearer as to what could have triggered his bender. "That they're going to come out sooner than expected?"

John says yes, then goes on to explain, "An intern in HR contacted him first thing. She's new. She thought she was helping. It's being dealt with."

Mistakes happen, I know this better than anyone, but this understanding doesn't help the situation we've all found ourselves in.

"I don't know what to do to help him. He's up in his room, basically killing himself. He won't listen to me."

"Then make him." As blunt as his answer is, it isn't unexpected. "You deal with these situations all the time. Nothing is different apart from the fact it's personal. What would you do if this wasn't Ryan?"

"Tear him a new A-hole?"

John chuckles. "Then make sure you have a sharp knife, because he's as stubborn as they get."

I laugh, then laugh some more. The words 'it takes one to know one' have never been truer. My laughter stops abruptly when it hits me that I need to confide in John the not-so-minor detail I've found out. "I know about his allergy."

"I didn't think it would take you long to figure it out."

"I've known Ryan for almost four years," I reply. I should have known from the day we met. I should have figured it out. But I was too busy being angry and hating him to take in all the details staring me directly in the face. "I feel like an idiot for not figuring it out sooner."

"Sooz. Ryan might be stubborn. At times, he might be impossible. Others, the laziest of the group. But he's also clever. Capable of achieving the outcome he wants. It's a craft he's had to perfect, because he doesn't want anyone to know."

I frown to myself, taking in everything John is saying. "Am I right in assuming, if he's wearing a band, his milk allergy is serious?" John remains silent. "Please. I need something, because Ryan is giving me nothing. I need to know the extent of what I'm dealing with."

"Yes."

159

That's it. I wait for him to continue. To tell me *how* serious. But he doesn't.

"Mr. West …"

"Ms. Van Rensburg, I would like to take this opportunity to remind you that you're the best at what you do, and I'm saying that when I have a PR department who currently earn double your wage for half the results. Take your emotions out of the situation."

"And do what I'm paid for?"

"No." I can practically hear him shaking his head. "Do what Ryan asked me to hire you to do."

The room tilts as John's words slam into me.

"I'm sorry, what?"

"I need to go. I called to ask you to get Ryan out in some social situations tomorrow. Get any positive media coverage you can. We need the world to love him before they hate him, because we're taking control. We're leaking the images."

"What do you mean, Ryan asked you to hire me?" It's the only part of what John said that I'm able to register.

"Don't ask questions you already know the answer to."

He sounds like he's going to hang up. I pull my professional hat on, needing to salvage this last part of the phone call. "How long until you leak them?"

"Just over twenty-four hours. Our PR department is getting everything ready and will set up an interview with Allure magazine for tomorrow afternoon. Make sure you're ready, because the media are going to come at you like wolves. I've already spoken with Abby. She's briefing the girls. Jake will stay with her and Clara. Sam with Sophie and Russ. You can stay at S.C.A.R.A.B.'s place. Security teams will be stationed outside."

"How long will we need to hide out?"

"A week, at least."

"A week!" My voice comes out unnaturally high.

"It's not ideal. I know." He sighs. "Merry Christmas … right?"

With how busy everything has been since I returned, and how absorbed I've been in all things Ryan Alvarez, I'd forgotten we were even in December. An easy thing to do, considering there isn't a trace of anything festive in the house.

"Christmas isn't my jam, anyway," I admit.

John lets out an unamused laugh. "I really do need to go. Speak with my PA if you need anything."

"Okay."

"Oh, and Sooz?"

"Yeah?" I try to sound positive. It's all but impossible with the enormity of what we're going to deal with sitting on my shoulders.

"Remember what I said. Take your emotions out of this situation. Do whatever you have to do to make him fall in line. This isn't about what he wants, it's about what he needs."

The line goes dead, and I'm left trying to frantically figure out what the hell I've gotten myself into. After half an hour, I tell myself to get it together. I did not get this far to fall over one not-so-small, Ryan-shaped hurdle.

Following a stern inner-talking to, I call the one person I know has questionable morals and ask her to bring the cuffs I know are sitting on display on her nightstand.

"He could call the cops and have them arrest us. You know that, right?" says Zoe after I've rattled off my plan.

After hanging up with John, I made my way back up to Ryan's room and found him passed out on his bed. Unsure how long the effects of his overindulgence would last, I seized the moment, and whatever I could find. No surface, no cubby hole and no corner were left untouched. Every spirit I could find went down the sink. Because I'm not a total biatch, I made sure to keep two bags of weed aside, in a safe hiding place. I don't need Ryan to stop smoking completely, I just need him to not have access to so much he could kill himself. Rations are the way forward—I hope.

"He won't call the cops," I reply.

She arches a brow. "How do you know?"

"Zoe. He has more weed in his room than a dealer, and I don't care that he says it's medicinal. There's no prescription anywhere in the house. I checked."

"He's going to be pissed." She shoves the final bag of Ryan's habit into her tote.

"And you're going to be gone," I reply. "What does it matter?"

I watch, amused, as the cogs turn in her mind. She's struggling to decide what to do. I know she's come to a conclusion when she looks dejected, defeated, and everything in between.

"You don't tell him I was involved." She waggles her finger at me. "I don't want any part in your enemies to lovers crap."

"You don't need to worry."

"And why's that?" She folds her arms across her chest with a wry smile.

"Because we will never be lovers."

"Fuckers then," Zoe responds without hesitation. "Enemies to lovers has always sounded pansy. Enemies to fuckers. Now, that's where it's at."

I roll my eyes and push her toward the front door. "Just get rid of his stash."

"In our office." She shoves the straps of her tote higher up her shoulder. "You realize how wrong this is. Abby will kill us if she finds out."

"Which she won't, because you're not going to say anything. Plus, she's going to be stuck in the apartment for seven days."

"Maybe I should drop her some off." Zoe snickers. "Clara is going to turn feral." I give her a hard no by narrowing my eyes. "Fine. I'm leaving. If this goes wrong, I had nothing to do with it."

"Nothing's going to go wrong."

"You keep telling yourself that," she says, passing through the door. "And FYI, it's three left, then a wiggle right to get them to unlock. Remember, because I'm not coming back to uncuff him from whatever dirty shit the two of you give in to."

I swat her away before she can enlighten me with any cruder comments, then make my way up to the attic, swinging the metal cuffs in my hand as I go.

"I still can't believe you fucking cuffed me," Ryan mutters, rubbing at his wrists as he walks by my side.

You wouldn't believe a lot of things if I told you what you got up to.

"You gave me no choice. I needed you coherent." I chew on the inside of my cheek and decide to tag a small truth on

163

the end to give him some insight—besides his pounding head—of how messed up he was yesterday. "And alive."

When Ryan came round in the early evening, he had no idea why he felt like he'd been part of a train wreck. He also had no clue he was, in fact, *the* train wreck.

It doesn't feel right to go through the motions of everything he said, despite his words keeping me awake for most of the night. I pretend like nothing happened at all. A relatively easy task, considering Ryan can't remember a thing.

Regardless of the prior day's angst, there's a spring to my step as I walk with Ryan along the streets of Manhattan. It's the first beautiful day there's been since I returned. The sky is the bluest of blues and the air is crisp. The weather's taunting us, knowing we're going to be stuck in for who knows how long. Trying not to dwell on what's coming in twelve hours, I think on positive things, like the fact we'll have a week of reprieve, camping out away from the press. I can't remember the last time I had a daytime date with Netflix. I need to make a list. A rank, so I make the most of my time. Thank God the girls are all over the New Year's Ball, because if they weren't, we'd officially be stuck.

"Where's my weed, Sooz?" Ryan grunts, his breath clouding the air.

"Somewhere safe." I beam at an old couple passing by, hand in hand. It's pairings like theirs that could convince me true love exists, regardless of how my parents' marriage deteriorated.

"You're stealing." Ryan's inaccurate comment breaks me from my romance-themed daydreams. "Technically, I could report you."

"Really?" I scoff at the same time I stop walking. Placing my hands on my hips, I turn to face him. "You're going to report me. For theft." My brow arches. "Theft of your *drugs*."

Ryan folds his arms with a huff. His face is obscured by a cloud, and he drops his voice as a woman with a labradoodle walks by. "I've already told you. It's medicinal."

I let out a shrill laugh. A pigeon sitting on the car next to us startles and flies away. It's when Ryan looks ready for dropping to his knees and begging, that I reach into my black leather tote and undo the zippy bag containing the emergency joints.

"You're on rations," I say, holding one out.

My arm remains extended as the joint hovers in midair.

Ryan's eyes turn to saucers before he snatches it away, throwing out a "Seriously?"

"I thought it was medicinal?"

"It is," he hisses. "But with what's going on, the last thing I need is this getting out, too."

He turns abruptly and walks away. Thanks to his exceptionally long, jean-clad legs, he's five car lengths away after only a few strides. At least, it feels that way when I sprint.

"Believe me," I pant, catching him up. "You've been anything but discreet."

He takes a sharp right and then we're walking along a narrow alleyway. We're halfway when he steps behind a dumpster. I remain standing where I am, with a visual of the street. Ryan looks at me as if to ask why I'm not following.

"I'm not hiding behind that."

Admittedly, it's impressive how he manages to make his huge frame small enough to slide down the wall and hide himself. He's like a flat-pack drummer.

"Then go somewhere else. You're making it look like we're doing something suspicious."

"That's because we are!" He's too busy getting himself ready to spark up to reply. "Two minutes," I say, before heading back in the direction we came.

"Yes ma'am," Ryan calls after me.

I hear the click of his lighter and then all goes silent as he inhales his way into bliss.

Chapter Fifteen

"We're going to the label?" Ryan asks, a line forming between his brows.

"No," I say, when his steps slow. "We're going for a wander."

"A whatty?" He stops walking altogether.

"A wander," I repeat. "A perusal of the area. An amble. A leisurely stride."

"Why couldn't you just say we're going for a walk?"

I shrug and try to keep my lips in a flat line, but it's no good, they curl up. "The sky is blue and I'm feeling poetic."

Ryan looks at me like I've lost my mind. "Did you dabble in my stash?"

"Erm, why would you think that?"

"I dunno. Because you're being all weird and playful and I guess not very ..." He reaches up and scratches the side of his head, gifting me with a slither of his midriff. It's the reminder I don't need that I know exactly what's hidden beneath the denim wrapped snugly around his hips. "… you."

My eyes snap back up. I have to stop myself informing him how very much himself he was being yesterday. His comment is irritating, upsetting, but I'm distracted by how low his cap is sitting on his head and wind up laughing.

Ryan gives me another confused look as we start walking again. The crowds carry us through Times Square. A few stragglers in front dart out across the road, dicing with death when a yellow cab almost clips their heels. Ryan seems none the wiser—something I strongly suspect is down to our pit stop. I fling my arm out to the side to stop him and my hand collides with a ridiculously hard set of abs. He stares at me from beneath the peak of his hat.

"Careful, the robot's changed."

"Robot?" I point at what I'm referring to. "You mean the crosswalk light?"

"The robot," I confirm, as it changes back to green. When the crowds begin moving across the road, we go with them.

"Is that a South African thing?" Ryan asks, matching my pace with ease.

New York roads make me nervous, so I refrain from answering until we're on the other side, with our feet safely on the sidewalk. "Other cultures call it a robot, too."

"I've never heard it before." I flatten my lips while glancing at him out of the corner of my eye. "Don't you dare call me uncultured again."

"Oh yeah," I reply. "I keep forgetting all that experiencing you do while high on tour."

Ryan stops walking again. People grumble as they sidestep him. "You're seriously making another dig at me?"

168

Acid burns my throat. Seeing these different sides to him, ones where he has emotions besides being a weed vessel, makes me uncomfortable. I have no idea how to handle him. Ironic, considering he's on his best behavior. I prefer it when he's flying off the handle. At least then it makes it easier to keep my own emotions out of the situation. Something that's proving a struggle currently, because I have the strong urge to close the gap between us and give him a hug.

I don't hug. Unless it's Henrik. My brother at a push. Clara's a given.

"Can I ask you something?"

It's not the best time for a heart to heart, surrounded by hundreds of people, huffing out their annoyance as they push their way past us. But it feels like we're tiptoeing on the edge of another truth. One that isn't an inebriated slip. A rare one. Willingly given. One I'm going to take. Regardless of our poor choice of place and audience.

"You're going to anyway," Ryan says, shoving his hands into the pockets of his pants. His giant frame continues to cause a block in the middle of the sidewalk.

"Most of the time, you're like this happy-go-lucky kind of guy. But not with me. Why?"

It's a stupid question. One I already know the answer to. Kind of.

'I hate myself for wanting what I can't have.'

Still, I need to hear it from him now. Sober. I need him to help me make sense of it all.

He's never given the slightest suggestion that he wants me. Quite the opposite. Avoiding me any chance he can. Now, we've done a complete one-eighty, resulting in him demanding we do the dirty and him having John West contract us into working together.

I don't know what to think anymore. He's not the person I thought he was. The scary part is how easy it is to be around him. How I'm starting to care too much. For him. His health. The outcome for his career when the images get out.

Wobbling on the line of professional and personal, I don't know how to stop myself from tumbling to the wrong side. He's creeping his way under my skin and I'm beginning to enjoy his company.

Zoe was right. We're giving off major enemies to lovers vibes. We're surrounded by red flags.

Knowledge is power, and the more time we spend together, the more we know what makes the other person tick—and what has the potential to bring them down.

One of the only things Mother taught me that's proven useful: you have to drive through life fueled by goals, not by matters of the heart. She would know. Rather than crumbling when our father left, she came back stronger. But as much as I know all this, Ryan's making whatever is developing between us impossible to ignore.

Totally unaware of my inner turmoil, he glares at me. "I've had over three years of you breathing down my neck. Picking out my faults. Not caring why they exist. Over three years of you making me feel like I'll never be good enough …"

He doesn't get a chance to continue. A woman tuts, breaking his flow as she shoves her way past him. I'm left wondering if he was going to give me the same truth as yesterday. A sober one. Finishing with, *'for you'.*

It's not what I continue to focus on, though, as Ryan stares me down in the middle of Times Square.

My brain is busy trying to process all the hurts I've sent his way. The frustrations I've caused him when I thought I was doing my job. I never figured that Ryan might see it otherwise, taking some of what I've said personally.

I open my mouth to respond, maybe even apologize.

But Ryan has one last thing to say. "I'm tired, Sooz." His face crumples. "I'm tired of it all."

The back of my neck goes clammy as I try to figure out how we get past this. Seconds tick by, and I feel no closer to navigating us into safer waters. So, I reach for the only reliable and consistent thing there is in my life. Work. It's the perfect excuse. The perfect escape.

With Ryan distracted, I jump. High enough I'm able to flip his hat off. I shove it in my bag before he can grab it back.

"Hey!"

"The point of this morning is for you to be seen," I explain. "Come on. We're behind schedule."

Hurrying ahead, I feel like I can breathe again as I leave the emotions of the past few minutes behind. I assume Ryan is following.

It doesn't take long to get to our destination and my face lights up, when I step inside the store. I go as far as squeaking with excitement when I race to where I know I'll find what I need.

"Disney?"

Turning at the perfect moment, I watch Ryan attempt to duck through the fake castle arch, misjudging and cracking his head.

"Errands!" I squeak again.

This time, to hide my laughter, I walk toward the yellow gowns—away from his glower.

Ryan comes up behind me when I'm skimming through sizes. "This is a kid's store. You might be small, but you're not *that* small."

"So pessimistic." My positivity wobbles the closer I get to the back of the row of dresses. I'm ready to give up, then catch sight of a tag with my size.

Over excited, I spin around fast, colliding into the wall that is Ryan. Hands like paddles grip my upper arms as he steadies me.

"Thanks," I mumble into his chest.

He smells good. Too good. Even with the marijuana undertones. *Focus,* I tell myself. The zip of his coat presses against my nose, and one of the drawstrings catches against the lashes of my left eye.

With his hands still on my arms, Ryan pushes me back far enough he can look at me.

"What are you dressing up for?"

"New Year's Eve," I reply, relieved he hasn't picked up on the fact I smell the same as him.

The corners of his mouth lift. "I meant what event?"

"The New Year's Eve Ball that Next Level has been organizing for, like, six months …" My answer doesn't draw so much as an eye twitch from him. I let out a frustrated sigh. "S.C.A.R.A.B. were invited months ago. Before anyone else."

He looks sheepish. "I don't think we got it?"

"The invite is stuck to your refrigerator."

Feeling the temptation to get stroppy, I shrug out of Ryan's grip and walk toward the checkouts. I've been looking forward to this event since I decided to add it to the calendar with the girls.

It's when Ryan's dragging a hand through his flattened cap hair after I've paid, and we're walking out of the store, that a guy stumbles in front of us. I wince at the thud his body makes when he hits the ground. Thanks to it still being wet from the downpour earlier this morning, he's now drenched, making the situation even worse.

The scenario plays out in true New York style. It's like watching Moses parting the Red Sea when the crowd separates. Some people continue walking with no concern for the heap of a man on the floor. Then, the ones who do stop hold up their phones and capture the moment.

Ryan stares at the guy sprawled in front of us, who's groaning in pain.

"Well, help him up," I hiss.

The guy looks up as Ryan takes a step forward, offering out his hand. "Oh my God. Aren't you in S.C.A.R.A.B.?"

People stop walking, and over thirty phones capture the exchange. Some are brazen enough to use their flashes. Not that they're really needed. Times Square is like the brightest place on Earth. When the guy takes Ryan's offered hand, I let out a sharp breath of relief. I don't want to think how awkward it would have been if he hadn't.

"What a hero." I clap my hands with what I hope is the right amount of enthusiasm. "Swoon." Ryan gives the stranger a tight smile. "It was *so* lucky we were here to help."

The guy's brushing himself off when Ryan lowers his head and under his breath says to me, "Because the other hundred people wouldn't have been able to."

"I know, right!" I beam and throw an arm around the guy's shoulders, dragging him back so he's sandwiched between Ryan and I. "Smile!" Ryan does the opposite as camera shutters go off. It's impressive they can be heard over all the noise.

Eventually, things die down, and the crowd moves on from the show.

"Sorry," I say to the injured guy while gesturing for Ryan to follow me. "We have places to be."

We're two blocks and one right turn away from Times Square when the guy catches us up.

"Great job." I hand him twenty dollars. "Stellar performance. Oscar worthy."

The guy frowns at the money in his hand. "I ruined my pants."

"Fine."

There were more photos taken than I pre-empted and it's worth the extra forty I hand him. He snaps it away and disappears.

Ryan stares at me. I can't tell whether it's humor or disbelief swirling in his eyes.

"You're unbelievable," he says. "You know that, right?"
Disbelief it is.

"I'm going to take that as a compliment." I slide my purse back into my bag.

"I thought you might. Where to now?"

"It's a surprise."

Ryan's brows draw together. "That means you're not telling me because you know I won't like it."

I shrug. "Would you have come at all if you knew what we were doing?"

"No."

"Exactly."

Walking away, I pray his loyalty to his band shines through. I cross a few extremities for extra luck.

It's when I hear Ryan's sneakers splash through a small puddle that I smile to myself.

Chapter Sixteen

Help an injured stranger. Check.
Perform randomly in the street with another artist. Check.

Smile at a child. Check—although, it took three attempts, because Ryan kept doing this weird thing with his mouth, making him look creepy.

We've completed *help an old person across the road* and I'm checking through the list to see what we have left. Some tasks need to be delegated to after the photos leak. We're out of time and need to make our way to Ryan's interview with Allure Magazine.

"Hey."

I'm focused. In the zone. Nothing can break my concentration.

There's another "Hey." Louder this time, and much closer. Close enough I startle.

My phone slips out of my grip and falls to the ground. It misses a puddle by less than an inch.

"Gah!" I shriek.

I drop down at the same time Ryan does. Our heads collide when we both reach to grab it.

"Shit," Ryan hisses, as I yelp.

We remain crouched, rubbing our foreheads. Ryan's cheeks are red, and he laughs. The sound is awkward, but infectious. I laugh too. Until our eyes lock and he stops abruptly. Wanting the moment to be done with, I reach to pick up my phone. I'm a second too late, and my hand lands on top of his.

My cheeks burn. I have a feeling they're a shade deeper than Ryan's. Not knowing what else to do, I snatch my hand away. Ryan picks up my phone and dries it with the sleeve of his coat. He hands it over and neither of us says a word. Still crouched. Avoiding each other.

When he stands, I copy. Then, I remember to check my phone. The reason for all our awkwardness. My face scrunches when I take in the damage. There's a giant crack through the middle of the screen.

"Oh no."

"Sorry." Ryan scratches the back of his neck. "It was my fault. It probably works. But I can still buy you a new one?"

The potential of losing my lifeline to work has me feeling narky. Just like that: *I'll buy you a new one.* A phone that will cost the better part of a thousand dollars, he's offering to pay for like he's purchasing a half-price coffee. He's a rock star, I remind myself. He has the cash to splash.

I'd be a fool not to take him up on his offer, which I know deep down is a kind one. Unfortunately, today is the worst possible day this could have happened. I shake my head and hold back a huff. There are already way too many being exchanged when the two of us are together.

"We don't have time," I reply.

A couple of taps on the screen confirm he's right. My phone still works, for now.

"I'm sure cuddling puppies can wait a day or two."

I stop tapping. "How do you know about the puppies?"

"I didn't. It was a joke."

"Yeah. Well, they were supposed to be next, but we need to get to your interview."

Ryan groans. "Can we at least take a break?" He's midway through dragging a hand over his face when he peeps at me through the cracks between his fingers. "Get coffee?"

I stare at him suspiciously. "Why?"

"Why not? Everyone loves coffee."

"That's a big assumption to make." Wrapping my arms around my middle, I pull my coat tighter. Coffee to any team member of Next Level is like water. When the workload is impossible, like it is currently, caffeine is my kryptonite. I refuse to admit he's got me. "Not everyone loves coffee."

He rolls his lips. "Who doesn't love coffee?"

"Children."

"Children?"

"Yes. Children don't love coffee and there's around one-point-nine billion, making up twenty-seven percent of the Earth's population."

"You have percentages. Wow." He takes me by surprise when he smiles. "Sooz, all I want is a coffee. You're already withholding my weed. Don't deprive me of this, too."

"Fine." I drop my arms. Over the morning, we've stayed in the same area, doing one big loop around the Times Square area. In the planning stages, it seemed easier and more time efficient to keep everything close. Another benefit is that there are a ton of places where we can make a pit stop. "There's somewhere near."

The place I'm referring to is a block away. When we get there, I glance at the couple sitting in the window on stools. From the outside, it looks basic. Especially in comparison to the high-end coffee shops close by. Inside, the décor is modern. The exposed brick walls and black metal surfaces are industrial chic. It feels like the coffee shop equivalent to Riffs.

"Cool?" I glance up, expecting a comeback. My heart does a weird little leap in my chest when he grins.

"Very cool." Ryan pulls out his wallet when we get to the counter and says, "I'll get these."

I go to argue that I can buy my own when my thumb catches on my screen. I let out a hiss of air.

"You're bleeding."

I don't get a chance to make a quip that he's stating the obvious. Blood is already trickling down my hand, toward the cuff of my coat sleeve. Because white and red don't mix, I hurry away to grab a napkin.

"What do you want?" Ryan calls after me.

"Honey latte, please," I reply.

I've bandaged my thumb tightly and stashed some spare napkins in my bag when Ryan walks over. There's a takeout cup in his left hand and a bottle of cold black coffee in his right.

"Thanks." I eye the screw-top lid of his drink, fighting the urge to pry. Outside, I wrap my hands around my paper cup, decorated with dancing snowmen. After attempting to soak in whatever heat I can, I raise my drink to my lips. I inhale before I take my first sip, then frown. "Honey latte? Yeah?" I wrinkle my nose and sniff again.

Ryan unscrews the top from his bottle. "Yep."

I wait until we're walking to ask, "What'cha got?"

The words black coffee read clear as day on his bottle.

"Coffee." Ryan gives me a sideways glance. "Black."

"Hmm." I give my drink another sniff. A small taste confirms it's a variation of what I requested. "This is soya."

"It's all they had."

My feet stop moving, and I scowl at Ryan's back. Why won't he open up to me about his allergy? Besides it being frustrating, especially considering *he's* the one who wanted to work with *me*, it's also unnerving. Not knowing meant I could have put him at risk.

I don't have long to simmer on Ryan's lack of information. He's getting smaller, and I realize how far he's moved away. I chase after him, because he's showing no signs of stopping.

"It's a coffee shop," I say when I've caught up. "Like they wouldn't have regular milk."

"I'm looking out for you." Ryan shrugs, continuing to stride forward. "You'd think with all that yoga you do in the morning that you'd be more on it."

"On what?"

"Keeping your health under control."

"I'm thirty, Ryan. You're making me sound like a geriatric. What exactly is unhealthy about dairy?"

"Didn't you hear? Too much kills."

My mouth drops open. There it is. *The* truth. The one I've been waiting for. And the asshole has the audacity to cover it in a f'in joke. I give him a tight smile and he wiggles his brows.

I can't decide if he knows I know. I think he knows I know. But I don't want to ask if he knows I know. In case he really doesn't know that I know.

"So, where are the puppies?"

"Screw the puppies," I snap.

"Sooz." He gives me a mock, horrified look. "Leave the poor puppies alone."

"I can't help you if you don't tell me what's going on," I say, tempted to flip him off. "Why black?"

"Nothing's going on. I like black coffee." I rummage in my bag while he's talking. "What are y—"

I thrust the zip-lock bag containing his rations at him. I'm done trying to help someone who won't let me.

"People *pretend* they like black coffee. Nobody really does. Especially not iced."

"Sooz, if I want an iced coffee, I can have an iced coffee."

We're getting louder with each comment, but I can't stop myself from continuing. "It's thirty-five degrees. Who drinks *cold* black coffee when it's freezing outside?"

"Me." He steps toward me and lowers his voice. "I will drink what I want, when I want. I don't have to explain the reason why to anyone. Especially not you."

"You're a dick, you know that, right?" My eyes drop to the red band hidden among the other multi-colored ones around his wrist. I might as well have slapped him for the look he gives me when I dare to move my eyes back up to meet his. "You're going to lose everything you've worked for." I look at his wrist again, barely able to get my next words out. "I can't help if you don't let me in."

I take two steps back, then turn away and walk to the curb.

180

"Where are you going?" Ryan asks, when I fling my arm out to hail a cab.

"You have an interview with Allure Magazine." I let out a laugh fueled by irony. "It's to tell the story behind the images. Maybe you'll trust a stranger more than you trust me."

"How much further?" Ryan grunts after barely speaking a word to me during the journey.

"It's over there."

I point a few buildings in front, tracking the address John West's PA sent over on Google Maps, because I haven't heard of the place before. The little blue dot shows us close to our destination.

"Where?" Ryan stares straight ahead to where I'm pointing.

Thanks to roadworks and a ton of congestion, the cab driver asked us to get out early. Ryan's spent the block we've been walking six steps ahead. It's a pattern we seem to have settled into. Him doing whatever he can to leave me behind after I tell him something he doesn't want to hear, or make him do something he doesn't want to.

"There," I say, jogging at his side.

His stride falters as he tries to find where I'm pointing. "I can't see a sign. Where are you talking about?"

"There isn't a sign."

He stops walking and lifts his shades that seem to have been magicked out of nowhere. The '*seriously*' I can tell he wants to fire my way isn't needed. I already know this is the kind of place he refuses to come to, regardless of it being a label requirement.

"No."

He goes to turn and walk back in the direction we came. My hand flies out to stop him, finding itself tangled with his. We both look down. His thumb moves, enough that I feel it everywhere. A guy passing by coughs, and I snatch my hand away.

"Sorry," Ryan mumbles.

"Please, will you do this?" I'm pleading, and he still looks like he's going to say no. "For me?"

Times are desperate when I use myself as a bargaining chip.

Ryan drops his shades. "Fine." I gawp. "Ten minutes. If they piss me off, I'm leaving."

He starts walking again, but there's no way I can let him with those terms. Already in a grouchy mood, and with minimal weed in his system, the odds aren't in anyone's favor.

"Forty minutes."

He stops, but he doesn't look back.

"Fifteen."

I shake my head even though he can't see me. "Thirty-five."

"Twenty."

"Come on, Ry." His shoulders tense. "There's no way you can make a valid assessment of a situation in twenty minutes. It could take that long for us to be seated and order our drinks. Thirty. Please."

"Fine." He moves ahead without me.

Outside the restaurant, he stops abruptly.

"We really have to do this?" he asks, staring at the blacked-out door.

I sidestep, then shuffle, so I'm standing in front of him. My hand itches to reach out and give his a reassuring squeeze, but I stop myself.

"I promise," I say, trying to reassure him with my words when I can't with my touch. "If it's awful, we leave."

He lifts his shades off his head, then does this effortlessly cool thing where he slides one of the arms into the pocket sitting above his left pec. He's the epitome of a rockstar and I appreciate every detail.

It's when the muscles in his throat cord as he swallows that the hairs on the back of my neck raise.

"Ry. What's the real reason you don't want to go inside?"

He stares unblinking at the glass doors and my eyes move over him. I'm halfway down his body when the band of red I hate catches my attention.

"What are you doing?" Ryan asks when I hook my arm through his.

"What I should have to begin with."

I flash him a smile, then drag him away.

Two blocks later, we're officially clear of the restaurant. Ryan calls for a private car after the unhelpful cab situation earlier. When it arrives, it's the most cliché of moments, serving as a reminder of who exactly is at my side. It's becoming easy to forget.

The vehicle is sleek and black. Its wheels glide along the tarmac in a way that makes it look like they're not moving.

We're about to climb in when my phone starts ringing in my bag.

"Give me a minute," I mouth. Ryan nods and slides into the backseat. I frown when I pull my phone out and find John West's name on the caller ID. "Hello?"

"Sooz, is everything okay?"

"Um. Sure. Why?"

"I've had a call from the woman who was due to interview Ryan. She said he's late?"

Ryan's in the back seat of the car and likely not listening, but I need more privacy, so I back away. A crowd of teenagers ambles past, laughing and chattering. Combined with the noise of the traffic, I can barely hear myself think. I plug a finger into the ear that isn't pressed against the phone and turn away from the road, hunching in on myself.

"Sorry. It's really loud."

"Where's Ryan?" John's voice is stern and laced with suspicion.

"He's in the car. He froze."

"He froze?" I hear him shift in his seat. "Why?"

"Because your PR team organized for the interview to take place in a restaurant," I hiss.

I don't know any part of Ryan's story yet. God, I hope it's a yet. And I have no idea how deep the damage goes or how dark his history is. But what I do know is that standing outside the restaurant, there was fear in his eyes. The kind that renders you immobile. Makes you forget who you are and why you should keep going.

Ryan never should have been put in that position. If he isn't ready to fight, then he needs someone in his corner. I'm more than willing to wear the gloves and throw the punches, if it means I don't have to see that look on his face again.

"Ah," says John.

There's a stretched silence.

184

"Why did this happen? Should there not be a disclaimer or something for the department?"

John sighs. "Under normal circumstances, there would be."

"And what isn't normal in *these* circumstances?"

"Ryan doesn't want *anyone* to know."

My chest expands for a second at the knowledge it isn't only me he's shutting out, but everyone. The relief is short-lived, because the enormity of what John's saying sinks in. I feel like banging my head against the brick wall directly in front of me.

"This is ridiculous! People need to know something like this. He's putting himself at risk. He has an allergy band, for Christ's sake!" Somewhere in my frustration, I stop caring if Ryan can hear me.

"These are concerns you need to raise with Ryan."

"That's it?" I snap.

"Sooz, I've worked with S.C.A.R.A.B. for over six years." John's voice remains level. There's a soothing tone to it that calms me. "All these worries you're having, I've had them too."

"I'm not worried."

John chuckles. "Then why are we having this conversation?"

His question throws me, and I take a moment to think how I'm going to reply. One moment extends to another, because I can't come up with an answer, other than that he's right. I am worried. The way my chest feels like it's going to cave in on itself each time I see a flash of red makes it blatantly obvious I am. I'm well into my third moment when John clears his throat.

"These feelings are normal when you care for someone."

185

"I don't care about Ryan," I reply on autopilot.

"I meant as a friend."

"Right." I cringe, glad he can't see how hard I'm blushing. "What now?"

"We rearrange the interview. The magazine owes me a favor, so it's fine. We can work it in for after the photos have gone public, and things are starting to settle."

"That could be months," I mutter.

"I know you don't like the festive period, but here's a reminder to help you warm to it. The holidays mean parties. Time off for everyone. To relax and let their hair down."

I cotton on to what he's saying. "Including celebrities."

"There will be another scandal before the New Year, I guarantee it. I'd just like you to make sure that, after tomorrow, the next big one doesn't involve S.C.A.R.A.B.'s drummer again."

"And what do we do while we're hiding out? We're going to be sitting ducks."

"You're the pro." John laughs. "Have fun with it. Get Ryan's media accounts back up to scratch. Fans love to see the real people behind all the glamor." I don't point out that glamor is one of the last words I'd use in the same sentence as Ryan. I keep listening, because John is on a roll. "Look at Michael Becket and that piece that ran a few years back. The world hated him and now he's the NFL's golden boy. This situation isn't good …"

"… but it doesn't need to be bad," I finish. "Got it."

"One thing," John says, before the inevitable end to our call. "No more old women in the street."

I cringe and laugh. "You didn't exactly give me much time to come up with anything better."

"And maybe you didn't think he could be likeable otherwise."

He's right. "No comment."

"I have another meeting, so I need to go. Everything is in place for tonight. Just keep looking out for him. It will be over before we know it."

We say goodbye, and I hang up.

When I turn around, Ryan is peering out of the back of the car. "Everything good?"

"Yep," I reply.

"Where are we going now?" he asks as I walk toward him.

"Somewhere I think you'll prefer."

Chapter Seventeen

With a new sense of purpose, I give the driver the address of one of my favorite places to visit for food when I'm in Manhattan and need something far from the city vibes.

"Where are we going?" Ryan asks again, staring out of the tinted window as the city rolls past.

"Food." His body tenses. "I promise this place will be more your jam."

The left corner of his lips twitch and he twists in his seat to face me. "My jam?"

"I'm trying to be cool." The right corner of his mouth lifts. "Maybe I should have said I was trying to be funny?"

He shakes his head, amused, but doesn't say anything else. When he goes back to staring out the window, nerves get the better of me. I hope he likes this place, and it isn't as big a disaster as the last. After a while, he glances over at me.

"Why are we going for food, anyway?" There's an unmistakable growl and I arch a brow. He shrugs. "We were running low on food."

And there it is. The pinch point. The subject I don't know how to broach or navigate. A world I have too many questions about. Questions I'm unsure if Ryan will ever want to answer, because so far, he's done an excellent job of putting them off.

"Exactly." I smile overenthusiastically. "And we can't take on the day if we aren't fueled adequately." Ryan stares, and I shift in my seat. "Gotta keep that engine stoked if we want to perform at our best." I go as far as throwing a playful arm jab his way. "In it for the long haul." I'm tempted to wink. Ryan staring at me like I've lost my mind stops me.

"You're kind of awkward sometimes."

Truer words have never been spoken.

"It's you," I admit. "When you're being all serious and behaving, you make me nervous."

I realize my error when our eyes lock and Ryan smirks. "Would you rather I misbehave?"

My cheeks burn. "You know what I meant."

He carries on smirking. "Sorry. I don't." I narrow my eyes, but Ryan's far from done. "You'll have to explain it to me." I look away. "Go on. Call me an ass. You know you want to." Ignoring the laughter in his voice, I continue staring out the window. "Why won't you say the word ass?"

"I don't cuss," I answer. "You know this."

"Technically, ass is a body part."

"Buttocks is a body part. Ass is a derogatory term often used to intensify a statement." Ryan doesn't say a word, and when the silence becomes uncomfortable, I look over at him. "What?"

Our eyes meet and it feels like the walls of the vehicle are closing in. There's too little space. Miles wouldn't be enough. But I can't look away.

Short staccato stabs fill the silence.

"Better get that!" My pitch comes out as high as the *Psycho* shower scene score playing in the background. My hands tremble as I pull my phone out. "Mother?"

"Where are you?"

No '*Hi*' or '*How are you?*'.

"I'm working," I reply.

She tuts down the line. "And you didn't think to let me know?" Sorry, what? I do a quick mental log of all the times she's ever wanted to know where I'm at. I come up with nothing. "Suzanne?"

"I didn't realize checking in with you had become a requirement." The car starts to slow and comes to a stop right outside where I want to take Ryan. "When did you start worrying about people outside of the firm?"

"Stop acting like a child, Suzanne. I'm trying here."

She huffs and hangs up. I'm left with no clue as to why she rang—for the first time in a decade—in the first place.

"*Psycho?*" Ryan smirks.

"It's fitting." I lock my phone and put it back in my bag, then stare out of Ryan's window.

Ryan's laughter stops, and a small line appears between his brows. I don't look at him, but I can feel him watching, trying to read me. "You don't get on?"

"Everything is about Willem." I try to feign nonchalance.

"Who's the eldest twin."

My eyes flicker to his, widening a little with surprise. I didn't know anyone knew about him. I've hardly made the details of my family public knowledge this side of the Atlantic.

"Yeah. We call him Will." Ryan watches me as if he already knows this, too. "Most people assume he's a year or two older. That he's aged well."

"Why?" Ryan scoffs. "It's pretty obvious you're twins."

I give him a 'how-the-hell-would-you-know' look, before answering, "Because he's got his life together, and I, well, compared to him, I don't."

"You're the most put-together person I know."

"Tell that to my mother." I laugh. "Things are different in South Africa. Especially in the circles my mother and Will swim."

"Have you told her how you feel?"

"You heard what I said, right? I think how I feel is pretty obvious."

Ryan goes quiet, tapping his fingers against his knee. "If I make an assessment, are you going to bite my head off?"

"Depends." I sniff.

"Right." He smiles and winks. "I forgot you were into biting and shit. Anyway, what I was going to say, before you came over all bitchy, is—"

"Gee thanks. Don't hold back."

"People aren't mind readers, Sooz." I wait, intrigued by where he's going with this. "No one knows how you're feeling, and no one knows your story, unless you open the book and start to tell it from the very first page."

I don't point out the irony in this profound statement coming from him, the person whose story is all but shackled shut.

"She's my mother. She's supposed to just know."

Ryan's gaze softens, and he reaches over to grab my hand. I think it's for reassurance, but I'm not quite sure, because all it does is send me into overdrive, psychoanalyzing every little detail of the moment.

"It took my parents years to figure out how to cope with their fears. And then, when their own battle was over, they had to help me with mine." He smiles. "It's still a work in progress."

It's then that it hits me. The reason why he's holding my hand isn't to reassure me, it's to reassure himself that it's okay to tell me a part of his story. It hits me how monumental the step is, even if what he's telling me isn't from the very first page. Some stories aren't meant to be linear. The beauty comes in the journey, in piecing them together so you can find your way to the end.

I look down when Ryan squeezes my hand again.

"Why are you telling me this?"

"Because," His voice cracks, "sometimes, the best way to see things differently is to step into someone else's shoes and see it through their eyes. Be an outsider to your own circumstances."

I go to ask what he's getting at as far as my mother and I are concerned, when the privacy window separating us from the driver rolls down. I startle and snap my hand away. Ryan's scowl gives away exactly how he feels about my reaction.

"Is this the right place, Ms. Van Rensburg?"

"Do you want to stay?" I ask Ryan. "We don't have to."

He shrugs. "We're here already. Might as well."

He opens the door on his side, which is closest to the sidewalk.

My pulse picks up as I slide along the leather seat, and I can't decide if it's because I'm excited, or nervous.

My confidence waivers when we enter the restaurant.

The interiors don't leave much to be desired. Light spills down from dusty chandeliers, highlighting the chips and ring marks on the old, glossy wood tables. Then there's the aroma. The one which isn't coming from the kitchen. It's musty, and the source could either be the carpet with a medieval print sitting beneath our feet, or the suede green material covering the booths and chairs. It looks like once upon a time, it might have been a shade of emerald or green like new spring grass. Now, it looks more like moss.

"I don't think there's going to be anything I can have here," Ryan says, apprehension pouring off him.

"Wait here."

I hold my hand up to stop him from walking further in. I didn't think as far as checking this place could accommodate an allergy. But I've gotten to know the owners over the years, and although the restaurant itself might not be easy on the eye, the food they produce is perfection on the palate.

"What are you going to do? Try to entice them into making something with all that charm you have?"

I'd fire a comment back, but it's a relief to hear him trying to make light of the situation by letting old Ryan off his leash. I offer him the prize of an eye roll and walk away. I'm at the bar-slash-counter used for everything when the door leading to the back of the restaurant swings open.

A small, older woman walks out, stopping in her tracks when she sees me. She glances to the side and her eyes widen when they settle on Ryan in the background. Without a word, she holds a finger in the air for me to wait, then turns back and opens the door. She doesn't disappear, just rattles off a ton of Danish at the top of her voice, which I know Ryan won't understand, but has me laughing.

Finally, she turns back and walks around the bar.

Her face breaks into a huge grin when she holds out her arms. "Suzanne!"

The next thing I know, I'm bundled in her arms receiving the kind of affection Mother's never thrown my way.

Hearing Ryan shuffle from behind, I lean down and rush whisper in her ear the situation, asking if she can help.

"Ja!" she beams, pulling back and glancing over at Ryan again.

I wave him over, but he doesn't move.

"Come on," I laugh. He drags his feet as he walks over. "Ry, this is Dora." I turn to Dora, even though she's made it perfectly clear she knows who he is. "Ryan."

"Ik weet."

The back door flies open and two girls, mid-teens, barrel through. An older man—Dora's husband—follows behind them with a pace that says this is the last thing he wants to take part in.

The girls begin chattering with a speed that makes it hard for me to translate, and Dora stands, staring at Ryan like Jesus has walked into her premises. I chew the inside of my cheek, trying not to laugh again. After everything that's happened recently, and everything I'm learning about Ryan, a good dose of ego stoking feels more than appropriate.

Dora's older daughter, Layla, pulls her phone out of the pocket of her jeans and asks if I can take photos.

"Do you mind?" I ask Ryan, waving the phone in explanation.

He schools his expression and shrugs. "Whatever."

Not the reaction I was expecting. I frown to myself, but hold back from asking what his problem is.

"Give me your phone," I say when the girls are primping themselves ready for the photoshoot of a lifetime.

"Why?"

"So we can post it on your socials." He frowns, so I start to explain further. "Let's show people who you really are."

"And who do *you* think I am?"

"A nice guy who's been misunderstood by everyone. Including me."

A smile plays on his lips. "I knew you liked me."

I roll my eyes. "Can we take the photos now?" I glance over at Layla and Bertie. "I think they're going to combust."

He nods at the girls and they both start jumping up and down, squealing with a pitch that could shatter the glassware. I raise Layla's camera in the air first. My eyes start to water and I can barely keep the phone still when she wraps her arm around Ryan seductively. She juts her hip out and trails a finger down his chest. Ryan stands stock still, mortified. Bertie, trying to copy her older sister, is the icing on the cake. When I've finished taking a few photos on Layla's phone, I end up in a coughing fit to cover up my giggles.

'*I hate you,*' Ryan mouths when I've calmed down and handed Layla's phone back, ready to take more photos with his.

"Say cheese!" I wink, fully aware of what I'm saying.

Ryan's guard falls, and he laughs hard. I capture the moment, and when Ryan's trying to understand what Layla is saying to him, I quickly send it to my phone.

Mini photoshoot complete, the girls babble to each other and coo over the images.

"Bedankt," Dora says to Ryan, then ushers the girls behind the bar.

"Where do you want to sit?" I glance around the room.

Ryan shrugs, and his voice comes out cold. "It's not like we're stuck for choice."

"Grouchy much?"

He brushes me off with a question. "So, we're staying?"

"If you want to still?" Ryan looks unsure. "You can go with Dora's choices. Or they can make whatever you want."

He stares. "Just like that?"

"Do you not trust me?"

The air sits between us, thick and heavy. I think he's going to say no, but then he points at a random table.

"There?"

I nod and walk away before he can see the smile that feels like it's going to break my face. I can't look at him when we first sit down. If I do, I'll start grinning like a fool again.

It's a couple of minutes in, that I realize using the word grouchy was an understatement. Ryan's now staring at the table like he wishes he could destroy it with his eyes. His mood reminds me of the summer we first met, when he'd flip flop between being high, and the lowest of lows.

"What's wrong with you?" I ask, dropping my voice.

He toys with the edge of the napkin sitting in front of him on the table.

"I'm going to have photos circle of me on the internet," he says, his voice as grim as the expression he's wearing. "Ones that aren't suitable for S.C.A.R.A.B.'s younger fans. Soon they're only going to remember me for one reason. The fact they hate me."

"They won't."

I don't know this—I don't know anything—but it feels like the right thing to say.

With uncanny timing, a familiar melody starts in the background. One of S.C.A.R.A.B.'s older songs, where the opening is heavy on the drums. The music gets louder. Too loud for a restaurant. I learned a long time ago that, like the interiors, the people who run this place are outside the norm. I look over my shoulder and find Layla and Bertie making a show of air drumming with their arms, tapping their fingers against the countertop, and impressively, matching the beat. Dora laughs at them while dancing around, drying a plate.

I raise a brow at Ryan. He watches them thoughtfully, then suddenly, the feet of his chair scrape along the floor when he pushes it back to stand.

"Where are y—"

He walks over to the girls and joins in with them. They look ready to combust again, but keep going.

Remembering what John said about using Ryan's socials, I hurry over. Dora lets out a loud whoop and I try to keep my phone still as I film it all.

Every laugh. Every facial expression. Every euphoric moment.

The problem with good things is that no matter how hard you try to make them not, they come to an inevitable end.

Nothing good last forever.

Cold. Hard. Fact.

As the final chords to the song kick in, I can see the inevitable crash as the room erupts in applause.

Ryan switches off from everyone, including me, maybe even himself. He walks back over to the table with a thundercloud above his head, and I give Dora and the girls a half-hearted smile. Layla and Bertie don't pick up on the change in atmosphere, already getting into the next song. Dora gives my arm a small squeeze and tells me to go sit, because Steve, her husband, will have our food ready soon.

My steps are heavy as I make my way back to the table. I try not to think about the next battle coming our way. How Ryan is going to feel having all control taken out of his hands.

"I like it here," he comments when I drop down across the table from him. Our eyes lock. "You speak Danish?"

"Yeah."

"How many other languages do you speak?"

"Um …" I look down, wringing my hands together in my lap. "Fluently, ten, made up of some of the usuals. French. German. Spanish. Italian. The rest are native South African ones. I know dribs and drabs of five or six more, like Danish."

"Wow."

Dora walks over with a tray of drinks. She sets down a stein of pilsner in front of me. Ryan's eyes widen, and I shrug.

"I'm on Cape time."

I wait for Dora to place Ryan's drink down. At first, she doesn't. Her hand pauses above Ryan's left one, which is resting on the table. He looks up, seeing the question in her eyes, then nods. Dora lowers her hand and touches the permanent red fixture wrapped around his wrist.

She turns it and reads. Understanding crosses her face, finished with a sad smile, before she lifts her hand away. She grabs the bottle of beer I ordered for Ryan and sets it down on the table. A glass appears next to it and Dora speaks quietly in Danish to me.

"What did she say?" Ryan asks when she walks away.

"She pulled the glass out of storage for you."

Right before Dora disappears into the back of the restaurant, she looks over her shoulder and Ryan gives her a thankful smile.

"I like it here," Ryan comments.

"Yeah?" I grin.

"It feels like the restaurant version of me. A bit rough around the edges, but there's more to it than meets the eye."

"You're not rough around the edges."

Ryan gives me a look as if to say, *oh really*. Out loud, he adds more Ryan finesse. "Bullshit."

"Yo—"

"Forget it. It was a comment."

"Fine."

I look away because the temptation to snap at him is strong. It feels like we're tumbling backwards after all the progress we've made, and I don't know how to stop it.

"Food is a sore subject," he admits eventually.

I drum my fingers against the table and find the courage to admit what I know out loud.

"Are you embarrassed by it? Your allergy."

"No." Ryan drops his gaze. "It's—I dunno. I spent so long when I was younger dealing with it all, now I—"

"Don't want it to ruin things?"

He looks back up. "Stubborn?"

"A little," I answer, then pause. "By not being honest, you're putting yourself at risk."

"I know the score and so do the people that matter." The meaning of his words feels harsher than I think he intends. I want to ask why he didn't tell me, but it doesn't feel like the right time. Not here. "I have my own way of dealing with it."

"Like weed?"

He lets out a huffy laugh. "Yeah."

I watch him, waiting for more. I should know better by now, because there's only so much he's willing to give.

"I have questions," I say, staring at the band. "A lot of them."

"I know," he replies, at the same time the kitchen doors swing open.

Dora and the girls walk out with their hands full. Our somber conversation is forgotten temporarily.

My mouth starts to water as the smell of fried onions and potatoes reaches my nose. It's only when they start to set everything down on the table, pulling another over because there are that many dishes, that it registers: everything is on disposable serving trays. Layla disappears, and when she returns, paper plates, then plastic knives and forks are set down.

Dora leans over and speaks low in my ear.

"Everything is made fresh. No contamination," I explain to Ryan. I point at the paper plates and plastic utensils. "They wanted you to feel safe."

Rather than saying something, Ryan pulls out his phone and begins tapping the screen. I go to comment on how he's being rude when his brows furrow in concentration. When he looks back up, his cheeks turn a faint shade of pink.

"Tak," he says and Dora beams. After looking around at all the food, he takes me by surprise again when he drags out one of the chairs. "Please."

Dora turns and says something in a hushed voice to Layla, who then rushes off. Dora sits in the chair offered by Ryan, then less than a minute later, Bertie reappears with Dora's husband.

The hour that follows is more relaxed than I could have anticipated. Dora spends her time describing the dishes, and I translate. This is some of the best food in the city, and the taste journey each dish provides is an experience the most glamorous of interiors could never achieve. When we've finished, I realize I'm reluctant to leave.

We're waving goodbye, both of us carrying a stack of takeout boxes, when Dora steps forward and places a hand on Ryan's forearm.

She smiles and says carefully, "Take. Care."

"Thanks for that," Ryan says when we're back in the car.

"Anytime," I reply.

A second passes, then Ryan scratches the side of his head. "I was wondering if you wanted to make some breadcrumbs with me sometime."

My heart skips a beat, but I keep my expression neutral while trailing the tips of my fingers across the seat. "It depends. Will they be the selfie kind?"

"Like they would be any other type." He beams.

The car pulls out into the road, and I spend the entire journey back to Ryan's place trying to get my breathing under control.

Chapter Eighteen

Three hours later, I'm making my way back and forth between the Uber and S.C.A.R.A.B.'s place with the many paper bags it's taken to pack everything I thought we might need to keep us fed over the next week. The many, many, many paper bags.

I was approaching the checkout with the cart filled by maybe an eighth when it hit me that I was going to be living with two exceptionally large grown men. Two men whose single cereal portions equate to a week's worth of my own. My trip to the store was extended by thirty minutes and, by the end, it was impossible to push the cart.

I go to climb the steps with the last two bags when I hear footsteps approaching from my right. I glance and dismiss the figure approaching slowly. My foot is on the second step when I turn around and reassess.

"What are you doing?"

"Taking a dog for a walk. What does it look like?" grunts Ryan, his face hidden by a fir tree larger than his frame. "Well?"

"What?"

He huffs somewhere behind the pine needles. "I know watching me be all manly gets you wet, but it would be nice if you could give me a hand. This thing is heavy."

Deciding to ignore most of his comment, I reply, "There's something missing in all those words you spewed at me."

"Help and I'll give you that orgasm I know you've been dying for."

I want to laugh, but equally, I want to curl up and die. I've never been happier for the abundance of green between us, because it means Ryan can't see the red stain covering my cheeks.

"You're vile sometimes."

Vile but funny. Now we seem to be getting over our deeper issues, I see it. The humor. Why others like him when I've been too busy being high strung.

"Coming from the woman who said I turned her on."

Huh. I don't get chance to over-analyze his comment, or panic over how much of yesterday he remembers, because Ryan wobbles dangerously and I find myself dropping the brown paper bags and darting to the trees' rescue.

Said tree moves with speed toward the ground along with my buttocks. I land with an 'oof'.

"You good?" Ryan grunts.

The words 'comedy sketch show' come to mind. I dread to think what we must look like to anyone passing.

"Wet, but good." I cringe, thankful again for the tree buffer.

"Wet is always good, baby."

"I've already told you not to call me *baby*," I snap at the same time Ryan shifts the tree. My mouth is filled with needles. "Plergh."

Ryan manages to get a grip on the tree and lifts it away. I'm left a hot, wet mess on the ground and for none of the right reasons.

"You good?"

"Depends." I blow a rogue piece of hair that's escaped from my bun out of my face. "Are you going to stop with the baby talk?"

"Why don't you like it?"

"It's derogatory."

Ryan's eyes glitter in the light spilling from the open door behind me. His irises are three shades lighter to what they are when he's in a less than stellar mood. "Wrong."

"Excuse me?"

Apparently, my help is no longer required, because he shifts the tree so it's better positioned in his arms. I wait for him to lift it and disappear up the steps. He manages to maneuver it, along with his body, so he's crouching beside me on the step.

"You're not the only one who knows fancy words, *Sooz*. It was meant as a term of endearment."

I'm left alone on the bottom step, blinking into the night, while Ryan's feet thud on the cold stone leading up to the house.

"So, what have *you* been doing?" Ryan asks when I'm standing at the front door with the last two bags.

I stare in surprise when he takes both from me. "Buying food."

Ryan rolls his lips and glances at the other bags filling the entryway floor. "I figured that. Why?"

"We're potentially going to be stuck in here for days. If the press doesn't eat us alive, then our stomachs might."

I glance at his arms, looking for a tell-tale sign of them tiring. The last two bags were *heavy*. But then, he was carrying a tree along the sidewalk like a Mountain Man, which is why it isn't surprising when he remains statuesque. There's not a muscle twitch in sight. It's like his arms are filled with feathers.

"You're being dramatic."

"I'll sharpie everything I've bought with my name, then, three days from now, ask if you still think that." Left in an awkward silence, I continue with the first thing that comes into my head. "Are you going to help move all these into the kitchen?" I cross my arms over my chest. Ryan's eyes remain trained on my face. "Or do I actually need to sharpie them?"

The corners of his mouth twitch. "You're being playful?"

"Jovial."

"Same thing."

"Whatever. Will you help me?"

"I already am."

He shuffles the bags in his arms. The brown paper crinkles and crunches, emphasizing his point.

When he moves back, I do what I can to slide the rest of the bags across the floor with my feet so I can close the door. I triple bolt it, making sure the encroaching night, and any uninvited guests, remain outside.

Ryan has already walked into the kitchen when I grab two of the lighter bags. I follow him, finding the tree leaning against the long dining table, taunting me. I turn my attention away from it to Ryan, which isn't any better, as he's staring into the bags he carried in with a weird look on his face.

"Have I unknowingly offended you?" I ask, adding in a hint of jovialness.

I place the bags that I'm carrying on the counter near his.

He mumbles something to himself before disappearing back into the hall. He returns with another two bags, sets them down on the central island, does another quick perusal of the contents, and walks out again. He repeats the process over and over, until I'm sure there are no bags left, but unsure why the fact makes him look like he wants to set me alight with his eyes.

What happens next really throws me. Ryan turns to face me with his hands hanging limp at his sides, then he stands, watching me. The fancy over-head lights feel like lasers burning my skin.

"Why are you looking at me like that?"

"You bought everything dairy free?"

"Why wouldn't I?" Ryan's silence tips me over the edge. I'm done tiptoeing around the milk cow in the room. We *have* to talk about this. "Would you like me to take it all back? Serve you a death sentence instead?"

Okay, maybe I could have been more tactful, but I'm a control freak. Everyone knows this. I know this. Ryan knows this. Yet, since the moment my flight landed back in the US of A, I've had none. I feel like a chess piece being moved around. And I'm always a player, not a piece on the board. I make sure of it. But recently, I've found myself being the pawn—and I hate it.

"Sooz." Ryan warns.

Too riled up to conduct the appropriate assessment for the potential damage it will cause, I laugh out a 'Ry'. It comes out sounding as empty as I feel, tainting the white flag in the form of the two lettered nickname I've given him.

Ryan looks like he's been slapped. It's a look I'm becoming used to when we're together and something I'm far from proud of. A look that tells me that, despite all my efforts not to, I've ended up becoming my mother.

The sad part is—having learned from the master—I've enough years ahead of me that if I continue like I am, I could become worse. So much worse.

"I'm sorry." It's not much, but it's something. "I don't know how to do this. How to talk about … it … when you give me nothing back. But we need to. Please. Meet me halfway."

Nothing about this is easy. It's a subject that's so wrong. So cruel. But so many things in life are. People are dealt bad cards each day. I'm lucky enough that mine fall close to the bottom of the pile in significance. I might not understand Ryan's struggles, but what I have learned through the few I've had is that how you approach them makes the world of difference.

"This isn't a fucking joke, Sooz," Ryan snaps, with a level of anger I didn't know he was feeling.

The question, though, is whether that anger is at me, or his circumstances. Because we've never done this, the serious and everything that comes with it. I can't read him.

"You think I don't know that?" I straighten my spine, stand a little taller, and raise my chin. "I quote: 'too much dairy kills'. That was you. This morning. When I was trying to broach the subject like an adult."

"By analyzing my drink order?" he sneers.

"Because you gave me nothing to work with!"

"Because all you do is judge!" Ryan throws his hands up and then they drop, slapping against the countertop.

This is a disaster. How did we go from dancing around outside with a Christmas tree, firing sexual innuendos at one another, to this? Unfortunately, neither of us is done.

"And you make things hard when all I've tried to do is help navigate you through everything." I suck in a breath. "All I've ever tried to do is my job," I say, resigned.

"I've never needed you to do your job, Sooz. All I've ever needed was …" Ryan swallows, "… for you to be my friend."

The words stun me. My eyes widen. "What are you trying to say? That I'm bad at being your friend?"

Ryan looks down, his face invisible from my view. His laughter fills the air.

At first, I watch him. It goes from soft to hysterical. I refrain from uttering a quip when I find myself starting to laugh right along with him.

Eventually, we both stop. We don't look at each other. Don't say anything. My chest rises and falls more dramatically than I'd like. Getting to the end of a marathon would be easier than this conversation and I've never run in my life. Not even for the subway.

Ryan drums his fingers against the slab of marble beneath his hands, then looks up.

I might not know a lot about him, but the one thing I've learned over the years is that his eyes are the key to what he's thinking. The problem is that I don't always know how to interpret what I see.

For instance, now, they're clear. Irises still light, after our word war. And I'm gifted with a grin that stumps me after all the angst we've thrown each other's way. "For someone so intelligent, your perceptiveness is shit."

"Thanks?"

Some of the humor slips from his face. "No. Thank *you*." I must look confused, because he gestures at the brown paper bags I'd forgotten were on the countertop. "For this. I really appreciate it. It's just a sore spot."

Judging by the reaction I receive any time I try to broach the subject, I'd say it's more like a gaping hole.

"Okay." I don't really know what else to say. "Are we good?"

"We've never not been." This is news to me, but I decide after the rollercoaster that's been this conversation, not to make a comment. It's becoming perfectly clear that *my* assessment of our relationship and *Ryan's* assessment don't line up.

"Be kinder sometimes, yeah?" he says, giving me a lopsided, vulnerable smile.

I'm finding it hard to believe that I once thought he was a waste of my time, when now, I'm finding myself willing to give him all of it.

"Okay." I give him what I think is my own lopsided smile in return.

Another silence creeps in. It's an amicable one that I'm more than happy to let stretch for however long it wants, if it means that the warm, fuzzy feeling that's filling my chest gets to stay with it.

"I can help unload if you want?" he says.

"Yeah. Sure."

Cool, Sooz.

I try to concentrate on the task at hand, but it becomes impossible. What with Ryan stripping his jacket off and doing the thing I originally claimed to despise. A gun show. The way his biceps keep bulging is distracting. And the tattoos — the eye, the woman with the finger to her lips on the inside of his arm. They feel significant. Like a warning.

"There's a lot of food here," he comments, after unpacking two densely packed bags.

"I almost put my spine out of alignment on aisle three in Wholefoods," I say, hammering home the effort and energy expended to make sure the three of us—Zach included—don't starve.

"Dramatic," he says, humor in his voice.

"There was a small child involved. I was trying to avoid mowing them down. I'm not being dramatic."

"Wow." Ryan grins. "You're starting to care about things with a heartbeat. Maybe there's hope for you."

He winks and I give him a dismissive wave of my hand in return, then we both go back to unpacking. Whenever I get stuck with where to put something, Ryan shrugs and says it goes wherever. A few bags in, I'm annoyed and decide to take matters into my own hands.

"You can't put things *wherever*," I huff on his fourth wherever. "You need a system. Organization."

"Sooz. It's a kitchen. *My* kitchen. I can do whatever I want."

I narrow my eyes at the can of mixed beans he's holding. We both glance at the cupboard that's been at the receiving end of my magic organizational touch.

Don't do it.

He places the can at the front of the row. Two centimeters out of alignment.

He did it, and with a smirk.

"What's wrong?" Said smirk gets bigger, verging on a grin. "Is there something you want to say?"

"Anus."

Ryan throws his head back and laughs so hard his entire body shakes. "You're weird, you know that, right?"

"And you're a pain in my anus." I give the can another glance. My eye twitches. I'm sure it's moved to three centimeters out. "Where are you going?" I call out, as Ryan starts to disappear through the kitchen doorway.

"To get something," Ryan throws over his shoulder.

"What about the groceries?"

He stops walking and looks back. "What about them?"

"We're not done."

He shrugs. "They're not going anywhere. Live on the edge. Do it later."

"Just like that?"

"Yeah." He disappears out of sight, leaving me alone with a repeated "just like that," and an abundance of grocery bags taunting me, calling to be packed away.

Feeling Ryan's expectation for me to continue in the room, I purposefully don't, opting for the pointless task of standing and wringing my hands together. When he returns, he smiles at the grocery bags still sitting unpacked on the countertop.

"Careful, Sooz. Next, you'll be putting your diary in the trash and saying fuck the system."

"I don't have a diary." Ryan looks shocked. "At least, not a paper one." I tap the screen of my phone. "Meet my life in the form of a small digital object." I don't bother commenting on the way Ryan shakes his head, because I'm more concerned with the delay in my phone's response.

Three hard taps and a six second further delay, the screen lights up.

"Everything okay?"

"Not sure," I mumble, typing in my passcode. Everything is taking longer than it should to register.

"I can get you another phone."

I look up and give him a tight smile when it's unlocked. "No need. I'll figure it out."

Lines of frustration begin to appear on Ryan's forehead. "It's not a big deal. It was my fault."

"And I said I'm fine."

"Why won't you let me help?"

Where Ryan's brows are lowered, merging into one thick line, mine work their way up my forehead, creating a perfect arch of disbelief. "We're doing this again?"

Ryan presses his lips together and his cheeks puff out.

"What are you doing?"

"Tryingnottosaysomethingishouldnt …" is all I'm able to make out as his cheeks remain full.

It's the comedy element needed to diffuse the situation before it escalates. I decide to roll with it. "You look like a puffer fish when you do that."

"And you look gorgeous when you're pissed."

My mouth opens in surprise.

"And you look like a goldfish when you do that," he says.

I stand, staring, no clue what to say.

"We've got our own finding Nemo cast going on." Ryan chuckles and sets the box he'd retrieved earlier down on the countertop.

"Want to help me decorate the tree?"

"I'm good," I reply. The blood drains from my face, his comment forgotten.

Ryan watches me carefully, unmoving.

"Are you not going to decorate it?"

He shrugs. "I'll wait until you're ready."

"You assume I'm going to change my mind," I say, folding my arms across my chest. When he doesn't comment back, I wrack my brain for something else to say as the silence becomes unnerving. I go to speak, when Ryan grabs a chopping board and an onion. "What are you doing now?"

He pulls a knife out of the wooden knife block. "Cooking."

My brows shoot up. "You cook?"

The knife he's holding hovers over the onion, then the pointy tip starts to create the smallest of incisions. "Is that an issue?"

"No, it's just …"

The words, '*You were being judgy*' hang unsaid between us.

I start to play with the edge of a bag of pasta for a moment.

"I mean … your breakfast cereal choice …" I continue.

The knife slides through the middle of the onion and the two halves fall apart and rock on the chopping board. "What does my cereal choice suggest?"

"That you're like a child? That you can't cook?" That sounded worse out loud than it did in my head.

Ryan sets down the knife. I flinch in anticipation of an onion half being launched my way. A deep rumble of laughter fills the room, warming the minimalist interiors that I wouldn't have put with S.C.A.R.A.B. The kitchen is the only place in the house that reflects the growing wealth of its inhabitants.

"You're not what I expected you to be like when we first met."

"What did you expect?"

His eyes move from my white blouse up to my golden hair, pulled back tight in my go to bun. "That you'd be more uptight."

"Now who's being judgy?"

He holds his hands up. They seem impossibly large for someone who spends most of their day working with fragile little drumsticks. And then there are the tattoos on the insides of his fingers, which are impossible to see because of the constant movement. With hands like his, it brings forth a very real question. How doesn't he impale the sticks through the skins of his drums?

"You got me."

He smiles and a butterfly awakens inside me. "You're not what I expected you to be like either." He glances up, waiting. "When you're not high or wasted ..." I sniff, "I guess you're kind of likeable."

He frowns and goes rigid. "But I'm unlikeable otherwise?"

"No. I didn't mean it like that. It's just—" I don't know what to say. I've basically said I don't like two of the things that make up who he is. "Sorry."

"No need to apologize." He grabs a hand towel, wipes his palms against it, then tosses it down on the countertop.

"Where are you going?" I ask when he starts walking toward the kitchen door.

"To my room. I'm suddenly not hungry."

"Wait." I'm clutching at straws because I don't know how to make any of this better. I grab the rest of his stash that I'd picked up from the office earlier and hold it out. At some point today, it hit me that he doesn't need a babysitter. It's the last thing in the world he needs. He needs someone to believe in him and to guide him towards a better outlet for whatever demons he's fighting.

My gesture is misconstrued though, and if I screwed up with the comment I made, then I've obliterated whatever progress we've made based on the look Ryan gives me. He stares at the bag of weed, his expression grim.

Holding my breath, I wait for a snide remark, maybe even some shouting. All he does is shake his head and go to leave the room.

Before he disappears, I voice the question that's been bugging me, even though there's a strong possibility he won't answer. "Why did you say that before?"

"Say what?" he asks, his voice flat.

"The gorgeous thing …"

"Because it's the truth," he sighs, and my gaze lowers to the countertop. "Why do you think I go out of my way to piss you off?"

When I find the courage to look up, he's already gone.

Chapter Nineteen

I 've only just closed my eyes when something stirs me from sleep.

Bleary-eyed, I stare into the darkness, finding nothing that could be the source of the noise. I go to close my eyes and go back to sleep when I hear it again.

"What the?" I grumble, pushing away my sheets and sitting up. My hair settles around my shoulders, hanging so low it hits just above my waist.

I'm greeted with silence and let out a frustrated exhale. Then I hear it again. A deep rumble which stops abruptly, then voices. Another rumble follows, then a flash of light pours through the cracks in the floor-length curtains covering the window. Throwing my legs over the side of the couch, I let out a squeak when my bare feet make contact with the cold floorboards.

When I move toward the window, I do so hesitantly. I stop, standing to the left. When I move the curtain back, it's by a millimeter, if that, but it's enough that I'm able to see what's happening outside.

There must be at least thirty vans creating a roadblock. It doesn't seem enough in comparison to how many people there are. At least a hundred. Maybe fifty more. I'm not sure, because I can't see clearly. Not unless I move the curtain, which would draw attention to where I'm standing.

Carefully, I set the curtain in place, then shuffle back over to the couch. I use it to guide me toward the small side table, grunting when my big toe collides with one of the table legs. Blinking through watery, pain-filled eyes, I tap my phone screen, making out it's after three. Actually, it could be five. The cracks are distorting the numbers. Relying on my internal clock, I decide it's closer to three.

Time feels irrelevant though, especially considering I have two hundred and fifteen notifications. I blink and the number jumps to two-thirty-six. I don't dare blink again. At least I don't until it registers my phone isn't bleeping. Or vibrating. It isn't doing much of anything apart from receiving hundreds of messages and updates without informing me of it. I give it a little shake. Then a tap. Still nothing. I should have taken Ryan up on his offer after all, because this malfunction couldn't be happening at a worse possible time. What's worse: when I go to open my messages, the screen freezes. I'm in notification no-man's-land.

My phone remains lifelessly illuminated. I toss it down on the couch and sit, staring into the darkness. There's no way I'm going to be able to sleep, not with the world standing outside in the street. When there are more voices and commotion, I grab my phone, then pad through the darkness, not wanting to make the front-page news in my jammies.

I've entered the kitchen when I hear a noise. I freeze as my brain jumps from one worst-case scenario to another.

Heart hammering, I blindly move my hand left to where I know the knife block is sitting. There's another shuffle as I pull a knife out. Clutching it shakily in my left, my right stretches to the wall on the other side of the doorjamb, carefully searching. My fingertips make contact with the plastic square, then find the switch. I count to three before flicking it down.

Light floods the room and a rainbow of fruit loops fly through the air. They cascade down like multicolored raindrops, pitter pattering when they hit the ground.

Setting his now empty bowl down on the kitchen counter, Ryan folds over and attempts to catch his breath. "Jeez, woman," he gasps. "Give a guy some warning."

In the absurdity that has become my life, a giggle slips out.

Ryan rests his elbows on the central island. His hair looks freshly washed, no products in sight, and falls across his forehead. He glances up with a smile. A smile which drops when his eyes settle on the silver butcher knife glinting in my left hand.

"I wanted to protect myself."

His brows shoot up. "And kill someone."

"You've seen outside, right?"

"Violence is never the answer, baby."

My mouth parts at his slip after what he revealed a few hours ago. The word has a new meaning, and I'm not sure how I feel.

"Sorry," he says, pushing away from the counter and standing tall. I tilt my head back so I can keep looking at him. He's a human tower. "I know you hate it."

I almost drop the knife. "Since when do you care if I hate what you say?"

Green irises bore into mine. "I've always cared. I'm not a dick."

My heart does a dangerous thud and my instincts flare, telling me to snipe back, so this can't move to somewhere it shouldn't. My mouth parts ready, and Ryan's eyes glitter. Waiting. Expectant. I press my lips together and look away, realizing I don't want to.

"So, why are you up?"

"Why do you think?"

"The papz woke you, too?"

"I was hungry."

The memory of clearing away the red pepper makes me grimace. "Sorry."

He shakes his head. "Stop apologizing. It's weird."

"But yo—"

"Look," he sighs. "Can we be normal with each other?" I watch him, confused. Ryan's shoulders start to shake, and he chuckles. "I like you, Sooz." I gawp. "I like us, together. I don't want us to change."

No matter how hard I try to process everything he's said, combined with everything he said earlier, his words won't register properly.

"I thought you hated me?"

It's Ryan's turn to look confused. "Why?"

I make an 'Um', which sounds more like a 'Duh', then let out a huffy laugh. "Because when there's no one else around, you're angry with me?"

"When have I ever been angry with you?"

I laugh hard. "All the time."

"When?"

"Are you being serious?" His expression says yes. "Erm, like now ..."

"Right now, I'm annoyed that you think I've ever been angry with you. Plus, I'm not asking about right now. Tell me when in the past."

"Whenever we're together. You're frowning." I drop my voice low. "Making remarks with a super low, deep voice like you're piddled." He blinks, so I spell it out. "P-I-S-S-E-D."

"I knew what you meant." I look away, my cheeks warming. "Sooz." I refuse to glance back. "I swear, I've never been angry." I still don't say anything, and my eyes burn from the strain of staying focused on anything but him. "No, that's I lie. I was angry."

My head turns back and I point an accusing finger in his direction. "I knew it. I was right."

He smiles. "I was angry at myself that I was too much of a *waster* to convince you that we could be friends when we first met."

At first, I don't know how to reply. If he notices how much his words have affected me, he doesn't point it out. When I manage to gather my thoughts together, I say, "With everyone else, you're the life and soul of the party. But with me, well, you're a bit of an ..."

"Ass?" He smirks.

"Yeah."

"You mean like how you have this weird leadership respect thing going on, but with me you're a bit of a ..."

"Beyatch?"

"Yeah." His eyes move down my body and I become hyperaware of the fact only a thin layer of cotton is covering me, and that I'm not wearing a bra. "Nice pajamas."

I'm not sure if he's referring to the two pairs of avocados dancing hand in hand over my nipples, or the pink wording beneath. I shift my feet and wrap my arms around myself. As I do, my hair falls forward again, covering my face. I brush it out of the way and find Ryan's been watching me the whole time. At least he has until he gets caught and tears his eyes away.

He pointlessly moves his spoon across the counter. "You should wear your hair down more often."

"Why? Because it makes me look less uptight?"

"No, because it's beautiful."

I splutter at another compliment he's openly throwing my way. I go to ask if he's high again, but I don't get a chance, because there's a hammering at the door so loud it sounds like it's going to come off its hinges.

We both look at each other with wide eyes, our conversation forgotten. Ryan walks quickly toward me then we both make our way out into the hall. I'm near the door with Ryan close behind when there's a second round of hammering.

"Who the hell is that?" asks Zach, rubbing his eyes as he trudges down the stairs in a pair of black boxers that complement his dark hair.

I purse my lips and hold back a comment that this whole scenario is a bit cliché. It would potentially send him back up the stairs to find a shirt and pants, and there are worse sights to be forced to look at than a couple of rock stars wandering around in minimal clothing.

"No idea," replies Ryan.

The frosted glass panels surrounding the front door light up from all the flashes outside.

Zach looks at them, confused. "What's going on?"

Ryan rolls his eyes. "Dude, seriously? Please tell me you remember what was happening tonight?"

"With the photos?" Ryan nods, and Zach's brows shoot up. "That was today? Fuck, I booked a hair appointment for before lunch."

"That's a joke, right?" I ask in disbelief.

"I feel like I should say yes, so I'm going to." Zach gives me a thumbs up. "Yes."

Ryan gestures at the door. The huge chunk of ivory painted wood stands, taunting us all, hiding whoever is on the other side. "I guess we should open it?"

"The press wouldn't knock," I muse. Knocking would give us a chance to prepare, and they're after the most candid photo they can get.

"What if we like, stand behind it and open it far enough someone can slide through?" suggests Zach.

"Yeah. Who cares about murderers and crazy fans, or whoever else could come in?" I reply.

"Get your butcher knife and we'll be safe." Ryan winks when I don't respond. "That *was* a joke."

"Just open it." The unknown is making me antsy, and I sound shrill.

Ryan walks to the door as Zach and I both shuffle away, pressing our backs against the wall in preparation for the onslaught that is undoubtedly going to come.

"Thanks for the support," says Ryan, undoing the bolts. He turns the key in the main lock, then twists the intricately decorated iron handle. The door opens a crack, illuminating the entryway.

"Christ." Zach's mutter is barely audible over the noise that floods in from outside.

"You're going to have to open the door wider to let us in." All the blood drains from my face. "Well?"

I race forward, shoving Ryan out of the way, ignoring his grunt as he crashes into the wall and Zach's protests as I fling the door wide open.

Everything amplifies. The flashing of lights. The roar of the press and their demands for a photo slamming into me. It would be terrifying. Should be. But what's standing in front of me is much worse.

Clad in all her bouclé glory, with the majority of New York's paparazzi swarming behind her, is my mother.

My mouth opens and closes at least four times before I manage to say, "What are you doing here?" The words feel garbled as they come out. The way she looks at me suggests I haven't spoken any sense. When I tear my eyes away from her, I find Henrik and Willem flanking her sides. Their matching navy suits look too perfect and pressed to have endured a transatlantic flight.

"I could ask you the same question," my mother says with a smile. She's had passive aggressive nailed since she was in the womb. The term was created solely for her. "But this hardly feels like the place to be having a family reunion." Passive gone; she shoots a venomous look over her shoulder at one photographer in particular who gets too close. Luckily, he takes two steps back. He must sense she has the ability to kill someone with her eyes alone. With her personal space clear, and all well in her bouclé bubble, she turns back to me. "Well …"

"Let us in," Will says under his breath.

"Right," I stammer. "Sure."

Flattening myself to the door, when the trio have passed by, the flashing intensifies. I cringe at the realization my jammies will, in fact, be making the tabloids, and hurry to close the door then lock it. While doing so, I try to figure out what's worse, being under the scrutiny of the press, or my mother.

"Why are you here?" I ask, turning and finding five pairs of eyes watching me, each wanting a different explanation to what is going on. Something I don't quite know myself.

Mother's lips flatten into a line as tight as the bun she's made sure I wear my hair in since I was little. "In the entrance? Really, Suzanne? We might as well be standing outside with the press."

"Where exactly are you expecting to have a conversation?"

It's then that my eyes move down to the travel case sitting at her feet. The one so tall it sits at waist height. It's super chunky, with enough space to fit a couple of weeks' worth of clothing, meaning this isn't going to be a short trip.

"Somewhere a little more comfortable." She smiles at Zach and Ryan. "We're guests after all."

"No," I mutter, as Ryan leads the way back to the kitchen. "Guests suggest you're invited."

"I heard that," she whisper-hisses back.

She stops abruptly when her feet crunch. She looks down, raises her foot and tilts it to the side to check the bottom of her right Louboutin. The sole now resembles a crushed rainbow.

I shrug when she stares at me, waiting for an explanation. "Fruit loops."

Her smile falters. "Of course."

Will and Henrik have somehow managed to tiptoe their way through the kitchen with minimal crunching involved and are now both watching our interaction like we're two bombs ready to detonate.

"So!" says Zach with a big grin stretched across his face. "I'm Zach." After shaking hands with Will and Henrik, he makes his way to my mother. The crunching beneath his bare feet does nothing to lighten the moment, and when he's standing with his hand stretched out between them, her eyes drop to the ink on his bare chest.

"Is that …"

"A scarab." His smile grows larger, and he waits for the penny to drop. Metaphorical tumble weed rolls on by and his hand, still hovering between them, lifts to the back of his neck and rubs. "It's the name of our band, although it has dots in because we thought it looked fancy." He gestures back at Ryan, and my mother blinks. "I'm the bassist."

"How lovely." Things get worse when she leans to the side to look around Zach and finds Ryan again. "And you are?"

"The drummer."

She straightens and faces me. Her eyes drop down to my baby pink night shirt and she reads the '*It's a good day to av-o-cado*' slogan. Her nostrils flare, making it perfectly clear she finds my nightwear choice as offensive as my current living arrangements. "And let me guess, you're singing?"

"No, Mother," I snap. "I'm doing my job. The one you've refused to acknowledge for years."

My foot itches to stomp and crunch a ton of Fruit Loops to tip her over her pretentious ledge.

"And the press?"

225

"My fault," admits Ryan, raising a hand in the air. I hold my breath and wait for the cannon to fire. "I got pictured getting a few blow jobs. The pictures just leaked."

Boom.

The shrug he adds on the end finishes Mother off.

"A few," she squeaks. I try to block out that the quantity is the only part she's surprised by. "Well then."

Will clears his throat, giving both Ryan and Zach an apologetic look. "I'm sorry. We appreciate you letting us come inside your home. But do you mind giving us a few minutes?"

I'm taken by surprise when Ryan looks over at me for confirmation of what they should do. The tense nod I give does nothing to lessen the deep line between his brows. Zach starts walking out, and Ryan follows, but pauses at my side as he passes by.

His voice drops low so only I can hear him. "I'll be in the next room. Call if you need anything."

A wave of calm washes over me and, out of nowhere, I have the urge to lean into him.

"Thanks," I reply.

And then there were four.

My mother is like a vulture and doesn't waste a second to swoop in and attack. "You told me you came to Brooklyn to work, when really you've been living with a band?"

Will opens his mouth to jump to my defense, but I hold a hand up to stop him. I'm tired of him fighting my battles with her.

"No, Mother. I have an apartment with Abby, my business partner." The name drop doesn't draw a single ounce of recognition. "You've met. Twice."

226

She casts her eyes off to the side and shows a considerable level of interest in one of the kitchen units. "I don't remember."

"Because you have selective hearing." Will and Henrik both share a worried look, but I don't care about pushing her buttons right now. She's standing in my territory. I'll happily push them all. "In fact, no. It isn't selective. You don't hear anything I say, unless it's to do with Will."

She has the audacity to widen her eyes and look shocked by what I'm saying. "That's not true."

"Why are you here?" I ask, ignoring her second lie.

"A visit has been long overdue."

"I've lived here for three years. You've never once shown any interest in seeing me. Seeing what I've made of myself. What. Is. Going. On?"

Her forehead does the unthinkable. It crinkles. Then she glances over at Will. They share a look, but still she doesn't reply.

Always the one to save the day, Henrik steps forward and pulls me into his arms.

He lowers his head and whispers in my ear, "She wants to apologize for the party, but she doesn't know how. Give her a break. I've never seen her as restless as on the flight here."

Finished, he rests his chin on the top of my head. He feels warm. Familiar. I bury my face into his shirt, when I feel like I'm going to cry. I don't cry.

After a shuddered exhale, I pull back and give him a wobbly smile. The smile he returns is a half one. I go to ask what's wrong when I realize it isn't directed at me. I turn and find Ryan standing in the doorway. He looks different. His usual lazy gaze is nowhere to be found. His eyes are hard, and his expression is completely unreadable.

"We have spare rooms." His words are directed at me, but his eyes remain focused on Henrik.

Will jumps and says, "We don't want to intrude," at the same time Mother claps her hands together. "Perfect."

I'm tempted to bury my face back in Henrik's shirt, because this has disaster written all over it. The look on Ryan's face stops me.

"Thanks."

All I get in return is a nod. A nod that fills me with guilt, because I can't help feeling like he's disappointed with me. The confusing part is what I think is the reason why.

Mother takes Sam's room and Will and Henrik take the other spare ones.

By the time everyone is settled, and I'm back camped out on the couch, it's already five AM. I should be tired. Exhausted. But I can't settle, no matter how hard I try.

Phone still dead as a dodo, I fire up my laptop, needing to see what we're dealing with and how the press has decided to spin the images.

After opening the internet browser, I type in *Ryan scarab,* before I can second-guess myself.

Instantly, I wish I hadn't.

There are pages, one after another, all with similar headlines. None are as bad as I predicted they might be, because the press has picked up on a detail; one that isn't small; one I don't know how I missed. A detail which works in both Ryan, and the band's, favor. But a detail that has my mood turning sour.

Glancing over at the stairs, I listen carefully to check no one is around. When all I hear in return is silence, I walk over to my bag and retrieve the brown envelope John West gave me in his office. After pulling out the images, I set them on the bed one after another, next to each other, and take them all in.

I want to kick myself for missing this. It's so obvious it's ridiculous.

Each picture shows the same nose with a slight lift at the tip. The same harsh-lined brows and thick lashes lining the same crystal blue eyes. The same body that's left millions envious.

The only difference is the hair.

And as I slide the images back into the envelope and hide them away, I try to ignore the stab of jealousy that comes with accepting the headlines might be true. That I was wrong the day I berated Ryan for having a harem of women.

Because it's now very clear for the eye to see that there was only ever one.

Chapter Twenty

I t's mid-morning when I startle awake.

I don't remember falling asleep and I also don't remember getting a blanket. Hello, sleep deprivation, and all the fun that comes with it. In a wave of panic, I jolt up, expecting to find another digital screen cracked on the ground. It's empty, and I find my laptop sitting safely, closed on the coffee table.

After a couple of mental preparations, I stand and make my way into the kitchen, anticipating everyone will already be awake. It's empty apart from Zach and the sound of the fork he's using, clinking against a blue ceramic bowl.

"Morning, my South African sunshine!"

"Where is everyone?" I ask, climbing onto one of the stools.

Zach looks up from the eggs he's whisking. "If by everyone you mean your not-as-sunny South African counterparts, I think they're still sleeping." My body slumps. Zach doesn't miss the movement, because he chuckles out an exhale. "I know, right? Your mom. She's kind of …"

"Intense?"

"Much better way of putting it." He winks, and I laugh.

"I've had plenty of practice." I shift in my seat, then glance over at the Christmas tree no longer resting against the dining table, but standing tall and secure in an iron stand, still undecorated.

"Ryan went out," Zach says, answering my unvoiced question with his attention back on his eggs.

Images of Ryan being mauled by the press in broad daylight flash behind my eyes. "What do you mean?"

"Exactly what I said." Zach glances up. "He went out. Had shit to do apparently."

"But the press?"

Zach's eyes trail over to the back door. "He went that way. It comes in handy." A ghost of a smirk covers his lips. "But you know that already."

"Did he say when he'd be back?"

"Nope." He takes the bowl over to the stove and pours the contents into the waiting frying pan. They sizzle and bubble when they hit black cast iron. He looks over his shoulder at me. "Want some?"

"I'm good."

"You sure? I make mean eggs. They're the second thing I'm famous for." He grabs a spatula and starts folding the edges, which have already set, into the center. Liquid flows out into the pan and sizzles again.

"Zach."

"Sooz." He spins around with a ridiculous grin on his face and the spatula raised in the air. I frown as some of the half-

231

set eggs begin sliding down it like glue. "He has a security team with him. You need to chill. He's fine." The spatula lowers back into the pan right before the trail of egg drips off.

"I wasn't worried."

"Sure, you weren't." With the eggs finished, he scrapes them onto a plate, turns, places the plate on the central island, and slides it across the countertop toward me.

I frown, even though they do smell incredible. "I said I was good."

The sound of footsteps padding down the stairs fills the silence and Zach's eyes move to the kitchen doorway. They're too light to be Will or Henrik's.

"I know you did," he replies, still staring at the doorway. "But I think you'll need the energy more than I will."

I'm gifted another wink before he tries to make a quick exit. He's left it too late, though, because before he can dart out of the kitchen, my mother appears. She's wearing her usual bouclé, but a color I've not seen her wear before. Baby pink with a thick white border lining all the hems. She looks like a marshmallow.

"Morning, Ma'am." Zach goes as far as saluting.

Mother looks at him like she's sucked on a lemon. "You're clothed today."

That's it. No hello. Good morning. Thank you for providing us with a bed to sleep in.

Zach proves he doesn't do well under scrutiny like hers when he scratches at his head. "I mean, I could take them off?"

Mother's wide eyes find mine. I want the ground to swallow me up.

"Zach, it's fine," I answer, knowing she won't know how to. He's managed to do the unthinkable and shock her. "You can leave."

He throws a thankful look over his shoulder, but sadly, the awkwardness doesn't end. He takes a step left as my mother takes a step right. He makes a strange sound as she huffs. Zach then takes a step right as my mother takes a step left. This time, the sound that comes from him is more of a strangled one. Mother narrows her eyes. Zach then does some weird shimmy with his hips and his arms thrown out at each side. He looks like he's going to gyrate against her leg.

My forehead has a near miss with the eggs when I groan in the background and face plant the counter. I refuse to look up until the sound of Zach scurrying away reaches my ears. When I hear Mother walking to the opposite side of the central island, I contemplate keeping my head down.

"Suzanne."

One deep breath, and I'm sitting up straight, smiling.

"Yes?"

"What is going on?"

I take her in. All of her. Not just her outfit and hair pulled back in the same bun I wear each day. But the way her skin is tight over the bone structure of her face, not a line in sight. Micro-bladed brows, semi-permanent lined lips. It's a miracle she hasn't had fillers.

"I've already told you. Twice. I'm working."

"Here?"

"Yes. Here."

Her eyes move around, taking in the kitchen. With the fruit loops swept away, she looks less disapproving.

"Why?" she asks, looking back at me.

I drag my finger back and forth along the counter.

I'm not really sure why I can't quite meet her eye when I say, "Ryan summed it up pretty well."

"Living as a groupie doesn't seem like work."

I throw my hands up in the air. When they come back down, they slap against the marble countertop. I'm too irritated to wince. I barely feel the sting from the impact.

"Why do you have to do that? Belittle everything I've achieved." Her left brow twitches. "You know what, forget it. I'm going to get cleaned up." I push the plate of now lukewarm eggs toward her. "They're all yours." I'm at the doorway when I pause and look back. "And you need to find a costume."

"Why?" Mother asks.

"Because if you're staying for the holidays, then you get to attend the New Year's Ball."

"Organized by whom?"

"The company I helped build." I walk away, throwing out a final, "Not that you really care."

My sour mood from talking to my mother washes down the plughole with the suds from my shampoo, and I feel less grouchy after a long bath.

It's when I have a towel wrapped around me and my hair is hanging damp down my back, smelling of a certain drummer, that I realize my error. With Mother now camped out in Sam's room, I have nowhere to get ready. I deliberate going to the kitchen and asking her if I can use the room, but decide against it. I'll have to get ready in here, humid hair be damned.

I leave the bathroom, hearing the sound of guns firing and explosions as I go. The next door along the hallway from Sam's, open a crack, confirms the noise is coming from Zach's room. He lets out a whoop as I make my way downstairs toward the living room to grab my bag. When I get there, it's nowhere to be found.

Huh. I know left it down here.

Backtracking, I make my way to Zach's room, pulling the towel tighter around me as I go. The noise spilling out gets louder the closer I get. So loud, that when I call Zach's name, there's no response. I push the door open and almost drop my towel when I find Will and Henrik, sitting on the floor with their backs against the foot of the bed. Their legs are stretched out in front of them, games controllers are in their hands.

"Pew! Pew! Pew!" Henrik shouts.

"Burn, motherfucker!" says Will.

I watch my brother, bemused.

When he doesn't acknowledge my existence, my eyes move to where Zach is sitting. His back's against the headboard and Ryan's at his side. They also have controllers, and their eyes remain glued to the giant TV screen hanging on the wall.

"You're back," I say to Ryan. I wait for him to answer. A round of rapid firing starts. I jump and throw the screen an annoyed look. Still, no one acknowledges I've entered the room. "Have you seen my suitcase?" I all but shout. "It was in the living room, but it isn't there now."

Ryan looks over. A droplet of water falls from a strand of my hair and makes a path down my chest. His eyes follow the movement, snapping back up when it disappears beneath the towel. There's another huge explosion in the background. I squirm. I'm not sure if it's from the cool path being tracked between my breasts, or the dark look he gives me.

"Your case is in my room," he says.

Taking it as a signal I've been dismissed, I back out without another word. Because of the disaster that was the last time I was in his room, I walk toward the door leading to the attic, trying to figure out whether the smell of weed can permeate through plastic. Also, whether I need to go out and buy a new wardrobe.

When I'm at the end of the hallway, I hover, hold my breath, then grab hold of the door handle. I exhale, and before I can change my mind, fling open the door. I wait to be hit by an overwhelming fruity smell.

I wrinkle my nose. Sniff. Inhale deeply. There's nothing but fresh air.

Less reluctant, I make my way up, bracing myself for the war zone. The floor is empty. No empty liquor bottles in sight. The dark sheets have been replaced by white ones with a light blue damask pattern. With the shade up and the window open, the space is light and airy. Because it's the first time being in here that I don't feel on edge, I use the opportunity to take in the surroundings thoroughly, appreciating all the details now they aren't hidden by mess. There's an electronic drum kit sitting in one corner with a small stool. It's the acoustic guitar resting against the wall behind it that captures my attention. Another detail of many I didn't know made up Ryan Alvarez.

The spotless desk throws me. I never noticed it the two other times I was in here. But there it is, and sitting in the center is my laptop. That isn't what makes my chest go tight, though. It's the rectangular box lined up perfectly next to it.

I walk over, stop, stare, then remove the lid and pull out the Samsung Galaxy Z Fold4. When I tap the screen, it comes to life. A quick check of the SIM settings confirms my number is still the same. All my old contacts are saved with the addition of one new one. I click on it and send a message.

Me: *I can't accept this.*

I stare at the mini laptop sitting in my hand that costs more than my months' rent. Three dots appear, signaling that Ryan is typing.

Ryan: *Take it.*
Me: *No.*

When the three dots appear again, they remain on the screen. I go to text asking if he's writing something close to *War and Peace,* when I hear a click that sounds like a door closing. I pull the towel tighter around me and remain frozen, facing the desk. Footsteps move up the stairs. They stop at what, judging by the volume increase, is the top.

"Please, Sooz."

I set the phone down on the desk and walk over to the electronic drum kit. "These are cool."

"Don't change the subject," Ryan says.

"Are they silent?" I perch on the stool and shift to get comfy.

"Unless these are on. Yeah. Pretty much." I feel Ryan move in from behind. He towers over me as he reaches and retrieves a pair of headphones, resting on what looks like a control unit. "Want to try?"

My head tilts back. He glances down, gripping the headphones, waiting for my answer. I look back at the kit, before replying, "Sure."

His 'okay' comes out more of a croak.

Instinctively, I go to ask what's wrong, then decide against it. I have a feeling his what's wrong is similar to my what's wrong. A what's wrong where I feel hyperaware of everywhere Ryan is or isn't.

"Take those." He nods at the drumsticks, then frowns at my bare legs. "You need to move the stool closer for the pedals."

He walks away as I shuffle the stool forward.

When I look over my shoulder, I find him wheeling the chair from his desk over. He sets it behind the stool and sits, then scoots it in closer. So close, his front is against my back. His t-shirt shifts against where I'm uncovered by the towel when he reaches around to grab the headphones. Right before he lowers them, his head moves in toward me. His lips almost skim my ear.

Ryan's next words answer all the questions I've had about the other morning, and whether he remembers what happened.

"You seem to be spending a lot of time naked around me for someone so against fucking."

He's right. I'm barely covered. The top of the towel is low. The hem barely hiding my nipples, revealing one of the only jackpots I hit with the Van Rensburg gene pool. The bottom is bunched around my waist, hiding nothing depending on which angle you take me from. A shiver works its way through me, but I'm hot. Red hot from a moment that, to most, would be tame, but after years of bouncing between dry spells and inadequate sex, is verging on erotic.

238

Encouraged by my silence, Ryan inhales. He all but buries his face in my still wet hair. My back goes ramrod straight when he shuffles in and plasters himself against me.

"Why do you smell like me?" I squirm. The situation isn't helped by the rock-hard erection pressed against my lower back. "Do you smell like me everywhere?"

The everywhere he's referring to throbs as the headphones find their way carefully in place. The smallest of sounds disappears. My grip tightens on the drumsticks when our arms line up. Ryan's hands cover mine.

I want to move. Feel how he'd react. I must be giving away my apprehension, because my right hand goes cold as Ryan's lifts away. A couple of centimeters of air finds its way between my ear and the pad.

"Relax."

I do the opposite, as another shiver rolls down my spine. It settles as a small, dull ache between my legs. The kind that can only be satisfied by friction. Unfortunately, the only friction my body receives is from the vibration in my throat when I clear it.

"Do you get this close and personal for all the drum lessons you give?"

"Only the special ones," Ryan replies.

The ear-pad lands back in place with a light thud. I scowl. Ryan leaves me with little time to stew, giving my left hand a squeeze, before lowering it to the drum. The sound of the stick hitting the skin pours through the headphones. Ryan squeezes my right hand, encouraging it to join in with the motions.

For those few moments, I let myself forget everything. My mother's expectations. The harsh expectations I set upon myself. I forget all the reasons why I shouldn't be here, doing this, because it isn't a part of the path I've planned to walk along. I allow myself to settle into a beat I didn't know I could create, let alone enjoy. Allow myself to become lost in what the two of us create together. To some, it might be chaos. Noise. But, depending on who's listening, with the right perspective, it could be the most beautiful sound there is.

I'm taken by surprise when Ryan gives my right hand another squeeze. He lifts both our arms in the air and brings the stick down hard against the padded cymbal. Having become used to one steady rhythm, I startle at the crash. Firm upper arms lock me in place, keeping me still and upright as Ryan's t-shirt rubs against my back. His forehead drops to my shoulder. I feel a familiar vibration. Like the rumble of laughter. Then, the right ear-pad is shifted forward.

"Move like that again and this lesson will turn into a different kind." His warm breath coats the paper-thin skin of my ear in a shuddered exhale. "How was that?"

"Good."

I draw in a breath, trying to not to think how it feels having him pressed against me. How we're two completely different pieces, somehow fitting together.

"My favorite part of drumming is that you can have the same beat," he says, leaning to the side and folding himself around me. "And all it takes …" His hand wraps around my calf. Burns my skin. I manage to lift my leg with his help and set my foot against the right pedal. The towel works its way higher. I'm unsure how much he can see, but something takes over and I don't care. Ryan's fingers trail up as he straightens and continues, "Is one small change to transform it into something new." Right before the ear-pad is set back in place, he says, "Play."

Doing as I'm told, I move both sticks in the same basic rhythm he's taught me. His left hand settles at my waist over the terry material. The tips of his right fingers ghost over the bottom hem of the towel. They move lower. Then his palm flattens. I continue to play as his fingers wrap around the inside of my thigh, and he presses down.

A deep thud transforms the sound. He adds pressure, then releases. Over and over. Creating something the same, yet different, as his thumb skims back and forth at the apex of my thigh. I moan, and his thumb moves further up. Holding my breath, my lids fall shut. I become lost in barely there sensations. Playing forgotten, all I'm able to do is pray Ryan stretches his touch a centimeter or two higher.

Maybe he can read my mind, or maybe he's as lost as I am in whatever this is, because he does exactly what I'm ready for begging him to. His thumb slips up. Purposefully or not, I don't care. All I care about is how it feels brushing against my clit. The tight bundle of nerves sparks to life.

Where the first slip could be considered accidental, the second isn't. It's the third slip that has me going slack. I lean back into him. With the ear-pads still in place, I don't hear the clatter the drumsticks make when I let go of them and they drop to the ground. All I can do is feel. Feel the soft pieces of Ryan's hair beneath my fingers when I lift my arms. Reach back. Grasp. Drag him closer. Feel the way his heart hammers against my back. The way hot, ragged breaths coat my neck when he starts to lose control. His thumb is replaced by two fingers that circle, then slide down and dip inside me. The vibrations of his groan work their way through me. They heighten every sensation as he slowly draws them out, then back in. Hitting a spot I didn't know existed.

Everything builds with the pace of Ryan's fingers.

Then it hits me exactly what I'm doing and who I'm doing it with.

Ryan must feel me tense, because he stops moving. His fingers become a too-short memory.

"Wait," I say breathlessly as the headphones are lifted away. Sound slams into me. Panting that isn't only mine. "I want this. I do. But I need something. Anything."

More personal because I don't fuck.

Ryan pushes the desk chair back and spins me round on the stool. The damp skin on the backs of my thighs burns moving over the plastic.

"What do you mean?" he asks, frowning.

"All I ever get from you is half a truth. Then you leave me to put the rest of the pieces together."

There's a darkness to his gaze. His irises are a deep shade of green, suggesting he's going to refuse. If he does, then we'll continue doing the same dance. The same push and pull.

"Fine." I almost fall off the stool. "One truth for another."

"Okay. You ask first." I figure if I give him mine, he will be less likely to back out of what I ask him.

"Why won't you take the phone?"

Huh. I don't know what exactly I was expecting, but it wasn't that. I blink, then blink again, before accepting I need to give him exactly what I want in return. Honesty.

"Everything I have is mine. Everything I've earned, I've earned myself. I'm who I am now because I wanted this, and

I did whatever I had to, to get here. It's not because I'm a Van Rensburg."

I don't ask if he knows the enormity of the impact the name has on my life. I assume from the pretentious vibe mother has brought into his home, along with Henrik and Will decked out in their suits upon arrival, that he's beginning to put it all together.

Ryan watches me carefully. I know he won't say sorry, like he knows I won't say the same back to him. We've each had our own bad experiences. And in our own way, through this weird navigation of a messed-up situation, are showing our empathy in the ways that matter. By learning to understand one another.

I also predict that one of the truths he thinks I'm going to ask for is something related to his allergy. But for the first time since I found out, it's the last thing I want to know. Maybe it's the moment. Us working together to create a new beat. But suddenly, I want to try to figure out what we are, without it looming over us. I want to show him that people can see past this huge part of his life and still appreciate who he is at his core.

"What do you need from me?"

"You," he replies. "That's it."

A couple of seconds of silence pass.

"What does that mean?"

I expect the moment to flip. The highest of highs followed by the lowest of lows.

It doesn't though.

"Right now," he starts to explain. "It means whatever you want it to. Tell me what *you* need."

His tongue darts out, and he wets his lips. Mine burn with the urge to lean over and kiss him. The memory of his panic attack the last time the K-word was mentioned stops me.

One day, those lips will be mine, and I promise when it's the right time, every bad memory, whatever they are, will be erased.

The thought hits me out of nowhere, bringing me out of the moment, slamming me back down to earth with a painful thud.

"You," I say, ignoring all the doubts and toxic thoughts threating to ruin one of the strongest connections I've let myself have with anyone. "I need you."

"Lean back," he says.

I tense. Process.

"Where?"

"Rest your arms against the drums."

"What if I break them?"

"I don't give a fuck about the drums, Sooz."

"Ry …"

Ryan smirks. "Fine. I'll get some more."

"Get?" I quip. "Not buy?"

Ryan's hands trail up my legs. His palms settle on my knees. He parts them, and cool air moves beneath the towel. I feel more exposed than I ever have in my life.

"We're talking about the logistics of how I get my drum kits right now?"

His eyes drop momentarily between my legs. His irises disappear.

I decide to play him at his own game.

"And what else should we be doing?"

"There are a lot of things I want to do right now and none of them involve talking." My insides somersault. "*Lean back.*"

"Bossy," I huff. Ryan grins. "Should we be doing this?"

His smile falters. "Probably not."

"Why?"

I need a truth I don't think has anything to do with Warped Record's policies.

"Because I don't think I can give you what you really need."

"And what do you *think* I need?"

"It's not that." He scowls, then mutters, "It's about what you deserve."

"And what do I deserve?"

"Everything."

Our eyes remain locked. I go to open my mouth, to tell him to stop overthinking this all. Ironic, coming from the chronic overthinker. I want to tell him to do whatever the glint in his eyes is suggesting he wants to. But I don't get a chance, because there's a loud, distant creak, and then the squeak of hinges.

Before I can clamp my legs together and retain what little modesty I have left, something cold and hard drops high, between my thighs. It slots perfectly where it shouldn't. Becoming coated in the evidence of exactly how much I don't want this interruption.

"No returns," Ryan says smugly as he stands.

Zach's voice drifts up the stairs. "Yo, Ryan. You up there?"

Damn him.

"Yeah. I'm up here. Just teaching Sooz a few things," Ryan replies.

His feet thud as he moves away. When I look down, I find the phone I now have no choice but to accept.

A gesture confirming what I already know.

That all along, everything I've thought about Ryan Alvarez is wrong.

245

Chapter Twenty-One

"How are things going?" Abby asks.

I'm finishing up with work for the night. Well, temporarily. I've been hiding away all day and the hunger pangs have become unbearable. Not daring to go down and face Mother or Ryan. Each hour that's passed, I've told myself I'll give it one more, then act like an adult and face the music. One song I'm becoming appreciative of, the other, not so much.

The clock sitting on Ryan's nightstand changes to nine PM.

"Fine," I reply.

Clara giggles in the background and I hear Jake talking, trying to coax her to go to bed. Bedtime is a sore subject, but one I'd happily embrace over of what's potentially sitting downstairs waiting for me.

"Really?" Abby's skepticism pours down the line.

I glance around Ryan's room, avoiding the drum kit in the corner.

"My mother's here."

Abby chokes. "Sorry, what?"

"And Will." She coughs. "And Henrik."

There's a clatter, and I hear Clara shout, "Oh no. Phone!"

"What?" Abby hisses when she's picked it back up. There's rustling, then the sound of a door closing. "Why are they here?"

"I think this is Mother's version of an olive branch?" I say, perching on the end of the bed. The line goes quiet. "You there?"

"Yep."

"Why are you being quiet?" She remains silent. "What's wrong?"

"This is my fault," Abby admits. "Henrik messaged, asking where you were staying, and I gave him the address. I'm sorry. I thought he wanted to send you a present or something."

"It's fine," I reply, making a mental note to pull Henrik up for being sly. Abby is back to being quiet. "What are you thinking?"

"That in all the time I've known you, your mother's never made a gesture. Never mind one as big as this."

"I know, right?" Abby hums like she has more to say. "Yes?"

"Maybe she really does want to make up for the past."

"It will take more than a trip to Brooklyn. A vacation isn't exactly a hardship."

"This is your mother we're talking about." Abby laughs. "Stuck in a house with two rock stars. At Christmas."

"True," I muse, then focus on the last detail of what she said. "I didn't get a chance to get you a present. I'm sorry."

247

"You mean you've done what you always do. Avoided thinking about Christmas until the last minute. Ryan's *situation* has screwed you over, because you can't do your usual Christmas Eve scramble." I remain silent. "Do you even know what day it is?"

"Erm."

For someone who prides themself on being in control and organized, things tend to fall apart each year, usually around this point.

"You can't stick your head in the sand every year."

"Coming from the avoidance queen."

Abby tsks. "And I'm working on it. You should too. Take it from someone who knows. No good comes from holding onto the past. We can't change what's happened. But we can learn from it."

"Well, the lesson I've learned is that I'm better focusing on myself and my career."

"This could be a chance for you to work on your relationship with your mother. It's not like you have anything better to do."

"For that to happen, she'd have to talk to me like a human instead of belittling everything I do."

"Give her time," Abby says. "She might come round."

"Listen to you, being the levelheaded one."

"Regular orgasms will do that to a person."

I grimace. "And I'm hanging up. As happy as I am for you and Jake, I don't need the details."

Abby laughs. "Call if you need me. Or if you need a break for your sanity." Her laugh gets louder. "Trapped with your mother *and* Ryan under one roof. You can't make it up."

Rolling my lips, I keep to myself that being stuck with Ryan is becoming far from a hardship.

248

"Before I go," I say, changing the subject. "Is there anything you need me to do for the New Year's ball?"

The ball I've barely had a chance to do anything for apart from a few last-minute admin jobs today. I feel riddled with guilt that the team has had to do all the legwork, considering the idea was mine. Meanwhile, I'm here, doing things I shouldn't be, with the person I'm supposed to be 'babysitting'.

"Nope. You tied up all the loose ends earlier. The rest we've got covered."

"I feel bad," I admit.

"Oh, please," says Abby. "We've been fine. You did all the hard work. We've just made sure everything's slotted into place. Anyway, I better go. Get some rest. I'll speak to you tomorrow."

We both hang up. I go to do exactly as Abby said, and go to sleep, when my phone starts ringing again. I groan, tempted to ignore it, until I read John West's name. Panic sets in. I hadn't thought of calling him. Too busy messing around with his rogue drummer.

I answer before the call rings off.

When John speaks, I realize my worrying is for nothing because I'm greeted by his cheery voice.

"Sooz!"

"I'm so sorry," I blurt, pacing back and forth with the phone Ryan bought plastered to my cheek.

"For what?"

"Dropping off the face of the Earth."

"It's been a day," John chortles. "Want to know a secret?"

"Sure?" I reply, hesitantly.

"I've enjoyed having a reason to stay home."

"I'll make sure to pass the feedback on to Ryan."

My cheeks flush from saying his name in a work conversation. There's a reason boundaries are set in place for work-related relationships. They result in this. I curse, then start to berate myself for referring to whatever this morning was as a relationship. I'm spiraling, and I don't know how to stop.

"Anyway," says John, breaking me from my train of thoughts. "The reason I've called is that with you both being holed up together and the press blocking entry to the house, I thought it would be a good opportunity for you to do some work on the social media side of things like we mentioned. The board can't say no, because our team can't get down the street, and the offices close the day after tomorrow for Christmas Eve."

Christmas is that soon? When did that happen?

"I'll see what I can do," I manage to get out.

"Great! There's not much else we can do apart from wait out the storm. Have a great Christmas!"

"You too," I reply before hanging up, wishing some of his chipper mood could travel down the line and replace the impending sense of doom I'm starting to feel.

Perching on the end of the bed, I let out a long exhale at the same time my stomach rumbles. I'm starving thanks to being voluntarily stuck up here all day. There's no way I can make it through the night without food.

I tell myself to suck it up and go downstairs.

Considering how many people are in the house, and the fact it isn't late, I'm surprised to find the kitchen dark and empty.

Wanting to keep it that way, I opt for trying to find the most filling thing I can, that will make the least noise when preparing it. The refrigerator comes up trumps, filled with fresh produce, all of which would involve some sort of prep work and cooking to become anything substantial. Totally not worth the risk of drawing my mother back down.

After desperately rummaging through the freezer, I find a plastic bag filled with slabs of cake and do a little dance. They're going to be dairy free, but the fact I could eat my own arm means I'm not picky.

Because I don't have the patience to wait and let it thaw on its own, I shove the biggest slab on a plate and then into the microwave oven. Two minutes later, the kitchen-diner is filled with the smell of warm, chocolatey goodness. I salivate as I take it back out. Half a brownie in, the sugar starts to flow through my bloodstream. High off glucose and somewhat satisfied, I start to move around the kitchen, needing something to do.

The green fir tree—still bare—catches my attention, and I walk over to it. The box of decorations Ryan brought through last night is tucked away beneath it.

"I don't like you," I mutter at it with my hands planted on my hips. The tree does nothing back, which I find irritating. I feel the need to inform it of the fact. "I *really* don't like you," I say, louder this time.

"Hating on trees now?" comes a voice deeper and huskier than ever before.

The sound spreads warmth through my insides, then turns into an odd tickle. I fight the urge to giggle.

"It's being offensive."

My reasoning was sounder in my head.

When I turn and face Ryan, he's standing by the dining table, watching me with an amused expression.

"All that standing and being dead it's doing," he says. "The horror."

251

"Stop acting like a buttock or I'll go back to hating on you, too."

I return to staring at my evergreen nemesis.

"You know," Ryan says, walking over.

I stare at the needles and try not to think how my body is threatening to go haywire with the need to jump and ride him to the universe of orgasmic bliss.

"There could be some learning here," he continues.

"Enlighten me," I say, without looking his way.

"You hated me, and look where we are now. Maybe you need to spend more time with the tree. Get to know it. Bond."

"Bond? With a tree?"

Still refusing to look his way, I feel his eyes on me. He's grinning if the light tone to his voice is anything to go by.

"Yeah. Why not?"

"And how does one bond with foliage?"

"You're the one hating on it." Ryan shrugs. "You tell me."

I frown, then my eyes drop to the box beneath it. Maybe he's right? Maybe I need to bond. Move on from the past and create my own memories. Better ones that might make this time of year feel a little less depressing.

"Want to decorate it?" I ask, turning to face him.

I wish I hadn't, because the beam that takes over his face threatens to split my heart apart with how it makes it swell.

"I thought you'd never ask," he replies, crouching and pulling the box out.

He lifts the lid away, revealing a collection of decorations that looks older than the both of us.

"Oh my God." I crouch beside him and start to rifle through the contents of the box. "These are so kitsch."

"They were my grandma's." Ryan laughs. "I'm gonna try not to be insulted there."

I want to disappear, but because that's never going to happen, I decide to roll with my error.

"Kitsch is the new high end."

"Bullshit."

Ryan's chuckle turns into what can only be described as a belly chortle. I giggle with him. A giggle that lasts longer than I expect it to and continues when I find more of the tackiest decorations I've ever seen.

When I manage to stop and catch my breath, I remember I haven't finished my snack.

"You get started," I instruct him. "I won't be long."

He doesn't question what I'm doing, already busy pulling out the decorations and lining them up on the ground. I watch him wrap the tiny, warm white LED lights around the tree while I eat. I take my time, appreciating the bending and flexing show.

"They look like stars against the night sky," I comment, walking back over when I've finished.

"How poetic of you," Ryan says, then slides the first decoration onto one of the branches.

My nostrils flare as I struggle to contain my laughter. It's an elf-pixie-I-don't-know-what-the-hell-it-is. Kitsch taken to a whole other level. The pointed hat is a vivid blue. The left arm is missing along with the tip of its nose. And the mouth. I can't figure out if it's supposed to look like it's grinning or growling.

"Mind if I make a suggestion?" I say, attempting to flutter my lashes.

The movement is lazy and slow. My eyes feel like they're going to roll into the back of my head.

"Why do I feel like this is you prepping me for something I'm not going to like hearing?"

Because the lash fluttering isn't working, I swap for making my voice sweeter than the brownie I've consumed.

"Maybe move that one somewhere that isn't central."

"It's my favorite," Ryan says.

"It's terrifying." Ryan huffs, and I shrug. "You can explain to Jake why Clara's sleeping less than usual from the nightmares *that* has caused."

"It's an elf."

"It might have been once." I inspect it. It's creepier up close. "It's like a miniature festive *Chuckie*." I draw back with a shudder. "*I'm* going to have nightmares."

"It was also my grandma's favorite."

The 'was' in his phrasing has me feeling like the ultimate beyatch.

"I'm sorry," I say, preparing to backtrack. "Front and center it is."

"You don't have to be sorry for being honest."

Ryan scrubs at his jaw, which has considerably more covering than it did this morning.

Why can't I stop focusing on everything he does? If Zoe were here, she'd give it to me straight. Tell me it's an after effect of almost coming over someone's fingers. Emotional attachment through orgasms and pleasure. Because it can't be anything more than that. Right?

My question turns into my answer as I continue to roll with my inner monologue.

Of course, it's something more. I can't keep pretending to myself for much longer that it isn't. Not when we've been forced together like this. Because of the images. Images I was

254

appalled at, that now make me feel a stab of jealousy whenever they cross my mind.

The thing about proximity, when it's forced, is that there's no reprieve. There's a ton of moments. One relentless one after another. Where emotions are intensified, leaving you questioning how you got from A to B in the blink of an eye.

Which is where we're at.

Me, anything but hating the person I thought I did. Not having a clue how we got to this point, despite Ryan having the subtlety of a dumpster truck.

"Please don't be nice to me when I don't deserve it," I say, bending and picking up the next most grotesque decoration out of the selection.

"We all have flaws, Sooz. You're not immune."

I give Ryan a sideways glance, tempted to snipe back, because it's what feels familiar and right. Instead, I hang the next decoration close to the other. Ryan follows suit, picking out another.

The next twenty minutes are filled with decorating. Enough to give the tree the kitschiest of vibes.

"Weirdly, it looks good," I giggle.

Grotesque elf number one looks like he's waving at me. I giggle again. Because I like the feel of it, I keep going.

"Everything okay?" Ryan asks.

I've giggled for a minute solid and I'm showing no signs of stopping.

"Wonderbra!"

His brows shoot up. They look soft, and I want to stroke them. My hand gets the memo before my brain makes the decision. The tips of my fingers are skimming over them before I register what I'm doing.

"Sooz …"

"Yes?"

I continue moving my fingers in the same back-and-forth pattern.

"Please stop stroking me."

"But you feel so good."

His fingers wrap around my wrist, stopping me from moving.

"I'd be all for you telling me that if we were in another situation."

"What's wrong?" I hum, feeling hazy and not getting what the issue is.

"You're playing with my eyebrows."

"And?" I say, happily.

Ryan looks torn, like he doesn't want to ruin my moment. "It's kinda weird."

"You're weird." I go to poke him in the chest, forgetting my wrist is still locked in his grip. "You silly sausage, you."

I'd shoulder bump him if I didn't feel like I could fall over.

"Why are you looking at me like that?"

Ryan scrutinizes every inch of me. His gaze lingers on my mouth.

"Are you going to K-I-S-S me?"

"No." He lifts the hand that isn't playing the role of a vice. "You've got something …"

His fingers reach out and rub at the corner of my mouth. I lean into his touch for a brief moment. One that doesn't last long enough. In the next second, he's pulling his hand back and staring at the dark smear on the pad of his thumb.

"Sooz, what did you eat?"

"Chocolate brownie." I grin.

Ryan groans. "Where from?"

"The freezer," I singsong, as if it's self-explanatory. "They were delicious. I need the recipe."

"Yeah, you don't want the recipe." Ryan laughs.

The sound doesn't match the apprehension in his eyes.

"Why? What's wrong with them? Are they like space cakes or something?" Ryan doesn't answer, and it's my turn to groan. "There's no need for the 'or something', is there?"

He shakes his head, and I giggle.

Under normal circumstances, I'd be declaring things can't get any worse.

But with my rational side floating somewhere above me, dancing with my aura, I declare repeatedly to Ryan that things can't get any better.

Chapter Twenty-Two

The bed looks like a giant cloud, calling for me to jump on it and absorb its comfort. So, I do. After a run, then a leap, I soar through the air. I'm a bird, not a plane.

My arms extend above my head, making me more streamlined than an Olympic gold medalist diver.

The land is better than I anticipate, and I sink deep into the mattress. Forget cloud. It's like Jell-O, rippling around me. I keep sinking until the mattress pulls taut, then I'm thrown back into the air.

I hit the ground with a thud and an "oof" flies out of me. I don't feel a thing, but a little voice tells me that might change in the morning.

"What the fuck?"

Feet race up the stairs. The ceiling looks interesting, so I remain flat on my back, staring at it. Ryan's hair creeps into my vision. Then he's there, all of him, staring down at me with his hands on his hips, the gray material of his Henley stretched around his biceps. My mouth waters.

"I left you alone for two minutes."

"Sowweee."

He pulls his phone out and groans, then pockets it and drags a hand through his hair.

"Trust you to nail a whole space cake when you've never properly tried drugs before."

"Who said I've never taken drugs?" Ryan gives me a blank look and I pout. "I thought marijuana was *medicinal*?"

"It is." He holds out his hand to help me up. "But not in the quantity you've had it. You're off your face."

"High as a kite." I beam and take his hand. "Flying through the sky."

"From what I heard, there wasn't much flying."

I stick my tongue out, and he pulls me up, shaking his head. We're standing close enough that I notice he has a dimple. More like a half one. On his left side. Actually, that's my left. His right. God, it's true. I'm gone. Too gone to care I'm gone. Too gone to care about the consequences when I lean forward a little bit more, reach up, and stroke it.

Ryan looks down his nose with the same amused look he's been giving me since we met in front of the tree. The dimple deepens. He's trying not to smile. My eyes roam his face, then settle on his eyes. They're fascinating. I stand on the tips of my toes to inspect. It's like staring at a meadow filled with buttercups.

"Your eyes have bits of yellow in them. You're like a cat." I frown and my brain detours to the flaw in my comment. "Apart from the whole milk thing." Ryan's laughter fills the room. Even in my state, I can't mistake the way my heart skips a beat at the sound. "I like it when you laugh like that."

259

Something in his eyes changes. I try to lean in closer. His hands find my shoulders, holding me in place.

"What are you doing, Sooz?"

The yellow flecks move, and the green darkens. His irises shrink, replaced by his pupils.

"The yellow's moving," I reply. "I want to see."

Ryan's grip tightens, making it impossible for me to move. He takes a step back.

"I'm not doing this when you're high."

I blink, oblivious to what the problem is.

"Always coming up with excuses." I yawn. "I'm tired."

"I bet. I would be too if I'd talked for two hours continuously."

With my creeper tendencies back in their box, he drops his hands to his sides, and his eyes return to a more familiar shade.

"Wow. That's a long time."

"I know." He smirks. "I could have done without the in-depth analysis of each member of the Kardashian family. Forty-five minutes of my life I won't get back."

"You'd do it again in a heartbeat."

The air is sucked from the room when his gaze drops to my lips. It darts back up so quick I convince myself it's the weed making me see things.

"Yeah, I would." He fills his pause with a smile that warms my insides. "I get that you're career driven, but what's one thing you wish you could do?"

The question catches me off guard. "I don't understand."

Ryan shoves his hands into his pockets with a half kind of shrug. "I guess what I'm trying to ask is, that when work isn't there, what do you wish you had? What do you feel like you're missing out on?"

"I want to be swept off my feet," I answer. My mind wanders to happy places that feel impossible to get to. "Whisked to somewhere that steals my breath away."

"Where would you want to be whisked away to?"

"New Orleans." I frown, remembering we've already been there. "Again."

"That's very specific." Ryan laughs.

"I love the *Princess and the Frog.*"

"Isn't that a book?"

"It's also a Disney movie," I explain, letting out a dreamy sight. "And it's schaaaamazing."

Maybe the weed's made me become super in-tune to everything Ryan does, because I think I hear him swallow.

"Was New Orleans what you wanted it to be?"

My eyes snap up, becoming less lazy, more focused. "It had its moments." Then, because it feels like we're breaking down each other's walls, and nothing but the truth feels acceptable, I admit, "But there were parts that could have been better."

"I'm sorry I ruined it for you."

The torn expression he's wearing tells me he means it.

"I learned a long time ago not to pin all my hopes on fantasies."

Ryan reaches up to brush away a loose strand of hair that isn't there. His hand lingers, cupping my face. The warmth, combined with my inebriation, makes my resolve little to none. I lean into his touch, wanting more of everything. Whatever our everything is. Whatever we're becoming.

"Who dulled your sparkle?" he asks.

"The people who were supposed to help me shine."

We stand, staring at each other, until I find myself giving him more of my truths. Truths I've never told anyone, out of fear of being disappointed.

"I want the fairytale. I want to find my frog. Be challenged. Loved. Respected. I want to be kissed in the rain and know that there's the promise of a happily ever after sitting at the end of the rainbow."

This time, the sigh I let out is a wistful one, and I stare off to the side of the room.

When Ryan still doesn't say anything, I laugh awkwardly. "Am I setting my goals too high?"

"No." His eyes are filled with an intensity that makes it hard to breathe. "Not at all."

"Can we do this again?"

Ryan's brow pops. "Get high?"

"Maybe." I give him a mischievous smile, then sidestep him and walk toward the bed. "I meant hang out. Like friends."

Flopping back on the mattress, with less counter bounce, I return to staring at the ceiling. A minute goes by before I realize Ryan has gone quiet. I shift my weight up onto my forearms and take in his frown.

"What's wrong?"

Instead of answering, he walks over to the other side of the bed and starts to tug at the corner of the tightly fitted sheet.

"What are you doing?"

"Staying here," he replies. He's already under the sheets, lying back and getting himself comfy. "You've already tried to fly to the bed. I don't trust you not to attempt it out the window or some shit."

He closes his eyes and I clamber off the bed.

"You can't."

One of his eyes peeps open.

"Can't what?"

"Can't stay in here." *Because I can't guarantee what will happen if you do*, is the part I don't say out loud. "I promise I won't try to fly again. You're being dramatic."

"What's wrong? Scared you won't be able to keep your hands off me?"

"Don't worry." I glare at him. "That won't be an issue."

It's lies. Blatant lies. After this morning, we both know it.

"Then get into bed and go to sleep."

"Fine," I huff.

He closes his eyes again, but I refuse to move.

After standing and debating what to do, I figure he's going nowhere. Reluctantly, I draw back the covers, then find myself frozen on the spot once more.

"You can get changed," Ryan says, lids still shut. He's a mind reader. It's creepy. "I won't look. Promise."

"I bet you say that to all the girls."

Watching, I then search for the slightest facial movement that might suggest he's going to open his eyes so he can catch me half naked. There isn't a single twitch until maybe a minute has gone by. But the movement isn't around his eyes, it's around his mouth, which breaks into a sleepy smile.

"I don't know what the issue is. I saw your pussy this morning."

My cheeks set on fire.

"And I'd have done more than look at it if it weren't for Zach."

I shift uncomfortably at the memory of the interruption and the happy ending I never received.

"Stop watching me like a creeper and get dressed. I swear, I'm not going to look."

"Okay," I say, giving in.

He might not have his eyes open, but when my camisole passes over my head, I feel as exposed as I did this morning. My hands tremble when I pull on my nightshirt. I tumble when I'm pulling off my lounge pants, and stumble when I replace them with sleep shorts.

After climbing into bed, I turn off the lamp sitting on the nightstand.

"Hey, Ry," I say after a while, my voice thick with sleep.

"Yeah?"

"Thanks for looking after me."

"No problem. Apart from the Kardashians, high Sooz has been the highlight of my week."

I've thought something like weed makes you sleep better. It's deceptive, like it's good old friend alcohol. All I can do is toss and turn. Throwing the sheets off when I get too hot, then scrambling in the darkness to find them when I get too cold.

When sleep does come, it brings with it trippy dreams.

Dreams where I'm strapped in a chair and forced to drink a pint of full fat cream. Dreams where I'm stuck in a field of milk cows with no way out.

In each dream, Ryan is standing in the distance. It doesn't matter how hard I try. I can't help.

There's a particularly nasty one where Ryan is swimming beneath me in a sea of milk, gasping for breath. I jump off the cliff and my limbs flail, but I never get to the sea, or him. I land on the cold, hard floor with a bang.

Still stuck in a dream-like state, I let out a delirious whimper.

"Sooz!"

I whimper again when Ryan disappears in the white liquid, and then he's gone forever. I start to tremble with grief.

"Sooz!"

Forget tremble. I'm shaking uncontrollably.

No. Wait. I'm being shaken.

My eyes fly open, and I find Ryan crouched over me.

"You're alive?" I whisper.

His concern is swapped with relief. He moves back onto his haunches and smirks.

"Disappointed?"

If he's expecting some kind of smart reply, it isn't what he gets.

I lunge forward, wrapping my arms around his neck and my legs around his middle. I'm like a koala wrapped around a tree trunk as I bury my face in the crook of his neck and try to control my breathing. It remains ragged as I fail to keep control of my emotions. Ryan's skin grows wet with hot, salty tears. I've no idea where they come from.

"It's okay," he says quietly in the darkness.

One large hand is splayed at the small of my back, covering it. The other moves up and down. His fingers skim over the soft material of my shirt, lulling me into a sense of peace until the tears dry up. Why am I crying? If I weren't still trying to rid my brain of the memories of my dream, I'd be embarrassed. I never let anyone see me like this. Ever.

Ryan continues the soothing motion. If somebody said we could stay like this forever, my answer would be 'yes please', happily. My mouth parts and I let out a soft moan of ecstasy as I shift my hips, wanting him closer. I might as well have struck a match, because the movement lights something inside me. A familiar ache starts between my legs. An ache I know can only be satisfied in one way. An ache that leads to one conclusion. A conclusion I want to reach as I circle my hips again, desperate for friction.

Ryan's hand stops moving. In the silence of the room, I hear his pulse quicken.

"Don't."

The lack of conviction in his voice and his erection pressing hard against me leads to the opposite.

I roll my hips. Once. Twice. Circle. Then lift.

When I lower back down, Ryan's erection probes my center. I lift my hips again and drop my chin, finding in the dim light filtering up the stairs from the hallway, the outline of how much he wants me tenting his sweatpants. Fire courses through my veins when I realize he's not wearing anything beneath them.

Three thin layers of material sit between us when I lower my hips again. His head presses into me and a gasp fills the room. I don't know if the sound comes from him or me.

I lean back and watch when his tongue darts out, and he wets his lips. Heat pools in my core.

One break from reality. One pause in concentration. One lapse in judgment that we both need.

That's all it takes for his hand to press at the base of my spine. He pulls me against him. I hold on tight when he rolls back onto his feet and lifts us both from the ground. I cling on for dear life. He's my anchor, stopping me from floating away, as my heart hammers in a beat I didn't know was possible.

Only when he lowers me back down on his mattress, do I let go. It's temporary though, because my hands move higher. My fingers trail through the soft tendrils of hair at the base of his skull. Up and up. Finding thicker, coarser hair. Hair that I fist as I drag him down toward me, with one target in mind.

Lips filled with promises.

My eyes flicker shut in anticipation. Waiting.

Waiting for a kiss I have a feeling will be the kind I never forget.

But the kiss never comes.

Ryan plasters his body over mine. Presses me into the mattress with the heavy weight of him as he buries his face in my hair. His next words are the worst kind of torture, ripping away what we both want. "I can't give you what you need. I don't know how to do any of this."

"I don't care," I reply.

I should.

The evidence of why is sitting in a brown envelope in my bag at the side of the room. But the time we've spent together, and the Ryan I've gotten to know, has me believing that whatever I think I've seen, the conclusions I've come to, are far from the truth.

Ryan shakes his head and rises. He lifts his upper body, then, hovering over me, stares down. His eyes scour my face. Searching for an uncertainty he won't find. His hips remain centered between my thighs. His erection presses into where I'm aching to feel him.

Out of the corner of my eye, I watch, waiting for his arms to tremble holding his weight. They remain still. Solid at each side of my head. Pillars that I want to crush and destroy every past failing that's embedded itself and warped my perception of what love means. He's working his way under my skin. Burying himself into my foundations. Foundations I want to rebuild with him at my side. New ones that provide a solidarity and a future I never could have imagined wanting.

"We can't do this until we've talked."

"Why?"

"So that you can decide if this is what you really want."

"I want this."

I stretch up to kiss him, but he pulls away. His biceps look like they might snap from the strain. My gut tells me not to push him to fall, so I drop my head back, landing against the pillow with a soft thud.

"But I need you to know it all. I need you to see the parts of me I've never let anyone else see."

My eyes trail lower, and he lets out a throaty chuckle. I feel the rumble everywhere, including between my legs. My thighs clench around him and he drops to his elbows.

His forehead lowers and presses against mine. His lips are so close. So tempting. But he still doesn't close the gap.

"Baby, you're killing me."

I lift my hips and moan.

"I'm trying to do the right thing here," he says.

"Right is overrated," I reply.

Testing the waters, I lift my head so my lips are close to his ear.

"So is being good."

My right-hand skims across his stomach. His abs tense as he inhales.

"I've been good for years. Always done everything right."

Ryan exhales when my fingers dip beneath the band of his sweatpants.

"I want to do something wrong."

When he doesn't protest, I wrap my hand around him, then stroke. Up and down. Slowly. My thumb moves over his tip. Slides the evidence of exactly how much he really wants this down the full length of him. I keep the rhythm going as my hand continues to slide over hot, silken skin.

"Sooz, you have to stop or I'm going to come." There's an edge to his voice. It's a warning more than a demand.

I keep stroking and give him the simplest reply. "Then come on me."

Ryan groans and falls to the side, but he still doesn't stop me. With my free hand, I shift my shirt, so it's rolled up and sitting beneath my breasts, leaving the rest of my torso exposed. His hand moves over my stomach, then, hesitantly, moves lower. I wiggle in anticipation when his fingers hit the band of elastic wrapped around my hips.

His voice cracks. "Can I?"

"Stop being polite. You didn't ask this morning."

I throw my head back when his hand disappears beneath my shorts and two fingers rub over my underwear. Moan when they lift away and go back to playing with more elastic. I curse myself for wearing too many layers, making a mental note to never do it again.

"I've wanted to do this for years," Ryan admits, still toying.

"Then why didn't you?" I ask breathily.

The elastic lifts and his fingers skim beneath.

"We haven't exactly been on the same page."

His fingers crawl down. Dangerously close to where I think I might combust.

"I was waiting for you to need it as much as I did."

He makes contact with my clit, and I barely hold in a gasp.

"Do you need this?"

When I moan "yes", he circles the tight bundle of nerves, ending with a pinch that makes me see stars. Both of our hands move faster, setting an unbearable pace. Back arching off the mattress, my moans fill the room as my thighs start to shake. My hand jolts up and down over Ryan in frenzied movements.

Right before I fall apart, warm liquid spills over my midriff.

Then Ryan rasps out two words that undo me.

"Me too."

Chapter Twenty-Three

"**S**ooz."

I groan when whoever is calling distracts me from pouring milk into my glass. It spills over the countertop, spreading fast, right to the edge, threatening to start dripping on the floor.

"Sooz."

I turn and search for the cloth I set down. It doesn't matter how many times I keep turning, or how hard I search. I can't find it.

"Sooz."

The voice is louder this time. I wish they'd be quiet. I need to clean up the mess before one of the guys comes down. There's milk everywhere and I still can't find a cloth. Exasperated, I do the only thing I can think of. I begin scooping it along the countertop with my hands in the direction of the sink.

"Sooz!"

When I look up from what I'm doing, I find Ryan standing in front of me. I take a step forward with my hands outstretched. Milk drips from them, creating a pat, pat, pat sound in the silent room. It hits me how silent, as I watch Ryan. He keeps opening and closing his mouth, but no sound comes out. He starts to go purple. I feel it all, everything he's feeling, as my own breath is stolen from me. I don't know how to help as he stumbles forward. His large hands grab my shoulders, and he begins shaking me.

A silent, desperate plea.

I frantically turn my head from side to side, searching for something. Anything. That's when my eyes settle on her. The woman from the images. She's standing, arms folded across her barely covered chest, wearing a smug look on her make-up smeared face.

"If I can't kiss him, no one can."

"Sooz! Wake up!"

My eyes fly open, and I gasp. Henrik's grip on my shoulders lessens, but the concern written all over his face doesn't.

"Are you okay?"

I sit up and give him a tight smile.

"Bad dream." My answer comes out strangled.

Like I felt. Like Ryan looked. Ryan who isn't here.

It hits me who exactly woke me from my second round of horrific dreams.

Henrik.

After last night, Ryan left.

My lips pinch together at my first experience of what mother must have gone through when Dad walked out. For the first time since that day, I empathize with her and maybe understand, a little, why she is the way she is. Closed off from everything and everyone. I knew love had the potential to make a person feel that way, but now … I've barely had a

272

taste of what Ryan and I could be together, and already I'm gutted.

Everything is too much. Too intense.

The situation isn't helped with my head pounding thanks to my accidental marijuana indulgence. I fall back dramatically, landing on the pillows with a huff.

Henrik watches me. A knowing glint in his eye.

"So, you're shacking up with the drummer?"

"No," I reply.

The refusal of anything that associates the two of us together is a bad habit. The mind-blowing orgasm, fueled by soft whispers, and more emotions than I've ever felt with any other guy, has me correcting my answer. I don't want to devalue what the two of us shared, regardless of the fact Ryan was gone by the morning.

"Yes. Kind of."

Henrik grins. "You dirty bitch. Tell me all the details."

"There aren't many to tell."

Apart from me literally getting dirty. Something I've never done, having been a fan of all things vanilla in the bedroom up until now. There's no way I'm giving Henrik any details, though. He won't be able to keep his mouth shut, and this is a big enough farce as it is.

"The flush to your cheeks says otherwise. He's a headboard rattler, isn't he?"

Getting excited at the potential of sex gossip, he talks too fast for me to keep up.

"What?"

Henrik jumps to his feet and starts thrusting his hips forward. He throws a spanking motion in.

"I bet he taps as hard as he hammers those drums."

"I wouldn't know."

"Yet." He winks. "Limber up, Soozy. You're going to find out exactly why sex is better than work."

I feel nauseous.

"The fact you're married to my brother makes this conversation all kinds of inappropriate. Please stop."

Henrik laughs and, thankfully, stops thrusting and swiping his hand through the air.

"What are you doing up here, anyway?" It's then that I take in what he's wearing. "Is that loungewear?"

Henrik wiggles his brows. "I'm hunkering down like a mountain man."

He couldn't look further from a mountain man if he tried, given he's wearing a maroon velour onesie that clashes with his amber-colored eyes.

"Why?"

"We're in isolation. I'm embracing it. Getting into character."

"We're not in isolation," I tell him.

"Then why are we stuck in here?"

"We're hiding out from the press."

"Same thing." He shrugs, twisting and taking in Ryan's room.

Doing so reveals another side to his onesie that has me laughing so hard my brain feels like it's rattling against my skull.

"Are those …"

"Ears. Yes," he replies, referring to the two flaps stitched to the hood as he turns back to face me. "It was the only style with the color I liked." The humor of the moment disappears, and his expression becomes serious again. "You sure you're good? You had me worried there."

I smile like I don't have a care in the world. "I'm good."

"We've barely seen you since we got here."

He keeps watching me, searching for a crack to my façade that only he or Will can find. One of the joys of knowing someone for a lifetime: no privacy.

"You've been busy blowing things up," I say, distracting him from the direction I think he's trying to take.

He grins and takes the bait. "It was a good game. I forgot how much fun it was having time off work."

"I wouldn't know."

I give him a tight smile and we both go quiet. I pull the bedsheets up around me. They provide a sense of much needed comfort while my skin remains clammy. My nauseousness increases after the dream.

"How's Mother?"

"Pissed and waiting for you downstairs in the kitchen."

"Ah." My stomach rumbles with comedy timing. Food is the last thing I want, especially knowing who I'll have to face to get it. "The truth comes out why you're really up here."

Henrik pouts. "I would have come up, eventually."

"Sure, you would." The bed shifts when he stands. "Where are you going?"

"Downstairs, where you will be going, too."

I scowl, but when I shake my head too quick with a 'no' and there become two of Henrik, I accept that I have to face the music, which is confirmed by Henrik's next words.

"She made the effort to come here finally. Now, you can make the effort to come down. You can't avoid her forever."

"I can try," I call after him when he heads toward the stairs, although I have no intention of staying in bed.

"Like ripping off a bandaid," he calls back. "I endured a transatlantic flight. Brunch is the least you can do."

My phone vibrates, and I grab it, finding a string of messages in the Next Level group chat regarding a few details that need clearing up for the New Year's Ball—now a little over a week away. It's another thing fueling my anxiety, but I lock my phone, deciding I'll reply when I'm done.

For now, all I can think is how I'm going to survive a day with my mother.

"Well, well, well," says Will when I appear at the kitchen door, alerting Mother to my presence. She appears to be content reading a book at the dining table.

She looks up, scans my pajama choice for the day, sniffs, then looks back down at her book without a word. Today, she's wearing a black skirt suit. She looks like she's in mourning. Likely the loss of her sanity from being trapped here with three people who she would never usually allow herself to be seen with, her daughter included.

Henrik sits beside her, still in his onesie, reading something on his phone. It's miraculous how he manages to read without moving his eyes.

'I hate you,' I mouth at Will as I approach him. A cocky sibling smirk is returned. When I get to his side, he wraps an arm around my shoulder and pulls me in.

"Play nice," he says into my hair.

I turn my face into him and lower my voice. "I will if she does."

"The two of you are ridiculous," he says.

I feel him shaking his head, but he pulls me against him tighter. It feels nice. I can't remember the last time we were together like this. Where there wasn't a career motive and at least fifty people watching. It feels like I'm standing hugging my brother, the person I shared a womb with, rather than the man on a fast track to become one of the most successful senior partners in the Cape legal field.

"You and Henrik brought her. And she's the one who makes things this way," I grumble stubbornly, not caring how immature I sound. She brings out the best in me.

"*We*," Will replies, "Didn't bring her anywhere. *She* wanted to come."

"*She* is sitting right here." My mother looks up.

Caught out, Will and I both freeze. I try to muffle my laughter in the gray hooded jacket he's wearing over his white t-shirt.

"Oh, and here's one without a shirt again," Mother says.

Henrik's head snaps up and we all look towards the kitchen doorway where Zach stands, filling the space. He's standing super straight, like a meerkat, his eyes wide and expectant as he looks over at me. I give my head a slight shake, indicating I'm not going to share the news of Ryan's allergy over eggs.

Clearly, Ryan hasn't spoken to him about me knowing. Or the fact that he knows I know. Or that he doesn't care that I know.

Understanding, a relieved expression crosses Zach's face. He beams, scratches his bare chest, then waves his hands in the air dramatically at me, doing a weird zombie impression. "She's aaaalive."

I think he's referring to my absence yesterday, but I can't be sure.

Silence fills the room until Mother sighs and turns a page of her book. It's a knife being twisted in a socially awkward situation. The kitchen faucet drips, startling Zach.

I roll my eyes and move away from Will. Zach doesn't have to worry about me giving anything away. At the rate he's going, he'll do a fine job of it himself. His nervous energy is making me nervous. It's a bad idea to mix caffeine with my rising levels of anxiety, but because there's nothing better to do, I pour myself a cup from the half still left brewed in the pot.

"Eggs?" asks Zach, shuffling up beside me.

"Sure." I try for another reassuring smile, but it comes out tight.

"Anyone else?" Zach calls over his shoulder.

Mother doesn't answer, because she only eats between certain hours.

Will raises his hand. "Me, please."

"Me too," says Henrik. "Do you have any cheese? I'm craving dairy and there's literally none in this house."

Zach and I both freeze at the same time a throat clears from the back door.

"Nah, man," Ryan says, entering the room from outside, "you don't want any of that. It's bad for your cholesterol."

My pulse quickens, and I set my cup back down. I don't know how Ryan keeps something like this a secret and pretends as if it's nothing. Zach finds it a struggle, judging by the way he's twitching at my side. As for me, I'm not sure how I'm supposed to get through another couple of days of this. I'm ready to crack faster than the egg in Zach's hand.

There's a rustle of paper as Mother turns another page.

To distract myself from the dairy elephant in the room, I twist and face Ryan properly for the first time since last night. He's wearing a hooded black leather racer jacket over a white shirt, decorated with an abundance of skulls. I never took myself as a death-vibe lover, but the combination makes my

278

panties wet. He looks gorgeous with his ruffled hair and a pair of black sweatpants that sit low on his hips. I feel a little faint. Right up until it hits me, he's coming in from being out. He left me without an explanation. And now here he is. Looking like *that*, when I feel like *this*. Dejected.

"I'll have eggs," Ryan says to Zach.

His eyes meet mine, and his brows pull together.

"So, really, no cheese?" asks Henrik.

"No cheese," Ryan confirms, diverting his attention away from me.

He grabs a frying pan out of one of the units and hands it over to Zach. There's a huge tray of eggs waiting to be scrambled, but my appetite's disappeared. I'm stuck overanalyzing everything that happened last night.

"Sooz?" Ryan is clicking his fingers and waving his hand in front of my face. "Earth to Sooz."

Zach jabs me in the side. I squeak, then jolt. Mother looks up from her book.

"Are you okay?" Ryan asks.

Dazed, I blink. I'm not sure what's wrong with me. I think it's my mother's presence, combined with keeping Ryan's allergy secret, that's freaking me out.

"Grand!" I say with a choked voice.

"You sure?" Ryan's eyes roam over my face. "You look a bit … weird."

"I'm fine!" I move toward the door to the hall. I need to leave. "Sorry," I say, when I come close to colliding with Ryan. "I have to go check something."

With a speed I didn't know I was capable of, I take the stairs two at a time, intent on dressing and getting out of the house.

Barreling through the first partially open door I come to, I find myself in Sam's room where Mother is sleeping. I'm over by the window when I try to inhale. It comes out more like a gasp.

The window. I need to open it. I need air. Fresh. There's nothing a good old dose of O_2 can't fix.

Unless you're going into anaphylactic shock.

With a strong chance of vomiting, I rest my forehead against the cool glass and close my eyes. It's not the best idea with the press camping outside. I hear a click that could be the shutter of a camera.

"Are you okay?"

I squeeze my eyes shut tighter. Maybe if I ignore Ryan, he'll disappear?

"Stop ignoring me."

So much for that plan. I count to five. My forehead makes a suction sound when I pull it away from the glass. There's an attractive grease mark left on the window. I really need to take a shower.

Ryan says my name and I realize I've zoned out again. I'm delirious with stress. Maybe it's tiredness. Tiredness caused by lack of sleep due to stress.

"Sooz." Ryan's voice comes out as more of an order. I turn and find him looking at me like I'm deranged. I don't disagree with his judgement. "What's wrong?"

"What's wrong?" My laughter fills the room. There's an edge of hysteria to it. "I woke up and you were gone." I look down briefly. "Was it *that* bad?"

Ryan groans. "Sooz, really?"

"What?" A bead of sweat forms above my lip.

"I'm not playing the miscommunication game." He chooses his next words carefully. "Last night, was one of the best nights of my life. I kind of thought that was obvious."

"Then where were you?"

"I had something I needed to do."

"Right …" I huff, making it obvious I'm unimpressed with his answer.

Ryan does little to hide that he's also annoyed. "Don't do this. Don't send us backwards."

"How can I not when you won't give me anything? Telling me that you need me and that you want me isn't enough. You have to prove it by letting me in. I'm here, trying to help you, and it still feels like you're keeping secrets."

A muscle in Ryan's jaw ticks. "Says the queen of openness."

There's a sneer to his tone that I don't like, but that's what you get when you poke the bear with a stick. After last night, I'm ready to bulldoze my way to the truth. I have to. The line of what I want and what I need and what Ryan wants and needs is becoming blurry. Trying to find a middle ground when everything is so messy is confusing, and it hurts. The kind of hurt that makes it impossible to keep your feelings to yourself. The kind of hurt that makes tempers flare and words turn cutting.

"I don't like how you're acting right now," I snap.

"Because you hate me. Yeah?" Ryan snaps back.

He looks away, his shoulders dropping. I shake my head. He's right. In minutes, we've gone so far backwards we're almost where we started. It feels worse now though, because I didn't know him then. Hadn't seen those hidden parts. The soft, considerate parts. The broken vulnerable parts. Words

281

I never thought would be used to describe him. Words that describe the parts that make him who he is.

"Who's the woman in the photos?" I ask, wanting to know if that's where he was, with her. It's the place my brain keeps going to.

"Sooz."

"No. Don't Sooz me." My patience reaches its limit. "You did this to us. You pushed this. Now we're here, and you expect me to fall at your feet when you won't tell me the whole truth. Everything. You expect me to be okay with knowing half, or parts of it."

I can't tell him that I've figured it out, because I want to hear it from him.

Ryan opens his mouth to say something, probably to distract me from my question.

I continue before he can. "Regardless of what you think, my perceptiveness isn't *shit*."

He swallows at my cussing. "I'm trying, Sooz. I've been trying. I've been understanding. *I've* changed because of you. *For* you."

My chest grows tight, and I struggle to stop my feelings spilling into words, when Ryan takes a couple of steps forward then wraps a hand around my waist.

"What are you doing?"

I'd take a couple of steps back, but I'm already against the glass. My cow-print jammies are on full display to the press. It's the least of my worries because Ryan's free hand cups my jaw, making my head swim. I chew my bottom lip. Ryan's thumb drags it from between my teeth.

"I'm *really, really* trying. I haven't had a joint in two days."

His eyes lock on my lips. I've never wanted to be kissed more in my life.

"Why?" I whisper in a daze. I've forgotten what we were arguing about.

"Because you didn't want me to," he replies. The tension disappears from his face as the corners of his mouth lift.

I want to swoon at his answer, but that would be naïve. Jealousy, fueled by the images, stops me.

"Do you kiss her?"

He shakes his head. "There isn't a her. I swear. It isn't what you think."

Needing more of everything, to be able to understand, I whisper his name and add a broken "please."

"What do you want to know?" he asks, stroking the side of my face.

"Why can't you kiss me?"

My gaze settles on the skull tattooed in the middle of his neck. Ryan's hand moves from my jaw to my forehead, and he frowns.

"You're like a furnace." I feel dizzy and my eyes roll. "Sooz, you're freaking me out."

I want to shout 'same'. I want to tell him that I'm terrified for him. Especially how him refusing to tell anyone about his allergy puts him at risk.

"Please, *Ry*."

His words come out strangled when he gives me the truth, I wish I didn't need.

"Because my first kiss nearly killed me."

"Oh my God," I whimper.

Then my word vomit is replaced with actual vomit.

All over Ryan's front.

Chapter Twenty-Four

"**O**h." I rest my head against the edge of the toilet seat, taking a breather as another round of vomiting passes. "My." I moan. "God."

Ryan drags his fingers across my forehead, pulling back the sodden pieces of hair that've fallen forward and become unfortunate collateral.

"Stop talking."

"Please, don't touch that." I moan again when he moves more of my hair. "There's yesterday's carrot in there."

"Sooz, it's fine," he replies, ignoring my attempt at humor.

"It's not fine, it's gr—" I bury my head back in the toilet.

I don't know how long we've been in here. It's long enough that the muscles in my back and arms ache from holding myself up. I know the intricate details of the gray pattern painted on the tiles beneath my knees.

"You good?" Ryan asks over the sound of the water flushing, removing the evidence of another brutal few minutes.

"I think part of my brain is on a journey to the sewers."

I hear Ryan chuckle at the same time there's a firm knock at the door. I'm too exhausted to care when a familiar floral perfume reaches my nostrils. I close my eyes and focus on breathing.

"The doctor is on his way," says my mother. "I'll take over."

"I'm good," Ryan replies.

He sounds tense. My delirious mind pictures him squaring up to her. Filling the doorway and refusing to budge. My own alpha brute. All growly and demanding.

"You've been in here with her for hours," my mother says. "You need a break."

"I said I'm good. I want to make sure she's okay."

Under different circumstances, I'd revel in the faceoff, watching with a bucket of popcorn.

"And what exactly do you think I want to do?" snaps my mother.

"Lecture me on my poor life choices and tell me how they've led me to this point," I mutter.

"I heard that," she says, her voice too loud.

"You were supposed to," I manage to find the energy to reply.

She tuts and must be focusing on Ryan again. "I would like to help look after my daughter." I'm impressed with the amount of control she has over her voice when it's clear she's irritated. "Please."

There's earnestness in the final word that comes out of her mouth that I've never heard before.

285

I'm on the brink of death. It's the only explanation.

"You are not on the brink of death, Suzanne. Stop being dramatic."

"And this is why I'm not going anywhere," snaps Ryan. "She's sick. She doesn't need you upsetting her."

Mother laughs. "Her feelings aren't the ones that need protecting."

The nausea starts to build again. I must be making a noise, signaling that I'm going to go in for another round, because a pair of hands hold back my hair. There isn't the familiar warmth from before.

"Ryan. Please. Go. I promise, if anything changes, I'll come and get you. Get some rest."

"Okay, fine," he replies to my mother.

The door clicks shut and I'm left with the person I least expected to be helping me. Mother hates mess, and this is as messy as it gets.

"What is this shit?" I cry after a particularly nasty couple of minutes.

With Ryan gone, I let my walls come down and go with the emotions of feeling so sick. It's never-ending, and tears spill down my cheeks as I continue to spew up my internal organs.

"Don't cuss, Suzanne."

Somehow, between the vomiting and crying, I manage to laugh. A laugh that sounds more like a cackle.

The back of Mother's hand finds my forehead, and she hums to herself. "You're burning up again." Again? When did she check on me last? God, I really must be on my way out if I'm losing time. "The doctor should be here soon."

"Do you think I'll make it?"

She sighs. If I had the strength to look up, I'd find her shaking her head.

"Forget parading around with rock stars, you'd be better channeling all this dramatic energy into something like acting."

"I'm not being dramatic, Mother. I'm sick."

"Believe me, you're making the fact very much known."

I snort. The sensation makes my already poor, damaged nostrils burn.

"Seriously? You can't find it in you to be nice right now?"

"I could say the same thing to you," she quips.

"What's that supposed to mean?"

"I left the firm at our busiest period. Flew hours to come and see you, and you've not even given me five minutes of your time. You've been hiding away, and now all you can do is make it clear how much you hate me."

"After I walked away from *my* own company and did the same journey to come and help you and Will, you barely acknowledged that I helped."

"I offered you a job!" Her voice reaches a pitch I've never heard before and the statement echoes off the tile walls. "What more of a compliment do you want? Do you think I'd let any old dross into my company?"

"Oh my God," I groan.

"Is that all you have to say?" she snaps.

"No. I'm going to be sick again."

This time, it doesn't pass. It feels like it's getting worse as I become lost in one wave after another. At some point, the doctor comes, and I'm ready to pass out. But even in the delirium, I can't forget the sinking feeling caused by her words. Because, for the first time in years, my mother

287

showed she still does care, when she sounded something familiar to hurt.

"What are you doing?" someone asks, as I stand up. I yelp when I bang my hip against something hard. "Sooz, you have to lie down."

"I need to get out of here," I mutter. "I have work deadlines. I can't miss them."

Searching in the darkness, I can't find my coat. Never mind. I'm wasting time when I have to get to the office before everything falls apart.

"Sooz!"

A hand covers mine before I reach the stairs. I sway and stumble as my eyes roll and the room tilts. Suddenly, I'm being spun around. Pulled into a large, rock-hard frame. Another hand finds my jaw, grips it, and forces me to look at whoever it is that's talking.

"You're going to hurt yourself."

My nerves seep away when I realize it's Ryan holding me up. He doesn't move an inch when I slump against him.

"I need to work," I mumble.

"The only thing you need to do," Ryan says firmly, "is get back into bed. Doctor's orders. You have a bad case of the stomach flu and you're severely dehydrated. You won't get better unless you rest."

"So bossy," I say into his chest.

"Baby, you fucking love it."

I can't blame whatever's wrong with me for the shiver that works its way over my skin as his warm breath covers my ear.

"I do. I really, really do."

My cheek rubs against Ryan's chest as he shakes with laughter. The material of his shirt is soft yet scratchy. He smells one hundred percent man. Peppery, musky, and delicious.

"I know you're sick, but I could get used to this."

"What?"

"You being amenable."

"Nah. You love it when I rile you up."

There's a pause. Enveloped in his warmth with neither of us moving, I start to give in to the tiredness that hits me like a freight train.

"Yeah," I think I hear him say. "I do."

"So tired."

"I know. Come on. Back to bed."

My feet don't move, but moments later, I find myself being engulfed by his mattress with a blanket draped over me.

"Ry, can I ask you something?"

"Anything," he replies from somewhere close by.

"Did you ever really hate me?"

"Never."

I smile to myself at his answer as a hand strokes my hair.

"Did you ever really hate me?" he asks back, tucking me in.

"Nah," I yawn.

"Really?"

I bury myself into the blanket and, right before consciousness slips away, I admit what I've known deep down all along, but refused to admit to myself.

"How could I? You're you."

I can safely say, apart from the day Dad left, the hours I lose to being ill are the worst of my life so far.

There are hours of cuddling the toilet and having Ryan press a tepid cloth to my head while I volley between shivering and setting ablaze. I'm not sure how many hours in it happens, but I start to hallucinate. It's no longer Ryan caring for me, but my mother, even after our bathroom bust up.

Then, eventually, things halt. I don't get better. But I don't get worse.

Ryan's room becomes a conveyor belt of bodies.

Mother. Zoe. Henrik. Mother. Will. Sophie. Zach. Mother. Amanda. Mother. Mother. Mother.

I block out all thoughts why Ryan is nowhere to be found and weep when I see Jake, having spent more time with my creator here than I have in six years.

My emotional state gets the better of him, and twenty minutes in, he calls Abby, informing her he wants off the Sooz Care Rota. She fights a good battle until he plays dirty and throws out the nighttime Clara card. She's an hourly waking menace and I try not to be too offended by his choice.

"You look better-ish," says Abby from the top of the stairs.

I'm sitting with a glass of water—half consumed—on the nightstand beside me.

I force myself not to cry again, because I can't risk her leaving when I know who her replacement will be. My dreams are still on the crazy side of the line and all I see when my eyes close is bouclé.

"I feel better-ish," I confirm.

"We brought you this." She holds out a small, flat gift. The pale-pink gift wrap covered in ballerinas has me predicting what she says next, correctly. "Clara picked it."

"We?" I repeat, focusing on the first word that came out of her mouth.

"Yeah. *We*. Everyone is downstairs," she explains. "The whole gang."

I shift in the bed, trying to get comfortable. It's impossible because of how gross I feel.

"Um, why?"

Abby smiles. "It's a surprise. You'll have to come down and see."

My face remains blank. "I hate surprises."

She laughs and rolls her eyes. Blue eyes that are heavily lined with black liquid, framed by lashes coated in enough mascara to make them pop. Zoe's handiwork, because Abby can never be bothered to put in any extra effort. Even her hair is in soft curls, glossy and catching the light. My attention moves to what she's wearing.

"Why are you dressed so fancy?"

"Chill, Sherlock," she says. "Put your control freak tendencies back in their box and open the gift."

"Fine," I huff, gagging when I get a strong whiff of my breath. I smell like a garbage disposal unit. "Who knew Clara was so deep," I say, when I've torn away the paper.

A daily mantra journal is sitting in my hands. The outside is covered in sequins and what look like hand-drawn stars.

"She's not," says Abby. "She liked the pattern on the outside. I, however, loved the idea."

"You know yoga is as far as I stretch with the whole meditating thing."

291

Abby rolls her eyes again. There's a reason we named her the queen of it. Like there's a reason I tell her on the regular, that one day, when the wind changes, they'll end up stuck somewhere back in her head.

"They're mantras. It's nothing to do with meditating. Journaling could be another way of channeling all this stressy energy you have."

"I'm not stressed."

Abby arches a brow. "You've been the sickest I've ever seen anyone because you're so run down. Ryan looks like death after sitting with you around the clock."

"I've been awake, and he hasn't been here," I respond.

"Sooz." Abby gives me a concerned look. "You've been out for a while." My eyes bulge. Seeing my panic, she grabs my hand and gives it a squeeze. "Chill. It's fine."

"But the images and the press. Your dad will think I'm terrible at my job. The New Year's Ball." God, I think I'm going to puke again. This time it has nothing to do with the stomach flu.

"Sooz, my dad understands." Abby gives my hand another squeeze. "People get sick. We're human and we're not immune to everything. It's important that you take care of yourself. Why do you think this floored you? You've been working yourself into the ground for years. It was inevitable that something would eventually take you down. And this has. As for Ryan, he's fine, apart from worrying about you."

"I doubt Ryan's been worrying that much."

Heavy footsteps sound on the stairs. They keep getting louder, higher. Abby's eyes widen and I hold my breath.

"Ryan has been fucking terrified about you."

Abby might as well not be in the room, because the only place Ryan looks is at me. His eyes are dark. His expression is one I've never seen before. I can't figure out if he looks torn, angry, upset, a combination of all three, or, like he said, terrified.

My mouth feels drier than the dessert. I want to say something after his bold admission, but nothing comes out.

"I'll leave the two of you alone," Abby says under her breath. She covers the room and glances back over her shoulder when she's past Ryan, mouthing '*sorry*'. She knows I'm incapable of running away myself.

Ryan doesn't move until Abby's feet are off the bottom step and sound further along the hall.

"How are you feeling?" he asks.

Abby's right, he looks exhausted. Maybe she's right about other things, too. Maybe he hasn't left my side.

"Sooz?"

He tilts his head and gives me an earnest look. With eyes like emeralds amidst all his darker features, he's transfixing. It's the only way to describe him. Transfixing and caring. So much so, my heart flutters in my chest. There's no doubt about it. I'm on the path to becoming my mother. I'm going to get my heart broken. Become bitter and twisted. Then, everyone around me won't want anything to do with the secondary female menace in the Van Rensburg family.

"Yeah?" I reply.

Why am I whispering when he's smiling at me? And why am I talking to myself?

Abby's right. I need to work less. I'm stressed. Verging on a nervous breakdown. It's the only explanation for how I'm feeling. Or perhaps it's some weird, trippy version of Stockholm Syndrome. Technically, Ryan forced us together like this. The word forced might be pushing it. Placed? Ensured? Regardless, it's what this is. Stockholm Syndrome.

Suspecting I look as bad as I smell, I can blame any irrational or weird behavior I'm displaying on whatever I came down with.

"I asked how you're feeling," Ryan says.

He looks amused. Meanwhile, I feel like I'm losing my mind.

Messing around with each other is one thing, but how I'm feeling while staring at him? It's too much. There's no coming back from these kinds of feelings. They're poison moving through my bloodstream, leaving nothing untouched, altering the chemistry of everything I thought made me who I am.

"Great," I reply, wincing at the sound that reaches my ears. I do not sound fine. Far from it. "I'm feeling fabulous."

Ryan starts walking toward the right side of the bed where I'm sitting. His hand twitches at his side, like he wants to do something with it.

It becomes clear the 'something' is that he wants to check my temperature when he says, "Are you spiking a fever again?"

"Would that explain why I'm losing my mind?"

Why I think I might be f—

I can't even think it without my skin growing itchy.

"Partially. The rest is down to the fact you and your friends are batshit crazy." I narrow my eyes as he perches beside me on the bed and laughs. "You're fine. Mentally." His gaze moves down to my pajama top. "I think."

This time, a fried egg is sitting on each of my breasts. A yolk perfectly positioned over each nipple. Ryan's eyes track left to right as he reads the slogan 'I like my eggs perky'. I wish I was still delirious, so I wouldn't remember this moment. The only saving grace is that there's nothing dairy-related to make things more awkward.

"What's that?" I ask when I notice he's got something hidden under the arm that wasn't twitching to check my temperature.

"It's for you." He gives me a shy, boyish smile and shifts the package, which, when it becomes more visible, and judging by the marijuana-leaf-patterned wrapping, looks to be another gift.

"Why is everyone bringing me presents?"

"They're belated Christmas ones."

I take the gift from him when he offers it over. It takes a couple of seconds for his explanation to register.

"Christmas? Ry, how many days have I been out?"

"I thought Abby told you." Ryan looks sheepish, and he scratches at the back of his neck.

"She said a while. A while is like, what? Twenty-four hours. Thirty max?"

"It's been five days."

"Days? Five days? Five!" I shriek, wishing I hadn't, because the wall of my esophagus is still in the deep stages of repair.

"Sooz, calm down. It's not a big deal."

"Not a big deal? Do you know how much can happen in five days?"

"Yeah. I'm kind of aware."

The world could end in five days. Amongst a ton of other things. I zone in on what's crucial at this exact moment in time. Work. A bad habit I'm fully aware of.

"What's been going on with the press?"

Ryan shrugs, like we're not discussing a pivotal moment in his career—and not for good reasons.

"They went home and enjoyed Christmas."

"Ry, I'm being serious."

"And so am I. It's the holidays. They left."

My brain goes into overdrive as I work backwards, trying to remember pieces of the five days that I've lost.

"But we haven't done anything to counteract what's been said."

"The plan was always to wait it out."

"Wait. What?" I ask, feeling deceived. "Then why am I here?"

"For the exact reason I didn't want you to, but needed you to be. To babysit me and make sure I didn't do anything fucking stupid. Congrats, you did a great job. A-plus." His eyes grow hard as he goes on the defensive. I don't know what expression I'm wearing, but it's bad enough for him to say, "Stop looking at me like that, Sooz. I don't *want* to do anything. I've already spoken to John West. Considering the angle the press has taken with it all, the label is happy to let things die down on their own. Everyone wins."

What he's saying feels wrong.

"But you have to fight this," I argue. "You don't have to let them believe any of it."

"I'm tired. Of it all. And after this, with you." Ryan's worried eyes trail over me. "I just want to move on."

"And let the world think she's your girlfriend?" The words get stuck in my throat. "Whoever the *woman* in those photos is."

"Don't say woman like that. You're making it sound wrong."

"Isn't it?" I scoff. "How am I supposed to say it when that's pretty much how it appears, *Ryan?*"

He scowls. "Don't call me Ryan like that, either."

"Stop telling me what to do," I snap. "I don't know why we're doing this. We keep going around in circles. We've been pretending we can get along, but really, *this* is who we are together."

"Sooz."

"Ryan," I bite back, setting the present, still in my hands, down on the bed.

He stares at it. "You're not going to open it?" I shake my head. "Why?"

"Because I don't want to see what's inside," I reply, trying my hardest to keep my tone even. "People buy people presents when they care about them. People trust people who care about them, and gift them not just with things, but truths."

"I gave you a truth!" He throws his hands up.

I understand exactly how he feels, because I'm as exasperated with him.

"But not the full extent of it," I say.

"I didn't exactly get a chance. You puked all over me straight after." He laughs. One without any humor.

"You're not funny."

"I'm not trying to be."

The more we say, the more defensive each of us gets. We're not going to achieve anything if we continue, apart from destroying the progress we managed to make before I got sick. The thought of us going right back to the beginning makes me feel sad, so I decide to take a deep breath and soften my approach.

"Who is she, Ry? You keep telling me that what I think about the images isn't true. That it's not right what the press is saying. But all I have to go off *is* what they're saying. So, you tell me something else."

Our eyes lock. An eternity could pass, and I wouldn't care. Becoming lost in all the different shades and flecks of yellow and green that make up the unique coloring of his irises.

"Fine," he says eventually, looking away and rubbing a hand over his jaw. "I'll tell you everything. But not now. Later." I try not to frown, because it's better than nothing. "You need to go downstairs. There's food."

That's it?

After we've riled each other up, he's backing down? And he's so levelheaded. Calm. Even the guns are hidden beneath the grunge gray Henley he's wearing.

"I'm fine," I say.

His brows twitch, but he manages to stop them raising. "You used the word fabulous."

"And?"

"You're the least colorful person I know. You never use the word fabulous."

"Harsh."

"You wear white. Every. Single. Day."

He's right. A bottle of stain remover travels wherever I go. The corners of his mouth start to curl up. He's probably seen it in my travel case. Things get worse when his eyes drop back down to the yolks.

I squirm, and before he can comment on my pajamas, say, "Because it annoys my mother."

"She lives eight thousand miles away."

"I'm dedicated to the cause." I sniff.

"She's not that bad."

If it weren't for the fear of post-vom breath, my mouth would drop open. Self-care is really, really needed.

"Are we talking about the same person?"

"Yeah, we are."

"You were in the bathroom with us, right?" He doesn't answer, pushing off the bed to stand. "Where are you going?"

"Downstairs," is all I get back as he starts to walk away.

He has to stay central in the room so as not to crack his head off the plasterboard where the ceiling dips at the sides. His feet stop at the top of the stairs.

"Your mom's organized a group meal if you're feeling up to it."

"My mother? Why?"

Maybe the world did end in the five days I've been out, and I was transported to a parallel universe.

Right before Ryan disappears, he answers, "Because she thought it would make you happy."

Chapter Twenty-Five

A long shower and fresh clothing later, I make my way downstairs. My pace is slow because it's all I can manage without swaying, and also, partly, out of reluctance.

When Ryan said group, there was a small bit of me hoping he meant group, as in the group of individuals residing in his home before the world no longer made any sense.

He did in fact mean group, as in *our* group.

Band.

Next Level PR.

Shaun.

South African Nationals.

I think the reason Mother is the only parental is down to the limit on seating.

It's the epitome of a celebration. I just can't figure out why.

"You're here!" says Amanda, clapping her hands vigorously.

A few platinum strands come loose from the up part of her half up/half down do. She's definitely responsible for the white and gold balloon arch spanning the length of the central island.

I'm contemplating whether I can backtrack my way to the attic when Abby appears at my side.

She beams into the room. "Don't even think about leaving."

Sophie and Zoe are standing a few feet away, nursing their drinks. They wave, excited.

"How did everyone get in here?" I ask Abby under my breath.

"We walked through the front door, like we've been doing for days."

She moves away, grabs an empty glass, fills it with cold water from the faucet, then walks back over and hands it to me. Everyone else is holding flutes filled with Champagne. My mouth waters at the thought of alcohol, and not in a good way. Abby hands me a couple of Advil and I place them on my tongue, swallowing as little water as I can to get them down.

Starting to sweat, I fan the hand not holding the glass in front of my face.

"Is there no music?" I feel like a museum artefact with everyone watching and pretending to 'not' listen in on what we're saying.

"We thought it might overwhelm you."

"I feel like I'm on show," I whisper back. She shrugs and walks off, leaving me to stand on my own. Because Henrik is closest, I shuffle over to him. "Can we leave yet?"

He lowers his chin and speaks close to my ear. "Your Mother wanted to make up for the disaster birthday party."

I frown. "How does she even know I was upset?"

I'm assuming my not-so-subtle hint before I left, what now feels like a lifetime ago, went over her head. Over the years, all the other not-so-subtle hints have.

"You rambled about it when you were sick. Constantly. I swear, you're worse with a fever than you are when you're drunk."

"Great."

"Be kind," he finishes. "She's trying."

When he pulls back, my eyes settle briefly on Ryan, who's doing a poor job at hiding the scowl on his face after our conversation.

"What's on the menu?" I ask loudly to no one in particular.

"Vegetarian Bobotie," is the answer I get.

"What?" I say, turning to stare at my mother.

She's magicked up an apron and is standing by the stove, stirring something in a large stockpot. She wanders over to the oven, and when she opens it, steam billows out. I wait for her to tut and fuss that her hair is going to poof. She doesn't do either, just closes the door carefully and turns back to the group with a smile that's virtually unrecognizable.

"It's ready," she says.

Surrounded by the familiar smells of my childhood, for a second, I feel like I've been transported back in time. A lump forms in my throat as I watch her move seamlessly around the kitchen, like she's been doing the same old dance for years, when in reality, she hasn't done it for over a decade.

Twintuition must be blaring, because Will stands at my opposite side to Henrik and gives my hand a small squeeze.

"You good?" he asks.

I'm too dumbfounded by what I'm watching to give him a real answer. I say as much.

"What am I watching?"

"This trip has been good for her," Will says. "She's missed you."

He gives my hand another squeeze, then walks over to the central island. Mother begins pointing animatedly at the dining table, which is dressed and ready for everyone to be seated. Wine glasses shine and there are a couple of small vases with wildflowers sitting in them, acting as small breaks of color in all the white detailing. It's plain. Perfectly understated. Exactly how I would have asked for it to be.

Someone must have said something, because everyone has started moving in the direction of the table.

Who did all this?

"Your mom." The hairs on my arms lift as I watch Ryan walk away, then start talking to Jake.

The group is milling around the table when Mother moves past me with a bubbling dish of Bobotie.

Vegetarian Bobotie.

"Wait," I say when it hits me exactly what's bubbling away. I stare at the creamy topping, perfectly crisp and golden, in horror. "Ryan can't."

Mother rolls her eyes. "Do you think I'd try to kill him?"

I don't know what to think anymore, because I'm in an alternative reality where my mother is acting like one, Ryan is a nice, misunderstood guy, and somewhere among all the revelations, I've also lost five days.

"I swapped the dairy out," she says.

And just like that, we're being open about it all. Ryan's allergy is public knowledge. At least it is in this room.

Mother's answer should make me feel better, but it doesn't. I simply feel bad for doubting her, as she walks away shaking her head. My gaze drops to the floor. When did I become this person who assumes the worst in everyone? When did I become so negative? I don't like myself right now, but unfortunately, I'm stuck with me, and no matter how hard I try, I can't get out of my own head. My eyes burn again. I've been crying more recently than I have in years.

Cabin fever, mixed with my lingering one, is the only explanation I can come up with.

A prickle of awareness crawls its way over my skin, and I look up. I catch Ryan's eye before he goes back to talking to Jake. Because there's nothing to do but go with what's expected, I shuffle over to the table and sit. A third, large serving dish of Bobotie appears—without the meat.

Everyone is then distracted by the bananas Will sets down to accompany it.

Everyone apart from Ryan. He's busy watching me watch my mother. I wish I knew what he was thinking.

"Tuck in before it gets cold!" Mother chirps, sounding like a domesticated goddess.

Henrik takes the seat next to me and lets out a satisfied sigh before taking in my mystified expression. "You need to eat. You look startled."

"I feel like I'm tripping out," I reply.

"It's a lot to take in," he agrees. We watch her together as she fusses around everyone. "Will's right, this trip has been good for her."

"I don't understand what's changed."

I can't stop staring. Being in Brooklyn has felt like being home with the close group of friends I've been a part of. But

304

now, with Mother, Will and Henrik here, it feels even more so.

"Sometimes, you have to step away from where you're at to see what you've been missing all along."

My eyes snap to Henrik's. He smiles, then his gaze flickers to Ryan before returning to me.

His reminder of stepping away from things doesn't help with the knot of anxiety inside me, already growing at a rapid rate. If what Ryan's saying is true, I've not worked in close to six days. The most time I've taken off in six years is one. Usually, it's been due to flights and poor in-flight Wi-Fi.

My chest tightens. I don't have a clue what's going on with Ryan. Yet, here I am, with my family. Sitting in his home. Ready to tuck into a meal. Meanwhile, his career could be in the pits, and I'd be none-the-wiser. I'm tempted to dart away from the table and get back to work. It's the only thing that feels like it might make any sense.

I must still or shift in my seat, because Henrik reaches over and squeezes my hand, hard. A 'don't-you-dare' warning. Not that I'd get a chance, because there's a clinking of metal against glass, and when I look to my left, I find Mother standing at the head of the table, tapping a knife against her Champagne flute. Beneath the layers of foundation, she's glowing.

"I'd like to thank you all for being here tonight." The Botox must be wearing off, because when she smiles, her eyes crinkle at the sides. She sets the knife down on the table, then raises her glass in the air. "To Sooz."

You could hear a pin drop in the silence. Every set of eyes looks to me for acknowledgment of what to do, so I do the only thing I can.

In a panic, I grab my own flute, raise it in the air and put on the greatest performance of my life when I squeak, "To me!"

Zoe claps her hands, managing to knock her water over. Abby and Jake jumping up before they're hit by a monsoon breaks the tension.

Mother laughs, and Henrik pulls me in for a side-on hug.

"If I'd known it was going to be this much fun," he says, "I would have told Will to encourage her to fly over sooner."

I pull back. My smile says *I love you*. My eyes say *I want to kill you*.

"Eat before it gets cold!" says Mother, as if she wasn't the one to cause the interruption.

When I pick up my fork, it's hesitantly. A lick of fear passes through me, and as I'm stabbing into a slice of banana, I glance at Ryan out of the corner of my eye. His movements look confident. The way he grabs his fork. Raises it. Cuts through the layers of egg custard, spiced lentils and butternut. He twirls his fork. Then, repeats the movements again.

"How is it, Ryan?" asks my mother. She looks down at the mush he's created.

He freezes, mid fork twirl. I divert my gaze, but as quick as I do, it bounces back to him. My pulse elevates when he scoops a small amount, custard and all, onto the end of his fork, then raises it.

There's a second of a pause, then the food is in his mouth. He gives Mother a tight smile. I count, watching his eyes get wider as he chews. Twenty in, he swallows, and takes another mouthful. Larger this time. His frown relaxes, and the corners of his mouth lift.

"This is great," he says. "Thanks."

Mother smiles against the rim of her glass, then dives into her own meal.

Henrik nudges me, and I realize I'm the only one who isn't eating. I take a huge mouthful and allow myself to be comforted by the tastes of my childhood.

Dinner goes by without a hitch.

Until the plates are cleared and there's nothing to act as a distraction from the very obvious fact I want to be anywhere but here.

"So, how much longer are you staying?" Amanda asks my mother.

"It's an open-ended trip," Mother replies.

I almost knock my Champagne flute over. "Open-ended?"

"Oh, you'll have to come to the New Year's Ball," says Amanda excitedly. "Next Level has organized it and it's *the* event in the city."

"Yes!" Henrik bounces in his seat.

My mother blinks. "What date is it?"

I'm ready to slide under the table.

"The thirty-first," I answer.

"Aaaand we should go," Abby says, because the night has been a success, and the last thing it needs is to end with an argument. "Clara has daycare early. We have to pick her up from my parents." Jake nods in agreement and pushes his chair back.

"Us too." Sophie stands with Sam. "We have to get Russ."

"Can I get a ride with you?" Zoe asks Sophie.

When Sophie nods yes, Zoe jumps to her feet in a flurry of purple. The meal's been better than nice, it's been great, the atmosphere, too, but I can't help feeling like everyone is in a rush to get away.

Zoe turns to Mother. "That Bubbletee." She mimics a chef's kiss.

"It's Bobotie," I call after her.

She's already halfway out of the room when she calls back, "That's what I meant."

"I have to get back to the bar," says Sam's brother, Shaun, with an apologetic smile.

Being the hostess with the mostess she now believes she is, Mother walks everyone who's leaving to the front door. The five of us remaining sit quietly at the table. I use it as a chance to listen in on what's happening in the entryway.

There are lots of thank you's and comments that the food was great. Then, the front door opens. My ears prick at the sound of camera shutters going off and a few calls from the press to smile. I haven't had it in me to look out the window or check on what's happening. My head has been well and truly stuck in the sand.

My excuse is that I still feel weak and exhausted, although the meal has helped. I make a mental note to take snacks to bed. I need carbs, protein, anything, as long as it comes with a nutrition label, so I can get myself back in the game in the morning. Nothing else can hold me back from working, because if I don't lose my mind after being stuck in this house for so long, I might lose a ton of Next Level's clients instead.

After I hear the front door close, I shift in my seat as Mother's heels click against the hardwood flooring back toward the kitchen.

"Dessert time," she chirps, walking into the room.

Although my appetite's shrunk, I still have room for more. My mouth waters at the promise of sugar and I watch as she busies herself at the counter next to the stove. The guys all sit, doing whatever they're doing on their phones. Seeing them each totally absorbed in whatever is on their screens makes me realize I've left mine upstairs. For the first time in my career, I don't care. It feels good to be present in the moment, rather than trying to micro-manage something elsewhere.

Unlike the help yourself set up earlier, Mother walks back and forth with our bowls, setting down mine and Henrik's first. The contents look too delicious not to dive straight in, so I load my spoon with as much as it will hold, then shovel it into my mouth.

I all but devour the first half in a minute, only slowing when I feel a set of eyes on me. A glance up confirms it's Ryan. Caught out, he smiles to himself, then focuses his attention back on his phone, having passed on dessert.

"This is great, Mom," I say, content. I feel lighter than I have in a long time. Like a cloud. I could drift away. "Really great."

She smiles and tucks into her own bowl, the portion considerably smaller than everyone else's, because some things don't change.

All that can be heard is the clinking of metal against ceramic. Will takes the noise level up a notch when he finishes, scraping the bowl for non-existent scraps. He might as well have licked it clean for how little there is left and, when he realizes, he drops his spoon. It lands in the bowl with a clatter, and he lets out an exaggerated sigh.

Henrik shifts beside me and giggles. Will giggles at Henrik giggling.

"Is there anymore?" I ask.

Mother's busy staring into her bowl, as if the meaning of life is hidden in the bottom. When she starts to lean forward, I realize she's inspecting it. She drops her face so low and so close that when she sits back up, the tip of her nose is covered in cream.

While Henrik is still busy giggling, I swap our bowls.

"Mother," I say. "You have to share the recipe for this chocolate cake. I want to make this again."

"I didn't make it," she replies, filling her mouth with a gusto I've never seen. "I found it in the freezer and thought I'd use it with the cream left over from the Bobotie." She winks at Ryan. "Soya."

"What's wrong, Zachmy?" I ask when I notice him pale. I laugh at my own genius. "Get it? Like Sam-my, but Zach-my."

Ryan stares at Mother, mortified, then looks at me with eyes like globes.

"The freezer?" he says.

He's trying to tell me something. I just can't figure out what.

"Yes." Mother's mouthfuls become smaller the closer to finishing she gets. There's barely a piece the size of a chocolate chip on her spoon when she puts it in her mouth again. "Did you make it?"

Zach groans. "Oh, God."

"What?" I giggle. "What's wrong? Don't tell me I've eaten the space cakes again."

Neither Ryan nor Zach answer. I feel like I should be angry by the anxious looks they're sharing, but I'm not. All I can do is laugh. Will licks his spoon repeatedly. Like his bowl, there's not a drop of food to be found.

"I'm high? Again?"

Ryan and Zach both nod.

"Well," Mother claps her hands, "isn't this enlightening?" Her chair scrapes the floor as she pushes it back to stand. "I'm exhausted."

"Maybe you shouldn't go to bed alone," says Zach, standing after Ryan nudges him.

Mother's eyes widen. "Are you propositioning me, Zachmy?"

There's a break in Zach's paleness when his cheeks turn pink. "No, Ma'am." He scratches his head and looks down at Ryan. "What are we supposed to do with them?"

They glance around at us all. Mother is looking at Zach like she wants him for her next meal, Henrik is in a daze, and Will is still licking his spoon.

"We could put a movie on and ride it out?" Ryan answers.

Henrik snorts. "Ride it out."

His shoulders shake, and Will starts to laugh with him, forgetting the spoon and subsequently gagging.

Ryan stands up, shaking his head. "Come on, you bunch of comedians. Netflix …"

He really should know better than to leave something open like that.

"And chilllll," finishes Will.

Because there's nothing else they can do, apart from seeing the funny side, Ryan and Zach finally laugh.

They then lead us to the living room, declaring there will be no *chilling* of any kind.

Chapter Twenty-Six

I t's the morning after another long night filled with misdemeanors. More from Mother than anyone else. The weird part: I don't think I've ever laughed as hard—and not all of it was because of the weed. I forgot how funny she can be. Her humor is razor sharp, like her tongue.

"I can't believe you got me high again," I mutter into Ryan's room.

Bright morning sunlight spills around the outside of the window shade, adding a warm, murky hue to the surroundings.

"Technically, I didn't do anything," Ryan replies from his makeshift bed on the floor.

I lean over the side of his actual bed and my eyes cast a slow, lazy perusal of him. The sheets are wrapped around his waist, and thanks to him being without a shirt, I get to see exactly what he's been hiding beneath all those gun show shirts he loves so much.

"Done checking me out?"

There's no mistaking the cockiness behind his comment. I ignore it completely.

"You didn't have to sleep down there," I say.

"Sooz, the last actual conversation we had was an argument. I'm not gonna jump into bed with you when you're high."

"Firstly," I raise a single finger in the air, "Van Rensburgs don't argue. They discuss things in a heated manner." Ryan shakes, holding in his laughter at my mimicking one my mother's comments from last night. "Secondly," I raise another finger, "sleeping in the same bed doesn't have to result in the jumping of bone-ers." My words sink in and I cringe.

"And what would you suggest the result be?"

"Sleep." He looks at me like he doesn't believe a single letter making up the word. "Maybe with a big and little spoon scenario."

I'm digging myself into a crater, because no matter which way I try to spin this, the outcome results in the suggestion of sexual activity. Basically, Ryan's right, and I hate that he's right. Because I hate how him being all gentlemanly makes me swoon harder than one of those ladies from the cast of *Bridgerton*. There's nothing lady-like about all the things my hormone-riddled brain keeps imagining doing with him.

"Anyway," I continue, deviating away from the sexual innuendos. "Please, can you get rid of the space cakes? As fun as this has been, I'd like for it to not become a regular thing." I blink as my error registers. Three times is a charm, and this has already become a frequent occurrence. "*More* regular."

The fact we have multiple drug-fueled occasions to refer to is worrying. If Mother hadn't accidentally dabbled in the dark side last night, she'd murder me.

"Scared I'll rub off on you?" Ryan quips.

"We're past that point already," I mumble.

The room goes silent. Ryan and I watch each other. It's awkward with a capital A.

"So …" I say.

"So?"

"Are you coming up?"

I shuffle to the middle of the bed, pulling the sheets back as I go.

"Why does that feel more like a threat?"

"Because you know I haven't forgotten the promise you made last night."

"Sooz."

There's a lingering pause filled with reluctance. I wait for Ryan to continue, but he doesn't.

"You said that we need to talk, Ry. So, let's talk."

"I don't—" His face scrunches as his voice cracks. "When you know, there won't be coming back from it."

I think I know where he's going with this, so I say as much. "You're not going to lose me as a friend. I promise."

He sighs. "That's never been the issue."

"What's that supposed to mean?" I frown, feeling a little put out.

"Sooz." He gives me a lopsided smile. "I've never wanted to *just* be your friend."

He bunches the sheet covering him tightly in his left fist. His right taps a fast beat on the floor. Are the answers I want worth the obvious discomfort they're causing? I don't know.

"We don't have to talk about this if it's too much."

"We do," he says, fixing me with his serious gaze. "Because it's what you need. And when I needed you, you were there."

"Okay …"

"Then you can decide if this is really what you want."

My heart skips a beat at his words. I'm already so deep in this, I can't imagine there being any other result than the two of us being us … together? I'm not sure. I've been so caught up in everything to do with him and the images. Then being sick. I'm stuck on a rollercoaster that's picking up speed. I don't know what I want when I get to the end. But what I do know is that I don't want to slow down. I don't know if I can.

"What if I don't like what I hear?" I say.

He shrugs. "Then I'll take whatever I can get after. I might not want to *just* be your friend, but I need you in my life."

He rises, then drops onto the bed and shuffles next to me. I throw my sheet over him. I should keep a distance between us, because of the conversation we're going to have. But because nothing about us has ever followed the rules or fitted into the perfect mold, I scoot in even closer. Ryan's arm wraps around my shoulder. He tugs me in hard and tucks my head against his chest.

His inked skin burns hot against my cheek, and I wonder if, when he's told me the truth, I'll still have the urge to outline his tattoos with my finger. I wonder if I'll still want to memorize every part of him with my touch.

"I got sick when I was thirteen," he says.

I don't dare move a muscle, scared to breathe. Scared if I do, he'll freak out and stop talking.

"I can't remember what it was. It was nothing." He lets out a flat laugh. "Then I had some weird reaction to the drugs the hospital gave me. It started then. The allergy. Apparently, it's a thing. Not common, but it happens. I guess I was one of the unlucky ones.

"First, I felt weird. Kept getting all these symptoms, and we couldn't figure out what it was. They said bed rest would help. But it didn't. Some days, I was worse. They ran every test they could. When they ran out of all the possible things it could be, they started on the allergies, and that's when they came back with dairy. Milk to be exact. And that was it. Problem solved."

"Just like that?"

His fingers tap lightly against my upper arm. "Just like that."

The smile in his voice, like it's nothing, when it's everything, brings tears to my eyes. I'm glad that we're lying like we are, so he can't see my heart is already breaking for him. Especially when I have a feeling we've not even made it past the first page of his story.

"Don't consume anything with milk," he continues. "That's all they said. It was that easy."

"Milk is in a lot of things," I say.

"Tell me about it." He laughs, genuinely. "It was tough at first, because yanno, cheese …"

"Cheese is life."

"Was."

Heat floods my cheeks. "Sorry."

"Don't be." He chuckles, but it's forced. A token one. "Anyway, my parents were great. My friends, too. Things were fine."

"But?"

"I was sixteen. Her name was Lu. Well, Lulabelle."

Never in my lifetime would I have pinned Ryan Alvarez as someone who'd hook up with a Lulabelle. When I try to twist so I can look at him and check he isn't kidding, the muscles in his arm contract, and he locks me in place. "Don't be judgy, *Soozy*." With that firm reminder, I resume my position. "That's pretty much all I remember, apart from the fact she nearly killed me."

I still as his brutal words hang over us. "What happened?" I ask softly.

"Milkshake and hormones."

His answer breaks the heaviness that's settled around us, and I laugh.

"Under different circumstances, that could sound pretty dirty."

"Yeah." He blows out a long stream of air. "I wish. We went on a double date with her sister. Movies. Food after. I went to use the restroom. While I was gone, she drank some of her sister's milkshake. I told her ab—" He stops for a second. "I trusted her. She knew the deal, and it didn't make any difference."

"You kissed," I probe when Ryan goes silent.

His fingers halt their tapping.

"And I stopped breathing," he finishes.

Lost for words, I reach over him to switch on the lamp. My pajama top brushes against his chest as I move, and he tenses. Light floods the room when I hit the switch. It illuminates everything around us. I look over at him, my attention fixed on the skull tattooed on his throat and the scar underneath it.

Like the red band, the scar provides another part of the answer I've been looking for—one that's been right in front of me, staring me in the face.

"How long?" I ask, eyes locked on the symbol of death.

"Two minutes."

"Minutes …" My face twists in horror as I struggle to process what he's said.

He stopped breathing for two whole minutes. There were two minutes where he didn't have a place in this world. There were two minutes where there was a chance he never would again.

"Luckily, we were in a public place and there was someone who knew how to use my epi-pen. Small mercies. Right? I never thought I'd have to use it. We didn't know it would get this bad. But it's a precaution I'm glad my parents made me go with. Because even with it," he pauses, "there were issues."

"That resulted in this?" I reach up. My fingers hover above his scar. Still, he flinches, and my fingers freeze. When he relaxes, I lower them slowly. In some ways, the skin feels warm, silky, and familiar as the rest of him. In other ways, it feels alien. How can something so small have such a huge impact on someone's life? "What happened after?"

I try not to feel hurt or disappointed when Ryan draws away and sits with his back resting against the headboard. It feels like our closeness is slipping away with each page of the story we move past. I sit up as well, and wrap my arms around my knees, hugging myself.

Ryan clasps his hands in his lap. His thumbs dance around each other. I watch, waiting for them to stop. When they do, there's a small part of me that wishes they hadn't, because when he looks up and our gazes connect, I become

318

lost in the pain and fear that takes over his face with his next admission.

"I was scared, Sooz. I was fucking terrified of everyone and everything. I still am."

"Ry …" I go to grasp his hand. I want to be his anchor, stopping him from sinking beneath his emotions when he looks ready to drown.

Ryan moves his hands away and shakes his head. "I have to get through this. Okay?"

"Okay."

"My Grandma was the one who introduced me to weed." I try not to frown at his words. "I meant what I said when I told you it was medicinal. It was. For *her*. She had cancer. I escaped death while she was on a slow path to it, and she gave me her fucking treatment, Sooz, to help me get past it. She's the bravest person I've ever known." He goes quiet, as if he's remembering everything, then he lets out a huffy laugh. "Sharing's caring. That's what she kept telling me every time I tried to say no. My parents went with it, because things were pretty dark, and it got me through."

My brows shoot up in surprise that his parents knew about his habit. Ryan doesn't miss the movement, and goes on to explain, "A couple of years back, I asked my mom why they didn't stop me." His gaze drops to his hands as his thumbs start to dance again. Faster this time. "She said that losing my Grandma was an inevitable conclusion. That she'd come to the end of her life, and that the two of them had decided they'd do anything to make sure mine wasn't cut short." He looks back up. "The weed helped me when I wanted to give up, when I didn't see the point of fighting to keep going. I—It made things easier."

I'm not sure what to say. I opt for the unexpected with a smile. "Is this the same Grandma with the kitschy decorations?"

My pulse quickens as I anticipate his response. It can only go one of two ways.

A rumble of laughter fills the room and relief courses through me.

"You should see her Easter decorations. I inherited all the holidays she liked to celebrate."

"Lucky you." I don't shy away from my next question, given how open he's been about his grandmother so far. "When did she die?"

"A couple of months before S.C.A.R.A.B.'s first European tour."

I try to hide the rush of compassion, pity and guilt that fills me. The same tour, the same summer, where I berated him for his 'habit' any opportunity I could. A habit that wasn't a habit at all. More like a lifeline.

"Ry ..." I croak, overcome with emotion.

"No." He jumps off the bed to his feet, and the green in his eyes disappears when they narrow. "Don't you fucking dare."

"What do you expect me to do?" My eyes brim with tears as I move across the bed and swing my feet to the floor.

"This is why I didn't tell you," he says, pacing back and forth. "I don't want you to feel sorry for me. It's already done. I'm telling you because it's important."

With a sniff, I manage to get ahold of my emotions. "Keep going."

He stops walking and stares at his feet. "After my first attack, I was scared to go near anyone for months, because I thought I'd die if I did. I couldn't go anywhere without panicking. Eventually, I went back to school. But things weren't normal. I wasn't normal. I still don't feel normal. And the worst part was, everyone was scared to talk about it. Teachers gave me good grades because they felt sorry for me.

"I felt like a pariah. So, I stopped talking. I pretended nothing was wrong. Pretending it wasn't real made things easier. Only the people who needed to, the people who mattered, knew what was going on, what I was feeling. Everyone else was noise and didn't matter.

"And then there was the shit with women. Do you know how hard it is to try to start a relationship with someone when you're terrified of touching them? When you physically can't kiss them because it could kill you."

"Ry," I whisper brokenly. "When was the last time you kissed someone?"

The corner of his mouth lifts sheepishly, and he shoves his hands into the pockets of his pants with a slight shrug. "When do you think?"

I press my lips together to stop myself giving away how I feel. I want to weep for this poor, broken man. Instead, I hold myself together, because if he can do it after everything he's been through, then so can I. Even though he's been truthful, telling me more than I've asked for, or have imagined there being, I can't stop fixating on the issue that still hangs between us. "But the pictures ..."

"Sooz." He grimaces as he raises one hand and rubs at the back of his neck. "I was a virgin 'til I was twenty-two. I was terrified of touching someone, let alone kissing them. So, I kept my head down. Focused on the band. Then we started doing well." He drums his fingers against his thigh. "I'm gonna sound like a dick right now, but I couldn't enjoy it. Any of it. Life. I couldn't be with anyone 'cause I didn't

321

trust them. I didn't dare do anything. Then, Zach made a joke one day about hiring a hooker with the cash we'd made and making her sign a contract so I could get a happy ending that wasn't from my right hand."

"And you did it …"

A pink tinge spreads across his cheekbones. "I didn't tell the guys until after."

"How long?" I don't have it in me to ask directly, but I want to know.

"On and off, almost four years." My mouth opens in surprise. Ryan removes the hand from the back of his neck and holds it up to stop me from saying anything. It's a wasted gesture because I'm speechless. "For the record, they were the worst four years of my life, and I've had some pretty shitty ones in comparison. I felt cheap. Fucking dirty. But in a warped way, it wasn't the worst thing, because I got to do something kind of normal. Sooz, I swear, regardless of that, I didn't care about her. I paid a fuckload to get my dick wet on the regular. But I wouldn't if I—"

He stops speaking abruptly. I want to ask what he was going to say, but the warning glint in his eye tells me not to.

Because I have no idea where his 'but' was going, I go with my own roundabout one. "But you stopped."

"Yeah," he croaks. "I stopped."

"Why?"

"Right before my grandmother died, she told me it was time. That there was someone else ready to take her place in my life. Someone who would challenge me and help me to keep living when she couldn't."

My heart starts to race.

"The first day I saw her, I knew. It was this blonde. She was like a viper. She walked into my life and tore me down.

322

She picked me up on my shit, and I knew then I didn't want to be the person I was becoming. I wanted to be better. I wanted to be worthy of her, even if it took years for me to get there."

A heavy silence sits between us. Ryan stands in front of me while I stare at my lap, trying to get my thoughts together. It's a lot. Everything he's told me. Too much, maybe. But regardless of the circumstances he's been handed by life, he's still here, fighting. He's one of the bravest people I've ever met.

I tilt my head back and stare up at him. He searches my face, as if trying to predict what my reaction will be to everything he's said.

Chapter Twenty-Seven

"I might not deserve you," Ryan says, looking down. "And I might not be the best person for you because I've made a lot of mistakes, but I want to be better. I've been trying, I keep trying, really fucking hard. One day, I want to be what you need, even if I can't be right now."

"Look at me." His gaze meets mine and I decide I'll take whatever he can give. It's enough. "Ry, I want you to fuck me."

"No." He scowls.

"Why?"

"Because I know you don't want me to. Not really. You told me you didn't fuck. You need more, and I can't give you that." He gives me a pained look. "Sooz, I can't kiss you."

"No, you're right," I say, as an idea starts to form. "How about this …" He raises a brow. "We meet halfway."

Ryan laughs. "Are we talking in literal terms?"

"No." I lean into him. The tips of our noses are close to touching. "Fuck me now," I glance at his lips. "With the promise that, when you're ready, if you ever are, I can have everything I need. Maybe. One day."

"One day …"

"On your terms."

The muscles in his neck cord as he works on a swallow and his eyes search mine. If he's looking for doubt, he won't find any. I've never been surer of anything in my life.

Heat pours from his palms when his hands find my knees, warming my skin. He squeezes.

"You're sure?"

"Yep."

"Just like that?"

I match his smirk. "Just like that."

The words ignite between us, and Ryan forces my legs open. He stands between them, staring down like he's ready to devour me. Before he can change his mind, I rip off my pajama top. His eyes lock on my breasts, and then I'm falling back against the mattress. Ryan drags my shorts down my legs.

"Fuck." Standing at the end of the bed, he palms his erection over his pants. I let my legs fall open, appreciating the result when his hand moves faster.

"Why are you still there and I'm still here?"

"Savoring the view," he replies.

"If you don't join me in the next three seconds, I'll have to touch myself."

The corners of his mouth twitch and he remains standing at the end of the bed.

"One." His hand moves down over his dick. "Two." It moves back up. "Three."

My right-hand trails over my breasts, my stomach, then lower.

"Stop."

Ryan clambers over me and his left-hand pins mine back against the pillow. Spreading my legs wider, his pants rub against me, and I moan.

"Screw it," he grunts, shoving his pants down.

Hovering above me, naked, his arm muscles flex and contract. When I stroke him, he feels bigger than I remember. I grip him harder and up my pace. He swells in my hand, and I take his shuddered breath as an invitation, guiding him to where I need him.

"Shit," he hisses, when his dick connects with my slit. "I don't have any condoms."

"Seriously?" I groan.

He falls to the side then bangs the base of his palm against his forehead. His face scrunches up like he's in pain. Suddenly his eyes snap open. "Wait. Zach might have some."

"You are not going down," I say, as his words sink in, "when my mother, my brother and his always-horny husband are in the house, to ask for condoms. Sorry. Nope." I shake my head, hard. "Not happening. We don't need one, anyway. I'm good."

A line appears between Ryan's brows. "What do you mean, you're good?"

"I'm clean. Covered. Just do it."

"I don't want to fuck you, Sooz." He blinks and puts space between us. "I never did."

"Then what do you want?" I ask, uncertainty creeping in.

"I want more than that." He reaches over and the tip of his finger trails a path over my chest. "I want everything. All of you."

His head drops close to my ear at the same time his thumb and forefinger roll my nipple, finishing with a harsh tug.

"Imagine it's my mouth."

He soothes the pain with more gentle rolling, then tugs again.

"One day, I want your tits in my mouth. I want to taste you."

My hips buck and he groans.

"Where?" I pant. "Where do you want to taste me?"

"Everywhere."

His hand leaves my breast and moves down, between my legs.

"You're so wet."

His fingers slide through me, skimming where I'm desperate for him to touch. I move my hips, trying to encourage his hand to go where I need it.

"Greedy."

It won't take much for me to explode.

Ryan knows it, because when he does move a finger over my clit, it's too brief. I try to chase a sensation that's already gone. Then his fingers slide back through me.

One slips inside me, and I moan. A second joins and I cry out. When there's a third, I forget everything. He curls them and hits my favorite spot.

All I can focus on is us. The way his fingers fill me, yet I don't feel full at all, because it's not enough. Not unless it's him. Really him.

I must be talking out loud, because he says, "I love it when you beg." He goes to pull his hand away, but mine wraps around his wrist like a vice.

"Ry," I warn.

He stares down at me. "I need something from you."

"What?"

"I need to know what you taste like."

Excitement dances over his features when I open my mouth and no words come out.

"And I fucking love it when you don't argue with me, as much as I love it when you do."

His fingers are close to my lips when he hesitates.

"Do you want me to stop?"

I shake my head. He grins, then moves his fingers into my mouth. My insides clench as my tongue sweeps up my arousal.

"One word." His voice breaks. "One word to tell me how you taste."

He draws his fingers out and I smile. "Delicious."

There's a small thud when his forehead finds mine.

"One day, it will be me. I swear, Sooz. I'm going to taste all of you." He traces his fingers over the outline of my lips. "When I kiss you here, you'll forget anyone else did."

"I need you, Ry."

"Where?"

"Inside me. Now."

He climbs over and nestles himself between my thighs. Thighs that tighten around his hips, holding him in place. It'd be a perfect moment if it weren't for the troubled expression he's wearing.

"What's wrong?"

"I'm scared," he admits. "I've never been with anyone like this."

"Do you trust me?" I whisper close to his ear, being careful not to let my lips touch him without his permission.

"More than anyone."

Our eyes lock and the air crackles. I wait until he's ready. When his hips move it's like he's breaking through both of our walls. Slowly, he pushes all the way in, and I gasp into his neck. My nails bite his skin as I wait for him to pull out.

He doesn't move though, and it breaks my heart when I realize why.

Sliding my hand down from his shoulder, I rest my palm over his heart. "It's okay." His muscles loosen. "You're still breathing."

A couple of moments pass before he takes a breath, slides out, then back in. With more confidence, his pace quickens. Hitting somewhere deep, he works me into a frenzy. I don't care who can hear as I become lost in everything Ryan Alvarez.

His jaw's clenched when he cups my cheek with his palm, forcing me to look at him.

"I'm not gonna last much longer."

"Call me 'baby'," I moan as he thrusts in hard.

"I knew you loved it," he groans, picking up the pace so I tremble. "*Baby.*"

My body locks around him with the most intense orgasm of my life. I ride each wave, driving him to his own.

He's a plot twist. A detour I never saw coming, onto a path I never want to deviate from.

Exhaustion taking over, Ryan lowers himself carefully on top of me. I sink further into the mattress with him still buried inside me and our skin glued together.

And as he murmurs how it's never been like this, and that he needs to do it again, I'm filled with impossible hope, imagining how it will be, one day, when I get all of this, along with the feel of his lips against mine.

A while later, I raise my head a fraction, looking at him.

"Ry, you told me in New Orleans that even the strongest people have something that brings them to their knees. What is it for you?"

I expect for him to say without any thought that it's his allergy.

But he doesn't. He fixes his gaze on me intently.

"You," he says quietly. "It's you. Every. Single. Time."

Chapter Twenty-Eight

Hours later, more sexually satiated than I ever thought I could be, I'm restless.

"I told you we could spoon without there being any boner-age."

I feel Ryan shaking his head as well as something else, pressed hard into my back.

"Sooz, I have a boner."

When I shift and shuffle up the bed, Ryan grumbles something under his breath about me wearing him out. His erection nestles itself between my glutes.

"I'm sorry to say, Ryan junior thinks otherwise."

"Stop calling it that."

"Does senior work better? I mean, it's large. And you're past your peak. You're on the downward spiral to fo—"

Ryan's hand squeezes my breast. I wiggle against him again as pleasure shoots through me. He's awoken something. The Sooz beast. I'm insatiable, and I love it.

"Stop."

"Fine," I huff.

Focusing on his room, because I need a distraction, my eyes settle on the acoustic guitar still sitting in the corner near the drum kit. It's covered in a layer of dust. I go to ask about it when Ryan stretches his arm out over me. His hand waves in front of my face and my attention is drawn to his fingers.

I grab at his hand, bringing it in close to my face.

"Scarabs?" I say, taking in the ancient bugs scattered over his fingers.

Ryan's sheets pool around my waist when I sit up. His eyes are drawn to my nipples, peeking out from the blonde curtains, almost, but not quite, covering them. I click my fingers in front of his face.

"My face is up here, Alvarez."

"I know." His eyes remain where they are. "But right now, I'm enjoying these."

His other hand reaches out. I grab it before he can pinch and have me forgetting the one-sided conversation I've started.

While he's giving me the stink eye, I say, "I thought Zach said you all had *one* of these tattoos. As in, singular."

Ryan shrugs as our fingers intertwine. "I felt like being extra."

I roll my eyes before asking something that's been bugging me for years. "What does the band's name mean? With the dots, it reads like an acronym." Ryan blinks with no recognition whatsoever of what I'm saying. "An acronym is whe—"

"I know what an acronym is."

"What does the name mean?"

"Exactly as it reads."

I frown. "But the dots?"

"Made it look more like a fancy band logo."

"That's it?" Talk about anticlimactic. "What Zach said was true? I've spent years trying to guess what it means."

"It means scarab," he confirms. "That's it. New beginnings. It was mainly for Jake moving on from all the shit with his grandpa. But I guess we all had a fresh start with the band."

"Why are they on your hands?" I ask when he's still playing with my fingers a couple of minutes later.

"Because I drum with my hands," he replies. "And drumming was my new beginning."

"But I thought you'd always drummed?"

His hands stop moving, and some of the color drains from his face. I'm onto something he doesn't want me to know. This has false cholesterol vibes written all over it.

"No."

My attention drifts back to the acoustic guitar. The dust isn't a thin covering. It's a layer thick with significance.

"What did you do before drumming?"

"Nothing." He drops my hands, rolls onto his back and stares at the ceiling.

Pursing my lips, I decide to give him a break. Rather than laying down beside him, I grab my nightshirt and shorts from the floor, slipping them on before he realizes what I'm doing. I go sans panties because time is of the essence.

"Sooz," Ryan says, when I've walked across the room and bypassed the drums. "Don't."

I crouch in front of the guitar and blow out a steady stream of air. Dust particles fly everywhere. It looks like snow. When I glance over my shoulder, I find Ryan half-sitting, with his weight resting on his forearms. His hair is all over the place. His highlights, now not so fresh, stick out in all different angles.

"You told me that one day you would give me everything I need," I tell him. "Right now, what I need is every truth there is."

"Why?"

The corners of my mouth turn down. "Because I can't help you heal when I don't know what's causing you pain."

"It's a guitar. You're reading into something that isn't there. It's not causing me anything."

His words come out fast. At a speed that suggests the opposite of what he's saying.

"Then why is it here? I'm guessing it's not Jake's. So, why keep it here, catching dust?"

"Fine." The way he drags his hand down his face, revealing a resigned expression when he's done, confirms I've got him. "It's to remind me what I lost, but how far I've come."

I wait for him to go on, watching as one unreadable emotion after another, passes over his face. It feels like I'm watching him relive everything he's been through, and it kills me inside. But I know better than anyone, after witnessing everything with my mother, that emotional wounds, when they're left untreated, fester.

"Ry, please don't destroy us when we've barely started."

"I used to sing."

The air whooshes out of me. It's not an admission of what he lost, but an admission of how deeply that loss affected him. How hard he had to fight to find his way back into the world.

"Drumming was my new beginning when I thought I'd lost everything."

Not knowing what else to do, I jump up and grab my rogue panties off the ground next to the bed before returning to the guitar.

"I can come up with a ton of better things to do with them," he jokes, watching me clean away the dust.

"And this is the best thing I can think of," I retort, picking up the guitar when I'm finished, and walking back over to the bed.

I perch on the edge of the mattress and place it on top of the sheets.

Ryan gives it a pained look, then focuses his attention on me. "What now?"

"Can you play for me?"

"I'm rusty," he replies.

"I don't mind. I'm no roxpert."

"I could sing." My brows shoot up in surprise. "If you want?"

Trying not to sound too eager, I wait a second, then say, "I want."

"I've not done this in years." He runs his hands over the strings and gives one a hard pluck. The twang fills the room. "I can sing. Occasionally. Like, once in a decade occasionally."

"Does it hurt?"

Grabbing the guitar, he gets himself set up and starts to strum.

"From what I remember ..." He messes with some other things. I keep watching and come to the assumption he's tuning it. "A bit."

My fingers wrap around his arm to stop him playing what I've decided are avoidance chords.

335

"You don't have to do this. I don't want you to hurt yourself."

"Sooz, it's fine. It's one song."

But when he starts to play one I've never heard before, one that's as familiar to him as breathing, it becomes very much apparent that it's not just one song.

It's like watching Jake and Sam sing at Orensanz, yet somehow so much more. The chords are beautiful, intertwined with a rhythm he expertly manages to include. I expected him to be okay, good at most.

What he is, what he's producing, even to my own musically ignorant ears, is exquisite.

The worst part is that it's made magical—the depth of the song and so much more—because of the rasp that comes with every chord that escapes his mouth. An agonizing rasp that wouldn't be there if the circumstances were different. If life weren't so harsh and hadn't treated him so unfairly.

"Why are you crying?"

Ryan's thumbs move through salty wet tracks I didn't know had worked their way down my cheeks when he's finished. Forcing down a sob I don't want him to hear, it works its way out in the form of a sniffle, followed by a hiccup.

Each time I think I know it all, how much he's been through, how far he's come, he retrieves another piece of the puzzle out of his back pocket. I don't know how much more I can take before I crumble and let him see how much his pain is hurting me. But after earlier, after everything we've shared, I'd take every ounce of his pain and more if it meant that, somewhere down the line, we could erase his suffering together.

One day. That's what we agreed.

That there will come a time, there will be a 'one day', in the future, when all the truths are out.

And all that will be left to face are promises.

"I loved it. I loved your voice," I admit, when I manage to get myself together enough to form a coherent sentence.

He dips his chin and looks up at me through lashes as dark as night. "Most people would take that as a compliment. Why are you saying it like it's not?"

"Because I loved the parts that shouldn't be there."

A smile pulls at his lips, which then move so close to mine I can picture perfectly how they will feel.

One day. Maybe.

Then he says what makes my heart beat harder than it ever has. Harder than I think it ever will for anyone.

"But, without those parts, I wouldn't be here now, with you."

I try to swallow down my emotions, but it's no good. The tears have become a steady flow, no longer a track, but a stream, soaking my nightshirt each time one heavy drop after another slips off my chin and lands on the material. Ryan's gaze diverts to where my tears are starting to pool, and without a word, he sets the guitar on the ground, then lifts my nightshirt over my head.

Later, buried deep inside me, he shows me why the past is important.

Because without it, we wouldn't be here, like this.

Without the pain we've both been running from, there wouldn't be any promises to chase after.

And when his lips ghost over my skin for the first time, in the briefest of moments that barely makes a second, I remind myself, promise myself, that no matter what happens

337

after this, I'll stand by him, waiting for that one day, with the hope of a maybe.

Ryan walks back into his room, freshly showered. Droplets roll down his skin.

"Head out of the gutter, Van Rensburg."

"The water. It's making a pretty pattern." I refuse to take my eyes away from the show. It's Oscar worthy. "Right down to your dick."

I wink when his lips pucker into an adorable pout, framed by a slight scowl.

"Why are you looking at me like that?" I ask as he stands, towel hugging his hips dangerously low.

"I'm trying not to like it when you're sassy."

"I'm always sassy."

Shards of yellow glint in the green of his eyes, meaning he's gunning for one thing: banterful mischief.

"No, you're always bitchy. There's a difference."

I decide to throw a curveball his way. "I can leave?"

He bounces his weight between his feet at my empty threat. "No. Don't."

"Chill, Ry." I giggle at his sudden nervousness, knowing it's one hundred percent unnecessary. "I'm not going anywhere without a shower first." He turns to go back down the stairs. "Where are you going?"

"To lock the bathroom so you can't shower then leave."

All of my pulse points flutter as my heart does a flip, then a flop.

"I smell gross," I call after him when he's about to disappear.

"You smell like me," he calls back. "I fucking love it. Oh, and by the way …"

"Yeah?"

"You never opened my gift."

I'm not sure what he's going to do when he's only got a towel covering him, but I don't care, because I'm focused on the gift still sitting on his desk. Marijuana leaves in abundance on the wrapping.

My ears prick as I listen out for any sign he's returning.

When all I hear is silence, I shuffle off the bed and make my way over to his desk. At first, I pass the gift between each hand, trying to guess what it might be, judging by the weight. Coming up with no worthy guesses, I settle for tearing the paper away. I keep my grumbles to myself when I find a box, working on getting it open.

"What the?" I mutter to myself when I lift the lid and see what's inside.

It's the most random of gifts, but it feels significant. I set aside the plastic jeweled crown and do my best not to overthink it.

Chapter Twenty-Nine

The lingering effects of the stomach flu, combined with a night of barely any sleep, mean that by mid-afternoon, I'm exhausted.

When my eyes are heavy and I struggle to keep myself upright, Ryan forces me to lie down for a nap, declaring he has a ton of things to do. Too tired to pry, I agree, and crawl back into his bed, mentally high-fiving my small win when he agrees to partake in a sleepover later. With the sheets pulled over me so I'm snuggled and warm, and my muscles crying out with relief after my orgasm marathon, sleep comes quick, pulling me under into a dreamless slumber.

I've no idea how long I nap for, but when I open my eyes to take part in the land of the living again, the shade rolled up on the skylight window shows light giving way to darkness. I sit up and shuffle back, so I'm leaning against the headboard. A quick time check on my phone reveals I've been out for hours. Normally, I'd curse, fly out of bed and frantically try to steal back the time lost by completing an abundance of unnecessary tasks to make myself feel better for being self-indulgent.

Right now, I don't have the urge to even try. It feels like all my adrenaline-fueled oomph has been sucked out of me. Frantic, busy body, take-on-the-world Sooz has left the building. In her place is a Sooz who wants to lie in bed on a grim day and listen to the rain as it pitter patters on the ground. A Sooz who wants life to slow down. A Sooz who wants to be present and enjoy the little moments over the Sooz who used to want to take on the world like she had everything to prove.

It's a first, being present in my own life, and with it comes a feeling of contentment.

I'm contemplating getting out of bed and making my way down a floor or two when the sound of feet stomping up the stairs stops me. It's slightly alarming that I know, from a simple stomp, that it isn't Ryan, and I watch the top of the stairs, waiting to see who's going to appear. I'm not surprised when the top of Will's hair comes into view, then his face, followed by the rest of him.

Besides Ryan, there are only four people it could have been. Zach was busy with Ryan; Mother would never dream of stomping and Henrik declared he was going to source last-minute costumes for the New Year's Ball the day after tomorrow.

Really, there was only ever one person it could be.

"We need to talk," Will says, wearing a serious expression.

"Yeah," I reply, "we do." I scoot to the right and pat the mattress beside me. Will's brows raise in surprise, and I shrug. "Like old times?"

341

He dips his chin and walks to the left side of the bed. I go to ask what's wrong when he hesitates, but I don't get a chance, because he spins around and sits on the edge.

"Better," he says when his back has joined mine, resting against the headboard. With his long legs stretched out across the bed, he wiggles his toes.

"Gross." I wrinkle my nose. "Next time, please keep your socks on. Your claw toes freak me out."

"You're jealous I got the good genes."

"You keep thinking that. But remember, there's a reason Henrik won't buy you sliders or flip-flops."

Will laughs. "I'll make you a deal. I'll put my socks back on if you tell me why you've been ignoring me more than Mother."

I purse my lips and contemplate whether to take the deal. Will wiggles his toes again, sealing my choice.

"Sometimes, I feel like everything is about you."

I want to crawl beneath the covers and never come back out. Saying it out loud sounds more awful than I anticipated, and also makes me sound like a child.

"Wow," Will says. I feel even worse when I take in his hurt expression. "That stings."

"I'm sorry," I say, backtracking in my regret.

Then, I remember how many times I've encouraged Ryan to talk and not keep his past and feelings to himself, so he can move on. I decide to take some of my own advice and shake my head.

"Actually, no. I'm sorry it sounds so bad, and you might be hurt by it, but I'm not sorry for how I feel."

Will's brows pinch together, and he stares at his hands. "I'm not sure I follow."

"You know me. You know me better than anyone." I look down. "At least, you did. But I know you know I wouldn't feel this way without there being a reason for me to."

"Why do I feel like this has something to do with our parents?"

"Because it does." I take a deep breath. "Before Dad left, the wins we celebrated were always yours. Any of my achievements that were celebrated were an afterthought. Then, when he was gone, Mother spent all her time doing or talking about how to get you to be partner one day. Even more so after you came out." I let my pulse settle after the last part. "I hate that you've had to go through everything you have, so you can be true to yourself and be with the person you love. I'd fight every battle with you over and over again without a second thought. You know I'm your number one fan. But sometimes, it would be nice to have *my* achievements recognized for what they are, rather than compared to yours or belittled."

"Mother is proud of you," he says.

"Will," I sigh, "she doesn't know what I do."

"Of course she does."

Shifting myself on the bed, I face him directly. "She's made it clear on more than one occasion she doesn't."

Will mirrors my movement and we stare each other down, each believing we're right.

"And you know better than anyone," he says, "that what people let us see isn't what's always real. Just because someone smiles, it doesn't mean they're happy." I narrow my eyes, and Will huffs. "Look, I didn't come up here to start an argument. I came up here because I miss you. All the time. You're my other half, and I want that back."

"We're never going to get back to what we used to be, not when I'm living an ocean away."

Will tilts his head to the side. "There's this thing called technology. Text me back. Pick up the phone. Let's Zoom. You living on a different continent doesn't mean we can't still be close."

I raise my chin, feeling a flash of defiance pass through me that, if I'm being honest with myself, has nothing to do with this conversation.

"And what about what I want?"

"What do you mean?"

The crestfallen look Will gives me has me carefully choosing what I want to say next. Deciding whether I want to cover up the truth and expand the distance that's already between us or admit what's really bugging me.

"None of this is about you. Not really." I take a deep breath, then blurt, "Right before I came back to Brooklyn, Mother offered me a chance to work with the firm." Will's face scrunches up. "Exactly. It's like, whatever I do isn't good enough. Everything comes back to Cape Unity."

"Did you ask her why she was offering it to you?" Will says after a couple of minutes of us both being silent.

"What do you mean?"

"What I mean is, you're assuming it's because she's belittling what you've achieved, but what if it's simply a case of her giving you options? What if it's because really she's impressed by what you've achieved here, and she offered it to you because she thinks you're the best person for the job? What if she offered it to you with the hope of getting a chance to work with you?"

His words sound familiar. Like what she said to me in the bathroom. I chew on my lip, trying to figure out what to say next.

"Is your meaning the kind of knowing meaning?"

Will presses his lips together in a line. The creases at the sides of his eyes give away the true answer.

"You need to speak to her. For real. Not argue. Sit down and have a conversation, like two adults."

"I'll think about it."

Will rolls his eyes. "I guess it's better than a no." I laugh. "This time, when I ask: are we good? I want you to give me the honest answer," he says. "Are we good?"

Hopeful eyes wait for me to respond. I give it a second, then throw my arms around him with such force he lets out an 'oof'.

"We're always good." I bury myself into him, needing the familiarity that comes only with the two of us together. Something I've missed for years. "I'm s—"

"I want you to do me a favor," interrupts Will. "I want you to start owning your choices and your feelings." I tilt my head back and give him a questioning look. "I read this article on the flight here that talked about change."

I wiggle my brows. "Oh, your favorite thing."

"Yep. So, as I was reading, all the words, well, they resonated with me."

"Where was the article?"

"Gossip weekly." I press my lips together. "Don't judge and don't laugh. Your drummer boyfriend downstairs is a prime example of how we can find unexpected things in unexpected places."

"Fine."

"Anyway," Will says, "I started to think about why I pushed so hard to become partner. Rather than focusing on the position, I want to start focusing on what I want to achieve with it. Change."

"You're being kind of cryptic." I frown. "I don't really know where you're going with this."

"The article talked about drive. About what it takes to bring on change, but how that drive can be misconstrued as something else. For us to bring on change, we have to be open to all the difficulties that come with fighting for it. It doesn't have to be the kind of change that transforms the world, it can simply be the kind of change that changes *your* world. But change is hard. We have to talk. We have to be open about what we want. What we desire. What it will take to achieve a certain outcome.

"But those who are driven by change are often the ones judged the most. We've created this culture where we're encouraged to be different, go after what we want, but we have to be silent, because otherwise we're seen to be self-centered, narrowminded, and sometimes unlikeable.

"You can't please everyone, Sooz. But what you can do is be true to yourself. Have those difficult conversations. Be honest. Someone not liking your choices or what you say, doesn't make them wrong. And those who voice their dislike are usually the ones backing away from a truth that resonates with their own judgements. Stop apologizing for doing what's right for you."

"I feel like you're enjoying this speech."

Will laughs. "Can I say something else?"

"There's more?" I say in mock horror, but when Will scowls, finish with, "I'm kidding."

346

"Your career isn't you. I know Mother's pushed us hard, but you have so much to give, and you do, every day—to your job." I frown, and Will smiles. "But your job is one part of who you are. There's someone downstairs who thinks you're pretty good, regardless. Don't be afraid because of how things went with Dad."

"My job is always there," I explain, "but people leave."

"And sometimes they don't. It's a risk you have to take. Nothing is a guarantee, even our careers. You have so much of who you are to give. Give it to someone who wants to give you everything back. I hate thinking that you might be lonely."

"I'm not lonely."

I receive a disbelieving look that I don't bother arguing with, because I am, in fact, very much lonely. I didn't realize I was until recently, when I've been forced to take a step away from the life I've been fighting for. Admittedly, I feel a little lost, because now I don't know where I want to be, and it's terrifying.

"I'm a senior partner and even I don't work the hours you do."

"Because you have someone to go home to." Will arches a brow. "Okay. I get your point."

I nestle myself back into Will's side. "Does Henrik get these deep musings?"

"It's our bedroom talk."

"Gross."

I shake when Will laughs.

"You walked straight into it. So?"

"What?"

"Do you like him?" Will asks. "The drummer."

"Ryan," I clarify. "I—The whole time we've known each other, I thought I hated him. But ... let's just say, all along, I had him figured out all wrong. And now, even the parts I genuinely don't like, I can't imagine being without."

"It sounds like you know how you feel to me."

"Maybe."

And maybe, even though I already know, I'm not ready to admit it out loud, because there's so much fear surrounding everything to do with him.

"Love always has the potential to fail, Sooz," Will says, as if reading my mind.

I give him a tight smile. "But falling for Ryan. I don't know. It comes with so many risks."

"And?"

"His allergy terrifies me," I admit. My chest loosens with my admission. "I feel completely out of my depth. What if something happens?"

Again.

"Henrik could walk out into the road tomorrow and get hit by a car."

"Morbid."

"But the truth. We can't let our fears of what might happen hold us back from living. If we waste the chance we've been given, we might as well not be here."

"Yeah. You might be right."

"I'm the older one. I'm always right." I raise my hand in response to his comment. "Nipple twist and we're done here."

I lower my hand and pat Will's chest as if I wasn't going to do as he said. "I missed you."

"I missed you, too."

"I missed you three," says another voice from down the stairs.

I groan, then call out, "You've been there the whole time? I thought you were shopping?"

Henrik's head pops into view. "And I finished early." He beams. "We're a trio. A triangle. Forever. What did you expect?"

I yelp when he races over and jumps on the bed. I guess there's something to be said for building bridges, because a while later, I start to consider taking on another.

Henrik cups his hands around his mouth and yells out, "Warning! Warning! Rugged rockstar incoming!" when the door to Ryan's room opens and light spills from the hallway up the stairs.

"Did you get at the space cakes again?" I hiss as the thud of footsteps, making their way up, gets steadily louder.

Having spent the past hour watching a true crime series Ryan recommended in the dark, there's a chance I'm not going to sleep for a week. When Ryan appears at the top of the stairs looking tired, but exactly how Henrik described him—rugged—I decide not sleeping for a week might not be such a hardship.

"No. I just like to watch you squirm. Now, keep your panties on until we're gone, you dirty bitch," Henrik replies, not quite under his breath.

The way Ryan is watching the three of us, bemused, suggests he's heard it all. Will's too engrossed in the episode to pull his husband up on his potty mouth, though. When I clear my throat loudly, he still doesn't move.

"Will?"

He ignores me, so I opt for a more direct approach to get his attention and close the laptop. My timing is uncanny, and the scene disappears at a pivotal moment.

"Hey!" he snaps.

"And that's what you get for ignoring me." I stick my tongue out.

"Not ignoring," Will replies. "Engrossed."

"Be engrossed downstairs in your own room."

Will stares at me, expressionless, like he doesn't understand why I'm kicking him out. I widen my eyes and move them to the side in a subtle 'look who's here' movement. Unfortunately, my brother doesn't do subtle. He never has.

Ryan coughing is when Will realizes he's there.

"You shut me off at the best part so you can have sex?"

"No. I don't want to have sex." Remembering Ryan and how my comment could be misconstrued, I correct myself. "I mean, I do, but I can't right now."

"Don't worry, Soozy," says Henrik with a wink, before jumping off the bed. "Give her some rest and recuperation, and V will be ready for another sexathon tomorrow."

I mouth 'I hate you' as Henrik saunters off. Before passing Ryan, he claps a hand on his shoulder.

"Remember, Ry Ry, don't play too rough. Our Soozy Van Boozy thinks she can take it." He goes as far as wiggling his brows and lowers his voice a level or two, but not enough that I can't still hear him. "But really, she's a delicate flower." Ryan's shoulder is gifted a farewell squeeze. "Give her twenty-four hours and she'll be good to go."

Ground swallow me up because this is up there as one of the most embarrassing moments of my life. Ryan stands speechless as Henrik takes his wonderful insights down to the next floor with him. Neither of us gets a moment to breathe though, because Will then struts toward the stairs following his partner in crime. Being that he's the more levelheaded and less forward one in their marriage, I pray we're clear from any more awkward moments.

Unfortunately, as he's bypassing Ryan, his feet stop moving. He turns and lifts his head the couple of centimeters needed for them to be at eye level.

"Hurt my sister, and I'll smash your face in."

I snort. "Please, Willem. The only thing you've ever smashed are the potatoes Henrik gets you to make."

He flips me off before making his way down the stairs.

Ryan waits until he hears the door to his room shut before he turns back to face me. I remain still, anticipating him to say something like "Cya, Sooz. I didn't sign up to be a part of the Van Crazyburgs.

"They're cool," he says with a grin.

And just like that, the embarrassment is gone. It's easy to forget, with everything that's happened recently, and all the deep moments we've shared, that ultimately, it is still Ryan Alvarez standing in front of me. The same Ryan Alvarez who is, more often than not, inappropriate. The same guy who, at times, can be overbearing. The same one who needs more bleach in his mouth than a toilet. Especially after all the filthy things he said to me last night.

The memory of his words has me clenching my thighs together, and I decide Henrik wasn't far off the mark. Ryan's muddied me up, and I'd happily never be clean again if it means I get to feel all the things I did last night, and I'm not just referring to all the happy endings I received.

"You look happy," says Ryan, a while later, when we're climbing into bed.

The sight of him shirtless and only in a pair of boxers turns me to Jell-O, but I'm exhausted with a capital 'e'.

"Yeah," I reply, smiling to myself, remembering my bonding session with my brother. "I am."

"Any reason?"

"An abundance of earth-shattering orgasms?" Ryan gives me a heated look as he tries to get the truth out of me with a poke to my side. "And I cleared the air with Will."

I watch as Ryan rolls onto his side. He does this pose, like guys do in the movies, where they bend their arm and rest their head seductively against their hand. There's muscle bulge-age, tendon pulling, skin tightening, the works. It doesn't look comfortable. Whatever. I'm all for it, taking a snapshot in my mind that I hope never gets lost with whatever the future has in store for us.

"What air was there to clear?" he asks.

It's then that I remember I haven't really talked about any of my life away from Brooklyn with Ryan.

"There were sibling issues."

"Sibling issues that have to do with you leaving New York for months?"

"Yeah." I roll my lips. I wasn't aware my absence had entered his radar. I then berate myself, because of course it did, if everything he's said to me in the past couple of weeks is anything to go by. "Kind of."

He reaches over and grasps a piece of my hair and rubs it between his fingers. "Why did you go back to South Africa?"

"Will needed my help."

"Was he in trouble?"

"No. Not really. Mainly hurt."

Ryan gives me a confused look. "Will's a senior partner at my mother's law firm. His position is a recent thing, but he's been working toward it for years."

"Henrik?"

"Same firm, another department," I confirm.

"I bet that's ..." Ryan tails off, choosing his next words carefully. "Interesting."

"Yeah. No." I laugh. "They save all their extra-ness for outside the office."

It's then that Ryan frowns. "Is that why he needed your help?"

I nod. "They hadn't come out."

Ryan's eyes pop. "At thirty?"

I give him a sad smile. "I know, right? I never got why. Especially considering they've been in love since we were like thirteen. They make me believe in real love. The kind that's written in the stars."

Overwhelmed by all the prejudices the two of my most favorite people in the world have had to face, I start to trail my fingers over Ryan's bedsheets.

"Sooz ..."

Ryan's murmur makes me realize I've become lost in my own thoughts.

"Sorry," I say. "It's just frustrating." I pause, deciding I need to let him know it all. "Can I be honest with you?"

"Sure."

"One of the reasons I agreed to help you wasn't even to do with you. Not really." Ryan waits for me to keep talking.

353

"There were images of Will and Henrik together. Another partner who was running against Will for the senior position threatened to leak the images, knowing they hadn't come out."

A whistle fills the room, coming from Ryan. "That's harsh. At least I didn't know who was using the images against me."

"You know what they say. Keep your friends close and your enemies closer."

Bitterness, resentment, and rage all mix together, fueling the exasperated smile that takes over my face.

"Who was it?" Ryan asks, reading me like a book.

"One of their best friend's. In the firm, at least."

"Shit. That's fucked."

"Couldn't have put it better myself."

"What did you do?"

"Like what John suggested we do with you. We faced the issue head on. Played the guy at his own game. I arrived in Cape Town, told Will and Henrik they needed to decide whether their relationship was enough." Ryan smiles, as if predicting what I'm going to reveal next. "The next day, they were married, and we kindly gifted the images of South Africa's most prestigious female CEO's son being wedded to the biggest gossip magazine in the country."

Ryan trails a hand through my hair. "Baby, you're brutal when you want to be."

"You love it."

His eyes soften and his pupils go wide. I feel like the world tilts as my heart beats a little faster. "Yeah," he says. "I do." There's so much intensity to his gaze. It all feels so much so fast, that when he says, "Sooz, I—" I don't have the strength inside me to deal with the words I think are going to come out of his mouth next.

I interrupt him before he can say anything else.

"Anyway, it wasn't all smooth sailing. Turns out, half the board are narrow-minded idiots. Unfortunately for them, Mother would axe anyone who got in the way of Will's success. The situation just needed nurturing. Will had other ideas though and went into the boardroom all guns blazing. I think it's in the Van Rensburg gene pool. He demanded the inclusivity clause in the employment contracts be revised."

"I feel like there's an 'and then' coming," says Ryan, doing an expert job of making himself appear unaffected that I detoured our conversation.

"And then, he declared that he wanted to set up a legal department focused on diversity and equality. The two areas Cape Unity was lacking in."

"And?"

"Mother signed it off then and there. There was weeks' worth of media coverage to deal with. Things were busy, which is why I ended up extending my trip."

Ryan's eyes move over me. "You sound like you kind of enjoyed it."

"I love a good take down. Who doesn't?" I laugh. "But it's not what I want to do, even tho—" I try to stop myself before I tell Ryan something that might rock the boat.

He's too quick. "Even though what?"

"Mother offered me a position at the firm. A permanent one."

His face drops. "Oh."

"Yeah." I chew on the inside of my cheek. "Oh."

"Do you want it?"

"Truthfully? No. Dealing with corporate stuff like that, it can be exciting, but I love what I do here. I love what I've built with the girls. But there's a little part of me I can't switch off. One that would like to do something that would mean my mother respects me. That she remembers why I get up each day."

"Have you talked to her yet?"

"Apart from our bust up in the bathroom? No," I say, shaking my head.

"You should. Take it from someone who knows. Life is too short to hold grudges."

"So, what exactly would you call the almost four years of us knowing each other?"

"A courtship."

I throw my head back and laugh. Hard. After my own personal story dump, it feels good. Needed.

"It's a pretty messed up courtship if you ask me."

Ryan moves his hand from where he's still playing with my hair, over my cheek, and then his fingertips find my lips.

"It's just us," he says. "It's our story and whatever it needs to be. It might not be genre specific, but the best ones aren't."

Hot air fills my cheeks. I try to hold it in, but it's too much. It bursts from my lips and my laughter before resembles a giggle in comparison. It's belly-aching, eye-watering, soul-enriching laughter. The kind of laughter people live for.

"I never thought I'd hear you say the words genre specific," I tell him when I manage to calm myself.

He scoots toward me with his hips, flattening our bodies against each other. Then his fingers move lower, away from my lips, their destination toward another kind.

"Tell me, how gentle do I have to be?"

I hold back a moan when his hand moves past my breast and lower, choosing to ask something that's been bugging me since Will gave me the third degree.

"What are we doing?"

"I know what I'm doing," Ryan answers cryptically. "What about you?"

When his hand dips between my thighs and his fingers draw my favorite pattern, I forget what we were talking about and give in to bliss.

Chapter Thirty

It feels like I've been asleep for all of five minutes when someone shakes me. Grumbling, I roll over and give whoever it is my back. When I'm jostled again, I roll back, ready to tell whoever it is exactly what I think about them waking me at an ungodly hour. I don't get a chance, because a finger presses firmly against my lips. My eyes fly open, and I find Ryan smiling down at me. Raising his other hand, he presses a finger against his own lips as he slowly lifts the one against mine away.

"Fancy going on that adventure?"

"It's the middle of the night," I grumble.

"You have two choices. Come with me. Or don't. Either way, I'm going."

"Can we not ju—" Ryan's finger finds my lips again.

"I feel like I'm suffocating here. And there's something I promised to do." My eyes lower, and he moves his finger away. "So, are you coming?"

I contemplate what to do. My record for tempting him into snuggles isn't great and because the look he's giving me says he's deadly serious and that he will leave without me, I decide if I can't beat him on this, I'm going to have to join him.

"Maybe after a vat of caffeine." I sit up and shove the sheets away. When Ryan doesn't respond, I shoot him a quizzical look. "Have I finally silenced you?" I squint, then catch the way Ryan is looking at me as his eyes continually drop down, then back up. The flames wrapped around his neck move as he swallows. When I look down, I realize why he's gone silent. "I thought we had somewhere to go?"

He groans, and my cheeks burn hot. "Get dressed into something you don't mind getting dirty."

He shuffles away, and when he's gone, I press the backs of my hands to my cheeks. After choosing suitable clothing, I get dressed, then, once ready, make my way downstairs, finding Ryan waiting by the front door.

With how many days it's been since the label leaked the images, the press is less rife, and they've stopped camping on the street through the night. Their daytime only attempted harassment means we make our way out to the Range Rover that's ready and waiting with its driver in the front without any hassle.

"Where are we going?" I ask when I'm buckled safely in the backseat.

"It's a surprise," Ryan answers. "But it might take a while. You can go back to sleep if you want. I'll wake you up when we get there."

"Promise you're not taking me somewhere you can dispose of my body easily?"

Ryan leans in and my pulse skyrockets when he whispers so the driver can't hear, "There are a lot more things I'd like to do with your body. But that isn't it."

With my head swimming, I shift in my seat as he pulls back, the corners of his lips lifted by a millimeter. I wrap my arms around myself and rest my head against the cool glass, settling into a restless sleep filled with vivid dreams about the drummer sitting at my side.

"Sooz," a voice says loudly, reaching my subconscious.

I bolt upright, colliding with something as I go. A searing pain radiates through my skull.

My hands shoot up, straight to the source of the pain, at the exact same time, "Motherfucker," is bellowed.

Blinking through the pain and sleep haze, I turn in my seat and find Ryan clutching his face.

"I think you broke my nose," comes out all muffled through his hands.

"I'm so sorry." I continue rubbing at my head, mortified. When I go to pull his hands away, he draws back, wide eyed. "I want to see if you're okay," I explain. Ryan stills, then ever so slowly, lowers his hands, revealing bright red palms and an even redder face. "Oh God."

"*I know,*" he grunts, cupping his hands below it, catching what is still a steady flow of blood streaming out.

When we climb out of the car, Ryan tilts his head back while pinching the bridge.

"There's a lot of blood."

"Yeah. Well," I can just hear what he's saying, "you have a hard head."

"Wait there. I'll see if the driver has a first aid kit."

All I get in return is another grunt as I make my way to the driver's door. I tap my knuckles against the window, and the driver rolls the glass down with a smile. I make sure the one I give back is a sweet one, partly because I need his help, but also as an apology for contributing to the destruction of the back seat.

"Do you have a first aid kit?"

Thankfully, he's friendly, and laughs. "I was wondering how long it would take you to ask."

I lower my voice so Ryan can't hear. "That bad?"

"Like watching a train wreck."

"I'm so sorry."

"Don't be. Most entertainment I've had in a while." He shifts, then reaches across the fancy console and opens the glove box on the passenger side. "I'm first aid trained," he says, passing over the box.

I glance at Ryan. "I think we'll be okay. I'm not sure how his ego will handle it."

"His ego is fine," Ryan calls. "And I can hear you."

Touchy, I mouth at the driver as he rolls the window up, holding back a smile.

"Here," I say, walking toward Ryan with the first aid kit outstretched. His hands are still covering most of his face, but his eyes stare down at me in disbelief. "What?" I ask when he continues to stare.

"Blood is pouring out of my nose like water. What exactly do you expect me to do with it?"

My right hand finds my hip and I tap my foot impatiently on the ground. "I thought you didn't need help. And FYI, I think you're being a little dramatic." He drops his hands briefly, which results in me dropping the first aid kit when I raise my hands mid gasp. "Oh my God, it's a bloodbath."

Ryan looks down at the first aid kit, having returned to cupping his nose. "Can you help, please?"

I crouch to pick it up. Ryan, meanwhile, stands with his chin still raised. "Do you think we need to get you to an emergency room?"

"Should be fine soon."

"You sound like you have experience."

"There have been a few fights growing up."

"Oooo hardcore."

"You mean hard ass." I think I can make out the hint of a smile from the small part of his face I can see.

When I move toward him with an antiseptic wipe, he launches himself back like I'm going to take him down.

"What?"

He reaches over and plucks the wipe from between my fingers. The other hand covers his nose, protectively. "I'll take it from here."

Finally, he drops his other hand. The bleeding has stopped, but my mouth still forms an O at the sight of him. He gives me a half eye roll and chooses to busy himself with cleaning his face.

Five wipes down and he looks less *Walking Dead* more *Rocky*.

With his face clean, and with less chance of him scaring small children, he stands. Once he's discarded of all the used wipes in a nearby trashcan and I've handed the first aid kit back to the driver, I walk over to him.

"So." I look around, nervously. "Why are we here?"

Ryan smiles. "Do you trust me?"

"Yeah?"

He grabs hold of my hand.

As he walks, I follow him blindly, and it hits me exactly how much I do.

Ryan's bloody look is fitting, considering where we are.

It really is like a set from the *Walking Dead*, being that we're passing through an old, abandoned warehouse. Outside, there were the tell-tale signs of what we were going to walk into. Signs I didn't pick up on, but I now remember them for what they are. Glaring red flags. Warnings to run. Run far away. Things like discarded rubbish, chain-mail fencing torn in key places, tears that have been turned into gaping holes. And well, simply the fact it would appear we're in the middle of nowhere. Apart from the filthy trailer in the distance, framed by bare scraggly trees. This has slasher vibes written all over it.

"Stop being antsy," says Ryan, squeezing my hand.

"A giant animal ran across my feet. How else do you expect me to be?"

"A rat is not a wild animal."

"It was huge! Like, how does it get that big? We're at the end of the Earth. The only way it's surviving is off dead bodies."

Ryan stops walking. Being that I'm holding his hand still and lost in my own rambling, I come to an abrupt halt that threatens to pull my arm from its socket.

"Sooz, you were asleep for the ride, so how would you know where we are? And for the record, there's a town five minutes away."

I ponder the information he's given me. "So, if we're about to die, there's a possibility we can run for help?" This is good. Maybe this won't end that badly. "Wait. Where are you going?" I rush after Ryan, who's already taken five long strides away from me. Strides which, given our situation, feel like miles. When we pass through a hole in the wall that I assume used to have doors attached to it before the buildings' apocalypse, I stop abruptly for a second time. "Xavier?"

"Sooz! Hey!" beams Sophie's youngest brother. He doesn't look anything like her. All of his features are dark, whereas Sophie could only be described as bright, in all senses of the word.

Rather than smiling back, I grimace. He's simply another one to add to the potential murder tally. This is a disaster. Where I'm too young to die, Xavier might as well still be in diapers. "Do your parents know you're here?"

He gives me a scared look. "No. Please don't tell them." I narrow my eyes. "Nawww, just kidding. Of course, they do."

A glance to the side reveals Ryan hiding his laughter behind his hand. When he drops it, it's Xavier's turn to grimace.

"Ryman, what happened to your face?"

Ryan's eyes twinkle mischievously. "I had a run in with some guys outside. They were beasts."

His macho act draws an eye roll from me. "I head butted him." Xavier looks between us, back and forth, forth and back, as if he can't figure out who's telling the truth. I want to remind him of the fact we're in the middle of nowhere, but he already looks like he's losing interest, while my attention lasers in on the drum kit in the background, surrounded by colored bottles on the ground. "What's going on?"

"Paint drumming!" chirps Xavier, like it's perfectly obvious.

"Paint drumming?" I repeat.

"Paint drumming," Ryan confirms, walking over to the drums and picking a bottle up. He turns it in his hands and holds it out for me to read the label. There it is. The word paint. Clear as day.

"Um …" I glance around the large decrepit room. Assessing. Analyzing. "Why are we paint drumming?" My eyes drop to the ground surrounding the drums. I shuffle in closer, finding old, multicolored stains. "And why do I feel like you've done this before?"

Neither answers me, but Xavier looks busy on his phone, so I wait.

The next thing I know, he tosses his phone, and I'm watching one TikTok video after another with a white-masked figure playing the drums in different scenarios. Some of the locations I recognize as where we're currently standing.

"Meet Ryan's alternative persona," Xavier grins. "My idea."

My right brow remains skeptically arched as I scroll down the feed, then back up. The view count steadily increases the closer I get to the most recent post, which, when I open it and check the date, was a week ago. Because Ryan spent a good chunk of said date holding back my hair, the odds are that it was filmed the morning I woke up when he was nowhere to be found.

While I assumed he was regretting what happened between us the night before, he was … glitter drumming? And the sparkly video alone has received … I blink, then narrow my eyes, bringing the phone screen closer to my face to make sure I'm not reading the numbers incorrectly.

"This video has twenty-three point eight million views." I look between them and get nothing. They're acting like this is nothing. Completely normal. Some of the best artists in the world struggle to get this number of views. Because they both remain silent, I start to assess the actual profile. "Rogue drummer has over sixteen million followers."

Xavier bounces on his feet, excited. Ryan looks as far from excited as it gets.

"Xave," Ryan says. His eyes meet with mine. "Can you get everything set up while I talk to Sooz?"

"Sure, man," Xavier replies, walking away and giving us space.

Ryan grasps my arm and gives me a gentle tug so we can move to the side of the room.

"What is this?" I hiss. "Do the rest of the band know?"

"No. And I'd appreciate if you kept it that way."

"How did this even start?" I search his face for answers, finding nothing. Right now, he's as much of a mystery as his TikTok persona.

"I've been teaching Xavier how to play the drums for the past couple of years."

"That's nice, but it doesn't explain this." I wave his phone, which I'm still holding with the profile open, in the air.

"We were messing around one day. Xavier was on TikTok and he found some funny videos. He said it would be cool if we did it with drumming. So, we did and," he shrugs, "I guess it took off?"

"You guess? Ry, you've accumulated over one hundred million likes."

He shrugs again. "Xave is the mastermind behind it. He runs the account. I show up and drum."

"But with everything that's going on with the label, this could help. This is huge. There's the potential for some major sponsorships here."

Shaking his head, he takes his phone back, locks it and shoves it into his back pocket. "That's not what this is about."

"Enlighten me." I fold my arms tight across my chest with my feet anchored to the ground, making it clear with my body language that I'm going nowhere without a better explanation.

"Remember what I showed you with the singing thing …" Ryan says, resigned.

"Yeah?"

"My allergy ruined it." He sighs. "And now the band … almost ruined again."

A lightbulb switches on in my head. "You think it's you?" Without thinking, I step forward, wrap my arms around his waist, and squeeze him tight. His arms fall down, and he pulls me in tighter. "It's not you. You know that, right?"

"Yeah." He doesn't sound convinced. "But I like this. That's it. I like doing it and Xave fucking loves it. There's no pressure. No reason for it, other than to have fun."

"Which means the likelihood of it being ruined is less."

"Sooz … sometimes shit can get dark. And this, it makes things lighter."

"I guess it's a better coping mechanism than weed." I smile against him as his chin rests on the crown of my head.

"Yeah. It is."

"Ready," calls Xavier, breaking our moment.

"So." Ryan pulls back enough that he's able to look down at me. "Ready to have some fun? Live on the edge?"

I'm considering my answer at the same time Xavier shouts, "Dude! Are we doing the fire as well this time?"

"Fire?" I squeak.

Ryan ruffles my hair while laughing, then walks away. "Yeah, man. Let's burn shit up."

Because I have two choices: either skulk around where there's the potential to run into a serial killer, or play with flames, I go for the latter. At least, if my life's at risk, this could be fun at the same time.

"Let Sooz pick the colors," Ryan says when I walk over to the two of them.

"What a compromise," I scoff. Xavier snickers and gestures with his arms at all the different paint bottles. "Green and yellow."

"Bold choices." Xavier beams.

"Yeah. They're my new favorite colors." Ryan's eyes find mine and I wink.

"Dude, you need to get changed," Xavier tells Ryan.

"Yeah, okay," Ryan replies. "Back in a second."

Not quite true to his word, he reappears a few minutes later.

"Wow, talk about an alternative persona." I gawp as Ryan walks in, wearing a Henley instead of a gun show shirt— which I assume is because of the fire—jeans and sneakers. All of which are white. There's even a white mask, dropped down by his side in his right hand.

"Makes the paint show up better," explains Xavier, emptying another green bottle of paint onto the snare drum. "And it looks cool."

When he grabs a fire lighter and dips the ends of a pair of drumsticks into a small bottle of gasoline, my mouth drops open. "You weren't kidding about the fire?"

Xavier gives me a 'duh' look. "Why would I be kidding?"

"Because fire is dangerous? There's a reason your parents have told you not to play with it."

"Ah …" He winks. "You're forgetting a small detail."

"Which is?"

"My parents aren't normal. So, they never told me not to."

I turn to Ryan, finding it ironic that, for once, he's the more sensible person I'm trying to communicate with.

"Dude, you ready? We're running out of time." I stare at Xavier, waiting for him to give me another riveting explanation. "Peak posting time on the Tok. Gotta hit it or the vid will bomb."

"Of course."

I must be oozing disapproval, because Xavier frowns, then scratches the side of his head. "Will it make you feel better if I pull out the extinguisher?"

"Not at all."

Ryan chuckles from the stool he's silently moved to during our back and forth. I watch him slide his mask into place. He looks freaky, and the image simply adds to my nerves.

"Everything is flame retardant," Xavier says. "Even the paint. We're more at risk than him."

"*That* doesn't make me feel better." Images of out-of-control flames dance behind my eyes.

"Ready?" Xavier calls out, blatantly ignoring me.

"Yep." Ryan's answer comes out muffled.

"Oh God," I mumble to myself as they both start to go about their business.

My nails bite the skin of my palm when Xavier does a final check over everything, then opens TikTok on his phone.

"Sooz, hit play on the other phone. It's connected to the speaker for Ryman to follow. I'll count you in."

Ryan shifts on the stool, getting in the zone, while I contemplate not hitting play at all. The odds of it deterring the two of them are slim-to-none, so I decide it's better to get it over with.

Xavier counts me in. When he gets to one, and I hit play, it's not the song I expect. A slow reverie of Kat Dahlia's "I think I'm In Love" fills the room. I've heard it a few times recently. I guess it's become a trending sound.

The more surprising part isn't the song choice, but that Ryan plays along expertly, like he wrote the song himself. It leaves me mesmerized as paint flies through the air. Plumes of spray jet out in all angles each time his sticks make contact with the skins. Waves of green interrupted by speckles of yellow. The colors merge, combining and creating a shade almost a perfect match to Ryan's eyes. His clothing is covered. A brief glance down confirms I am, too.

There's paint everywhere.

And then Xavier shouts out, "Make fire, baby!"

Ryan tosses the sticks he's been using to the side, magicking another set out of nowhere, along with a gas light. Fire sparks at the ends of the new drumsticks as the song lulls. When the beat kicks in straight into the crescendo, he brings them down hard on the cymbals with a resounding crash and flames shoot into the air.

With my fear gone, I grin so hard my cheeks feel ready to split. And then, I'm laughing at Xavier as his hoots and hollers come out louder than the music still pouring through the speakers. Only when the song's finished, rolling into another, and Ryan's tossing the firesticks into a bucket of water, do I realize my chest is heaving. Not from exertion, but adrenaline.

The whole thing was exhilarating. It's then I understand why he wants to keep this part of his life private. It's an opportunity to create magical moments that would be sorely missed if anything destroyed it.

"That was fucking epic!" shouts Xavier, so loud his voice breaks.

I press pause on the new song playing before he can cause unnecessary damage to his vocal cords.

Ryan pulls off the white mask, laughing. "I for sure thought I was gonna set on fire, man. That was awesome."

I stop smiling and narrow my eyes at them both. "I thought you said everything was flame retardant?"

Xavier shrugs. "Accidents still happen."

When I turn my attention to Ryan, he laughs. "Don't look at me like that. You wouldn't have let us do it if you knew."

"And rightly so!"

"Chill, Sooz," says Xavier. "You're about to take part in history. This is gonna break records on drumtok."

"Drum watty?"

"Drumtok," Xavier repeats, as if he's given me a better explanation and the answer isn't still weird. "Watch. We're gonna put the sound back over it so you can't hear me." He does just that. "Add a quick filter because the lighting in here isn't the one." He does as he's explaining and the colors in the video pop. "Drumtok hashtags with a bit of the old 'for you' love for all the people who need Ryman's beats in their life …"

Done filling out the caption, he hits post.

"Now what?" I ask.

"We wait."

"How long?"

I expect the answer to be an hour, maybe more. Xavier comes back at me with, "A couple of minutes. We'll know if it's gonna take then."

So, we wait. Like he said, two minutes later, Xavier reopens the app and the three of us, crowded closely together, stare at the screen.

"Fifty thousand views in two minutes," I balk. "How is that even possible?"

"Because Ryan's a fucking legend," says Xavier.

"And Xavier's a toxpert," Ryan says.

"What a dream team," I say, bemused.

"Anyway, guys, this has been stellar, but I've got shit to do. Ryman, you clean up and I'll shoot by and get everything later."

"Where are you going?" I ask as Xavier grabs a satchel bag from the ground and slings it over his shoulder.

He grins. "Got a date with a hot piece of pus—"

I hold my hand up, stopping him before he finishes. "It's okay. I don't need to know."

Xavier's smile droops as if he doesn't get what the issue is with the crude comment he was going to make. "See ya, Sooz. Come for the next video. We can do bigger shit if we have extra hands."

My mouth opens and closes as I watch him leave. "He's …" I can't finish what I'm saying, because there are no words to describe what he is.

"It's Grams' influence." Ryan chuckles. "Want to know the worst part?"

"Not really."

"He's taken Russ under his wing."

I groan. "Sophie will kill him."

"Yeah." Ryan laughs again, but it comes out flatter. "That's if he doesn't kill himself first."

"What do you mean?"

"He likes to live life on the edge," Ryan explains. "Sometimes, he leans out too far, though."

I start to understand. Not all of this is about Ryan. "Is that why you do this with him?"

"Kind of. He's reckless. I saw it when I started working with him. This gives him an outlet for all the crap he wants to do."

There isn't much else I can say or do without letting myself go down the path of psychoanalyzing Sophie's brother, so, I opt for a simple, "That's nice of you."

"Didn't you know?" Ryan wiggles his brows. "I'm a nice guy."

"Yeah ..." I grin. "You are. So, what now?"

"We clean up?"

I glance around at all the paint then take in the room again, remembering exactly why I was initially reluctant to stay here. "The paint is probably covering up blood spatter patterns. I think we could get away without doing any."

Ryan glances over his shoulder. Xavier is long gone, and everything is silent. When he turns back, he gives me a heated look. One that could restart the fire he's put out.

"Take your clothes off."

"Why?" My question comes out with 'no way' undertones.

"So we can clean up."

"This is not the place to get naked."

Ryan walks toward me, a smirk on his face. "Go on. Live on the edge."

The inside of my cheek finds its way between my molars as my resolve and reasoning take the same path Xavier has, right out of the building. "And what if I fall?"

"I'll catch you every time."

It's impossible to say no to anything that comes out of his mouth when he puts on his alpha bravado with a sprinkling of sweetness to seal the deal.

Hands find the hem of my shirt. It takes a second to register they're my own.

Ryan's eyes don't move from mine. Not when my bra drops on top of my shirt on the ground. Nor when my jeans join the pile, or when my black lace panties follow the path of gravity like a feather.

His gaze only diverts when he rips his own shirt away, laying it on top of all the dirt and paint, along with the leather jacket he was wearing when we arrived. Then it's me joining all the items of clothing, horizontal on the ground. Small stones bite into my muscles. The pain is obliterated by pleasure when Ryan's hands move over me, manipulating and massaging my muscles in a way that has soft moans falling from my lips and my body turning to mush.

"Say my name like that again."

"Ry," I moan. His touch disappears and my head snaps up when there's a weird sound like squelching. "What are you doing?"

"Lie down."

I do as I'm told, squeaking when something cold and wet makes contact with my skin. The contrast is polar to how much I'm overheating.

"Seriously, Ry ..." I mutter, when the cool, wet substance feels like it's covering my whole body. He smirks and looks down, as if to say, 'see for yourself', so I do. Hundreds of small, vivid green circles cover my skin. The ones bold and clustered hint toward the answer I'm going to get when I ask, "What have you done?"

"Circled everywhere I want to kiss you."

"You missed a spot." I frown.

Mischief flickers in his eyes, then he squirts some more paint onto his fingers.

"Don't you dare, Ry."

He's too quick, and before I have a chance to react, a ring of green lines my lips.

"Very mature," I quip, going in with my own attack.

Caught off guard, Ryan falls to the side, and his back hits the ground after my hard shove. Straddling his hips, I smile at him seductively as I reach to the side for the yellow paint.

"My turn."

His dick presses against the inside of my thigh, hardening beneath the paint-covered white denim, when I move and rub against it. A few yellow rings later, I make a choice to do exactly as he's said, and live on the edge. Midway through a circle, right above his heart, I fold in half. My breasts press against his stomach, and his head lifts when my breath moves over his skin.

I lower my lips a fraction, then wait. Move a tiny bit closer, and wait again. I'm so close, the smattering of hair on his chest tickles my lips.

Without the request for me to stop, I remove the final gap and my lips meet with his skin. His temperature is sky high. A chill rolls down my spine, ending with the roll of my hips. I glance up through my lashes and his nostrils flare.

I lift my head enough to ask, "Did she?"

He shakes his head no, vigorously, and a sense of pride washes over me. I'm the only one who's kissed him like this. Safely. Intimately. No contracts and no clause. A kiss sealed with trust. A kiss I have no intention of being the last. No maybes. Just a one day.

And when he's inside me and I ride us both to the break of our orgasms, it's the knowledge of the hurdle that we've overcome that tips me over the edge.

Later, as we make our way back out to the car, a perfect mix of greens and yellows, each other's works of art, I can't stop smiling, anticipating all the other hurdles we might be able to take on. Together.

Chapter Thirty-One

S taring in the mirror, I start to question my decision. My hands skim over the soft silk of my dress.

"Wit woo."

I smile as another joins mine from behind. "Does it look okay?"

"Better than okay. You look incredible." Henrik moves closer, so he's standing right behind me, then reaches up and helps pin one of the loose curls in place. "If you ever decide to go brunette. I'm all for it." He leans in and his eyes drop to the yellow straps hanging loose around my shoulders. "But you're being very naughty."

The choice was made before the three of you were in the country."

"Speaking of three. And speaking of the verbal kind. There's one person I've still to see you have any kind of prolonged communication with."

"Please." I move closer to the mirror and check my lipstick. "Mother doesn't care."

"Sounded otherwise to me, if what she was saying in the bathroom when you were sick is anything to go by." I watch his reflection. "Half of Brooklyn heard you both."

"Dramatic."

"Whatever. There's this little thing called communication. We grown-ups do it sometimes and it works fantastically." I scowl and Henrik tuts. "Don't frown, your foundation will sit in your lines."

"Gee thanks."

"I love you." Henrik winks.

"I love you, too."

"Anyway, I better go get ready." Right before making his way out of Ryan's room, Henrik glances back over his shoulder. "Oh, and be careful."

"When?" I frown.

"When you kiss your prince. Make sure it's right, because you don't want to break his heart."

Watching Henrik's retreating form, I give myself a final once-over before following him downstairs, deciding he's too astute for his own good.

Downstairs, there's no one to be found, and I assume everyone's still getting ready.

With nerves getting the better of me, I write a quick note and leave it on the kitchen counter, explaining to everyone where I've gone, then order an Uber. A few minutes later, I leave the house, more than thankful for all of the over-the-top festive celebrations. There's something about New Year's Eve. It brings out people's wild sides—celebrities in particular. My theory is, most people want to go out of one year with a bang before starting a new year with resolutions that are going to be kept for no more than a couple of weeks. Three max.

On the flip side, it means when my Uber arrives, there's not a soul to be found, because there is too much potential for the press to catch other celebrities doing and flashing things they shouldn't. I amble my way down the front steps and into the vehicle, like I have all the time in the world.

Another positive that could come from tonight is that someone else could do something so crazy, Ryan's scandal—a vague memory already now the storm has passed—is forgotten entirely. We're already halfway there. All it would take is one little push. A bit of extra weight to tip the scales in his and Warped Record's favor.

When the Uber pulls up outside the right address, I climb out as gracefully as one can while wearing a ball gown, without any assistance. Thanks to a downpour earlier, the sound of water splashing as cars roll by accompanies the blare of horns filling the night.

Luckily, we predicted unruly weather and thought ahead far enough in advance we were able to hire a canopy to keep the gold carpet dry. Oh, and the press, a few of which are already setting up, even though the event doesn't start for another hour. One waves at me, then holds his camera up, right in my face. The flash goes off, then all I see are colored dots until my vision clears.

"Thanks for that," I mutter, blinking rapidly.

Missing my sarcasm, the guy beams. "No problem. Almost didn't recognize you without your pajamas on." Oh God. "Excellent taste, by the way." His gaze drops to my breasts where, the night Ryan's images leaked, there was a pair of avocados dancing. "Ordered the same ones for my wife."

"Great!" I squeak, then hurry off before he can get any creepier.

The moment I set foot inside the venue, I let out a small squeal. Totally uncool, but totally necessary, because the place is perfect. Some might say *next level*. But seriously … the months of hard work, late nights communicating with the girls after working long days back in South Africa, have all paid off. I want to pinch myself at what we've managed to achieve, and I've only set foot in the main entrance.

Admittedly, when I left for Cape Town, there was a small part of me reluctant to let go of all the main projects I'd locked in. Some people have pets. I have a work portfolio. But as I walk through to the main room—a literal ballroom—and make my way down the sweeping staircase, past the gothic arches, gargoyles and all, I can't help feeling like it still won't be enough to please everyone. One person, in particular.

The months spent searching for the perfect location.

Hours spent pouring over the details.

Like shades of red for the drapes hanging from the roof.

Amaranth. Crimson. Rufous. Carmine. Firebrick. Sangria. Vermilion.

In the end, we went for Henrik's personal fave: Burgundy.

You name it. I know it. Codes and all. Adobe color drop tool has got nothing on me.

After that, it was finding the most authentic fake stars money buy. Don't get me started on trying to find realistic flameless candles, which are sitting on top of the black silk cloths covering the tables. One word: chore. Still worth it, as the last thing we needed was to make it into the history books with the Great Fire of New York. Goodbye, London! Yeah … no thanks. Then, there was the challenge of how to make the tackiest decorations we could find, a Saks kind of experience. Zoe and her creative flair nailed it.

It's perfect. All of it. Even the theme: couples through the ages. I can't wait to see what everyone's come up with for their costumes, and I hope it's an amazing night. A small, child-like part of me prays Mother will think it is, too.

When Abby, AKA Meg from Hercules, approaches me, I grin. "You look different," she comments.

"I'm wearing a wig," I deadpan.

She twirls the end of her dark hair, which is scraped back into a high ponytail, around a finger and casts another look over me. "No, it's not that …"

"I agree," says Zoe. She looks fantastic, especially with her hair the exact shade of violet for her character. She was brought into the world to be Mindy McCready. "You seem less … stressed?"

"Days of no work will do that to a person," I reply.

"Nope," says Abby.

"The bar looks so cool." It has the appearance of being solid gold, and it's magnificent.

Abby narrows her eyes. "Stop changing the subject."

Zoe moves in closer and lowers her voice. "Did you get laid? That's it, isn't it …"

It's my turn to roll my eyes. "Sex isn't the only way to destress."

"But it helps." Zoe winks. "And considering your mother's here, I'm surprised we haven't had to cart you off to an asaylum."

"It's *asylum* …"

Zoe throws her arm around my shoulders, beaming. "And this is what I love about our friendship. There's so much giving. You give me knowledge and facts I will never need …" She lowers her voice. "And I'm going to make you look fire for you-know-who later."

"I know you're talking about Ryan," says Abby.

"And I don't know what you're talking about," I lie.

"Please," laughs Zoe. "You've never been good at hiding the truth." She fans herself. "And watching the two of you together …" She mimics a chef's kiss.

"Is this a thing now?"

Zoe shrugs. "I'm working on my expression."

"I think you'd be better working that expression on Sh—"

"I'm getting major enemies-to-lovers vibes," she says, cutting me off. "It gets me horny thinking about it."

A waiter walks past with a tray of cocktails made to look like liquid gold. I snatch one and give him a thank you smile. "You're gross."

"And you love it." Zoe shimmies at my side, then hip bumps me so hard my drink spills over the rim of the glass. "And you'll love me even more when I work my magic on your face, and make your friends …" Her eyes move between my breasts, "pop so high you'll risk taking Ryan's eye out."

"I like how I look," I huff, then take a sip of my drink through the black straw. Vodka and some kind of soda/syrup mix coats my tongue. I can't put my finger on the exact flavors, but they're perfectly balanced, and the result is delicious. So delicious I could drink the whole thing in one go without thinking.

"You look like Belle," says Zoe, pointing out the obvious.

"That's the point," I reply.

Abby nods in agreement with Zoe, picking up on something I haven't. "Belle is too sweet. Tonight, we need to bring out sexy Sooz."

"I don't have a sexy Sooz," I say.

"Everyone has a sexy." Zoe grins. "We just have to tap into it." She links my arm and steers us both in the direction of the restrooms, grabbing her bag from the bar en route. "I have a feeling, when we find her, she's going to be a vixen, and impossible to put back in her box."

Zoe continues talking about ideas she's already having for my make-up, while I avoid revealing that Ryan has already brought Sexy Sooz out. I want to keep the two of us in a bubble for a while longer, before something can come along, pop it, and then we're tasked with navigating real life together.

"What have you done?" I ask, staring at myself in the mirror.

"Made you shine!" Zoe stands at my side, also staring. Her eyes are filled with pride. "Ryan's jaw is going to hit the floor when he sees you. Turn." I do as asked, and she rubs the tip of her finger beneath my eye. "Perfect."

I turn back to the mirror and notice how the smokey effect she's created looks that little bit smokier, thanks to her simple touch. The jet-black lines surrounding my eyes are as smooth as the amber shade of my irises, a match to the finest bottle of Scotch. From the expertly applied line, deep brown fades to rust, merging into an opulent gold that transforms the color blend Zoe's created into something magical.

"Anyone ever tell you that you're good at this?"

"All the time." She winks. "And I'm not good, I'm outstanding."

"Incredibly modest, too."

"We work hard. We need to celebrate our successes more." She starts to pack away the make-up items scattered around the sink. "Too many people are waiting to tear us down, so if we don't do it, no one will."

I watch her move as the truth behind her words sinks in. "I never thought of it that way."

She places the last item into her silk carrier, then slides the zipper shut. "You should. You look stunning." An approving eye roams over me. "And Ryan is going to think so, too."

Instead of belittling myself and passing off her comment as false, I say, "You think?"

"I don't think. I know." The smile I give her must be an uncertain one, because she smiles back and runs a hand over my hair, making a show of adjusting what she's already fixed. "I've never seen you with anyone since you moved to Brooklyn." She pauses. "Hell, ever."

"I've been busy. Working. Helping."

Her hand stops moving. "Doing whatever you can to avoid all the personal stuff in life."

"You're aware of the irony that this is coming from you, right?"

"We're not talking about me and Shaun." She drops her hand and turns away, making a fuss of placing her make-up bag into her actual bag. "We're talking about you, and the fact you spend so much time helping everyone else, you're neglecting your own needs."

"I'm fine. I'm happy."

And I'm happier now, after the past couple of weeks, than I've ever been in my life. The thought's terrifying.

Zoe purses her lips. "For now. But what about when Abby moves out? Because it's inevitable." My gut sinks as I realize she's right. "What about the nights when work isn't as busy and you come home to an empty apartment? There's more to life than work, and happiness can come from doing things for yourself, not just others. It doesn't make you selfish. We all have needs. We're human."

"I'm scared," I admit. I try to smile, but I don't have it in me. Zoe has managed to jab her finger against all the buttons I hate being pressed.

"Of?"

"Not being enough for someone to want to stay." Zoe frowns and waits for me to expand. With a sigh, I lean against the marble surrounding the sink. "When my dad walked out on us, my mother ... she ..." I blink. "She shut off. Used her firm to cover up all the pain." Zoe gives me a sad look. "He was her everything, and when he left, it's like he took her away. She wasn't always the way she is now. But she's never been happy since, and I'm terrified of that. Letting someone else have control of my happiness."

My voice cracks on the last part. This conversation, it's forcing me to face up to the doubts I've tried to block out. The ones that have been fighting harder to get to the forefront of my mind, threatening to sour the closest thing I've had to a proper relationship in so long.

"But that person could also make your life richer."

"I want the fairytale. I do. I want the prince. The happily ever after."

"Life isn't perfect, Sooz. And by setting such high standards, you're making it impossible for anyone to succeed. You're setting your dreams and desires up to fail."

"Because it's easier."

Zoe reaches over and gives my arm a squeeze. "Ryan will never be a prince."

"I know." And then it hits me. I've never favored Prince Charming. I love the beast, the frog, and I have a soft spot that's more the size of a crater for Shrek. "I don't want him to be. I like him the way he is."

Maybe she's right. Maybe temporarily, I can put my long-term plans to the side and try something new. Really give this thing with Ryan a go, outside of the band's home, when the dust has settled, and we're no longer forced to be a part of each other's lives.

"Well." Zoe throws the straps of her bag over her shoulder and fluffs her already poofy hair, then lowers the tone of our conversation. "Fuck fear. Deal with all the questions and shit later. Let's go find him."

With a new sense of purpose, we stride out of the restrooms together and, for the first time since I started falling for him, I feel confident about my future with Ryan.

Chapter Thirty-Two

Half an hour later, crowds fill the room in droves.

"There are so many people here," says Abby in awe.

"Of course, there are." Zoe checks her nails, feigning nonchalance. "We bossed it."

"This is so exciting," squeals Amanda, bouncing in her stilettos, impressive, considering their height. "Soph! Over here!" Amanda waves hard and I fear for her safety. Her heels really should come with a warning.

In the next second, Tracy Turnblad appears in front of us. Dark hair in a bouffant, wearing a yellow and black checkered skirt that sits below her knees, and a white frilly blouse.

It's the person standing at her side which has us all gawping.

"Sam …" Abby says, her voice shaking as laughter threatens to spill out. "Are you …?"

"Edna Turnblad. Yes." Sam lifts his arms to adjust the wig he's wearing, causing the pink sequins of his dress to shimmer under the strobe lighting. His gaze moves to Zoe. "Why are you looking at me like that?"

"Awe, Sammy. It's awe," she replies.

He gives her the middle finger, a tight smile and a, "Fuck off," in response.

That's all it takes for all of us to break, doing a stellar impression of a pack of hyenas. Each time we manage to settle, all it takes is one of us to glance back at Sam, and we all set off again. By the time we're finished, my muscles are cramping harder than after a Barry's Bootcamp ab session.

"Shoot," says Zoe, moving in front of me. "Keep still. You've ruined your make-up." When she's reversed whatever damage our laughing has caused, she waves a finger in front of me. "No more fun. Your face is a work of art, you're not meant to look like Zombie Belle."

"Harsh." I glance over her shoulder at Sam and smile. He eyes me warily. "I'm picking up on major Russ vibes."

"Hairspray is now banned," he grumbles.

Sophie wraps an arm around his waist and leans into him. "You should have seen his face when we walked out."

Sam places a kiss into her hair. "Yeah," he agrees. "I guess it was worth it. Anyway, I'm gonna go find the guys."

He moves away from Sophie, and we wait until he's gone to crack once more.

"He's like a human glitter ball," says Zoe, her shoulders shaking.

"You don't want to know how long it took me to convince him," Sophie giggles.

"Please tell me you got photos," grins Abby.

Sophie winks and pats the small bag she's carrying. "Already backed up." She spins on the spot, taking everything in. "This place looks incredible. You're going to be refusing clients left, right, and center after this."

I hold both of my hands in the air with my fingers crossed. "Hope so!"

So far, Next Level's main stream of income has come with working one-to-one with clients, helping to improve their image and presence in the media. But the long game has been about expanding. Becoming a one- stop shop for … well … everything. Events will play a huge role, helping to showcase exactly what we can achieve, while drawing all our potential clients under one roof. At least, that's the plan. I hope intuition pays off and, after tonight, we start to reap the benefits of months of hard work on top of our already full plates. We're ready to expand, to move up the industry ladder by at least five steps, which is a huge jump, but we need the extra business to fund everything.

Rather than letting my nerves get the better of me, I plaster on a smile, turn to Abby, Zoe, and Amanda and say, "You did an outstanding job."

Abby shrugs with a smile. "I've already said it. This was all you."

"This is a celebration, and you know what celebrations call for," Zoe chimes. We all groan in unison. "Shots!"

"No." I shake my head. "No celebrating until tonight is over." Zoe pouts. "Don't look at me like that." She flutters her lashes and I find myself holding up one finger with a huff. "One. That's it."

Zoe blows me a kiss and disappears to the bar. While she's gone, I spend my time catching up with all the girls. I'm midway through my story about Mother appearing on the doorstep when Abby, Sophie, and Amanda all look over my shoulder. Their eyes widen.

I freeze, then turn, painstakingly slow, but nothing could prepare me for what's standing behind me.

My mouth parts, and I suck in a sharp breath at the same moment Zoe returns with a tray of shots.

She grins. "Would you look at that, you've found your beast." Her face scrunches up when her eyes move beyond Ryan to Will and Henrik. "And your clock and candlestick too." She laughs. "This feels more like a musical gathering than 'couples through the ages'. And where's my partner in crime?"

She searches the crowds, and her question is directed at Ryan, but he doesn't get a chance to answer, because then there's a loud, "here" over all the music. A figure resembling Batman, without the yellow bat symbol on the chest, appears at her side. The eyes beneath the black, half face mask, resemble Zach's.

Zoe beams. "Hey, Big Daddy!"

"Don't be getting any ideas …" Zach replies. There's no warning in his tone, suggesting he's not entirely opposed to the idea.

Ignoring him, Zoe raises the tray she's still holding, higher in the air. "Drink up everyone!"

Henrik moves to my side and wraps an arm around my shoulder, poking me in the cheek with the tip of his faux flame. "You looked beautiful before, but you look exquisite now. That make-up …"

"My handiwork," chimes Zoe. There are only a few clear shots left on the tray. "Come on," she urges me.

Bummer.

I take one and knock it back. When the liquor hits the back of my throat I splutter. "Sambuca?"

Zoe laughs. "What did you think it was?"

"I don't know," I grumble, already feeling the effects of the alcohol as it hits my bloodstream. "But not that."

"Help me," says Henrik. When I give him a questioning look, he waves his arms in the air. "No hands."

I laugh and take a shot off the tray for him, then raise it to his lips and guide it as he tilts his head back to drink it. I take a quick glance to the side and I find Will, who's struggling with his own shot, thanks to the giant fake mustache he's wearing. Fed up, he rips it off so he can drink it.

"Where's Mother?" I ask.

"At the bar," he replies, sticking the mustache back in place. "Zoe tried to entice her with shots, but she was having none of it."

"I left as she was getting them to make an Ama-Lekkerlicious?" says Zoe, and I groan. "She was making sure they went heavy with the brandy. I left Hercules with her to make sure she could find us."

I give Abby a look at the detail Zoe's dropped. She beams. "Our first year doing his and hers costumes." She runs her hands over her purply pink dress. "I couldn't not."

"We need to work the room," says Amanda with purpose.

I can't take her seriously when she's dressed as Barbie and end up giggling. When I stop, I keep my eyes glued to her, although the urge to look back over at Ryan is strong. I can't though, because each time I get a glimpse of what he's wearing out of the corner of my eye, I feel like I've been charged with electricity. He's making my head feel fuzzy. Or

391

maybe that's the shot? Whatever it is, I need to stay focused until the event is in full swing and all the guests have drunk enough not to care how much I have.

Mother appears with Jake as the group is about to disperse. The red liquid in the tumbler she's clutching is multiple shades darker than the silk gloves she's wearing, thanks to the extra rum. Heavy is an understatement. By the bucket load would be a better way of describing the measurements used in her glass.

Her drink isn't what's surprising, though. It's what she's wearing. My eyes start from the top, taking in the black and white hair, then work their way down, right to the bottom, where a classic pair of black heels are wrapped around her fishnet-covered feet.

"And there was me thinking you were terrifying before. Cruella takes it to the next level," laughs Zoe. Her honesty has nothing to do with the alcohol she's consumed.

"It's all in the details," Mother replies, raising the cigarette holder to her lips to pose.

"Is that …" I move in closer to see what's peeking out of the top. "A joint?!"

Mother lifts it out of my reach before I can whip it away. "It's a prop."

I shoot daggers at Ryan. "You're letting her parade your drugs around?"

He shrugs. "She asked. I gave."

"You're a bad influence." He gives me a smile, dripping with amusement. My cheeks burn as I realize what I've said and what he's insinuating with a look. "Got to work!"

I stumble away, trying to put as much space between us as possible.

Tonight, I can't screw up. I need to focus. Need to walk, talk, schmooze. Ten minutes pass, and not much of any of them is achieved. The only thing I manage to do successfully is keep finding Ryan in the crowds. My eyes are like magnets. Wherever he is, they follow. Lock in. Refuse to move away, no matter how hard I try. It's the regal blue suit jacket he's wearing with the gold buttons. It's making me feel funny. We're a duo. Two opposites that somehow work in unison, better than a matching pair.

Around the fifteen-minute mark, I become desperate for a drink. The more bodies pack into the room, the hotter it gets. The air is stifling, and my skin starts to feel damp. I'm at the bar when a sense of awareness washes over me. I grip the edge of it, needing something to keep me upright, when nylon rubs against the exposed skin on my back.

"Thirsty?"

"Gagging," I croak.

Ryan laughs, and my internal temperature skyrockets from a combination of embarrassment and the sound coming from him. It's like bathing in an elixir. "Dirty talk. Careful. We might have to clean you up."

I whimper. I'm a hussy. Ready to drag him home. Or to a dark corner for a quickie.

A group of people move past us, already well on-board the drinking train. One takes a minor tumble directly into Ryan.

"Sorry," he mutters when his front presses hard into my back. I stare at his knuckles, which have turned whiter than white next to mine. I shift my feet, and he groans. My skin flushes and I shift again. "Sooz." There's a warning in his voice, but rather than scaring me off, it lures me in.

393

A bartender appears, and I fire off a random drink order, praying it has an alcohol percentage that could rival Mother's Ama-Lekkerlicious. When they move along the glowing bar to make it, I tilt my head to the side. Brown fur tickles my cheek as I speak as close as I can to what I think is Ryan's ear. "What do you want to drink?"

"I'm good," he answers. The words come out deep and raspy. I frown and turn a little more toward him. I go to ask if he's sure when he rumbles, "Seriously, Sooz. Stop moving."

I pull my head back, trying and failing to stop the rest of my body from doing as asked. Green eyes blaze down at me, and everything disappears apart from the faint sound of Lady GaGa playing in the background.

"Here you go," says the bartender. I barely hear him, but the cool of the glass when he pushes my drink along the bar and it touches the tips of my fingers brings me back into the real world.

"Thank you," I say, as I twist to get it.

Ryan's eyes catch everything. When I pick up the glass. When said glass touches my lips. When I lift my chin and take a small drink. It's ice cold and tastes a million times better than the Sambuca Zoe ordered. The cool liquid does nothing to cool my insides, though. All it achieves is a gurgle when it hits my stomach, then it feels like thousands of bubbles are popping in their own little party.

"You sure you don't want something to drink?" I ask Ryan.

He shakes his head and remains uncharacteristically quiet. In the background, the DJ chatters into his mic about taking the tempo down for a song. I go to ask Ryan if everything's okay when a familiar tune fills the room.

Gone are the party vibes. All I can think is how I can get away with murdering Zoe without being locked up. Beneath all the fur, Ryan finally looks more like himself. The brown paint on his nose moves when he wrinkles it, and Zoe appears out of nowhere, unsurprisingly with another tray of shots.

"If you can't beat 'em, join 'em," she says, ushering the tray in my direction. Ryan is busy looking anywhere but at me, when she leans in. "For Dutch courage."

She's mid-wink when I take one and shot it like a pro. I'm busy wincing when I watch her move a couple of steps away to speak to Ryan. He glances over while she continues to speak, and a wry smile transforms his face. His nod appeases her, and then I'm taken by surprise when he takes a shot himself. Zoe disappears as quick as she appeared, without so much as a backward glance.

Ryan extends his hand and I stare down at his outstretched palm. "Dance with me?"

I look up, chew my bottom lip, then reply, "I guess it would be rude not to." After having another large swig of my other drink, I set my glass back down on the bar and take his hand.

"After you, Ma'am."

"I prefer it when you call me baby," I say under my breath as we move through the crowds, feeling like we're stuck in one of the super cheesy, cliché parts of a movie, where everyone moves apart, watching the hero and heroine with hearts swimming in their eyes.

All we need is a collective sigh when we hit the dance floor, plus a round of applause at the end, to make it into the top ten for the cheesiest rom coms of all time.

"I know," Ryan rumbles. He walks close behind, flanking me like the beast he's dressed to be. The dancefloor is already full when we get there. People move out of the way for my dress, and Ryan gives my hand a sharp tug, drawing me into his arms. My left hand settles on his shoulder while his eyes settle on the yellow love heart line of my dress. Thanks to Zoe's handiwork, the material no longer covers my chest, but skims above my nipples, barely holding everything in place. "I remember this having less material in the store." I think he's talking about the skirt and what feels like the million layers I added in, now sitting beneath the silk. I wanted over the top and dramatic. I got it. I can barely sit down, and with all the moving we're doing, it makes it impossible for Ryan to get close. "And I like that you're wearing my present."

I touch the over-the-top ring of bejeweled plastic resting on top of my head. Rather than the princess crown that came with the costume, this is a full-blown crown.

"I love it," I admit. "But Belle's a princess. My tiara would have been fine."

Our gazes lock when Ryan starts to spin me expertly round the dancefloor. My dress sways and swirls as we glide, the tails of his jacket fan out.

"I didn't know you could dance." I struggle to get out the words, "You're good."

"I didn't know you could be nice," he quips. "I guess there's a lot about each other we still don't know." My lips press together, and his eyes sparkle mischievously. "And I know Belle's a princess." One of his hands drops to my waist. We swoop to the left and the bar glows behind Ryan, right before he leans in. His hand squeezes my side. It feels like he's squeezing all the oxygen out of me, and my head goes light. When we move to the right, I catch sight of Zoe, hovering at the edge of the dancefloor. She gives me a thumbs up. Beauty and the Beast—the Angela Lansbury version—hits the crescendo and Ryan lowers his head. His breath warms my ear. "But to me, you're a queen."

His nose skims the tip of my ear, and his grip on my waist tightens. When he pulls back, he looks like he wants to devour me, and my lips tingle in response.

"What's happening right now?"

The muscles in his neck cord, making the inked skin on his neck visible above the crisp white of his shirt collar move. His eyes drop to my lips and my pulse elevates. "Can we talk somewhere more private?"

"There's a terrace thing," I bumble, not sure why I'm whispering when everything around us is so loud.

Ryan lets go of my waist, and his other hand continues to clutch mine. "Lead the way."

My feet ache like they've covered miles by the time we get to the doors. I make a mental note to pack these shoes— possibly the most beautiful pair I own—back in their box where they belong when I make it home. They're the kind you look at, totally unsuitable for walking. The tell-tale signs of impending plantar fasciitis confirm they're a health hazard when it comes to dancing.

The terrace thing serves as an adequate distraction from the pain in my feet. Ryan lets go of my hand, and the cold air that replaces his touch is a shock to the system.

Spinning around, I expect to find the same playfulness from on the dance floor, but there's nothing playful about the way he's staring. He takes a few steps toward me, and my heart stampedes against my ribs. He takes a few more, and the toes of his fancy black dress shoes disappear beneath my dress. My breathing falters when he reaches out and grasps my wrist. He tugs me in toward him. It requires little effort, because with his eyes on my lips, he's rendered me incapable of doing anything.

"Is everything okay?" I ask, feeling uncertain, verging on shy.

Emotions run riot with his features and the butterflies swarming in my stomach are equally troublesome.

He scratches the back of his neck. "I've not been honest with you."

"Oh …"

The butterflies stop flapping their wings and I anticipate that I'm not going to like what he says next. I start to mentally prepare myself for the worst. My chin drops of its own accord. I don't think I have it in me to face him when he tells me that this isn't going to work out. When he tells me the thing I've been dreading since the second I realized I was starting to develop feelings for him. That he's leaving, in the vague sense of the word. There was a small saving grace when my dad left: that he was gone. But if this thing with Ryan ends, then there will be no escaping him, because Next Level will still have to work with the band.

"Hey," Ryan says, his hand moving from the back of his neck to cup my jaw. His fingers lift and then he's staring me straight in the eye. There's nothing between us. No distractions. No noise. Just me and him. "It's not like that. What I wanted to tell you was to do with the images … I know I said I wouldn't change anything, because it means that we get to be here, but I swear, if I knew that one day I would meet you, I would have waited a lifetime. I never thought I'd get the chance to be with someone like you."

"I'm scared …" I blurt, searching his face, because everything he's saying is a lot, and I feel it all. Feel the same.

But it doesn't stop me being terrified. His eyes widen and he shakes his head as if he's trying to shake off my question. I wait for him to tell me I have nothing to be afraid of, but he doesn't, so I start to ramble. "Sorry. I freak out after my dad left. It's a thing I like to do."

When he still doesn't say anything, I take in his painted face, framed by the fake beast mane he's wearing. He looks different, and I can't put my finger on why. He starts to frantically pat at his jacket, like he's searching for something. This couldn't be more awkward, and I feel like I need to salvage it in whatever way I can.

"I like you," I blurt, glancing into the night and focusing on the lit-up skyscrapers surrounding us. "That's why I'm scared. I kind of like like you. You know, *like* like."

I wish I'd chosen a better costume, one that hides my face, like I wish we'd never started down this line of conversation.

When I turn to face him, the next words disappear from my lips when I find fearful eyes surrounded by puffy lids. My gaze moves down to his lips. Beneath all the face paint, it's becoming clearer with each second that ticks by that they're equally as swollen.

"Ry ... what's wrong?" I ask, starting to panic.

A strangled sound crawls up his throat and the hairs on the back of my neck prickle.

I dive forward. Grab his arms. I want to shake him. "Ry?!" He opens his mouth like he's trying to suck in. Nothing happens. Nothing comes back out.

His hands fly up and claw at his neck.

"Oh my God. Oh my God. Oh my God."

The world starts to fall apart. I don't know what to do. I need to get help, but I can't leave him on his own like this.

When he sways, instinct kicks in and I help him to the ground.

"I'm coming back!" I call out as I stumble toward the terrace doors. My hands are trembling so hard I struggle to get them open. When they do, I fall through. People jump out of the way, and someone makes a joke that I'm wasted.

I've never been so happy to see my mother when she appears in front of me.

"Sooz? What's wrong?" Panic flares in her eyes.

"It's Ryan." I choke out. "I don't know what to do."

Bodies start to press in around us, trying to see what's going on.

Mother curses, then says frantically, "Where is he?"

"Terrace." I barely manage to get the word out.

"Go back." I can't move. "Now, Suzanne!" she snaps. The harsh bite in her voice whips me out of my panic. "I'll find Zach."

The word "hurry" comes out close to a sob and then I race back out to the terrace. I drop to my knees when I get to Ryan's side.

"I'm so sorry," I whisper.

Rain drops track down his face, creating wet sticky paths through the paint coating his skin.

The doors to the terrace fly open.

"Shit!" hisses Zach, charging forward with my mother close behind.

"I don't know what to do," I whimper. "I'm sorry. I'm so sorry."

The silence surrounding the four of us is more terrifying than anything I've ever seen or heard.

Zach's hands roam over Ryan's legs. "Come on …" He thrusts his right hand into the left inside pocket of Ryan's

400

suit jacket. "Fuck!" He pulls his hand out and shoves it into the right.

When he pulls it back out, I make out a red pouch as he shakes.

The reality of what's happening slams into me, and I stifle a whimper.

Zach's eyes dart up and meet with mine for barely a millisecond, then he's ripping the pouch open.

The sound of Velcro pulling apart tears through me as I watch him spur into action.

There's a tap, tap, tap as something bounces on the cold stone ground.

Then a click over the ringing in my ears.

And when I look up to pray, my eyes settle on a star in the clear night sky.

Chapter Thirty-Three

The drive from the ball to the hospital is the longest of my life.

The hours that follow are longer.

Whenever I've watched movies in the past, in particular those harrowing scenes where something life altering happens to one of the main character's nearest and dearest, and they sit in the hospital corridors as medical teams rush by, I've always wondered what goes through their mind. I mean, they're actors and actresses, so the likelihood is that really, they're sitting, thinking whether they're pulling off the art of devastation or whether they're going to can their career. The cockier of the bunch doesn't give a damn and is counting down the seconds until the camera stops rolling, while thinking what's for dinner.

My mind plays on a loop in those hours as I go over it all.

Every minute.

Every second.

Every little detail.

I question it all.

Should I have seen the signs sooner? Should I have known?

Why didn't I react faster? What if he doesn't make it through this?

Then I replay it all over.

And when I think I'm done … I start again.

It's a slow form of torture.

It's nothing more than I deserve.

I should have helped him, but I couldn't.

I didn't know what to do and I should have.

"This isn't your fault," says Zach.

Jake and Sam stayed behind at the ball with the girls to make sure the night continued without a hitch. I struggled to get my head around it until Zach and John West pulled me over, before we set foot outside, and informed me that how things were being dealt with was how Ryan wanted them to be—part of an emergency plan already in place. Because there was a strong chance something like this would happen to him again. There will always be a strong chance it will happen in the future.

I was wrong, believing we were living in a bubble, anticipating the pop. We've been sitting in a glass box together. One risk after another passing us by, until one decided it was time to wreak devastation. And when the impact came, and the broken glass sliced through the air, the damage the pieces caused was the lasting kind, the kind you don't recover from.

Zach and I left in the emergency vehicle and John West stayed behind to help keep the chaos at bay with a simple lie to the guests and press lingering outside. That Ryan had gotten wasted, passed out and hit his head.

So simple. So wrong.

"It feels like it." My voice comes out hoarse.

"But it's not."

"I should have done more to help. I should have known how to."

Zach's hand settles over my knee. He goes to squeeze it, but all he ends up doing is scrunching the yellow silk of my dress into a ball. "How would you have known how to?"

I turn and face him. "Because I should have spent less time living in the fairytale and should have been doing whatever I could to keep him safe …" Zach's mouth twists into a grimace. "Why wouldn't he show me how? He has a fucking emergency plan, Zach!" My voice rises and a nurse passing by glances over at us. "Why wouldn't he tell me if it meant I could keep him safe?" I break on the last word and raise my hand to quieten what is becoming an endless stream of sobs.

When I've settled, Zach shifts in his seat, turning so his whole body is facing me. He reaches up and grasps my face. "He didn't want to scare you." His thumbs rub away some of the wet trickling down my cheeks. He pulls back his hands and drops them into his lap. When I look down, out of the corner of my eye, I see the pads of them are now black.

Another hour passes before footsteps squeak along the linoleum floor.

Zach and I both look up. My heart starts to race when I realize that the on-call doctor—the one wearing the grim expression—is walking toward us.

404

When I was little, I dreamed of being a princess.

Just for one day.

I've been Belle for twenty-four hours and can confirm it's nothing like I hyped it up to be in my head.

"Hey, you," says Abby, as she slips into the room carrying a large bag.

I look over from where I'm sitting and give her a tight smile. "Hi."

She closes the door quietly and sets the bag down. "I brought you some things. You know, like a toothbrush ..." Her eyes move over my crumpled dress. "Some clothes, for if you want to freshen up."

I look back over at Ryan. A steady beep, beep, beep fills the room.

"I'm good."

Abby moves around the bed and sits in the chair beside me. She rests her forearm on the side of the chair with her palm facing up at the ceiling.

"Hand." I place mine in hers. She squeezes it tight, then we sit in silence. After a while, Abby says, "Any updates?" I give my head a small shake, and she sighs. "This isn't your fault."

"That's what Zach said. But it doesn't feel that way."

"Have you spoken with my dad?" I shake my head again. My phone died hours ago, and I haven't thought about sourcing a charger. "It was no one's fault, Sooz. It was an accident. Dad spoke with all the bar staff. The one who prepared the second round of shots for Zoe had been handling a milk-based cocktail before it."

"They touched his glass." I frown. "That's it?"

Abby glances at Ryan and her eyes drop to his wrist. "There's a reason he wears a band. It could have happened anywhere. At any time."

"I should have prepared."

"You worked with what he gave you, which wasn't a lot." Her frown turns to a sad smile. "He's probably listening, laughing that he's managed to piss you off while being unconscious."

"He's such an ass." I let out a huffy laugh, shifting in my seat. "You hear that?" I call out, cupping my ear. "I said it. *Ass*. I called you an *ass*. You can wake up now." Abby watches me. "Ass. Ass. Ass. Ass. A-S-S." My chin wobbles. "Please wake up."

The tears start again.

"All I want is for him to wake up. I just figured out I don't hate him, and now I might lose him." My voice cracks and Abby wraps her arm around my shoulders. She pulls me in and holds me tight until I stop shaking and catch my breath.

The door to Ryan's room opens, but I don't look away from the bed resident in front of me.

It shuts, and the room remains silent. There's shuffling and then a pair of large red sneakers creep into the side of my vision.

"How's he doing?" asks John West.

"I don't know." My words sound as empty as I feel.

"You could go get some rest. I can watch him for a while."

"Thank you, but I'm fine."

"You look exhausted."

"I'll sleep when he wakes up."

The expected, frustrated sigh that I've been gifted from everyone else doesn't come. John isn't the type.

Hours feel like they pass as we sit quietly, but in reality, it's minutes. Time is the hardest marathon on earth right now. I knew there was a reason I despised running.

"Ryan's parents are trying to get a flight back from Australia," John says. "Given the time of year, they're struggling. They might have to do the journey separately."

The mention of Ryan's parents makes my skin prickle. Irrational irritation blown up by heightened emotions, as I live with my thoughts for too long, focusing on details, creating reasoning that isn't really there.

"They encouraged his weed habit instead of getting him the help he needed."

A second passes. Then another. All that fills the room are the beeps from the machine Ryan's hooked up to. Beeps that have embedded themselves in my brain and will haunt me for a long time.

I'm contemplating whether John didn't hear me when he clears his throat. "Sometimes, as a parent, our biggest flaw of all is loving our children too much."

I want to make a comment about how I wouldn't know. I go for something that makes me sound less bratty.

"How can loving someone be a flaw? Especially your children?"

"Because we forget that they need to see the world and all the negative things that come with it. To experience pain. The hardest thing as a parent is letting go, letting our children fight their own battles, while standing on the sidelines, watching as they get hurt or fail."

His words come with experience. It doesn't take a genius to figure out it's his own. Especially after everything he went

407

through with Jake and Abby. I can't decide if hearing him talk like this is humbling or alarming. The pillar providing each of us strength, admitting his own flaws and weaknesses. There's something in his voice, suggesting he needs this though, that has me sitting silently, eyes trained on Ryan, waiting for him to continue.

"We can become so blinkered in wanting to protect the people we love the most, we don't see their own wants and needs. We become blind to what helps them grow."

"Allowing Ryan to develop a weed habit is hardly helping him to grow," I say without thinking, wincing when I play my words back in my head.

"If Abby was hurting like I know Ryan has been," John stumbles on his words, "like I know he is, I'd give her anything she asked for if it helped her cope."

"It doesn't make it right."

"But when someone is going through something like what Ryan has to face, what others do every day, it isn't about what's right. It's about the middle ground. About helping the person survive in the gray until they're strong enough to fight again."

The finality of his statement has me leaving the conversation where it is. I'm not sure how to take his words—how to process them. They resonate on so many levels. Bring up so many memories with my own parents. I just can't figure out why.

"What happens after this?" I ask when we've had a break from talking.

"I'm not sure," John replies honestly.

I try not to hyper-focus on the fact he's become somewhat of a role model to me, always certain, always strong.

Apart from when it comes to Ryan. A constant uncertainty.

I was right the first summer I met him. He's still a loose cannon ready to fire at any second. But now, knowing him—knowing the kind, misunderstood, generous man he is—when the cannon fires, the after-effects are so much worse.

"Will he need help?"

It's a ridiculous question, one I already know the answer to.

"Maybe. And you might, too."

"Me?" I look away from Ryan.

John looks different in non-work attire. He's sporting a pair of jeans, a baseball shirt, and those oversized sneakers so red they're practically glowing. He looks like Abby's dad. The father figure that doesn't leave without an explanation. Even when he makes mistakes.

"Trauma doesn't only impact those going through it. It impacts everyone around them."

"Ryan needs me to be strong."

"But it's okay if there are days when you want to crumble."

"I won't."

"Sooz …"

"Please, don't."

Please don't make me relive what I saw. Please don't remind me that I almost watched him die.

John sighs, and a large hand finds my shoulder. He gives it a squeeze.

"Call me if he wakes up."

He stands and leaves, and only when the door to the room clicks shut, do I give in to my emotions.

The word *if* becomes the next key player in my carousel of thoughts.

If not *when*.

It's been seventy-two hours.

Sitting. Watching. Waiting.

It feels like I've been here forever, when it's no time at all.

"Is he in a coma?" I hold my breath and wait for the man, mid-forties, standing in front of me, to give me that look they do in Grey's Anatomy, right before they give the bad news.

"No. He's not in a coma."

"Then why isn't he waking up?"

"When severe anaphylactic shock takes place, each time, it gets progressively worse." His words sound simple, but I've no doubt the meaning behind them is much more complicated. "The stress on the system is immense. His body is tired and trying to repair."

"He's resting?" I frown to myself. "No, that's not right. It's more like unconscious resting." I shake my head. "Sleeping?" The doctor smiles. I sit when I start to lose the feeling in my legs. There's one thing that doesn't make sense in what he's saying, because Ryan still hasn't revealed all of his history. "How many times?"

"I'm afraid I can't disclose that information."

"Please, I'm trying to understand."

He moves around the room. Checks some notes on one of Ryan's clipboards, then sets it back in its holder. I watch him intently. Watch when he walks over to the IV drip, raises his hand to check something, then lowers it, and rests it on the side rail of the bed.

He looks down at Ryan. Thoughtful.

"I never understood why people say 'third time's a charm'. It rarely is, because it's rarely down to luck. I don't believe in luck. I believe in hard work. Perseverance." He pauses, pushes away from the rail, then says quietly, "But, if I were to believe in luck, it would be less of the lucky kind of luck."

I blink, struggling to keep up.

"The sixth time is where it'd be at. Goodnight, Ms. Van Rensburg."

The door to the room opens and I startle.

Everyone's already visited today. But it isn't an expected anyone who appears.

"You're still wearing the yellow?" I roll my eyes and turn away from my mother. "When was the last time you showered?"

I look down at my dress, then back up. Her expression remains blank.

"Do you think I have a wardrobe filled with ballgowns?"

She walks toward the bed and watches Ryan. "You know I don't like yellow." She gives me a sideways glance. "Although that shade is more tolerable. It suits your complexion."

"Thanks?" I reply as she settles in the chair next to mine.

"Do you want to know why I hate yellow?" It's never interested me to delve into the real reason why, but three days sitting at someone's bedside, only moving to do a quick restroom trip, will do funny things to the mind. I nod. "It was your father's favorite color."

"That's it?"

411

"Emotional scars take many forms." She purses her lips. "It's what makes them so hard to heal, because usually, they find a way to become the one thing we can't escape."

"I'm sorry."

I'm not sure if the tight smile she gives me is acceptance, but it feels somewhere close.

"He seems nice," Mother says, her eyes back on the unconscious drummer.

"Yeah," I croak. "He is."

"I want to tell you to be careful with your heart. But I won't."

"Why?"

"Because life is full of risks. One of them is falling in love and giving your heart to another. As is getting it broken. It hurts, but it's a luxury not everyone gets to experience."

"I don't love him."

Mother gives me a knowing smile and leans back in the seat with her hands clasped. It's the most relaxed I've seen her. Even her bun doesn't have its usual level of tension.

"Funny …" she muses.

"What is?"

"That's the same thing Ryan said to me when he refused to move from *your* bedside for days." My heart feels heavy. "Go get a shower. Freshen up. I promise I'll come get you if anything changes."

I remain frozen in the chair. The thought of leaving him is terrifying.

"Go, *Sooz*."

"Okay." I stand slowly.

After grabbing the bag Abby brought me a couple of days ago, I look back a final time before leaving the room, struggling with a riot of emotions from Mother's words, which I can't wait to get away from.

The nurse sitting at the main station gives me a bemused look when I approach to ask where I can shower. I guess it's not every day they have a Disney princess wandering the corridors. It's the other nurse—an older lady—who's been caring for Ryan on and off for the past few days, who guides me to where I need to be.

God, I hope her eagerness doesn't have anything to do with how bad I smell.

"Use this as much as you need," she says, writing down the code. "It's for patient's family and loved ones."

"I'm not family," I reply.

"I know." She passes over a small piece of paper before walking away.

Getting into the room is as much of a struggle as getting into a chair, and I promise myself that I won't be wearing taffeta again for a very, very long time. The battle is worth it though, because the room is like being in a hotel suite. The carpet is soft and plush and there's a couch with a selection of colored cushions. There's even a kitchenette station and, beside it, a hamper filled with toys.

Deeper in, I find the bathroom, and set the shower running with the water temperature to as hot as my body can tolerate. I try not to inhale when I peel the layers of fabric away, but it hits me how gross I feel. No wonder Abby started moving her chair further away.

Steam has already filled the room when I open the bag and pull out what I need. I send a mental 'thank you' to Abby for packing my favorite body wash, the one I use when I need to relax.

When I step under the water and it runs over my body, my muscles loosen in a way they've been unable to for days. Exhaustion hits me. I don't have the strength to keep my walls up. I close my eyes and see Ryan lying on the ground in front of me, barely breathing.

My hand flies up and I use the tiles for support when my legs threaten to give way.

I need a break. I need it all to stop.

But more than that, I need Ryan to open his eyes. I need him to tell me everything's going to be okay. I need him to make me laugh. I need him to smile at me in that infuriating way he does right before he says or does something he knows will irritate me.

I need him.

Him and all his imperfections.

Eventually, when the tidal wave of emotions passes, I laugh. Laugh at the irony that the person I thought knew me the least is still the one who knows me the best. Then I switch off the water and make quick work of getting dry and into a comfy lounge set. I leave my hair damp and tangled, pack my things, and make my way back to Ryan's room.

"You're right," I say, barging through the door.

I go to tell Mother that I care for him. That I maybe more than care for him, but I stop when I take in her eyes, wide as saucers.

She turns toward the bed, and I follow her movements.

"Would you look at that …" she says with an awkward laugh, "he's awake."

Chapter Thirty-Four

My feet remain glued to the spot, and all I can do is stare.

"You're awake …" I breathe.

This has to be divine intervention or something, because you can't make the timing up.

Mother's head moves left to right as she looks between the two of us. "I'll leave the two of you alone and get the doctor." She's out of the room before I have a chance to tell her not to go.

The beeps from the monitor sound more ominous now than when Ryan was unconscious. The silence between us stretches out taut like a sting, and everything in me tenses as I wait for it to snap.

"Are you okay?" I ask when I can't bear it anymore. "How do you feel?"

Ryan doesn't answer, and I feel nauseous at the thought he might hate me, even blame me for what's happened. He continues to stare blankly at me, and I want the ground to swallow me up. I've had this whole life-changing epiphany, jumping past the part where we get to know each other as friends and test whether we can stand being around each other for prolonged periods of time, straight into the whole developing feelings part. Feelings for someone who's looking at me like they don't have them back.

There's a knock and the door to the room is opened by the doctor I remember because of his 'sixth-times-a-charm' comment. Doctor Magic Number Six walks in with a grin brighter than his green scrubs. Needing a distraction, I decide a shorter name is required. The name on his badge doesn't work for me, so I settle on Magic.

"My favorite drummer is awake." Magic claps his hands together, then rubs them before moving to Ryan's side. "I'm glad to see you nice and alert. I have a Spotify playlist reserved for the band's next album." I think if it wasn't against hospital policy, he'd give Ryan an elbow dig and ask for his autograph. Ryan watches, still not saying a word. Observing his side profile, I catch the small movement when Magic's brows pull together. He raises a hand in the air, then lifts a finger. "Follow this for me." Ryan does as asked. "Good."

I struggle to get the words out when I ask, "Is everything okay?"

Magic's lips sit in a line. He watches Ryan, who isn't doing a lot of anything.

"Can you give us a few minutes?"

It might sound like one, but it isn't a question.

"Sure." I slip out of the room and close the door.

My chest is tight, and I bite down on my lip when Mother moves in front of me. Her left hand wraps around my arm while her right lifts my chin so she can look me in the eye. "What's wrong?"

"I don't know." Doom and dread creeps in, akin to when I was crumpled beside Ryan on the terrace, watching his chest, waiting for a sign he was still breathing. "He wasn't talking. And he looked really confused." I've been watching too much of Grey and the clan, because my brain jumps to the absolute worst-case scenario. "What if he can't remember anything?"

"He can remember everything …" Mother's eyes dart over my shoulder. "That's the problem."

I spin around as Magic closes the door to Ryan's room, catching a glimpse of him stroking his bed sheets before he disappears from sight.

"How is him remembering everything a problem? It's a good thing?" My words come out so fast I jumble them. "Right?"

"He's overwhelmed. In shock." I frown. "This is expected, Ms. Van Rensburg." Magic smiles, and I want to wipe it off his face. Nothing about this situation feels smile worthy. "What Ryan went through was traumatic and he's lost a few days. Give him a chance to come round." The vibe I'm giving off must be a reluctant one, because the card Magic pulls out next is the reassuring one. "All his obs are within the normal range." I'm glad when he doesn't throw the word healthy around.

"So, what now?"

"Now you give him time. He'll talk when he's ready." He looks along the corridor. "If you'll excuse me. I have other patients to see. Call if you need anything."

I step to the side so he can pass. He's taken a few steps away from Ryan's room when I spin around and shout, "Wait!"

I'm greeted with an amused arch to Magic's brow. "Yes?"

"Sorry for being ... abrupt."

"Patients aren't the only ones hurting in here," he replies before walking away.

When Mother and I are alone, I blow out a long, shuddered breath. "I don't know if I can do this."

"Of course you can." Mother sniffs. "You're a Van Rensburg."

"Speaking of, where are Will and Henrik?"

"On their way back to South Africa."

"What?" I splutter.

"Our flights were booked for yesterday. Will wanted to stay, but something came up and he had to get back. He will call you when he's home."

"Why didn't you go with him?"

"Because you needed me here."

If her face were closer to a Botox renewal, she'd look more surprised when I step forward and throw my arms around her. She pats my back in an unsteady rhythm.

"How long are you staying?"

"As long as you need me to. Now ..." Mother pulls away before the hug can move into awkward territory. "While you're giving Ryan time, let me give you something that will make you feel better."

"Motherly warmth and affection?"

She loops her arm through mine, and we start to walk along the corridor. "I was leaning more toward caffeine."

With Ryan now conscious, I become more than aware of how exhausted I am.

A vat of coffee couldn't keep me awake. Fact. I make my way through two large black ones with Mother, and they do nothing. After an hour of yawning and head lolling, she declares I need to sleep. Admitting defeat, I make my way to the family room and pass out for three hours on the couch with my head in her lap. I wake up abruptly when an emergency alarm sounds out overhead and we both dart out of the room. The staff running in the opposite direction of Ryan's doesn't make me feel any better. I can't wait to see the back of this place.

"Ready to go see him?" Mother asks.

"No," I admit. "Is it bad that I preferred it when he was asleep?" It sounds worse saying it out loud, but I can't hold in how I'm feeling. Delirious with tiredness—even after the three-hour nap—I'm an emotional pressure cooker ready to combust.

"It sounds completely normal." I eye her warily, holding back on admitting that I also preferred it when she was standoffish and harder to communicate with than a brick wall. Between her and Ryan, I feel like I'm stuck in *The Twilight Zone*. "Stop looking at me like that. You both went through a lot the other night."

It's tempting to laugh that she's using such a word in association with the two of us.

My sneakers squeak against the floor and my skin crawls the closer we get to his room. "I'd happily go back a few weeks and still be in South Africa." I'm a foot or two ahead when I realize I'm walking alone and turn back. "What's wrong?"

"Ryan needs you to be stronger than regretting anything that's happened between the two of you. Even the bad stuff. You mean more to each other than that."

When I turn my head back to face his room, guilt hits me hard, and I realize she's right. "Do you mind if I go see him alone?"

"Not at all." Mother gives me a smile I've not received in a lifetime. A proud one. "I'll be right here if you need me."

Pausing at the door, with my hand resting on the handle, I take a deep breath before opening it and walking in. I needn't have worried about some grand word dump happening or a life-changing heart to heart, because Ryan's fast asleep.

The only difference from the past few days is that all the wires and drips are nowhere to be found. Needing to be as close to him as physically possible, I bypass the chair and climb onto the bed, shuffling myself into the tiny gap between his and the bed's sides. I still when Ryan sucks in a harsh breath, waiting a second before I wrap my arm around his middle and carefully rest my head on his chest.

When he lets out a long, slow exhale, his breathing goes back to a steady rhythm, in and out like waves breaking against the shore. I glance up at the clock on the wall above the door, watching as the hands move so they're sitting in a perfectly vertical line.

Before closing my eyes, I pray that Magic is right, and maybe there's some luck in the number six after all.

"Sooz."

My name washes over me like the softest lyric.

"Sooz."

A grunt-slash-snore comes out.

"Baby, wake up."

My lashes flutter as my lids part. "Don't call me *baby*."

"Scared you'll like it too much?"

"I think you're being optimistic."

Ryan's chin rests on top of my head. "What can I say? I'm a wishful thinker." He inhales slowly, then lets out a long sigh. The over-exaggeratedness of it is like he's practicing. Testing. "This is the way I'd have preferred to wake up the first time."

Eyes burning, I bury my face into his chest so he can't see that I'm going to cry.

He inhales again while his hand rubs up and down my arm. "Lavender and wild iris," I tell him. "Before you go all cliché and demand to know why I smell so good."

"Is that what they do in those shitty movies you tried to get me to watch?"

"Sometimes. More in the books Amanda lends me."

"I thought you preferred guidebooks?" I jab a finger in his chest, and he chuckles. "What else do they do in these books?"

Drawing circles over his hospital gown, I decide to play along. We're tip-toeing around everything we need to talk about, but after the past few days, I don't care.

"She loves a good alpha. There's usually lots of dirty talk. Hair pulling. Nails scratching. Sex against random surfaces."

"Where can I get these books?"

"I have one back in your room." Ryan shifts, and I smile to myself.

"We should schedule in a buddy read date."

My hand stops moving. "We?"

"Yeah. We."

421

"Then we need to talk." I start moving my hand again, needing something to do with all the nervous energy that comes with each long pause.

"I know," Ryan says, quietly. "But I've imagined this for a long time, and I don't want to ruin it."

"You imagined us like this in a hospital?"

This time, I'm at the receiving end of a jab. "I'm trying to be all deep and profound here."

Shaking my head, I move away from his chest. Ignoring my racing pulse and clammy palms, I give Ryan what I know he needs more than anything right now.

"I don't need deep and profound, Ry. I just need you."

When he swallows, the bandage wrapped around his neck moves and he winces. "You've always had me. Right from the start."

Seventy-two hours felt like forever.

It takes less than twenty-four for everything to feel like it's getting back to normal.

"You need to wait for your parents to get here."

"I don't *need* to do anything," snaps Ryan.

"Then where are you going to go?" I stare at him in disbelief.

"Home."

"As in, the band's place?"

"Yes," he huffs, shoving a couple of his things into the small bag Zach brought by so he could freshen up before being discharged. "That's the place I now refer to as home over the place where I was raised."

I throw my arms up and turn toward the door. "Tell him he's being ridiculous!"

Magic watches us both, entertained. "I'm not allowed to do that," he replies. "I'd be fired."

"But ..."

Magic holds up his hand before I can go off on another rant. "Mr. Alvarez is able to discharge himself."

"Because I'm a grown man," Ryan adds to the end. "It would be nice if you started treating me like one."

"What's that supposed to mean?" Fists clenched at my sides, I'm seconds away from stomping my foot.

Ryan steps toward me, green eyes blazing. "It means *this* is the reason I didn't tell you about *everything*."

My hands unclench and find my hips. "And that worked out so well for you. Didn't it?"

He turns away, dragging a hand over his jaw. "I'm sick. You're supposed to be being nice to me."

"This *is* me being nice. People that care want to make sure you're safe. Wait for your parents to get here."

His shoulders slump at the same time Magic clears his throat, making us both aware he's still in the room. "I have to agree with Ms. Van Rensburg on some of this. You might want to make sure you have someone around to help so you can recover."

"Fine." Ryan turns to me. "Looks like you're stuck with me again. This time you get to play nurse."

Magic leaves the room, shaking his head.

Deciding Ryan needs time to cool off, I follow him out, smiling, because even though Ryan's words are supposed to come across as a threat, they're not.

Not even close.

The ride back from the hospital is a quiet one.

Our moment yesterday in Ryan's hospital room feels like a dream. A long-ago one.

"Are you sure you're feeling okay?" I ask, closing the front door.

"Yes," replies Ryan abruptly. "I feel okay now. I felt okay a minute ago. The two before that and each time you asked me in the past hour."

"You're being dramatic." I fold my arms across my chest. "I haven't asked you that many times."

"Yes." He pats his hands over his coat. "You have." Not finding whatever he's searching for, his pace increases, and his brows knit together when he starts patting his pants.

"What's wrong?" I rush forward. Ryan looks up at the ceiling. "Are you counting? Why are you counting?"

He takes a step back. "I need a break."

I feel like I've been punched in the gut. What he's referring to isn't the recess kind.

"From me?"

He heads toward the stairs. "From everything."

Before he disappears at the top of the first flight, I try not to panic but it's hard not to. Standing alone, I listen to the slow, steady thuds of his feet as he makes his way up the next three. My feet want to follow, but my brain tells me not to.

Later, when Ryan hasn't reappeared, I make my way upstairs. I stop at the third floor when I'm greeted with a familiar smell.

Feeling completely out of my depth, I head back down to the living room and pass out on the couch.

Chapter Thirty-Five

I t's dark when I wake up in a panic.

"He's fine," says Zach, sprawled over an armchair to the left of where I'm laying on the couch. The TV is playing quietly in the background, a true crime episode I didn't get round to watching with Will and Henrik. "I checked on him a half hour ago."

"But he's okay?" I ask, needing more reassurance. "Does he need anything?" I jump to my feet. "I could make him something?"

The world feels like it stops spinning when Zach removes his attention from the TV.

"He doesn't want to see you."

"Why?"

Zach drags a hand down his face, then grabs the bottle of beer sitting on the coffee table. "He's doing what he does when shit like this happens."

I'm ready for swiping the bottle away when the sounds of him glugging the amber liquid down replaces his words.

"Why are you talking like this is normal?" I snap.

"Because for Ryan, this is." Zach sets the bottle down. "Leave him to go through his processes."

My arms fold across my chest, and my nostrils flare. "I watched him almost die, Zach. I'm not going to stand back and watch him waste another second chance."

The response I get is cold. It doesn't sound at all like the friend I thought I'd found. "Do whatever you want, Sooz. But don't say I didn't warn you."

He goes back to watching the TV as I leave without another word. I spend the night in Sam's old room formulating a plan—controlling whatever I can in an uncontrollable situation, ready to tackle another hurdle with Ryan in the morning.

It's all I can do to stop myself hurting after the rejection of the two people in the house, who, without me realizing how much, have become a key part in my life.

"I mean," sighs Abby down the line. "It's a good plan. A great plan. But it's only as good as Ryan wanting to do it."

"Why wouldn't he want to?" I skim my hands over my outfit as I give my reflection a final once over. I look put together. Like I mean business. Not like I'm constantly teetering on the edge of crying. Thank you, good make-up. "Then the images will be meaningless. People will sympathize with him, *and* it will help keep him safe."

"Can I say something without you biting my head off?" I don't reply, knowing whatever is going to come out of Abby's mouth next, I'm not going to like. She takes my silence as an invitation to continue. "What if Ryan doesn't want people's sympathy? Sooz, there's a reason he's made it to thirty without telling anyone."

I scowl at myself in the mirror. "He's putting himself at risk."

"And it's his choice to make."

"Why are you fighting me on this?"

Abby sighs. "I'm not. I'm preparing you, before you go to him, all guns blazing, and maybe get a response you don't want."

"He will agree. I know he will."

He has to.

"Okay," says Abby, sounding unconvinced. "Call me later. Let me know how it goes."

"Sure."

I hang up, and as I leave Sam's room and make my way toward Ryan's, my steps are filled with purpose.

"No."

"What do you mean no?"

"I mean no. I don't want to."

I blink in the darkness.

"But it's a good idea."

"It's a great idea, but it doesn't mean I want or have to do it."

Frustrated that I can't see Ryan properly, I walk over to the skylight window and roll up the shade.

When I turn back, I wish I hadn't, finding a similar-looking empty bottle to the last time we were in a standoff like this, and a couple of stubbed out joints sitting on his nightstand.

"Because what you're doing is *so* much better?"

Ryan gives me a blank, lazy look. His eyes are so red, they look painful. Because I can't watch him do this to himself, I rush over and snatch away the evidence of what, if he lets it, will be his demise.

"You're on pain meds, Ry. You're going to kill yourself."

"What if I want to?" The joints and bottle fall from my hands. There's a loud smash as the glass shatters on the floor. "Do you know what it's like to almost die?"

"No," I reply quietly. "But I know what it's like to watch and not be able to help."

The effort it takes not to cry is too much. A tear spills over and rolls down my cheek.

"You said you would give me whatever I need. I need you to let me help you. Please, Ry. If you do the interview with Allure magazine, tell them about your allergy, it could help keep you safe."

Ryan lets out a bitter laugh. For a moment, I let myself hate the person sitting in front of me. Hate him because he's done the worst thing he could. Found my weakness. Made promises. And now he's ripping them away.

He climbs off the bed and walks toward me.

"You're going to hurt yourself."

I glance at his bare feet moving over the shattered glass.

His hand finds my waist and I don't have it in me to step back or push him away.

"I'm already hurting."

A sob falls from my lips. One that comes from deep within my chest. It's painful. But not as painful as when Ryan reaches up with both hands and cups my cheeks. He starts to lean in, and his eyes drop to my lips. His ragged breaths and dark pupils make it clear what his intentions are.

428

"What are you doing?" I whisper, before he gets too close, and we can't reverse the moment.

"I know what I'm doing …"

He tries to close the gap, but I give him my cheek.

"Don't. Not if you won't give me what I need. Not when you're not willing to fight for us."

"I'm still here, aren't I?" he says with a coldness I didn't know he was capable of. Not after everything we've been through. Everything we've shared. "This is me fighting."

"No." I shake my head abruptly and take a step back. Then another. "This is you accepting less than what you deserve."

"And what about you?" The hurt of my rejection drips from his sneer. "Why do you hate Christmas, Sooz? Why do you work all the time? Why is it all you ever do?"

"Stop."

"Admit it. You're scared. You walk around pretending you have everything together. That you're strong and in control, but you're fucking terrified of letting anyone in after your dad left."

"Please, stop."

But he doesn't. He keeps going. Spilling out everything I've never wanted to accept about myself. Hurtful, flawed truths.

"You're terrified of becoming your mother, but guess what, *baby,* you already are."

"All I'm trying to do is help, Ry!"

He takes some steps back himself, and when I look down at the ground, there's blood shining on the glass. Evidence of what we are together outside of the box.

"And all I've ever wanted is for you to see me. But all you ever do is focus on my flaws. I guess we're both losing out here."

My hand itches to raise; to cut through the air and make contact with his cheek. I don't though, because I learned from the best—even though she might be different now—that wounds caused by words cut deeper and last longer.

"I was happy hating you. Now I need you, and you're what …" I throw my hands out. "Giving up?"

Ryan's anger breaks, and his eyes start to resemble the ones I thought I could lose myself in forever. I lost myself, alright, and now I don't know if I stand a chance of getting what he's taken back. You should never show your enemy your weakness, because then they know how to tear you down. Like Ryan is now. He's breaking parts of me I didn't know existed.

"Sooz …" It comes out too gentle; too much of a contrast after the past few minutes. "Baby …"

"No," I snap. "Don't baby me. You knew what I was afraid of. You've made that perfectly clear. I told you I wanted the chance at a happily ever after. I told you dreams I've had that I've never told anyone. You let me believe that maybe we stood a chance, and now you're tearing it away." Ryan goes to move forward. Retracing his thoughtless steps. I stop him, holding my hand up. "Stop hurting yourself. Stop hurting us both.

"We can still have the happily ever after."

"Not if you're fucking dead we can't." He blinks at my cussing. I don't have it in me to care. "How can we ride off into the sunset together if you're buried six feet in the ground?"

"That won't happen …"

430

"Oh really? Because you've been doing an excellent job of managing the situation so far. How many times is it now that you've almost died, Ryan? No, wait." I laugh bitterly. "It's okay, because the doctor, a perfect stranger, gave me the details that the person I was falling for couldn't."

Ryan's eyes darken.

"Sooz."

This time, my name is a warning to stop pushing. What he hasn't figured out yet, because he's still riding the high of his toxic crutch, is that we've already fallen, and we're now fighting against the tide. A tide so strong it's already pulling us under.

"I had to watch you stop breathing." Glass crunches beneath my feet. "I waited for you to move, but this ..." my hand rests on his warm skin, above his heart. "Had already stopped beating." I lift my chin and try to make him see my pain. "I had to prepare myself for what life would be like without you in it." My eyes drop and my hand snaps away as I take a step back. "And it all could have been avoided if you let the world know."

"What are you saying?"

"That if you're not willing to fight to stay alive, then I'm not willing to fight for us. You make your allergy known, or we're done."

Ryan's eyes narrow. "You're being unfair."

"No." I pause, inhale the sweet, scented air, using it to give me the strength to say what I need to next. "I'm being reasonable. I'm willing to face my fears, knowing there's a chance this might not work out between us in the end, if you're willing to face yours."

"I gave you everything I could. How can you not see that?" Ryan says desperately.

I shrug. "Maybe that's the problem. Maybe we were never meant to be together like this. We started out as enemies. Maybe it was inevitable we'd use each other's weaknesses to break whatever we could become."

"We're not breaking," he snaps, removing the space between us again. His hands find my face; they're harsher—more forceful—this time. I pull away. "Why won't you let me kiss you?"

"Because I don't want to fall anymore in love with you. Not if there isn't a future for us." I walk away before we can spiral any further, stopping at the top of the stairs. "You deserve the same as everyone else, Ry. A fair chance at life that only you can give yourself—by speaking out."

"My allergy makes me weak, Sooz," he says, before my feet make contact with the steps.

"No."

I shake my head and look back over my shoulder, breaking a bit more at what I see. A Ryan who resembles the one I first met.

"It makes you relatable." Clutching at the last straw, I give him the final truth, one I hope resonates with him. If not now, then later. "Do you know how many of your fans might be struggling with something similar to what you are? Might be feeling everything you are, with no outlet. The odds are a lot. You could help them like you've been helping Xavier. You could inspire them. Show them they can achieve whatever they want to. Because you did. Even if you don't believe it yourself."

Ryan doesn't say anything else, and neither do I.

I make my way downstairs and throw my things into my bag, preparing to leave.

"I'm sorry for what I said last night," says Zach from down the hallway, right before I reach the front door.

"I get it now," I reply.

"Don't give up on him. Please."

I don't give him a direct answer, because I don't want to hurt him after his apology.

"Do me a favor? Give him a couple of days before you tell him I'm going back to South Africa with my mother."

My hand twists the handle and I step out into the dank Brooklyn morning. I leave Ryan before he can leave me. And I run to the only person I know truly understands.

"Suzanne?"

My mother stands, holding her hotel room door open.

Both of our faces are shocked. Hers, likely because she can't believe I'm standing in the doorway. Mine, because her golden hair is soft around her shoulders and she's wearing loose yoga pants with a hooded jumper. There's not an ounce of bouclé in sight.

"Can I come in?"

She gives me a curt nod and steps to the side so I can pass by her and into the room. The room she booked because she wanted to give Ryan and me alone time. The reminder is a painful stab to my heart, and I sniffle.

"Are you okay?" she asks.

"I'm fine."

"Is Ryan okay?"

"He's fine."

"Everyone is … fine?"

"Yes, Mother. Everyone is dandy."

Because she's never been the type of parental figure to do things normally, she laughs.

"Is something funny?" I frown, discarding my bag and settling on the plush, velour couch.

"Dandy is what people say when they're not fine." Her eyes search my face. "What's really going on?"

"Why would you think anything is going on?" I sniff, looking away before I start to cry again. The probability of her seeing exactly how not fine I am with the blotchiness of my skin is high enough.

"Because you're voluntarily entering a room where I'm staying, and judging by the bag you've brought with you, it looks like you will be staying too."

Right before she goes to sit on the couch opposite mine, I ask, "When is your flight back to South Africa?"

She turns to face me. "The day after tomorrow."

"Do you know if there are any seats left?"

"Why?"

"Because I'd like to come with you. I want the job at Cape Unity." When she doesn't answer, and looks at me like I've lost my mind, I say, "What? This is what you wanted, right?"

She rolls her eyes. "Stop with the dramatics."

"Gee," I mutter, "don't be happy that I'm giving in and doing what you want."

"The job isn't available anymore." My eyes widen. "And why would I be happy when you're sitting, being bratty over the fact you broke up with your boyfriend?"

"He's not my boyfriend," I snap. "And I think I'm allowed to be dramatic."

Mother sighs. It's not a huffy, frustrated one. More of a sad one. And then she takes me by surprise when, instead of

434

sitting on the couch she originally intended to, she chooses to sit next to me.

"*He* almost died," she says, giving my knee a squeeze. "Not *you*."

My chin wobbles as I stare down at where she still has a firm grip on me. "He's falling apart."

"And he's entitled to, I think. Don't you?"

"But he's had years of this …"

"I'm still not understanding the issue here." Her words are firm, but their meaning isn't unjust.

"He's ready to give up. I told him I wanted him to do an interview about his allergy, so he would be safe." I fill my cheeks with air, then puff it out. "He has an allergy band, and he hides it beneath a ton of others. It's like he wants to give up. He isn't fighting for us."

My shoulders slump, and Mother watches me for a couple of moments before speaking again.

"You say Ryan isn't fighting, but by walking away from what the two of you have, are you giving him a reason to?"

A heavy weight sits in my gut as it hits me that she's right.

"You're making me feel shitty right now."

"Don't cuss, Suzanne." I roll my eyes. "You're a Van Rensburg, and now you need to act like one."

"Because we have such a stellar rep," I sulk.

She's right, I'm being bratty.

When she tilts her head to the side, amusement plays on her lips. "Shall I tell Willem you said that, after everything he's had to fight for with Henrik?"

"I wasn't referring to Will."

"I know." Her words sound cold, but her gaze is warm. "Sooz, this has to stop."

"What?"

"You making me out to be the villain. Like I'm narrowminded and hurtful when I'm not."

"You've never given me any reason to think otherwise," I admit, hating myself when she looks hurt.

"Do you really think that?"

"When Dad left, you might as well have left, too. At least for me. Sometimes it genuinely felt like you'd forgotten I existed."

"I was being strong and holding things together in the only way I knew how."

"You never did anything for me ..."

"I'm not talking about you, Suzanne. I'm sorry you felt like I was abandoning you, but don't you see?" She reaches over and runs a hand through my hair. "I never had to hold you together, you were doing fine yourself. You're a true Van Rensburg. A fighter. Look at everything you've achieved."

"Then who were you being strong for?"

She gives me a bombshell that changes everything I've believed throughout my adult life. "Willem." She looks away, then her gaze hardens, and she faces me again. "I promised myself I would never tell you this story, but sometimes promises are made to be broken."

"Okay?"

There's a faint ringing in my ears as my gut kicks in, telling me I'm going to hate the story to come.

"Your father walked in on Willem and Henrik being ... intimate." My mouth falls open. "I won't tell you the details of the fallout. I'll give him that much respect, because he gave me the two of you. Let's say that two days later, he walked away, leaving behind a broken son who thought he

436

couldn't achieve what he wanted in life because of who he'd chosen to love."

I thought I knew what it was like to feel my heart break, but this is a different kind of pain. I thought I understood everything my brother had been through. Now I know I'd barely touched the surface.

"Willem never came out with Henrik, because of ..." I blink rapidly, trying to process the information she's giving me. "Dad?" Mother nods. "Why didn't you tell me? Why did you let me think that he left because your marriage fell apart? Because of you?"

"Because I didn't want him to taint your view of men. He was your knight in shining armor. Always had been."

"Mother, when he left without a goodbye and never got in contact again, he destroyed that belief spectacularly." Mother's lips form a line. "Is this why Will went so hard for senior partner?"

"Yes. He wanted to prove to everyone he could do it. And I wanted him to see for *himself* that he could." I sink back into the couch, physically and emotionally exhausted. "I never meant for you to feel the way you did, or plan for you to hate me as much as you have, but then we were heading down a path it felt like we'd never be able to detour from."

"It's okay," I say quietly, looking up and giving her a small smile. "I'm glad we're detouring now."

In case it didn't already feel like the world was ending, Mother pulls me into her arms and presses a kiss into my hair. "I'm proud of you. Don't ever think otherwise."

"So, is the job really not available?"

"No," she replies. "Because you're a Van Rensburg, and I refuse to let you give up on what you really want."

I don't ask her if she means my career, because for the first time ever, what my heart wants outshines everything, and I know she's referring to Ryan.

Chapter Thirty-Six

T rue to her word, Mother leaves on the flight she booked.

There was a part of me that wanted to ask her to stay. Wanted to lean on her. I never asked, though.

Not because I thought she'd say no. Because her confidence in me, that's unknowingly been there all along, made me believe I can fight the hardest battle of my life on my own.

The one for my heart.

"Why did I agree to help with this?" asks Zach, four days later, pacing back and forth in S.C.A.R.A.B.'s living room.

"You need to chill out," I reply. "You're making me antsy."

"He's going to go fucking mental, you know that, right?"

"And then we have something that will soften the blow."

Zach frowns at my wink.

"Is that meant as a sex reference?"

"No," I laugh properly for the first time in over a week since that fateful night.

Thinking about it makes me nauseous. I don't know if there will ever be a time when it won't. Despite all the worry surrounding that night, and the hurt still very much raw from the words spoken after, I've accepted that I can't change anything.

And even if I could, I wouldn't.

Without it all, I wouldn't be here now, ready to walk a new path with absolute certainty it's where I want to be, with Ryan Alvarez by my side.

Everything I've organized feels like wasted effort—an unnecessary fight—when a text from Xavier comes through claiming that Ryan never showed up, and that he doesn't know where he is, because he isn't answering his phone. The plan was for Xavier to keep Ryan as long as needed under the false pretense of filming Rogue Drummer's next video. Now, it looks like our plan was never needed to begin with.

Zach carries on rambling that my idea is going to result in him being murdered when the sound of a key being turned in the lock of the front door reaches us.

"Shhh," I hiss, because there's only one person it can be.

The front door swings open, and Zach remains standing, frozen on the spot.

"You're going to give it away," I say under my breath.

"Fuck it, I'm out of here," he hisses, rushing out of the room before I can tell him to stop. He pauses at the front door, speaking to the figure still to set foot through it. "Hey, man. Sooz is here to see you."

I roll my eyes at his lack of subtlety. I should have known Zach would be the worst person to help with my surprise.

"Where are you going?" I hear Ryan ask, as Zach's footsteps sound like they're hurrying toward the stairs. He's bolting.

"Got shit to do …" is his explanation, then his feet are thundering upwards.

Listening to the front door close, my palms go clammy. I wipe them against my white denim jeans, then run my hands over my hair, checking there isn't any out of place.

"Sooz?" Ryan calls out.

God, I've missed his voice. It's only been days, but it feels like a long, distant memory. One I thought I might not get a chance to make a reality again.

"In the living room."

I don't want to move, because if I do, it will disturb … things.

The thudding of my heart increases in volume, matching Ryan's footsteps as he gets closer.

And then he's in the doorway. I take in all of him. His long thick legs, clad in black denim. The crisp white t-shirt and leather jacket he's wearing. There's a bandage still covering his neck. It looks like a fresh one. He's even styled his hair. He looks clean. Put together. A far cry from the man who fell apart in front of me days ago. Mother was right. So was Zach. He needed time to process. Process, while I ran away scared because of the wrong beliefs I've based my life on.

People always leave.

But sometimes they don't, if you ask them to stay. If you communicate what it is that you really want.

It's when our eyes meet and I find his are bright, not an ounce of red in sight, that I burst into tears.

Time speeds up, and he's down on his knees in front of me, wiping each one that falls away.

"Still bringing me to my knees." His chuckle takes me by surprise. I predicted there to be more of a fight. More angst. "You don't hate me?" I blubber.

Ryan shakes his head, and the corners of his mouth sit high. "*You* don't hate *me*?"

I give him a wobbly smile in return. "I never did."

"And I never could, even when you piss me off."

"For calling you out on your bull?"

"For calling me out on my bull." The sound of scratching followed by panting is when his gaze diverts away from me. He pales when he sees what's off to the side of the room. "Sooz?"

"Yeah?" I keep my tone sweet and innocent.

"What the fuck is that?"

"I never got a chance to get you a Christmas present."

Ryan frowns, remaining stock still where he's kneeling. Even his hands are stuck in place, cupping my face.

"Why are there holes in the gift wrap?"

I push his hands away. "Why don't you stop asking questions and open it to get your answers?"

"I don't know if I want to," he mutters, getting up. He groans when the present moves. "What did you do?"

I don't answer, just watch as he walks over, then pulls away the paper.

"You didn't ..."

He stares at what is now savaging a blanket in its crate.

"We never did get to go see the puppies." I clap my hands excitedly, which results in a round of yapping from our new furry friend. A literal ball of fluff. "I heard dogs are good for anxiety," I start to explain. "I'm not saying I want to change you, or that I want you to give up weed altogether." I crouch and open the crate. The fluff ball jumps at me and goes straight into licking my face. I hold it up in the air. "I'm asking you to meet me halfway and consider other options when things feel like they're getting too dark."

Ryan gives the puppy a skeptical look. "You're missing a few key points. I'm in a band. I tour. Travel a lot. Where will it be when I'm not here?"

I grin. "With me."

Ryan's gaze snaps away from the dog. "How can it stay with you when you're moving back to South Africa?"

His jaw clenches, as if he's holding himself back from believing I'm going to tell him exactly what I am.

"Because I won't be in South Africa. I'll be here."

"Is that so?"

His hand finds my upper arms, and when he pulls me toward him, the puppy starts licking his mouth. The same lips that have only touched once. My eyes widen in panic, and I wait for Ryan to tell me to take it back. What he does is throw his head back and laugh. My heart, which already feels impossibly large with all the emotions it's carrying around, swells.

Something that's been bugging me since our fight comes to the front of my mind, and while Ryan's stroking the puppy, I watch his hand moving, and say, "Remember when you said you knew what you were doing? What did you mean? Can you tell me what you were going to say?"

I've had an inkling what it was and I'm glad he didn't ruin it by admitting it in a moment where it didn't belong.

Rather than giving me my predicted answer, he shakes his head. "I can't, because it's not relevant. I don't think it ever was." I feel a wave of a disappointment, but then he continues, "It's not relevant anymore, because I was going to tell you that I thought I was falling in love with you. There's no thinking. I'm not falling. I'm already there. I'm in love with you, Sooz."

I open my mouth to tell him that I feel the same, but he places a finger over my lips, stopping me.

He sounds pained when he admits, "I don't know if I can kiss you."

It's an out. One I refuse to take, swatting away his hand.

I raise my own finger carefully, and when he doesn't flinch, I trace his lips. "These are one small part of everything you have to give. I'd take a forever without them if it meant the potential of a forever with you. I'd sacrifice a lifetime of kisses for a lifetime of what we are."

"You sure this is what you want?" Ryan asks a final time. "I don't know if I have it in me to watch you walk away again."

"I'm sure." I smile up at him. "I'm sure, because I love you, too."

He still looks unsure. "Sometimes we bring out the worst in each other. It might not be the fairytale you wanted."

I move my hand from his face and run it through his hair.

"No, we don't bring out each other's worst. We bring out what's real. Fairytales are overrated anyway."

Ryan sets the puppy down on the ground, and then he really pulls me into his arms. Literally engulfs me.

I don't wait for a kiss. And I'm not disappointed when I don't get one.

I meant what I said.

I can wait forever, because he's enough for me.

Two days later, an article is published in Allure Magazine that rocks the music world.

It's an article that serves as a harsh but needed reminder to people that they shouldn't take what they see at face value. It's a reminder that, just because you can't see someone's pain, doesn't mean it isn't there. That sometimes, those who appear happy and carefree are the ones hiding the most.

The article tells the story of a guy who only ever wanted to be normal, who was dealt a life that was anything but.

When asked why he always smiled, he replied that those who smile are often left alone.

And when the interviewee answered the final question, why he wanted to speak out about his story, his answer was that he wanted to do better.

Be better.

Inspire those going through the same thing to believe they could chase their dreams.

His final admission was that he was telling his story because he wanted to increase the odds of his happily after, unknowing at the time, that it was already waiting for him.

That it had been all along.

Epilogue
15 Months Later

"You know I hate it when you keep secrets," I say, as Abby steers me to I don't know where. "And remember when you told me to inform you when you're being a control freak?"

"Yeah," I reply into complete darkness.

The blindfold she has around my eyes is tied with enough tension it's cutting off the blood supply to my brain.

"You're being a control freak."

"I've not been able to see for hours on a plane, what do you expect?"

"For you to last a couple more minutes. We're nearly there."

We carry on walking. The air feels cool on my skin, but I'm still not sure where we are.

It's when my foot splashes in a puddle that I start with the third degree again.

"Are we outside still? We're outside, aren't we?"

"Yes," Abby sighs. "We're outside and we're here."

"Can I take the blindfold off?"

She laughs. "You're relentless. You know that, right?"

I'm too busy giving my eyes the freedom they've been dying for to answer her. I never would have predicted what I find when I'm gifted with sight, and I gawp at the Old French Quarter surrounding me.

"We're in New Orleans?" I ask in alarm, turning to her. "What about Zoomie?"

Zoomie is the name compromise for mine and Ryan's Pomeranian, which he often prefers to refer to as 'that damn dog,' each time she poops in his shoe and he doesn't notice until said shoe is already being slid onto his foot. Thinking about their antics has my excitement being replaced by sadness. He's been away for a month touring in South America. Four whole weeks. Not quite as bad as the world tour that he had to leave for two months after we made things official, but still …

"Zoomie is with Zach," says a deep, husky voice that has me jumping up and down.

"No way!" I screech, spinning around.

"Yes, way," says Abby, smiling at Ryan. "My duties here are done. I'm off to go find me one of those Hurricanes."

I barely hear anything she says, too focused on Ryan.

"You're really here?" I sprint the distance between us.

"Really here," he laughs when I jump into his arms.

"Why are *we* here, though?" I ask, not quite able to get my head around the fact I'm on Bourbon Street.

"I'm here," Ryan starts to explain, setting me down, "because I missed you. We're here because I wanted you to

447

have a do-over and have the vacation here you should have the first time, without me ruining it."

"You didn't have to do all this though," I laugh.

"I know nothing about us has been normal ..."

Ryan looks like he's going to puke. I go to ask why when a raindrop hits the tip of my nose. Holding my hand out, I tilt my chin, lifting my face to the sky. Thick clouds circle above us and a few more, heavier raindrops land on my palm.

"We should find a bar or something. It's going to rain."

A frustrated huff comes from Ryan, and I drop my chin, ready to ask what his problem is, but he's nowhere to be found. A throat clears, and I lower my gaze toward the ground.

"Did you drop something?"

I try to assess why Ryan looks paler now than he did a few seconds ago. Then my eyes connect with the small black box sitting open in his hand.

"Like I was saying," Ryan repeats, scowling when rain drops start to pitter patter against his face. "I know nothing about us has been normal. I know some people will say I'm moving too fast, but I need to ask you something."

Tears well in my eyes. "Because you missed me, and you don't hate me?"

"Because I missed you and I don't hate you. I never did." He grins. "So, will you marry me so we can do all the fairytale crap?"

"Oh, fuck."

Forget Ryan being pale, there's a strong chance I'm going to pass out.

"I thought Van Rensburgs don't cuss," he laughs, as I fist his now wet shirt and drag him to his feet.

Rain falls down around us, sparkling like the diamond ring he's slipping on me. I flex my fingers, testing it out.

Out of all our messy, disjointed pieces, this one's a perfect fit.

"I guess it's a good job I won't be a Van Rensburg for much longer then."

"Is that a yes?"

I glance up, because there's a softness to his voice, like there's more to come.

"Yeah," I say, so only he can hear, so this moment can be ours and only ours. "It's a yes."

"Good." The oxygen in my lungs evaporates when he starts to drop his head. And when there's only a sliver of space between us, he murmurs, "Because I'm ready to kiss you better than I fuck you now."

My brain doesn't get a chance to catch up as he holds up his increasingly excellent rep of keeping promises, pressing his lips against mine.

I sag against him. I was right all along.

A kiss from Ryan Alvarez is unforgettable. It's one I never want to end, because it's so perfect, but equally, it's one I do, because with its end, there's the promise of another, and another after that.

Happiness and euphoria coat my lips as Ryan steals whatever kisses he can.

With soft murmurs against my skin, his mouth moves away from mine, and he kisses along my neck. My head falls back with the waves of pleasure that roll through me, ones I'd have happily lived without, but ones, now I know how they feel, I'm glad I don't have to.

When I open my eyes, I'm hit with the realization that I got my own version of a fairytale as our tongues dance together with rain falling around us, beneath a neon rainbow sign on Bourbon Street.

And months later, when I think things can't get any better, that our own perfect has hit its peak … hidden by willows disturbing the calm waters with their leaves, with our closest family and friends around us, Ryan and I kiss after saying I do, finding our happily ever after, deep within the Bayou.

The End.

Acknowledgements

Finishing The Always Trilogy I thought things would get easier. I was very, very wrong.

Each book I write seems to get harder. I hope maybe after this one I'm due an easy story, because Ryan was as much of a handful to write as he was for Sooz to handle.

And there were rewrites. So many. A ridiculous amount. For a while I thought getting to this point would never happen, but here we are!

After almost giving up too many times, I'm glad I persevered, because there's something about this story that will stay with me for a long time. I love Ryan and Sooz, even at their worst, because it makes their growth that much sweeter. I hope you love them too.

Behind every challenge there's a team. I have an amazing one.

To all my betas, the gang, thank you for keeping me going, reading this in its shittiest form and helping me make it shine.

Hayley, thank you for being the best editor, being honest and making the most painful process better.

Kris and Babs … I wouldn't be where I am now without either of you. Your expertise and support have helped me become the writer I am, and with each book you help me to grow right along with my characters.

Carley. Where do I even start? I didn't know I needed you in my life until you were. You make the days so much more enjoyable, and I love the bants as much as I love your passion for books. I couldn't imagine doing this with anyone else and I can't wait to see where the future takes us together, and you on your own journey, because whatever you do, you're going to smash it.

Mum and Peter, none of this would happen without either of you by my side.

And my babies. My inspiration and my drive. This is all for you. To show you that whatever your dreams are, you can chase them, and I'll be there cheering you on when you do, like you have with me.

Harold, there's no thank you for you because you bark too much and are massive pain. But you do give good cuddles when late nights are involved.

All my readers and anyone who has spread the word for my books, thank you so much for all your support.

**Right after I finished writing the acknowledgements, I unfortunately received some terrible news. Someone I was incredibly close to during some of my best years as a teenager, went through a terrible loss. My heart feels heavy writing this, but it's a reminder that life is so short and sometimes incredibly harsh.

The years spent with these people were filled with laughter, sometimes tears, but they taught me that it's okay to different, it's okay to not want to be put in a box and to dance to whatever beat resonates with you. Those years inspired some of the best scenes in my work, good and bad. So much of what goes into my stories is through experience and it was a great privilege to be a part of those people's lives. I probably never would have put pen to paper if it hadn't been for my time with them, so I guess this is my own way of saying thank you.

Thank you for all the incredible memories and giving me the confidence to be me.

Want to know more about Abby and Jake?

Keep reading for more information about The Always Trilogy!

Always You

**You never forget your first love, and mine and Jake's,
was the kind songs are written about.**

I thought we were forever …
He promised me the world …
Then tore mine in two.
With my heart shattered into a million unrecognizable pieces,
I ran.
Out of the city. Out of the state. Out of my life.
Now I'm back for one summer, with one life changing
decision to make, and one goal: steer clear of Jake Ross, the
person who ran me out of Brooklyn.
Unfortunately, fate has other ideas and when
our careers become entangled,
avoidance proves impossible.
Together we were magical …
Apart we're a disaster.
Everyone deserves a second chance.

**But what happens if that chance leaves you questioning
everything, even when he promises that it
was always you …**

Always Us

**What hurt more than losing Jake Ross the first time ...
was losing him the second.**

It's been two years since I turned my back on the one that
got away, doing what I thought was right
for both of us.
Instead, I'm more confused than I've ever been before,
fighting to forget what it felt like
being in his arms.
Now, it's another summer and another
life-changing opportunity.
This time I'm running around Europe,
surrounded by Rock Gods.
It's the life most would dream of, but things are never that
straightforward, and a chance meeting with a stranger is a
recipe for disaster.
The heart wants what it wants,
regardless of the consequences.
But just when I might finally be able to move forward ... the
tables turn.
The choice is no longer between my head or my heart.

It's a question of whether love, really is enough.

Always

My life's about to change and I can't decide if it's for better or worse.

There was a time when I thought meeting Jake Ross, was fate
. . .
When I thought our love, was written in the stars . . .
When I hoped we'd find our way back to each other . . .
Now I'm left wondering if the path I'm about to take, will be
one I'll walk alone.
The one I want. The one I need.
Doesn't want me back.
Then the person I least expect gives me exactly
what I need.
A break from reality.
But there's only so long I can hide, and when the truth
comes out, it's explosive.
They say what will be, will be.

But what if we were never meant to be together?

OTHER WORK BY LIZZIE MORTON

The Always Trilogy:

Always You
Always Us
Always

The Always Series:

Wanting You Always
Needing You Always

Fool Me Series:

Fool Me Once
Fool Me Twice
Fool Me Thrice

Summer Nights Series:

Just One Kiss